# ILLUSIONS

Also by Aprilynne Pike

WINGS

SPELLS

# ILLUSIONS

## APRILYNNE PIKE

An Imprint of HarperCollinsPublishers

HarperTeen is an imprint of HarperCollins Publishers.

Library of Congress Cataloging-in-Publication Data
Pike, Aprilynne.
Illusions / Aprilynne Pike. — 1st ed.
    p. cm.
  Summary: As her senior year of high school starts, Laurel is just
beginning to adjust to Tamani's absence when he suddenly reappears,
telling her he must guard her against the returning threat of the trolls
that pose a danger both to her and to Avalon.
  ISBN 978-0-06-166809-8
  [1. Fairies—Fiction. 2. Trolls—Fiction. 3. High schools—Fiction.
4. Schools—Fiction. 5. Interpersonal relations—Fiction.] I. Title.
PZ7.P6257Il 2011                                           2010040320
[Fic]—dc22                                                        CIP
                                                                   AC

Typography by Ray Shappell

11   12   13   14   15   LP/RRDB   10   9   8   7   6   5   4   3   2   1
                                ❖

First Edition

*To Gwendolyn, who was with me*
*for every minute of revisions.*
*Every. Minute.*

# ONE

THE HALLS OF DEL NORTE HIGH BUZZED WITH FIRST-
day-of-school chaos as Laurel wedged herself through a
crowd of sophomores and spotted David's broad shoulders.
She twined her arms around his waist and pressed her face
against his soft T-shirt.

"Hey," David said, returning her embrace. Laurel had just
closed her eyes, prepared to savor the moment, when Chelsea
caught them both in an exuberant squeeze.

"Can you believe it? We're finally seniors!"

Laurel laughed as Chelsea let them go. Coming from her,
the question wasn't exactly rhetorical; there had been times
Laurel doubted they'd make it through junior year alive.

As David turned to his locker, Chelsea produced Mrs.
Cain's summer reading list from her backpack. Laurel suppressed a smile; Chelsea had been fretting over the optional
books all summer. Probably longer.

"I'm starting to think *everyone* read *Pride and Prejudice*," she said, tilting the paper toward Laurel. "I knew I should have gone with *Persuasion*."

"*I* didn't read *Pride and Prejudice*," Laurel countered.

"Yeah, well, you were a little busy reading *Common Uses of Ferns* or something like that." Chelsea leaned in so she could whisper. "Or, *Seven Habits of Highly Effective Mixers*," she added with a snort of laughter.

"*How to Win Fronds and Influence Poplars*," David suggested, raising his eyebrows. He straightened abruptly, his smile widening and his voice getting just a touch louder. "Hey, Ryan," he said, extending a fist.

Ryan bumped him and turned to run his hands down Chelsea's arms. "How's the hottest senior at Del Norte?" he asked, making Chelsea giggle as she went onto her toes for a kiss.

Sighing contentedly, Laurel reached out for David's hand and leaned against him. She'd been back from the Academy in Avalon for only a week, and she'd missed her friends— more even than last year, though her instructor, Yeardley, had usually kept her too busy to dwell on that. She'd mastered several potions and was closing in on more. The mixings were coming more naturally too; she was getting a feel for different herbs and essences and how they should work together. Certainly not enough to strike out on her own like her friend Katya, who was researching new potions, but Laurel took pride in her progress.

Still, it was a relief to be back in Crescent City, where

everything was *normal* and she didn't feel so lonely. She smiled up at David as he swung his locker shut and pulled her close. It seemed monumentally unfair that she and David had only one class together this year, and despite having spent the past week with him, Laurel found herself clinging to these last few minutes before the bell rang.

She almost didn't notice the strange tingle that made her want to turn and look behind her.

Was she being watched?

More curious than afraid, Laurel disguised the glance over her shoulder as a toss of her long blond hair. But her watcher was immediately apparent, and Laurel's breath caught in her throat as her gaze locked with a pair of pale green eyes.

Those eyes weren't supposed to be light green. They were supposed to be the rich, emerald green that once matched his hair—hair that was now a uniform black, cut short and gelled into a deceptively casual mop. Instead of a hand-woven tunic and breeches, he was dressed in jeans and a black T-shirt that, no matter how good they looked on him, had to be terribly stifling.

And he was wearing shoes. She'd hardly ever seen Tamani wearing shoes.

But light or dark, she knew his eyes—eyes that featured prominently in her dreams, as familiar to her as her own, or her parents'. Or David's.

As soon as their eyes locked, the months since she'd last seen Tamani shrank from an eternity to an instant. Last winter, in a moment of anger, she'd told him to go away, and he

3

had. She hadn't known where, or for how long, or if she'd ever see him again. After nearly a year she had almost gotten used to the ache she felt in her chest every time she thought about him. But suddenly he was here, almost close enough to touch.

Laurel looked up at David, but he wasn't looking at her. He, too, had noticed Tamani.

"Wow," Chelsea said from behind Laurel's shoulder, breaking her reverie. "Who's the hot new guy?" Her boyfriend, Ryan, scoffed. "Well, he is; I'm not blind," Chelsea added matter-of-factly.

Laurel still couldn't speak as Tamani's gaze flitted from her to David and back again. A million thoughts spun through her head. *Why is he here? Why is he dressed like that? Why didn't he tell me he was coming?* She hardly felt David pry her hands from his shirt, lacing his warm fingers through her own, which were suddenly cold as ice.

"Foreign exchange, I bet," Ryan said. "Look at Mr. Robison parading them all around."

"Maybe," Chelsea said noncommittally.

Mr. Robison said something to the three students who were following him through the hallway, and Tamani's head swung so that even his profile was no longer visible. As if released from a spell, Laurel dropped her gaze to the floor.

David squeezed her hand and she looked up at him. "Is that who I think it is?"

Laurel nodded, unable to find her voice; though David and Tamani had met only twice before, both events had been . . .

4

*memorable.* When David looked back toward Tamani, so did Laurel.

The other boy in the group looked embarrassed, and the girl was explaining something to him in a language that was clearly not English. Mr. Robison nodded approvingly.

Ryan crossed his arms over his chest and grinned. "See? Told you. Foreign exchange."

Tamani was shifting the weight of a black backpack from shoulder to shoulder, looking bored. Looking *human.* That by itself was almost as jarring as his being here in the first place. And then he was looking at her again, less openly now, his glance veiled beneath dark eyelashes.

Laurel fought to breathe evenly. She didn't know what to think. Avalon wouldn't send him here without reason, and Laurel couldn't imagine Tamani abandoning his post.

"You okay?" Chelsea asked, stepping up beside Laurel. "You look kinda freaked."

Before she could stop herself, Laurel flicked her eyes in Tamani's direction—a move Chelsea tracked instantly. "It's *Tamani,*" she said, hoping she didn't sound as relieved—or terrified—as she felt.

She must have succeeded, because Chelsea only stared in disbelief. "The hot one?" she whispered.

Laurel nodded.

"Seriously?" Chelsea squealed, only to be cut off by a sharp gesture from Laurel. Laurel glanced covertly over at Tamani to see if she'd been caught. The tick of a smile at one corner of his mouth told her she had.

Then the foreign exchange students were following Mr. Robison down the hallway, away from Laurel. Just before Tamani disappeared around the corner, he looked back at Laurel and winked. Not for the first time, she was supremely grateful she couldn't blush.

She turned to David. He was staring down at her, his eyes full of questions.

Laurel sighed and held her hands up in front of her. "I had nothing to do with this."

"It's a good thing, right?" David said after they'd managed to detangle themselves from Chelsea and Ryan and stood together in front of Laurel's first class. Laurel couldn't remember the last time the one-minute warning bell had made her feel so anxious. "I mean, you thought you were never going to see him again, and now he's here."

"It *is* good to see him," Laurel said softly, leaning forward to wrap both arms around David's waist, "but I'm also scared of what it means. For us. Not *us*," Laurel corrected, fighting the unfamiliar awkwardness that seemed to be worming its way between them. "But it has to mean we're in danger, right?"

David nodded. "I'm trying not to think about that. He'll tell us eventually, right?"

Laurel looked up with one eyebrow cocked and after a moment they both burst out laughing.

"I guess we can't count on it, can we?" David took her right hand in his, pressing it to his lips and examining the silver-and-crystal bracelet he had given her almost two years ago, when they first got together. "I'm glad you still wear this."

"Every day," Laurel said. Wishing they had more time to talk, she pulled David close for one last kiss before hurrying into her Government class and grabbing the last seat next to the wall full of windows. Small windows, but she would take whatever natural sunlight she could get.

Her mind wandered as Mrs. Harms handed out the syllabus and talked about class requirements; it was easy to tune her out, especially in light of Tamani's sudden reappearance. Why was he here? If she *was* in some kind of danger, what could it be? She hadn't seen a single troll since leaving Barnes at the lighthouse. Could this have something to do with Klea, the mysterious troll hunter who killed him? No one had seen her lately, either; as far as Laurel could tell, Klea had moved on to other hunting grounds. Maybe this was some other crisis entirely?

Regardless, David was right—Laurel was happy to see Tamani. More than happy. She felt somehow comforted by his presence. And he had *winked* at her! As if the last eight months had never happened. As if he had never walked away. As if she had never come to tell him good-bye. Her thoughts drifted to the brief moments spent in his arms, the soft feel of his lips on hers in those few times when self-control had slipped through her fingers. The memories were so vivid that Laurel found herself lightly touching her mouth.

The classroom door swung open suddenly, startling Laurel

from her thoughts. Mr. Robison entered, Tamani following close behind.

"Sorry to interrupt," Mr. Robison said. "Boys and girls?" Laurel hated how adults could combine two perfectly serviceable words into such a condescending phrase. "You might have heard that we have some foreign exchange students from Japan this year. Tam"—Laurel blanched at the counselor's use of her pet name for Tamani—"isn't technically in the foreign exchange program, but he just moved here from Scotland. I hope you will treat him with the same courtesy you have always shown our other exchange guests. Tam? Why don't you tell us a little about yourself."

Mr. Robison clapped one hand against Tamani's shoulder. Tamani's eyes darted briefly to the school counselor and Laurel could only imagine how Tamani would have preferred to respond. But irritation showed on his face for less than a second, and Laurel doubted anyone else noticed. He grinned lopsidedly and shrugged. "I'm Tam Collins."

Half the girls in the class sighed softly at Tamani's lilting brogue.

"I'm from Scotland. A little outside of Perth—not the Australia one—and . . ." He paused, as if searching for anything else about himself that the students might find interesting.

Laurel could think of a few things.

"I live with my uncle. Have since I was a kid." He turned and smiled at the teacher. "And I know nothing about Government," he said, laughter in his voice. "Not this one, anyway."

The entire classroom was won over. The guys were

nodding their heads a little, the girls were twittering, and even Mrs. Harms was smiling. And he wasn't even Enticing them. Laurel almost groaned aloud at the trouble *that* could lead to.

"Well, pick a seat, then," Mrs. Harms said, handing Tamani a textbook. "We've only just gotten started."

There were three empty seats in the classroom and almost everyone near them launched into a silent campaign for Tamani's favor. Nadia, one of the prettier girls in the class, was the boldest. She uncrossed and recrossed her legs, tossed her wavy brown hair over her shoulder, and leaned forward to not-so-subtly pat the backrest in front of her. Tamani grinned, almost apologetically, and continued past her to claim a seat in front of a girl who had scarcely looked up from her book since he'd walked into the classroom.

The seat beside Laurel.

As Mrs. Harms droned on about daily reading assignments, Laurel sat back and stared at Tamani. She didn't bother to hide it; just about every other girl in the classroom was doing the exact same thing. It was maddening to silently sit just two feet away while a million questions whizzed through her mind. Some were rational. Many were not.

Laurel's head was spinning by the time the bell rang. This was her chance. She wanted to do so many things: yell at him, slap him, kiss him, grab his shoulders and shake him. But more than anything else, she wanted to wrap her arms around him—to hold herself to his chest and confess how much she'd missed him. She could do that with a friend, couldn't she?

But then, wasn't that why she'd gotten angry enough to send him away in the first place? For Tamani, it was never just a friendly hug. He always wanted more. And as flattering as his persistence—and passion—could be, the way he treated David as an enemy to be crushed was less endearing. It had broken her heart to send Tamani away, and Laurel wasn't sure she could go through that again.

She stood slowly and looked at him, her lips suddenly dry. As soon as his backpack was slung over one strong shoulder, he turned and met her eyes. Laurel opened her mouth to say something when he grinned and reached out his hand.

"Hey there," he said, almost too brightly. "Looks like we'll be desk-mates. Wanted to introduce myself—I'm Tam."

Their clasped hands were moving up and down, but it was all Tamani's doing; Laurel's arm had gone limp. She stood silently for several seconds until Tamani's meaningful look intensified and became almost a glare. "Oh!" she said belatedly. "I'm Laurel. Laurel Sewell. Pleasure." *Pleasure?* Since when did she say "Pleasure"? And why was he shaking her hand like a stodgy salesperson?

Tamani pulled a class schedule from his back pocket. "I have English next, with Mrs. Cain. Would you mind showing me where the classroom is?"

Was the feeling that rushed over her relief that they didn't share their second-hour class, or disappointment? "Sure," she said cheerily. "It's just down the hall." Laurel gathered her things slowly, stalling while the classroom emptied. Then she leaned close to Tamani. "What are you doing here?"

"Are you glad to see me?"

She nodded, letting herself smile.

He grinned back, unconcealed relief brightening his expression. It made Laurel feel on more even ground to know he had been unsure too.

"Why—"

Tamani shook his head slightly and gestured toward the hall. When she was almost at the door, Tamani took hold of her elbow and stopped her. "Meet me in the woods behind your house after school?" he asked softly. "I'll explain everything." He paused, and with an unnatural quickness he lifted one hand to stroke her cheek. The feeling scarcely had time to register before his hands were back in his pockets and he was strolling out the door.

"Tama—Tam?" she called, trotting to catch up with him. "I'll show you where to go."

He grinned and laughed. "Come now," he said almost too quietly for her to hear. "How unprepared do you think I am? I know this school better than you do." And with a wink, he was gone.

"Homigosh!" Chelsea squealed, assaulting Laurel from behind and practically yanking her fingers from David's grasp. She put her face right in front of Laurel's. "Faerie boy is totally in my English class! Hurry before Ryan gets here— you have to spill!"

"Shh!" Laurel said, glancing around her. But no one was listening.

"He's really hot," she said. "The girls were all watching him. Oh, and the Japanese guy is in my Calculus class even though he's only fifteen. When do you think American schools will get the memo that there's a global economy out there?" she demanded. Then she paused and her eyes widened. "Man, I hope he doesn't blow the curve."

David rolled his eyes, but it was with a grin. "That's what everyone else is thinking about *you*," he said.

"Listen," Laurel said, pulling Chelsea closer, "I don't know anything yet; I still need to talk with him, okay?"

"You'll tell me though, right?" Chelsea asked.

"Don't I always?" Laurel teased, smiling.

"Tonight?"

"We'll see," Laurel said, turning her around by her shoulders and pushing her in Ryan's direction. "Go!" Chelsea turned and stuck her tongue out at Laurel before ducking under her boyfriend's arm.

Laurel shook her head and turned to David. "One class together is not enough," she said in a mock-stern voice. "Whose idea was this, anyway?"

"Not mine, that's for sure," David said. They went into the classroom and claimed a couple of desks near the back.

After everything else that had happened that day, Laurel shouldn't have been surprised to see Tamani walk into her and David's Speech class. When Tamani entered, David tensed, but he relaxed when Laurel's erstwhile guardian chose a desk at the front of the room, several rows away.

It was going to be a long semester.

# TWO

SIGHING HEAVILY, LAUREL DROPPED HER BACKPACK on the kitchen counter. She paused in front of the refrigerator to stare at its contents, then scolded herself for her obvious delay tactics. Still, she grabbed a nectarine before closing the fridge door, if for no other reason than to justify her browsing.

She walked over to the back door and stared, as she often did, at the trees behind her house, searching for signs of the faeries who now resided there full-time. Sometimes she spoke with them. She even occasionally supplied them with defensive potions and powders. She didn't know if the sentries got any use out of them, but at least they didn't turn them down. It was gratifying to feel like she was helping, especially since having to guard her house had disrupted all of their lives.

But with the total absence of troll activity since last year it hardly seemed necessary anymore. Part of her wanted to suggest they go home, even though she knew better. Jamison had warned her that trolls preferred to strike when their prey was at its most vulnerable, and her experience had proven the truth of his words. Like it or not, it was probably safest if the sentries stayed, at least for now.

Laurel pulled open the back door and set off toward the trees. She wasn't sure where exactly she was supposed to meet him, but she had no doubt Tamani would find her, as usual. She stopped short when she rounded a scrub oak to discover him removing one shoe with a swift, violent kick. His back was to her and he had already pulled his shirt off; Laurel couldn't help but stare. The sun filtered through the canopy of leaves to illuminate the warm brown skin of his back— darker than David's—as he bent and pulled at a stubborn shoelace. With a quiet mutter he finally got it undone and kicked it into the trunk of a nearby cypress tree.

As if freed from shackles instead of clothing, Tamani's shoulders relaxed and he sighed noisily. Even though he was a bit short by human standards, his arms were lean and long. He stretched, flinging them out wide, his broad shoulders forming the top of a slender triangle that narrowed to his waist, where his jeans hung loosely at his hips. The angles of his back caught the sunlight and for a moment Laurel fancied that she could *see* him soaking in those nourishing rays. She knew she should say something—announce her presence— but she hesitated.

When he placed his hands on the hips she was eyeing and

14

lifted his face to the sky, Laurel realized she'd better make some noise before he took something else off. She cleared her throat quietly.

The sun tossed golden light through Tamani's hair as he spun, visibly tense. "It's you," he said, sounding relieved. Then a strange look took over. "How long have you been standing there?"

"Not long," Laurel said quickly.

"A minute?" Tamani pressed. "Two?"

"Um, about one, I guess."

Tamani shook his head. "And I didn't hear a thing. Damn human clothes." He dropped onto a fallen log and pulled off a sock. "They're not just uncomfortable, they're noisy! And what is with that school? It's so *dark*."

Laurel stifled a grin. She'd told her mother the same thing after her first day at Del Norte. "You'll get used to it," she said, handing him the nectarine. "Eat this. It'll make you feel better."

He took the fruit from her, his fingers brushing hers. "Thanks," he said softly. He hesitated, then faced forward and took a bite. "I trained for this. I did! But they never made me stay indoors for this long at once. I was focused on learning the culture and didn't even think about the consequences of being inside so much."

"It helps if you get a seat under the windows," Laurel suggested. "I learned that the hard way."

"And who the hell came up with jeans?" Tamani continued darkly. "Heavy, sweltering fabric? You're seriously telling me the race that invented the internet couldn't create a fabric better than denim? Please!"

"You said 'internet,'" Laurel said with a snort. "That is so weird."

Tamani just laughed and took another bite of the nectarine. "You were right," he said appreciatively, holding up the fruit. "This helps a lot."

Laurel stepped over and sat down next to him on the fallen log. They were almost close enough to touch, but the air between them might as well have been a granite wall. "Tamani?"

He turned to face her, but said nothing.

Not sure whether it was a mistake, Laurel smiled and leaned forward, circling her arms around his neck. "Hello," she said, her lips near his ear.

He wrapped his arms around her, returning her greeting. She started to pull back, but he held on tighter, his hands begging her to stay. She didn't fight it—realized she didn't want to. After a few more seconds, he released her, but it was with obvious reluctance. "Hi," he said quietly.

She looked up into his light green eyes and was disappointed to realize that the color still bothered her. They weren't *different*, really; they were still his eyes. But she found the new color irrationally disturbing.

"Listen," Tamani said slowly. "I'm sorry this was all such a surprise for you."

"You could have told me."

"And what would you have said?" he asked.

Laurel started to say something, then closed her mouth and instead smiled guiltily.

"You'd have told me not to come, right?" Tamani pressed.

Laurel just raised one eyebrow.

"So I couldn't tell you," he said with a shrug.

Laurel reached down, plucked a small fern, and began tearing it to pieces. "Where have you been?" she asked. "Shar wouldn't say."

"Mostly in Scotland, like I said in class."

"Why?"

It was his turn to look guilty. "Training."

"Training for what?"

"To come here."

"The whole time?" Laurel said, her voice barely more than a whisper.

Tamani nodded.

Laurel tried to push away the hurt that instantly filled her chest. "You knew this whole time that you were coming back and you still left without saying good-bye?" She expected him to look ashamed, or at least apologetic, but he didn't. He met her eyes without blinking.

"As opposed to waiting for you to come and tell me in person that you were choosing David instead of me and wouldn't be coming round anymore?"

She looked away, guilt crowding out her hurt feelings.

"How would that have done me any good? You'd have felt better—heroic even—and I'd have looked like a fool going off to the other side of the world to play scorned lover." He

17

paused, taking a bite of the nectarine and chewing thought-fully for a moment. "Instead, you had to feel the weight of your choices and I got to keep some of my pride. Just a touch," he added, "since, regardless, I *still* had to go off to the other side of the world and play scorned lover. I think my mother would say, 'Same fruit, different bough.'"

Laurel wasn't sure she grasped the idiom. Even after two summers in Avalon, faerie culture mostly eluded her. But she got the gist of it.

"What's done is done," Tamani said, polishing off the nectarine, "and I suggest we don't dwell on it." He concentrated for a second before throwing the pit hard at the trees.

A quiet grunt sounded. "Hecate's eye, Tamani! Was that really necessary?"

Tamani grinned as a tall sentry with closely cropped hair materialized from between the trees, rubbing his arm. "You were spying," Tamani said, his tone light.

"I tried to give you some space, but you did ask me to meet you here."

Tamani spread his hands wide in defeat. "Touché. Who else is coming?"

"The others are watching the house; there's no reason for them to join us."

"Great," Tamani said, sitting up straighter. "Laurel, have you met Aaron?"

"Several times," Laurel said, smiling her greeting. "Several" was probably stretching it, but she was fairly certain they had met once or twice. Last winter she had tried to go out and talk with the sentries—make friends. But they always simply bowed at the waist, which she despised, and said nothing. Still, Aaron looked familiar.

More importantly, he didn't correct her. He just nodded—so deeply it was almost a bow—then turned back to Tamani.

"I'm not here as a regular sentry," Tamani began, looking at Laurel. "I'm here to be what I was always supposed to be: *Fear-gleidhidh.*"

It took Laurel a moment to remember the word. Last fall, Tamani had told her it meant "escort," and it resembled a word the Winter faeries used for their bodyguards. But it was somehow more . . . personal.

"We had too many close calls last year," Tamani continued. "It's hard for us to watch you while you're at school, or protect you well in crowded places. So I went to the Manor for some advanced training. I can't blend in with humans as well as you do, but I can blend in well enough to stay close no matter what."

"Is that really necessary?" Laurel interjected.

Both fae turned to look at her blankly.

"There hasn't been any sign of trolls—or anything else—for months."

A look passed between the two sentries and Laurel felt a stab of fear as she realized there was something they hadn't told her. "That's not . . . exactly true," Aaron said.

"They've seen *signs* of trolls," Tamani said, sitting back down on the fallen log. "Just no actual trolls."

"Is that bad?" Laurel asked, still thinking that not seeing

trolls—for any reason—was a good thing.

"Very," Tamani said. "We've seen footprints, bloody animal corpses, even an occasional fire pit. But the sentries here are using everything they use at the gates—tracking serums, presence traps—and none of them are registering a troll presence at all. Our tried-and-true methods simply aren't finding the trolls we *know* are here somewhere."

"Couldn't they be . . . *old* signs? Like, from last year?" Laurel asked.

Aaron started to say something, but Tamani spoke over him. "Trust me, they're new."

Laurel felt a little sick to her stomach. She probably didn't want to know what Aaron had been about to say.

"But I would have come regardless," Tamani continued. "Even before you told Shar about the lighthouse, Jamison wanted to send me to find out more about Barnes's horde," Tamani said. "His death gave us some peace, but a troll like him would have lieutenants, or commanders. I think it's safe to assume this is merely the calm before the storm."

Fear was gnawing at her insides now. It was a feeling Laurel had grown used to living without and she wasn't happy with its sudden return.

"You also gave Klea four sleeping trolls, and it's probably too much to hope that they simply woke up, killed her, and got on with their lives. It's possible she interrogated them and found out about you, maybe about the gate."

Laurel snapped to attention, feeling panicked. "Interrogated? The way she talked, I figured she would just . . . kill them. Dissect them. I didn't even—"

"It's okay," Tamani said. "You did the best you knew how, under the circumstances. You're not a sentry. Maybe Klea did kill them outright; trying to interrogate them would be suicidal for most humans. And we don't know how much Barnes told his lackeys, either. Still, we have to prepare for the worst. If these troll hunters decide to become faerie hunters, then you could be in more danger than ever. Jamison wanted to address these new developments, so he changed the plan slightly."

"Slightly," Laurel echoed, feeling suddenly weary. She closed her eyes and covered her face with her hands. She felt Tamani's arm slip around her.

"Listen," Tamani said to Aaron, "I'm going to take her inside. I think we're done here."

A soft nudge brought Laurel to her feet and she headed toward her house without saying good-bye. She walked quickly, pulling away from Tamani's hand, wanting both to put distance between them and exert her independence.

What was left of it, anyway.

She pushed through the back door, leaving it open for Tamani, and walked over to the fridge, grabbing the first piece of fruit she saw.

"Do you mind if I have another one?" Tamani asked. "The one you gave me really helped."

Wordlessly Laurel handed him the fruit, realizing she had no appetite for it.

"What's wrong?" Tamani asked at last.

"I'm not really sure," Laurel said, avoiding his eyes. "Everything is just so . . . crazy. I mean"—she looked up at him now—"I'm so glad you're back. I really am."

"Good," Tamani said, his smile a little shaky. "I was starting to wonder there."

"But then you tell me I'm in all this danger and suddenly I'm afraid for my life again. No offense, but it kind of overshadows the happiness."

"Shar wanted to send someone else and just not tell you, but I thought you'd rather know. Even if it meant . . . well, all of this," he said, gesturing vaguely.

Laurel considered. Something inside her insisted it was better this way, but she wasn't so sure. "How much danger am I really in?"

"We're not sure." Tamani hesitated. "There's definitely something going on. I've been here only a few days, but the things I've seen . . . Are you familiar with tracking serums?"

"Sure. They change color, right? To show how old a trail is? I can't make them yet—"

"No need. We have batches specially made for tracking trolls and humans. I poured some in a fresh track and it didn't react *at all*."

"So, none of your magic works?" Laurel asked, her throat tightening.

"It appears that way," Tamani admitted.

"You're not making me feel any safer," Laurel said, trying to inject some humor with a smile. But the quiver in her voice betrayed her.

"Please don't be afraid," Tamani insisted. "We don't *need* magic—it just makes things easier. We're doing everything we can to patrol the area. We're not taking any chances." He paused. "The problem is that we don't actually know what we're up against. We don't know how many there are, what they're up to, nothing."

"So you're here to tell me I have to be super-careful again," Laurel said, knowing she should feel gratitude instead of resentment. "Stay at home, sundown is Cinderella time, all that?"

"No," Tamani said quietly, surprising her. "I'm not here to tell you anything like that. I don't do patrols, I don't go hunting, I just stick close to you. You live your life and continue with all of your normal activities. I'll keep you safe," he said, stepping forward to sweep a lock of hair back from her face. "Or die trying."

Laurel stood frozen, knowing he meant every word. He misread her stillness as an invitation and leaned forward, his hand cupping her cheek.

"I missed you," he whispered, his breath light on her face. A gentle sigh escaped Laurel's lips before she could stop it and as Tamani drew nearer her eyes began to close on their own.

"Nothing's changed," she forced herself to whisper, his face only a hair's breadth from hers. "I made my choice."

His hand stilled, but she sensed the slightest tremor at his fingertips. She watched him swallow once before smiling wanly and pulling back.

"Forgive me. I overstepped."

"What am I supposed to do?"

"Same thing you do every day," Tamani said, shrugging. "The less change to your routine, the better."

"That's not what I meant," said Laurel, forcing herself to look him in the eye.

He shook his head. "Nothing. It's me who has to deal with it, not you."

Laurel looked at the floor.

"I mean it," Tamani said, shifting subtly, putting more distance between them. "You don't have to watch out for me or try to be my friend in school. I'll just be around, and it will be fine."

"Fine," Laurel repeated, nodding.

"You know those apartments down on Harding?" Tamani asked, sounding casual again.

"The green ones?"

"Aye. I'm number seven," he said, his smile playful. "Just in case you ever need me."

He headed toward the front door and Laurel watched him for a few seconds before reality crept back in. "Tamani, stop!" she said, leaping off her stool and sprinting to the entryway. "Do *not* go out my front door with no shirt on. I have very nosy neighbors." She reached out to grab his arm. He turned and, almost instinctively, his hand rose to cover hers. He stared down at her fingers, so light against his olive skin, and his eyes traced the length of her hand, her arm, her shoulder, her neck. He closed his eyes for a moment and took a deep breath. When he opened them again his expression was neutral. He smiled easily, gave her hand a squeeze, then released it and let it fall from his arm.

"Of course," he said lightly. "I'll go out the back."

He turned toward the kitchen, then paused. He lifted his hand and touched the necklace he had given her when they first met—her baby faerie ring, which hung on its silver chain. He smiled softly. "I'm glad you still wear this."

# THREE

SCHOOL WAS ALMOST UNBEARABLY AWKWARD FOR
the next few days; Tamani's presence in Government drove
Laurel crazy and his presence in Speech drove *David* crazy.
The fact that apparently there were still trolls hanging around
Crescent City would probably have disturbed Chelsea more
if she weren't so happy to have a *second* faerie at Del Norte
High. But though he was always around, Tamani mostly
ignored Laurel and her friends. And while Laurel appreciated the occasional wink or secret smile, even those served
to remind her of the dangers that could be lurking around
every corner.

But with the return of homework and tests and research
papers, Laurel found herself slipping into her usual school
routine—trolls or no trolls, Tamani or no Tamani. She
knew from experience how exhausting it could get, living
in constant fear, and she refused to simply *endure* high school.

She wanted to live her life, and though Laurel hated to admit it, her life didn't have a lot of room for Tamani.

She wasn't sure whether to feel sad about that, or guilty, or exasperated. Whether or not there was room in her life for Tamani, Laurel knew that there was precious little room in Tamani's life for anyone or anything but Laurel. He lived to protect her, and he'd never failed her. Annoyed her, frustrated her, hurt her, maddened her—but never once failed her.

Sometimes she wondered what he did when she wasn't around. But, especially in the afternoons, when she would lay snuggled up on the couch with David, she thought she was probably better off not knowing. She and David didn't discuss it—she'd told him what was happening, of course, but they had long since come to the mutually tacit conclusion that where Tamani was concerned, silence was golden.

The itchy feeling that she was being watched was almost continual now. Laurel tried not to dwell on how often it was real, and how often imagined. But she often *hoped* it was real, particularly when a suspicious-looking vehicle drove by her house.

Or when her doorbell rang unexpectedly.

"Ignore it," David said, looking up from his crisp, neatly tabbed notes as Laurel slid her messy ones off her lap. "It's probably just a sales guy or something."

"Can't," Laurel said. "Mom's expecting a package from eBay. I'll have to sign for it."

"Hurry back," David said with a grin.

Laurel was still smiling when she opened the door. But the instant she saw the familiar face her smile melted away and she tried to recover by pasting on a new one. "Klea! Hi! I—"

"Sorry to drop by unannounced," Klea said with a smirk to rival the *Mona Lisa*'s. She was—as usual—dressed from head to toe in formfitting black, her mirrored sunglasses drawn down over her eyes. "I was hoping I could call in a favor."

That seemed strangely direct, coming from Klea. Laurel's mind went to Tamani's words last week about the calm before the storm. She hoped she wasn't watching that storm roll in. "What kind of favor?" she asked, grateful her voice sounded steady, strong. "Can we talk out here?" Klea asked, nodding toward the front veranda.

Laurel followed her hesitantly, though she knew no one got this close to her house without sentries tracking their every move. Klea extended one hand toward a girl who was standing silently next to the wicker chair farthest from them. "Laurel, I'd like you to meet Yuki."

It was the girl Laurel had seen with Tamani on their first day of school—the Japanese exchange student. She was wearing a khaki canvas skirt and a light, airy top decorated with red flowers. She was a little taller than Laurel, but the way she stood made her seem very small—arms folded, shoulders slumped, chin tucked against her chest. Laurel was familiar with the posture; it was the same one she assumed when she wished she could disappear.

"Yuki?" Klea prompted. Yuki raised her chin and lifted her long eyelashes, settling her gaze on Laurel.

Laurel blinked in surprise. The girl had elegant almond-shaped eyes, but they were a shockingly pale green that seemed at odds with her dark hair and complexion. Very beautiful, though—a striking combination.

"Hi." Feeling awkward, Laurel thrust her hand out. Yuki took it, limply; Laurel quickly let go. The whole encounter was weirding her out. "You're our new foreign exchange student, right?" Laurel asked, her eyes flitting to Klea.

Klea cleared her throat. "Not exactly. Well, she *is* from Japan, but we may have falsified some paperwork to get her into your school system. Calling her foreign exchange was the easiest way."

Laurel's lips formed a silent O.

"Can we sit?" Klea asked.

Laurel nodded numbly.

"You may recall, I solicited the possibility of your assistance last fall," Klea began, leaning back in the wicker chair. "I hoped we wouldn't need it, but unfortunately, we do. Yuki is . . . a person of interest to my organization. Not an enemy," she added quickly, cutting off Laurel's question. She turned to Yuki and stroked her long hair, brushing it back from her face. "She needs protection. We rescued her from trolls when she was just a baby, and placed her with a host family in Japan, as far from any known hordes as we could manage." Klea sighed. "Unfortunately, nothing is foolproof. Last fall, Yuki's host family—um, foster parents—were killed by trolls trying to capture her. We barely got her out in time."

Laurel looked over at Yuki, who was staring calmly back, as if Klea had not just spoken of her parents' murder.

"They sent her to me. Again. She's been traveling with us, but she really ought to be in school." Klea removed her sunglasses, just long enough to rub wearily at her eyes. It wasn't even sunny out—but of course, Klea wore the stupid things even at night, so Laurel wasn't surprised. "Plus, we managed to clear out the trolls in this area last year. Anyway, I don't want to put her back in danger, and I certainly don't want any new trolls to discover her. So we've put her in school here."

"I don't understand. Why here? What do you need me for?" Laurel saw no reason to conceal her skepticism. She had seen Klea's camp—when it came to trolls, she couldn't think of anyone less in need of help than Klea.

"Hopefully, not much. But I'm in a real bind. I can't risk having her with me on a hunt. If I send her too far away, she's vulnerable to trolls I *don't* know about. If I don't send her far enough, anything that slips through our dragnet could come after her. You held your own against five trolls last year, and Jeremiah Barnes was an especially difficult case. Considering that, I suspect you could deal with any . . . *rogue elements* that might show up in town. And I just thought you'd be a good person to keep an eye on her. Please?" Klea added, almost as an afterthought.

There had to be more to this than Klea was saying, but

Laurel couldn't imagine what. Was Yuki here to spy on Laurel? Or was Laurel letting Tamani's suspicions make her paranoid? Klea *had* saved Laurel's life—twice! Still, her reluctance to trust Klea was an unscratchable itch. No matter how much sense the woman made, no matter how plausible her stories sounded, every word that came out of her mouth felt *wrong*.

Was Klea being deliberately mysterious now? Maybe it was because this was the first time Laurel had seen Klea in broad daylight, or because she was emboldened by the nearness of her faerie protectors, or even just because she was older and more confident now. But whatever the reason, Laurel decided she'd had enough. "Klea, why don't you just tell me what you're really doing here?"

This, strangely, made Yuki chuckle, if only a little. Klea's face was momentarily expressionless, then she too smiled. "That's what I like about you, Laurel—you still don't trust me, after everything I've done for you. And why should you? You know nothing about me. Your caution is to your credit. But I need you to trust me now, at least enough to help me out, so I'll give it to you straight." She looked over at Yuki, who was staring down into her lap. Klea leaned forward and lowered her voice. "We think the trolls are after Yuki because she's not exactly . . . *human*."

Laurel's eyes widened.

"We've classified her as a dryad," Klea continued. "It seems to fit. But she's the only specimen we've encountered. All we know for sure is that she's not an animal; she has plant cells. She seems to take nourishment from the soil and sunlight as well as external sources. She doesn't exhibit any paranormal abilities, like the strength or persuasion we see in trolls, but her metabolism is a little miraculous, so . . . anyway. I really do need you to keep an eye on her. It may be months before I can arrange a permanent safe house. My hope is that I've hidden her well enough for now, but if not, you're my backup plan."

It took less than a second for Laurel to understand. She turned back to Yuki, and Yuki finally looked up at Laurel. Her pale green eyes. They were mirrors of Laurel's eyes. Aaron's eyes. Katya's eyes. And, lately, Tamani's eyes.

Those were faerie eyes.

# FOUR

LAUREL PUSHED THE DOOR CLOSED, WANTING NOTHING more than to turn back time; to have ignored the doorbell like David suggested. Not that an unanswered door would be likely to deter Klea, but . . .

"Well?"

Laurel spun around, startled by the sound of Tamani's voice. He was standing next to David in the front room. Both had their arms crossed in front of them.

"When did *you* get here?" she asked, confused.

"About half a second before you answered the door," David replied for him.

"What did she want?" Tamani asked. He pursed his lips and shook his head. "I couldn't quite hear what she was saying. If I didn't know better, I'd swear she picked that spot on purpose—like she knew I was there."

Laurel shook her head. "It's the porch, Tamani. It's a

common place to sit and chat."

Tamani looked unconvinced, but he didn't press the issue. "So what's going on? Why was Yuki with her?"

"Who's Yuki?" David asked.

"The girl from Japan," Tamani said brusquely. "The exchange student."

Laurel stared at him for a second, wondering if he already knew. But she remembered that they had all toured the school together. Obviously Robison would have made introductions. Besides, he would have told her if he knew— wouldn't he?

"She's a faerie," Laurel said softly.

Stunned silence buzzed in her ears.

Tamani opened his mouth, then stopped and closed it. He laughed humorlessly. "Those eyes. I should have seen it." His grimace became a determined scowl. "So Klea knows about faeries—we have to assume she knows about you."

"I'm not sure she does know about faeries," Laurel said slowly. "She called Yuki a dryad." Laurel sat down on the couch—where David immediately joined her—and related the rest of the conversation as Tamani paced the room. "I don't like her and I don't trust her, but I don't think Klea actually knows what Yuki is."

Tamani stood still now, his knuckles pressed softly against his mouth.

"Klea did save our lives. Twice, even," David said. "But bringing another faerie to Del Norte seems like a pretty big coincidence."

"Right," Laurel said, trying to sort out her feelings. Part of her was overjoyed. Another faerie, living as a human! And not just for show, like Tamani, but raised from a young age by adoptive parents. That part of Laurel wanted to embrace Yuki and pull her inside the house and grill her about her life, her coping techniques, her daily routine. What did she eat? Had she blossomed yet? But revealing anything to Yuki surely meant telling Klea as well, and that was *not* something Laurel wanted to do.

"What do we know about Yuki?" David asked, looking to Tamani, who again crossed his arms and shook his head.

"Basically nothing. But she's involved with Klea, so we know she can't be trusted," Tamani said darkly.

"What if Klea's telling the truth?" Whatever her doubts about Klea, Laurel found herself hoping that Yuki was, at worst, an innocent pawn. She wasn't sure why. Perhaps just a natural desire to defend her own kind. Besides, she seemed so timid and shy. "I mean, if she's here to spy, why reveal herself at all?"

"There are a lot of different ways to spy," Tamani said slowly. "Yuki could be a diversion, or she could be hiding in plain sight. Knowing Yuki is a faerie isn't nearly as important as knowing *what kind*."

"Aren't most of you Spring faeries?" asked David.

"Sure," Tamani agreed. "And a strong Ticer surrounded by humans is as good as an army."

David blanched, but Laurel shook her head. "Klea said Yuki didn't have any powers."

"Klea could be lying. Or Yuki could be hiding her abilities from Klea." He paused, grinning a little. "In fact, *Yuki* could be the one lying to *Klea*. Wouldn't *that* be something."

"So what's the worst-case scenario?" David asked. "She Entices me or Chelsea into spilling your secrets?"

"Or she's a Sparkler and she's in here right now, invisible, listening to this conversation," Tamani said.

"Summer faeries can do that?" Laurel asked.

"Some of them," Tamani said. "Not that she's likely to figure that out without training. But until today, I would have told you that I knew the location of every faerie outside of Avalon, so I guess anything is possible. For all we know, Yuki could be a Winter." He closed his eyes, shaking his head a little. The thought made Laurel's stomach clench. "Or a Fall." He hesitated again, then spoke in a rush, as though afraid someone would stop him before he'd had his say. "She could even be the Mixer who poisoned your father."

Laurel felt like she'd been punched in the stomach. She managed to choke out a strangled, "What?"

"I—I—" Tamani stammered. "Look, the point is, she could be harmless, but she could be very, very dangerous. So we need to act quickly," Tamani said, avoiding the question.

But Laurel wasn't going to let him off that easy. "You mean two years ago—when he got sick? You said it was trolls."

Tamani sighed. "It *could* have been the trolls. But in centuries of dealing with the trolls, we've never seen them use poison like that. They're brutal and manipulative . . . but they're not Mixers. So when your father got sick—"

"You think a Fall faerie did that?" Laurel asked blankly. Suddenly it made horrible sense.

"Yes. No. We thought *maybe*—"

"And you didn't tell me?" Laurel felt her anger rising. What else had Tamani been holding back? He was supposed to teach her about the faerie realm, not keep her in the dark! "I've been to the Academy *twice* since then! Where basically all the Fall faeries live! You should have said something!"

"I *tried*," Tamani protested, "but Shar stopped me. And he was right to stop me. We investigated. Aside from you, no Mixers have been through the gates without constant supervision in decades. We don't let fae cross out of Avalon lightly."

"You let me," Laurel insisted.

Tamani smiled softly, almost sadly. "You are very, very special." He cleared his throat and continued. "No one wanted you to go into the Academy suspecting every Mixer you met of trying to kill your father. Especially since it probably wasn't one of them."

Laurel contemplated that. She knew several Fall faeries who were experts at animal poisons. Including Mara, who was still nursing an ancient grudge. "But now you think Yuki had something to do with it?" she asked, pushing that thought aside to focus on the threat at hand.

"Maybe. I mean, it doesn't seem likely. She's so young. And on top of that, Barnes showed resistance to our potions, so he could have been an unusually gifted troll in other ways too. All I know for sure is, Yuki shouldn't be here. No wild faerie should be here."

"Hang on," David said, leaning forward, placing a hand on Laurel's leg. "If Yuki poisoned your dad, then Yuki had to be working for Barnes—but if Yuki was working for Barnes, why is she with Klea now? Klea *killed* Barnes."

"Maybe she was Barnes's prisoner and Klea rescued her," Laurel said.

"Then why not tell you that?" David asked. "Why lie about Yuki being an orphan?"

"And we're back to Klea lying again," Tamani said wryly.

After a long silence, Laurel shook her head. "It doesn't add up. We don't *know* anything. All we have is what Klea told me." She hesitated. "What I'd really like is to get Yuki's side of the story."

"Impossible," Tamani said instantly.

Laurel glared, annoyed at his dismissal. "Why?"

Tamani saw the change in her expression and softened his tone. "I think it's too dangerous," he said softly.

"Can't you Entice her?" David asked.

"It doesn't really work on faeries," Laurel said. But it had worked on her, before she knew what she was—maybe David had a point.

Tamani shook his head. "It's worse than that. If it doesn't work at all, it will be because she knows about Enticement, and then she'll realize I'm fae. I can't risk that until we find out more."

"How are we supposed to do that?" Laurel asked,

exasperated. The impossibility of the situation was suffocating. "We don't know who's lying and who's telling the truth. Maybe no one's telling the truth!"

"I think we need to go see Jamison," Tamani said after a pause.

Laurel found herself nodding. "I think that's a good idea," she said slowly.

Tamani pulled something out of his pocket, and began tapping at it.

"Oh my gosh, is that an iPhone?" Laurel asked, her voice unconsciously rising in pitch and volume.

Tamani looked up at her, his expression blank. "Yeah?"

"He has an iPhone," Laurel said to David. "My faerie sentry who generally lives without *running water* has an iPhone. That's. Just. Great. Everyone in the whole world has a cell phone except me. That's *awesome*." Her parents still insisted that cell phones were for adults and college students. *So* behind the times.

"It's essential for communication purposes," Tamani said defensively. "I have to admit, humans are far beyond the fae in terms of communication. With this we can deliver messages instantly. A few buttons and I can talk to Shar! It's astounding."

Laurel rolled her eyes. "I'm aware of what they do." She paused, a pained expression clouding her features. "Shar has one too?"

"Granted," Tamani said slowly, not answering her question, "it doesn't work quite as well for us as humans. Our

39

bodies don't conduct electrical currents the same, so sometimes I have to touch the screen more than once to get it to react. Still, I can hardly complain."

David offered Laurel an apologetic smile. "You're always welcome to use mine."

Tamani growled and muttered an unfamiliar word under his breath. "No answer." He shoved the phone in his pocket and stood with his hands on his hips, looking pensive.

Laurel stared at him, his tense shoulders, his dominating posture. He'd been back for about two weeks, and everything in Laurel's life had been thrown into chaos.

Sexy, sexy chaos.

At least he had his shirt on this time. She cleared her throat and looked away, pulling her thoughts back where they belonged.

"We need to go to the land," Tamani said, pulling a ring of keys out of his pocket. "Let's go."

"What? Wait!" Laurel said, rising to her feet and feeling David do the same at her side. "We can't go to the land tonight."

"Why not? Jamison needs to know about this. I'll drive."

That sounded so wrong coming out of Tamani's mouth. "Because it's almost six o'clock. My parents are going to be home soon and I still have homework."

Tamani looked confused. "So?"

Laurel shook her head. "Tamani, I can't go. I have things to do here. *You* go. You don't need me. Besides," she added, glancing out at the purpling sky, "it'll be dark soon. This whole thing has really put me on edge and I would feel better if we were all home before sundown tonight. You're the one who told me there are still trolls around," she added.

"That's why I have to stay close to you," he insisted. "It's my job."

"Well, high school is *my* job," Laurel said. "Not to mention keeping my family and friends safe. Anyway, you have your phone. Call Shar again later; have him arrange a time this weekend for Jamison to come out and talk with us. We have a half day at school on Friday, so we can go then. Or Saturday, when we can be back in plenty of time before sundown."

Tamani was gritting his teeth, and Laurel could tell that although he didn't like what she was saying, he knew it made more sense than rushing off on an hour-long drive to the land just as the sun was starting to set. "Fine," he said at last. "But we're going on Friday, not Saturday."

"*After* school," Laurel said.

"*Right* after school."

"Deal."

Tamani nodded stoically. "David should probably head home, then. It'll be sunset soon." And with that he turned and headed toward the back of the house. Laurel listened for a door, but heard nothing. After a few seconds she peeked into the kitchen, but he was nowhere to be seen.

David came up behind her and nestled his face against her neck, his breath hot on her collarbone. She wanted to hold him closer, tighter, but knew it would have to wait. Despite

Tamani's assurance that he could handle things, Laurel was back to wanting David safe inside his house at sundown.

"You really should get home," she whispered. "I don't want you outside after dark."

"You don't have to worry about me so much," David said.

Laurel pulled back and looked up at him. "Yes, I do," she said softly. "What would I do without you?" It was a question that no longer seemed so hypothetical, and she didn't want to know the answer.

# FIVE

TAMANI SHUT THE DOOR NOISELESSLY BEHIND HIM, breaking into a silent run toward the darkening tree line. He didn't have much time—one of the less pleasant parts of his job was seeing that David got home alive once Laurel was safely in for the night. Keeping the human boy breathing didn't rate high on Tamani's personal priority scale, but since Laurel's happiness was second only to her safety, David was watched.

Aaron reached out to grab Tamani's arm as he passed the nearest tree. "What's happening?" he whispered.

"We have trouble," Tamani replied grimly.

Trouble was the least of what they had. Now that he didn't have to look confident and strong for Laurel's benefit, Tamani sank to the ground, ran his fingers through his hair—he still wasn't used to it being so short—and let his worst fears wash over him. Not for the first time, Tamani wished Jamison would simply order Laurel to Avalon for good. But Jamison insisted it wasn't time and that Laurel had to come willingly.

"Another faerie has arrived," he said.

Aaron raised one eyebrow. "Shar didn't say anything—"

"With the Huntress. Not from Avalon."

Aaron's other eyebrow went up. "Unseelie?"

"That doesn't seem likely. She's got to be some kind of . . . wild faerie."

"But that's impossible," Aaron said, stepping closer, his fists on his hips.

"I know," Tamani said, looking toward the house and seeing two silhouettes moving about the kitchen in the dying evening light. He recapped the visit to Aaron, fear gripping his chest as worst-case scenarios ran through his head.

"What does this mean for us?" Aaron asked.

"I don't know," Tamani replied. "More reinforcements, for one."

"More?" Aaron stared in disbelief. "At this rate we'll have half of Avalon here by winter."

"It can't be helped. We'll need at least one squad watching the new girl. Maybe two. Jamison promised me more sentries if we need them, and I don't want to take anyone from Laurel's house."

Tamani looked up at the sound of a car engine turning over. David's car—it had a distinctive tick that had become all too familiar the last couple weeks. It was time to go. Rising to his feet, Tamani pulled his phone out of his pocket.

He'd try Shar again as he tracked David. He turned and placed his free hand on Aaron's shoulder. "This faerie has the potential to destroy everything we've worked for. We cannot take her lightly."

He didn't wait for Aaron's reply before sprinting off after David's taillights.

Whatever Yuki was up to, it apparently required her to ignore Laurel at all costs.

At first Laurel thought Yuki was simply shy, as any attempt to approach her resulted in a murmured apology followed by a hasty retreat. But when Laurel settled for smiling at her in the hallway, Yuki pretended not to notice. By Thursday, even finding Yuki became a challenge, and Laurel's efforts were giving her a headache. Laurel didn't want to go to Jamison before she'd found *something* out about Yuki, but the elusive faerie wasn't giving her much choice.

On Friday morning Tamani wasn't in Government when Laurel walked in. She was beginning to worry when he plopped himself down in his seat just as the final bell rang. Mrs. Harms didn't mark him tardy, but she did raise one menacing eyebrow that seemed to say, *Next time.*

"Shar's still not answering," Tamani hissed as soon as Mrs. Harms turned her back to write on the whiteboard.

Laurel shot him a concerned look. "Not at all?"

"Not once." He was practically twitching in his seat. "It could be nothing," he added, sounding like he was trying to convince himself. "Shar hates his phone. He doesn't think we should be using human technology; says we always get into trouble when we do. So he's stubborn enough to not answer it on principle. But it . . . it could mean something's happened. We're still on for today, right?"

"Yes," Laurel said earnestly. "I told my parents and everything. We're good to go."

"Great," he said, sounding more nervous than excited.

"Are we still going to get to see Jamison?" Laurel asked.

Tamani hesitated and Laurel looked questioningly at him. "I don't know," he admitted. "Shar is really paranoid about opening the gate—especially without warning."

"We *have* to see Jamison," Laurel insisted in a whisper. "That's the whole point, isn't it?"

Tamani looked at her for a moment with a strange expression on his face that almost made Laurel think he was mad at her. "For you, I guess," he said darkly, then turned to the front of the room, doodling furiously as Laurel took notes. Laurel tried to catch his eye, but he looked steadfastly away from her. What had she said?

As soon as the bell rang Tamani stood and hurried toward the door without a backward glance. Just as he passed into the hall, Laurel heard a grunt and a scuffle. Craning her neck, she saw David and Tamani standing chest to chest, a couple of books on the floor at their feet.

"Sorry," David murmured. "Didn't see you."

Tamani glared at David for a moment, then he lowered his eyes and mumbled an apology as he retrieved his books and slid out into the hallway.

"What was that?" Laurel asked as she and David fell into step beside each other in the hall.

"It was an accident," David said. "The bell rang and he came barreling out. I didn't have time to move." He hesitated before adding, "He didn't look happy."

"He's mad at me," Laurel said, watching Tamani's back disappear into the crowd. "I don't know why."

"What happened?"

Laurel explained as they walked to their side-by-side lockers. Being a senior was not without its perks.

"Is it because I'm not that worried about Shar?" she asked.

David hesitated. "It could be," he admitted. "Don't you get mad at him when he doesn't seem worried about me? Or Chelsea?"

"Yeah, but that's different. You and Chelsea aren't like Shar. Tamani doesn't worry about you because you don't matter to him," Laurel said, stifling the anger she always felt at Tamani's general scorn for humans. "*I'm* not worried about Shar because he is totally capable of taking care of himself. It's . . . a respect thing."

"I get that, but if Tamani's worried," David said, lowering his voice, "don't you think maybe you should be too?"

It made sense, and Laurel felt her old grudge melt away—for the moment. "You're right," she said. "I should apologize."

"Well, you'll have plenty of time this afternoon," David said in a deceptively light voice.

Laurel laughed, giving a mock gasp. "David, are you jealous?"

"No! Well, I mean, I'd love to spend the afternoon with you, so in that way, yeah, I guess so." He shrugged. "I just wish I could go." He paused, then looked at her with transparent innocence. "I could wait in the car."

"It's probably not a good idea," Laurel said softly, thinking about the conversation she'd just had with Tamani. "We're trying to get into Avalon without advance notice as it is. Bringing you with us would probably just put them on edge."

"Okay." David paused again, then leaned his head closer to her and said in a fierce whisper, "I *wish* I could go through that gate with you."

Her throat tightened. Avalon was the one thing she could never share with David. And it wasn't just that the fae would never let him through the gate—Laurel was a little worried about how David would be treated even if he *were* allowed. "I know," she whispered, reaching her hands up to touch his cheeks.

"I'll miss you," he said.

She laughed. "I'm not leaving yet!"

"Yeah, but you're going to class. I'll miss you till it's over."

Laurel slapped his shoulder playfully. "You are so sappy."

"Yeah, but you love me."

"I do," Laurel said, folding herself into his arms.

When class let out for the day, Laurel headed straight for the parking lot, knowing how anxious Tamani was. And, admittedly, she was a little curious to see what kind of car he drove. She shouldn't have been surprised to see a convertible.

Tamani said nothing as he unlocked her door and lowered the car's top.

For the first couple of minutes, Laurel was simply fascinated by the sight of Tamani driving. The novelty of seeing him in distinctly human situations was starting to wear off, but it wasn't gone yet.

As Tamani pulled onto the highway, Laurel finally broke the silence. "I'm sorry," she said.

"For what?" Tamani replied, donning a convincingly unaffected air.

"For not taking you seriously. About Shar."

"It's okay," Tamani said guardedly. "I overreacted."

"No, you didn't," Laurel insisted. "I should have listened."

Tamani was silent.

Laurel sat, not knowing what to say next.

"If anything happened to him, I don't know what I'd do," Tamani finally said, his words coming out in a rush.

Not wanting to interrupt and make him clam up, Laurel simply nodded.

"Shar is . . . I would probably say he's like a brother, if I knew what that was like." He glanced over at her for a second before returning his eyes to the road. "Everything I am now, I owe to him. I wasn't even technically old enough to be in the guard when he took it upon himself to make a proper sentry out of me." Finally, Tamani smiled again. "He's the main reason I got to meet you again."

"He'll be fine," Laurel said, trying to sound confident rather than dismissive. "From everything you've told me and everything I know about him, he's really amazing. I'm sure he's okay."

"I hope so," Tamani said, edging his speed up a little higher.

Laurel watched the road, but out the corner of her eye she could see Tamani stealing glances at her. "You hardly talk to me at school," Laurel said a few minutes later as Tamani sped down the passing lane, overtaking a convoy of RVs. She was impressed. He had a manual transmission and was shifting through gears way better than she had when she was a new driver.

Tamani shrugged. "Well, we're not supposed to know each other, remember?"

"Yeah, but you talk to me in Government. You could at least wave in the halls."

Tamani glanced her way. "I'm not sure that would be a good idea."

"Why not?"

"Because of Yuki. Klea. Trolls. Take your pick." He paused. "I worry about too many faeries being together in one place. I'd like to," he added, smiling, "but I don't think it's a good idea."

"Oh, absolutely!" Laurel said in mock cheerfulness. "We should hide our friendship instead, and then if anyone sees us driving around like this they'll assume I'm cheating on my boyfriend. That's a *much* better idea. Why didn't I think of that?" She glanced sidelong at him. "Trust me, in a small town, scandal draws way more attention than group vegetarianism."

"What do you want me to do?" Tamani asked.

Laurel considered that. "Wave in the halls. Say hi. Don't ignore me in Speech class. In a couple of weeks, it won't seem out of the ordinary to anyone. Not even Yuki or Klea, assuming they care."

Tamani grinned. "Don't you think you're brilliant."

"I don't think," Laurel said with a laugh, leaning her head a little to the side so the wind caught her long, golden hair and threw it back behind her. "I know." After a pause she added, "You could be David's friend too." She glanced at Tamani when he said nothing. He was frowning. "The two of you really have a lot in common, and we're all in this together."

He shook his head. "It wouldn't work."

"Why not? He's a nice guy. And it would do you good to have some human friends," she said, hinting at what she suspected was the root of the problem.

"It's not that," Tamani said, gesturing vaguely with one hand.

"Then why?" Laurel asked, exasperated.

"I just don't want to cozy up to the guy whose girl I have every intention of stealing," he said flatly, without looking at her.

Laurel stared silently out the window for the rest of the trip.

# SIX

WHEN THEY ARRIVED AT THE LAND, TAMANI TURNED to her. "Stay here," he said, his eyes on the tree line. "Just until we know it's safe," he added. Laurel relented; after all, he was combat-trained and she wasn't. He unbuckled his seat belt and sprang out of the convertible without bothering to open the door.

Just before he reached the shadow of the trees, someone in green leaped out from Tamani's right and toppled him over. At first Laurel couldn't identify the blur that knocked Tamani to the ground, but as soon as she realized it was Shar she opened the door and hurried to them.

The two sentries were tangled in the dirt, Tamani with his arms wrenched firmly behind him, his legs wrapped around Shar's waist, pinning him to the ground. Each struggled to get free of the other, but it looked like a stalemate. Laurel crossed her arms and grinned as the faeries grunted out Gaelic epithets and outlandish faerie slurs.

"Rot-headed spore! Make me worry."

"Pansy sentry, totally unprepared."

Finally Tamani called truce and they got to their feet, dusting off their clothes and shaking leaves out of their hair. Laurel noticed that Shar's hair, like Tamani's, was no longer green at the roots. Apparently Tamani hadn't been the only one to change his diet.

"Why didn't you answer the phone, mate? I've been calling you all week!"

Laurel put up a hand to cover her smile as she listened to Tamani's accent thicken with every word. Shar reached into a pouch on his belt and pulled out his iPhone with the same look Laurel's mother reserved for leftovers found moldering in the back of the fridge. "I can't work this blighted thing," Shar said. "Half the time I don't feel it buzzing until it's too late, and even when I do, I put it up to my ear like you said and nothing happens."

"Did you slide the bar?" Tamani asked.

"What bar? It's as smooth as a holly leaf," Shar said, looking at the phone Laurel noticed he was holding upside down. "You told me it's as easy as picking it up and talking. That's what I did."

Tamani sighed, then reached out and punched Shar in the shoulder. Shar didn't even move, much less flinch. "There's not even anything to remember! It tells you right on the screen what to do. Let's try it again," Tamani said, reaching into his pocket.

"No point in that," Shar said moodily, his eyes darting toward Laurel. "I can hear you now." He turned and walked down the path. "Best get out of sight. Would be our luck that after six months with no trolls, one would wander by as we're standing out in the open, gawking at human trinkets."

Tamani stood for a few seconds, phone in hand, then shoved his hands in his pockets and tromped after Shar, looking back with a shrug to make sure Laurel was following. But Laurel could see the relief in his eyes.

About ten feet into the woods, Shar drew abruptly to a halt. "So why are you here?" he asked, his face serious, playful demeanor gone. "The plan was never for you to bounce back and forth. You are supposed to maintain your post in the human world."

Tamani sobered as well. "The situation has changed. The Huntress enrolled a faerie at Laurel's school."

Shar's eyebrow twitched; a big reaction, from him. "The Huntress is back?"

Tamani nodded.

"And she has a faerie with her. How is that even possible?"

"I don't know. Supposedly, Klea's people found her in Japan, where she was raised by human parents. We don't know what she's capable of, if anything." Tamani's eyes darted to Laurel. "I told Laurel about the toxin. The wild faerie—Yuki—looks too young to have made something like that, but who could say for sure?"

Shar's eyes narrowed. "How young does she look?"

"Younger than thirty. Older than ten. You know it would be impossible to say for sure. But from what I've observed of her behavior, she *could* be within a year or two of Laurel's age."

Laurel hadn't even considered that. She knew faeries aged differently from humans, but the differences were most pronounced in very young faeries—like Tamani's niece, Rowen—and middle-aged faeries, who might spend a century looking like a human in the prime of life. Yuki didn't look out of place at Del Norte, but that only meant she was at least as old as her classmates.

Shar was frowning thoughtfully, but asked no further questions.

"Now that I know your sorry pulp isn't crushed to death under some troll's boot, we need to see Jamison," said Tamani. "He'll know what to do."

"We do not just summon Jamison, Tam. You know that," Shar said flatly.

"Shar, it's important."

Shar stepped close to Tamani, his words so quiet Laurel hardly heard them. "The last time I demanded the presence of a Winter faerie it was to save your life. I have watched other fae die when Avalon could have saved them because I knew I could not put my home at risk. We don't call the Winters down for a *chat*." He paused. "I will send a request. When they bring a response, I'll let you know. That is all I can do."

Tamani's face sank. "I thought—"

"You did *not* think," Shar said sternly, and Tamani's mouth clapped shut. Shar chased his reproach with a scowl, but after a moment he sighed and his expression softened. "And that is partly my fault. If I had been able to speak to you on that ridiculous thing you wouldn't have been so concerned, and I could have made the request days ago. I apologize." He placed one hand on Tamani's arm. "It *is* a matter of great importance, but do not forget who you are. You are a sentry; you are a Spring faerie. Even your position of great notice doesn't change that."

Tamani nodded solemnly, saying nothing.

Laurel stood silently for a few seconds, staring at the two fae in disbelief. Despite her assurances to Tamani that she wanted Shar to be safe, *she* came to see Jamison.

And she wasn't leaving until she had.

Lifting her chin defiantly, Laurel turned and headed into the forest as fast as she could without breaking into a run.

"Laurel!" Tamani called immediately after her. "Where are you going?"

"I'm going to Avalon," she said, holding her voice as steady as she could manage.

"Laurel, stop!" Tamani said, wrapping one hand around her upper arm.

Laurel pulled her arm from his grasp, the strength of his fingers stinging against her skin. "Don't try and stop me!" she said loudly. "You have no right!" Without pausing to look at his face, she pivoted and continued the way she had been heading. As she walked, several faeries approached the path, spears raised, but as soon as they recognized her, they backed off.

When she reached the tree that disguised the gate it was guarded by five fully armed sentries. Taking a deep breath and reminding herself that, whatever else they might do, these warriors would never actually harm her, Laurel marched up to the closest one. "I am Laurel Sewell, Apprentice Fall, scion in the human world. I have business with Jamison, the Winter faerie, advisor to Queen Marion, and I demand entrance to Avalon."

The guards, clearly thrown by this display, bowed respectfully at the waist and turned questioning eyes to Shar, who stepped forward and also bowed. Guilt welled up in Laurel's chest, but she forced it down.

"Of course," Shar said softly. "I will send your request immediately. It is, however, up to the Winter faeries to decide whether they will open the gate."

"I'm quite aware," Laurel said, proud that her voice didn't quaver.

Shar bowed again, not meeting her eyes. He circled to the far side of the tree and Laurel wished she could go and see what he did—how he communicated with Avalon. But following him might destroy the illusion of power that, she had to admit, she was doing an excellent job of maintaining. So she averted her eyes and tried to look bored as silent minutes ticked by.

Finally, after what seemed like ages, Shar emerged from behind the tree. "They are sending someone," he said, his voice just a touch raspy. Laurel tried to catch his eye, but though his chin was raised as high and proud as hers, he would not meet her gaze.

"Good," she said, as though she were not the least bit surprised. "I will need to be accompanied by my, um, guardian." She indicated Tamani with a flick of her head. She almost tried the Gaelic word that Tamani used to refer to himself, but didn't trust herself to say it right.

"Of course," Shar said, eyes still glued to the ground. "Your safety is of highest priority to us. Sentries, my first twelve to the front," he ordered.

Laurel felt rather than saw Tamani start forward, but with a quick intake of breath he planted both feet again.

Twelve sentries filed past a large knot on the tree, each placing a hand on it. Laurel remembered with a twinge of sorrow the way Shar had lifted Tamani's nearly lifeless hand to the same knot when she'd brought him back—almost dead—after being shot by Barnes.

She tried to look unimpressed as the tree changed before her, transforming with a brilliant flash of light into the golden-barred gate that protected the faerie realm of Avalon. Beyond the gate, Laurel saw only blackness. Jamison had not yet arrived. Then, slowly, like the sun filtering out from behind a cloud, small fingers appeared and encircled the bars. A moment later the gate swung open, light flowing in to fill the space where there had been only darkness a moment before.

A girl who looked about twelve years old—*if she were*

*human*, Laurel reminded herself; the young faerie was probably fourteen or fifteen—stood in the gateway, dwarfed by
the height of the magnificent gate. It was Yasmine, Jamison's
protégé. Laurel lowered her eyes and inclined her head in
respect. Playing the role meant stepping into all aspects of it.
She straightened and glanced behind her.

And almost lost her nerve.

She hated seeing Tamani act like a Spring faerie. His
hands were clasped behind his back and his eyes were downcast. His shoulders were subtly drawn forward and he looked
very small, despite being half a foot taller than Laurel. Swallowing the lump that had formed in her throat, Laurel said,
"Come on," in the most commanding tone she could muster, and stepped forward.

The young Winter faerie smiled up at Laurel. "Lovely to
see you again," Yasmine said, in a sweet, tinkling voice. Her
gaze traveled back to Tamani and she smiled. "And Tamani.
A pleasure."

Tamani's face softened into a smile so genuine it made
Laurel's heart ache to see it. But he bowed the moment she
met his eyes, and Laurel looked away. She couldn't bear
to witness such obeisance from Tamani. Proud, powerful
Tamani.

Yasmine stepped back, beckoning them forward. Laurel
and Tamani passed by her, but instead of following, Yasmine
greeted someone else. Laurel turned to see Shar step forward
and present himself with a bow.

"Captain?" Yasmine asked.

"If I could, since you are here anyway, may I make use of the Hokkaido gate? I will be ready and waiting when you return with the scion."

"Of course," Yasmine said.

Shar skittered through the gate and Laurel turned to watch it close behind him, the blackness seeping in behind the bars.

"It will take just a moment for the sentries in Hokkaido to prepare for the opening," a small, dark-haired sentry said as she bowed to Yasmine. Yasmine merely nodded as the sentries on the Avalon side gathered around the east-facing gate. Laurel had never seen any of the other gates opened.

"You're going to see *her*, aren't you?" Tamani hissed to Shar.

A sharp look was his only response.

"Don't do it, Shar," Tamani said. "You're always depressed for weeks. We can't afford that now. We need you focused."

"It is because of the new faerie that I am going to her," Shar said seriously. He paused and his eyes darted to Laurel. "If this new faerie was raised as a human in Japan, her appearance could be evidence of the Glamour at work. And if that is the case, *they* may know something. Like it or not, they have knowledge and experience that we don't. I will do whatever it takes to protect Avalon, Tam. Especially if . . ." His voice trailed off. "Just in case," he said in a whisper.

"Shar," Tamani began. Then he pressed his lips together and nodded.

"Captain?" Yasmine's silky voice interrupted them.

"Of course," Shar said, turning away.

An arc of sentries lay just beyond the gate that Yasmine was holding open. They looked almost identical to the circle that always greeted Laurel, except that they were wearing long sleeves and heavy breeches—a strange sight among faeries. A gust of chilly air rushed through the gate, sharp enough to make Laurel gasp. She looked at Shar, but he was already striding forward, pulling a voluminous cloak out of his pack. Then he was gone, and the gate closed behind him.

"This way," Yasmine said, heading up the meandering path that led out of the walled garden. A half-dozen guards, clad in blue, fell into step around them—Yasmine's *Am fear-faire*, the young faerie's guardians and almost constant companions. For this alone Laurel would not have wanted to be a Winter faerie, no matter how powerful they were. She valued what little privacy she had.

They walked silently, passing through the stone walls that enclosed the gates and into Avalon's earthy resplendence. Laurel paused to savor the island's sweet air; the sheer perfection of nature in Avalon was enough to take anyone's breath away. Evening was already falling, and a brilliant sunset was painting itself across the Western horizon. "I'm sorry Jamison could not come and greet you himself," Yasmine said, addressing Laurel, "but he has asked that I bring you to him."

"Where is he?" Laurel asked. She hadn't intended to disturb Jamison in the middle of something important.

"In the Winter Palace," Yasmine said casually.

Laurel stopped in her tracks and looked up the hill to

where the crumbling white marble spires of the Winter Palace could just be seen. She glanced back at Tamani. He stared resolutely at the ground, but a slight tremor of his hands, clasped in front of him, showed her that the thought of entering the sanctuary of the Winter faeries frightened him even more than it frightened her.

# SEVEN

LAUREL LOOKED UP AT THE WINTER PALACE AS THEY approached it on a sharply sloped path. She had noted the green vines that supported large portions of the structure from afar, but as they drew closer she could see where tiny threads sprouted from the vines, enmeshing themselves in the shimmering white stone, encasing the castle in a lover's embrace. Laurel had never seen a building that looked so *alive*!

At the top of the slope, they came to an enormous white archway. On either side sprawled the disintegrating ruins of what must have once been a magnificent wall, and as they passed into the courtyard, Laurel saw that she was surrounded by destruction. Crumbling relics—from statues and fountains to sections of the destroyed wall—jutted incongruously from the beautifully manicured lawn. Nowhere else had Laurel seen such disrepair in Avalon. Everything at the Academy was fixed as soon as it was broken, every structure meticulously maintained. Everywhere else she had visited in Avalon seemed much the same—but not the palace. Laurel couldn't imagine why.

Inside, however, the palace was bustling with faeries dressed in crisp white uniforms, polishing every surface and watering hundreds of plants potted in elaborately crafted urns. It had the same familiar neatness and luxury that Laurel had gotten used to at the Academy.

She and Tamani followed Yasmine to the foot of a wide, grand staircase. The more steps they mounted, the quieter the chamber grew. At first Laurel thought it was a trick of acoustics, but by the time they were halfway up the staircase, the entire room was silent.

Laurel ventured a glance over her shoulder. Tamani was right behind her, but his hands, which had been trembling very slightly before, were now clasped so tightly Laurel imagined he must be hurting himself. Every faerie servant on the floor below them was staring, dusters and watering cans held limply in their unmoving hands. Even the *Am fear-faire* had stopped at the foot of the stairs, not following when Yasmine began her ascent.

"We're going into the upper rooms of the Winter Palace," Tamani whispered quietly, his voice strained. "*No one* goes into the upper rooms. Except Winter faeries, I mean."

Laurel looked up to the top of the stairs. Rather than opening into a wide foyer, as she had expected, they ended in a huge set of double doors, heavily gilded where they showed through a thick hanging of vines. They were the largest doors Laurel had ever seen. They looked too big, too heavy, for Yasmine to move at all.

But the young faerie didn't pause as she reached them. She raised both her hands in front of her, palms out, and made a gentle pushing motion toward the doors without actually touching them. There was visible effort in her movement, as though something in the air was pushing back at her, and gradually, with the rustling of greenery, the doors glided open, just wide enough to pass through single file.

Yasmine looked back at Laurel calmly, expectantly. After a moment's hesitation, Laurel eased through the door, followed by a slightly more reluctant Tamani.

It was like walking under the canopy of the World Tree. The air was alive with magic—with *power.*

"We do not frequently allow other fae into the upper chambers," Yasmine said calmly, "but Jamison felt that anything which would cause our scion to demand a meeting with him must surely call for secrecy only the upper rooms can provide."

Laurel was starting to regret her haste and the impulsive demands she had made to get here. She wondered what Jamison would do when he discovered why they had come. Was a wild faerie in Laurel's school worth all this concern?

"He's back here," Yasmine said, beckoning them through a cavernous room decorated in white and gold. An eclectic mix of items was on display atop a series of alabaster pillars—a small painting, a pearl-encrusted crown, a shiny silver cup.

Laurel squinted at a long-necked lute made of a very dark wood. Cocking her head to the side, she stepped off the deep-blue carpet that streaked across the room and headed toward the lute, obeying a pull it seemed unnecessary to question. She paused before it, wanting nothing else so much as to strum its delicate strings.

Just as she reached for it, Yasmine's hand wrapped around her wrist and pulled her arm back with surprising strength. "I wouldn't touch that if I were you," she said matter-of-factly. "My apologies, I should have warned you; we are all used to the lure. We hardly notice it anymore."

Yasmine padded softly back to the dark-blue rug, her bare feet making no sound on the marble floor. Laurel looked back at the lute. She still wanted to play it, but the pull wasn't quite as strong as before. She hurried away before she could dwell on it too long.

They turned a corner at the end of the vast room. By the time Laurel saw Jamison, he had already heard them coming. He turned from whatever he was doing and stepped toward them through a marble archway, gesturing broadly with both arms as he approached. From either side of the archway, two massive stone walls slid slowly together with a deep, echoing rumble. Over Jamison's shoulder Laurel glimpsed a sword, driven point-down into a squat granite block. The blade gleamed like a polished diamond before vanishing behind the heavy slabs.

"Any luck?" Yasmine asked.

"No more than usual," he said with a smile.

"What was that?" Laurel asked, before she thought to stop herself.

But Jamison just waved her question away. "An old problem. And like most old problems, nothing urgent. But you," he said, smiling, "I'm happy to see you." He extended one hand to Laurel and one to Tamani. Laurel was quick to grasp his hand in both of hers, while inclining her head respectfully. Tamani hesitated, gripped Jamison's hand in a traditional handshake, then let his hand drop and bent formally at the waist without saying anything at all.

"Come," Jamison said, gesturing to a small room just off the marble hall, "we can talk in here." Laurel walked into the finely furnished room and sat on one end of a red brocade sofa. Jamison took his place in a large armchair on her left. She looked up at Tamani, who stood, hesitating. He glanced at the spot beside her, then—changing his mind, or perhaps losing his nerve—stood against the wall and folded his hands in front of him.

Yasmine lingered in the doorway.

Jamison looked up. "Yasmine, thank you for escorting my guests. We have a great deal of training tomorrow. The sun has nearly set and I don't want you exhausted."

Laurel saw the beginnings of a pout form on Yasmine's lips, but at the last second she pulled it back. "Of course, Jamison," she said politely, then slowly withdrew, sneaking one last peek before disappearing around the corner. In that moment Laurel was sharply reminded that, in spite of being powerful and revered, Yasmine was still only a child—and so was

Laurel, especially to someone as ancient and wise as Jamison.

"So," Jamison said once Yasmine's footsteps had faded, "what can I do for you?"

"Well," Laurel said shyly, increasingly certain that her actions back at the gate had been rash and unjustified. "It's important," she blurted finally, "but I don't know that it justifies all this," she said, gesturing to the grandeur surrounding them.

"Better overprepared than overconfident," Jamison said. "Now tell me."

Laurel nodded, trying to stifle her sudden rush of nerves. "It's Klea," she began. "She's back."

"I did expect that." Jamison nodded. "Surely you didn't think we'd seen the end of her?"

"I didn't know," Laurel said defensively. "I thought maybe—" She cut herself off. That wasn't the point. She cleared her throat and straightened. "She brought someone with her. A faerie."

This time Jamison's eyes widened and he glanced at Tamani. Tamani met the old faerie's gaze, but said nothing, and after a moment Jamison returned his attention to Laurel. "Go on."

Laurel related Klea's story—how Yuki was found as a seedling, how trolls had killed her parents. "Klea asked me to keep an eye on her. To be her friend, I guess. Because she knows I managed to escape from the trolls before."

"Klea," Jamison said softly. He looked at Laurel. "What does she look like?"

"Uh . . . she's tall. She has short auburn hair. She's thin, but not skinny. She wears a lot of black," Laurel finished with a shrug.

Jamison was studying her, unblinking—a tingling sensation made her forehead warm. It was so subtle that Laurel wondered if it was just her imagination. After a moment his gaze grew unnerving, but as Laurel turned to Tamani for guidance, Jamison straightened and sighed. "Never was my particular talent," he murmured, sounding disappointed.

Laurel touched her forehead. It felt cool. "What did you just—"

"Do come sit," Jamison said, turning away from her question to address Tamani. "I feel I have to shout with you standing so far away."

Swiftly, but with a jerkiness that spoke of reluctance, Tamani pushed away from the wall and took a seat beside Laurel.

"Any sign this faerie has hostile intentions?" Jamison asked.

"No. Actually, she seems rather shy. Reserved," Tamani said.

"Any outward signs of power?"

"Not that I've observed," Tamani said. "Klea claims Yuki doesn't have any abilities beyond being a plant. She called her a dryad, but we have no way of knowing whether that's a ruse."

"Is there any reason for us to believe this wild faerie is a threat to Laurel or to Avalon?"

"Well, no, not yet, but—at any point—" Tamani stopped talking and Laurel saw him fix his jaw the way he always did when he was trying to put his emotions in check. "No, sir," he said.

"All right, then." Jamison stood, and Laurel and Tamani rose to their feet in response. Tamani started to turn and Jamison stopped him with a hand on his shoulder. "I'm not saying you were wrong to come, Tam."

Tamani looked at Jamison, his expression guarded, and Laurel felt guilt smolder inside of her—after all, *she* was the one who had been so insistent. She had wanted Jamison's advice so badly.

"We could not have foreseen this turn of events. But," Jamison said, raising one finger, "you may find that less has changed than you think. You already saw Klea as a possible threat to Laurel's safety, did you not?"

Tamani nodded silently.

"So perhaps this Yuki is as well. But," he continued, his tone intense, "if that is the case, then the place you need to be—the place you *must* be—is at Laurel's side in Crescent City. Not here." Jamison placed both hands on Tamani's shoulders and Tamani's gaze fell to the floor. "Be confident, Tam. You have always had a sharp mind and keen intuition. Use it. Decide what needs to be done, and do it. I gave you that authority when I sent you."

Tamani's head bobbed up and down, an infinitesimal nod.

Laurel wanted to speak up, to tell Jamison it was her fault, not Tamani's, but her voice died in her throat. She wished, strangely, that they hadn't come at all. Being reprimanded, even gently, had to be difficult enough without an audience to compound his embarrassment. She wanted to say something, to defend him—but she couldn't find the words.

"I do have one suggestion," Jamison said as he guided them back toward the large double doors that led to the foyer. "It would be wise to discern this wildflower's caste—as a precaution, but also in case she can be of use to *you.*"

That possibility hadn't occurred to Laurel. Whatever Klea was doing, if they could win Yuki over, perhaps she could be the key to unlocking Klea's secrets. *But if she's too young to blossom—*

Before Laurel could voice her question, Jamison turned to address her. "Discovering her powers could be difficult. A stop at the Academy, to consult with your professors, might be in order. Then back to California," he said firmly. "I don't like the idea of you so far from your sentries after sunset. But a quick visit should still get you back to the gate in plenty of time. I know it is later here," he added, gesturing to a picture window that looked out on a black, velvety sky with stars beginning to appear.

Jamison escorted them through the gilded doors—which opened wide without so much as a flick of his wrist—and all the way down to the foyer. It was mostly empty now, soft phosphorescing flowers beaming dimly throughout the capacious room. Jamison's entourage of *Am fear-faire*, however, were ready and waiting. They closed in around him as soon as he reached the bottom of the stairs.

"Yasmine has gone to bed," Jamison said as they crossed beneath a dragon-arched entryway, "so I will open the gate for you." He laughed. "But these old stems move much slower than your young ones. You go down to the Academy. I will head to the Gate Garden and we will meet there in a short while."

Laurel and Tamani left the courtyard some fifty paces ahead of Jamison. As soon as they were out of earshot Laurel slowed her steps, falling back to share the broad pathway with Tamani. "I should have told him this was my idea," she blurted.

"It wasn't your idea," Tamani said quietly. "It was mine, earlier this week."

"Yeah, but I was the one who pushed it and got us in today. I let Jamison scold you and he should have been scolding me."

"Please," Tamani said with a grin on his face, "I'd take a scolding for you any day and call it a privilege."

Laurel looked away, flustered, and hurried her pace. Moving downhill helped the walk go quickly and soon the lights of the Academy came into view through the darkness, guiding their steps. Laurel looked up at the imposing gray structure and a smile spread across her face.

When had the Academy started to look like home?

# EIGHT

WHILE THE WINTER PALACE SLUMBERED, THE ACADEMY hummed along, both students and staff. If nothing else, there was always someone working on a mixture that had to be cured by starlight. As they walked toward the staircase Laurel waved at a few faeries she knew and their eyes widened upon seeing her. But true to their carefully honed discipline, they returned to their projects without comment and left Laurel and Tamani alone.

As soon as Laurel's foot touched the bottom step, a tall female faerie scuttled over to them. She was dressed in the unassuming clothes of the Spring staff. "I'm sorry, but it's far past visiting hours. You'll have to come back tomorrow."

Laurel looked over in surprise. "I'm Laurel Sewell," she said.

"I'm afraid I can't let you go up, Laurelsule," the faerie said firmly, squishing Laurel's first and last name together.

"I'm Laurel. Sewell. Apprentice. I'm going up to my room."

The faerie's eyes widened and she immediately bowed at the waist. "My most abject apologies. I've never seen you before. I didn't recognize—"

"Please," Laurel said, cutting her off. "It's fine. We'll be done soon and then I'll be gone again."

The faerie looked mortified. "I hope I didn't offend you— there's no reason you can't stay!"

Laurel forced herself to smile warmly at the faerie—surely a new Spring, worried about being demoted from her position. "Oh, no, it wasn't you at all. I'm needed back at my post." She hesitated. "Could you . . . could you alert Yeardley that I am here? I need to speak to him."

"In your room?" the faerie clarified, eager to please.

"That would be perfect, thank you."

The faerie dropped into a deep curtsy—first to Laurel and then to Tamani—before hurrying off toward the staff quarters.

Tamani wore a strange expression as Laurel led him upstairs and down the hall. A smile blossomed on her face when she saw the curlicues of her name engraved on her familiar cherry door. She turned the well-oiled doorknob— that neither had nor needed a lock—and entered her room.

Everything was just as she'd left it, though she knew the staff must come in to dust regularly. Even the hairbrush she'd forgotten was still lying in the middle of her bed. Laurel picked it up with a grin and thought about bringing it back with her, but decided to tuck it away instead. A spare. After all, she'd bought another one when she got home.

She looked around for Tamani. He was lingering in the doorway.

"Well, come in," she said. "You should know by now that I don't bite."

He looked up at her then shook his head. "I'll wait here."

"No, you won't," Laurel said sternly. "When Yeardley comes I'll have to close the door so we don't wake the other students. If you're not in here you'll miss the entire conversation."

At that Tamani went ahead and entered her room, but he left the door open and stayed within arm's reach of the door frame. Laurel shook her head ruefully as she walked over and closed the door. She paused, hand on the knob, and looked up at Tamani. "I've been meaning to apologize for the way I acted earlier," she said softly.

Tamani looked confused. "What do you mean? I told you, I don't care if Jamison blames me, I—"

"Not that," Laurel said, looking down at her hands. "Pulling rank at the land. Snapping at you, acting lofty. That's all it was, an act. None of the other sentries were going to take me seriously if I didn't act like a pain-in-the-ass Mixer with a superiority complex." She hesitated. "So I did. But it was all fake. I don't—I don't think that way. You know that; I *hope* you know that. I don't approve of other fae thinking that way either and—anyway, that's an argument with no end." She took a breath. "The point is, I'm sorry. I never meant it."

"It's fine," Tamani mumbled. "I need to be reminded of

my place now and again."

"Tamani, no," Laurel said. "Not with me. I can't change the way the rest of Avalon treats you—not yet, anyway. But with me, you are never *just* a Spring faerie," she said, touching his arm.

He looked up at her, but only for a second before his eyes focused on the ground again, a deep crease between his eyebrows.

"Tam, what? What's wrong?"

He met her eyes. "The Spring faerie down there, she didn't know what I was. She just knew I was with you and I guess she assumed I was a Mixer too." He hesitated. "She bowed to me, Laurel. Bowing is what *I* do. It was weird. I—I kinda liked it," he admitted. He continued on, his confession spilling out with gathering momentum. "For just those few seconds, I wasn't a Spring faerie. She didn't look at a sentry uniform and immediately put me in my place. It—it felt good. And bad," he tacked on. "All at the same time. It felt like—" His words were cut off by a soft knock at the door.

Disappointment flooded through Laurel as their conversation was cut short. "That'll be Yeardley," she said softly. Tamani nodded and took his place against the wall.

Laurel opened the door and was assaulted by a mass of pink silk. "I thought I heard you!" Katya squealed, throwing her arms around Laurel's neck. "And I could hardly believe it. You didn't tell me you were coming back so soon."

"I didn't know myself," Laurel said, grinning. It was impossible not to smile around Katya. She was wearing a silky, sleeveless nightgown, its back cut low to accommodate the blossom Katya would have in another month or so. She had grown her blond hair down to her shoulders, which made her look even younger.

"Either way, I'm glad you're here. How long can you stay?"

Laurel smiled apologetically. "Just a few minutes, I'm afraid. Yeardley is on his way up, and once I'm done speaking with him I need to get back to the gate."

"But it's dark," Katya protested. "You should at least stay the night."

"It's still afternoon in California," Laurel said. "I really do need to get home."

Katya grinned playfully. "I guess if you must." She looked at Tamani, her eyes a touch flirtatious. "Who's your friend?"

Laurel reached out to touch Tamani's shoulder, prompting him to step forward a little. "This is Tamani."

To Laurel's dismay, Tamani immediately dropped into a respectful bow.

"Oh," Katya said, realization dawning on her. "Your soldier friend from Samhain, right?"

"Sentry," Laurel corrected.

"Yes, that," Katya said dismissively. She grabbed both of Laurel's hands and didn't give Tamani another look. "Now come over here and tell me what in the world you are wearing."

Laurel laughed and allowed Katya to feel the stiff fabric of her denim skirt, but she shot Tamani an apologetic grimace. Not that it mattered; he was back to standing against the wall and averting his eyes.

Katya flounced down on the bed, the silken folds of her

nightgown tracing her graceful curves, its low back revealing so much perfect skin. It made Laurel feel plain in her cotton tank top and skirt, and inspired a fleeting wish that she hadn't brought Tamani upstairs. But she brushed the thought aside and joined her friend. Katya prattled on about inconsequential things that had happened in the Academy since Laurel's departure only last month, and Laurel smiled. Just over a year ago, she wouldn't have believed that the daunting, unfamiliar Academy was somewhere she might laugh and talk with a friend. But then, she had felt the same way about public school the year before that.

*Things change*, she told herself. *Including me.*

Katya sobered suddenly and reached out to place her fingertips on each side of Laurel's face. "You look happy again," Katya said.

"Do I?" Laurel asked.

Katya nodded. "Don't mistake me," she said in that formal way Katya had, "it was lovely to have you here this summer, but you were sad." She paused. "I didn't want to pry. But you're happy again. I'm glad."

Laurel was silent—surprised. *Had* she been sad? She ventured a glance at Tamani, but he didn't seem to be listening.

A sharp rap sounded at the door and Laurel jumped off her bed and hurried to open it. There stood Yeardley, tall and imposing, wearing only a loose pair of drawstring breeches. His arms were folded across his bare chest and, as usual, he wasn't wearing shoes.

"Laurel, you asked for me?" His tone was stern, but there

was warmth in his eyes. After two summers of working together he seemed to have grown a soft spot for her. Not that you could tell by the amount of class work he gave her. He was—above all else—a demanding tutor.

"Yes," Laurel answered quickly. "Please come in."

Yeardley walked to the center of the room and Laurel began to shut the door.

"Do you need me to leave?" Katya asked quietly.

Laurel looked down at her friend. "No . . . no, I don't think so," Laurel said, glancing at Tamani. "It's really not a secret; not here, anyway."

Tamani met her eyes. There was tension in his face, and Laurel half expected him to contradict her, but after a moment he looked away and shrugged. She turned back to Yeardley.

"I need a way to test a faerie's, um, season." Laurel would not use the word *caste*. Not in front of Tamani. Preferably not ever.

"Male or female?"

"Female."

Yeardley shrugged, nonchalant. "Watch for her blossom. Or for pollen production on males in the vicinity."

"What about a faerie who hasn't blossomed yet?"

"You can go to the records room—it's just downstairs—and look her up."

"Not here," Laurel said. "In California."

Yeardley's eyes narrowed. "A faerie in the human world? Besides yourself, and your entourage?"

79

Laurel nodded.

"Unseelie?"

The Unseelie were still a mystery to Laurel. No one would talk about them directly, but she had gathered from bits and pieces that they all lived in an isolated community outside one of the gates. "I don't think so. But there is some . . . confusion regarding her history, so we can't be sure."

"And *she* doesn't know what season she is?"

Laurel hesitated. "If she does, it's not something I can ask her."

Comprehension dawned on Yeardley's face. "Ah, I see." He sighed and pressed his fingers against his lips, contemplating. "I don't think I've ever had anyone ask for such a thing. Have you, Katya?"

When Katya shook her head, Yeardley continued. "We keep meticulous records of every seedling in Avalon, so this problem presents a unique challenge. But there must be *something*. Perhaps you could formulate a potion of your own?"

"Am I ready for that?" Laurel asked hopefully.

"Almost certainly not," Yeardley said in his most matter-of-fact tone. "But practice needn't always lead to success, after all. I think it would be good for you to begin learning the basic concepts of fabrication. And this seems a fine place to start. An identification powder, like Cyoan," he said, referencing a simple powder that identified humans and non-humans. "Except you would have to figure out what separates the castes on a cellular level, and I'm unaware of much research in that area. It simply doesn't *lead* anywhere."

"What about thylakoid membranes?" Katya asked softly. As one, they all turned to face her.

"What was that?" Yeardley asked.

"Thylakoid membranes," Katya continued, a little louder this time. "In the chloroplasm. The thylakoid membranes of Sparklers are more efficient. For lighting their illusions."

Yeardley cocked his head to the side. "Really?"

Katya nodded. "When I was younger we sometimes stole the phosphorescing serums for the lamps and . . . um . . . drank them. It would make us glow in the dark," she said, lowering her lashes as she related the childish antic. "I . . . had a Summer friend, and she did it with us one day. But instead of glowing for one night, she glowed for three days. It took me years to figure out why."

"Excellent, Katya," Yeardley said, a distinct note of pleasure in his voice. "I would like to discuss that more fully with you in the classroom sometime this week."

Katya nodded eagerly.

Yeardley turned back to Laurel. "It's a start. Focus on plants with phosphorescing qualities that could show evidence of a more efficient thylakoid, and try to repeat the kind of reaction you get with Cyoan powder. I will work personally with Katya, here at the Academy."

"But what if she's not a Summer faeric?"

"Then you would be twenty-five percent closer to your goal, would you not?"

Laurel nodded. "I need to write this down," she said, not wanting to admit to Yeardley that she had no idea what

Katya was talking about. But David probably would. Laurel grabbed a few note cards from her desk where—after last summer—the staff always kept them stocked, and sat by Katya. Katya spoke quietly as Laurel wrote down the basics and fervently hoped that the biological terminology was the same in Avalon as the human world.

"Experiment when you can, and we'll see what Katya and I can come up with here," Yeardley said. "I'm afraid that's all I can do for you tonight." He paused, giving her an approving smile. "Glad to see you again, Laurel."

Stifling her disappointment, Laurel returned his smile as he left the room, closing the door behind him. After the near-fit she'd thrown getting here, the whole visit felt very unproductive.

"Did you hear that?" Katya said, her voice low but excited. "He's going to work with me personally. I'm part of your entourage now," she added, taking Laurel's hand. "I am going to help with a potion that might be used in the human world. I'm so excited!"

She grabbed Laurel's shoulder, pulled her in, and kissed both cheeks quickly before darting toward the door. "Next time you're here," she said, poking her head back through the doorway, "come see me first, okay?" She clicked the door shut behind her, leaving the room feeling quiet and empty.

"We'd better hurry," Laurel said to Tamani, walking past him without looking him in the face. She didn't want him to see her discouragement.

After a short and silent walk back to the gateway, they approached Jamison's circle of *Am fear-faire*, all standing at attention, but Jamison did not stir from his quiet conversation with Shar. After a few seconds, both men nodded, then looked up at Laurel and Tamani.

"Did your visit to the Academy bear fruit?" Jamison asked.

"Not yet, but hopefully soon," Laurel replied.

"Are you ready, then?" Jamison asked.

They nodded and Jamison reached out for the gate. As it swung open he looked first at Shar, then at Tamani. "The Huntress and the Wildflower should be watched closely, but do not let them consume your attention. What remains of Barnes's horde will surely be looking for an opportunity to strike. If you need anything—reinforcements, supplies, *anything*—you have but to ask."

"We will need more sentries. For the Wildflower," Tamani said. Here, away from the Palace and the Academy, he was confident again, speaking easily and standing tall.

"Of course," Jamison replied. "Anything you need and more. We *will* keep Laurel safe, but she needs to remain in Crescent City. Especially if we are to see how these events will play out."

Laurel was a little uncomfortable with how close that sounded to *Laurel is the bait.* But Tamani had never failed her before, and she had no reason to believe he would do so now.

# NINE

AS SOON AS THE GATE CLOSED, TAMANI TURNED TO Shar, hoping—and doubting—that his old friend was okay. "So, did you get what you were after?"

Shar shook his head. "Not really. But I probably got what I deserved."

*Don't be so hard on yourself,* Tamani thought, but he said nothing. Never did. However difficult it was for Shar to visit Japan, Tamani doubted the experience was half as bad as the emotional torment he always put himself through afterward.

"Who did you go to see, Shar?" Laurel asked.

Shar met her question with silence. Tamani placed a hand at the small of Laurel's back and gently urged her to walk a little faster. Now was not the time to be asking Shar about Hokkaido.

They stopped at the edge of the woods and a grin played at the corners of Shar's mouth. "Hurry," he teased Tamani. "The sun will be setting soon and you have school tomorrow."

Tamani swallowed his frustration. He hated his stupid classes and Shar knew it. "Just answer your blighting phone next time, okay?" Tamani said, getting in a parting shot.

Shar's hand flitted to the pouch where his phone was stowed, but he said nothing.

Once he and Laurel were in the convertible, Tamani pulled back onto the highway and set his cruise control considerably lower than he had on the way to the land. The sun was still an hour from setting, the breeze was cool, and he had Laurel in the car. No need to hurry.

They traveled a ways in silence before Laurel finally asked, "Where did Shar go?"

Tamani hesitated. It wasn't really his place to spill Shar's secrets, and technically he was only supposed to tell Laurel things she needed to know to fulfill her mission. But he preferred to think of that particular order as a strongly worded *preference*—and besides, it was at least plausible that the Unseelie had something to do with Yuki's appearance. "He went to go see his mother."

"In Hokkaido?"

Tamani nodded.

"Why does she live in Japan? Is she a sentry there?"

Tamani shook his head, a tiny, sharp movement. "His mother is Unseelie."

Laurel sighed. "I don't even know what that means!"

"She's been cast out," Tamani said, trying to figure out a better way to say it—something that sounded less harsh.

"Like, an exile? That's what Unseelie means?"

"Not . . . exactly." Tamani bit his bottom lip and sighed. *Where to begin?* "Once upon a time," he began, remembering that humans liked to start their most accurate histories this way, "there were two faerie courts. Their rivalry was . . . complicated, but it boiled down to human contact. One court was friendly to humans—the humans called them Seelie. The other court sought to dominate humans, enslave them, torment them for amusement, or kill them for sport. They were the Unseelie.

"Somewhere along the way, a rift developed in the Seelie Court. There were some fae who believed that the best thing we could do for the humans was leave them alone. Isolationists, basically."

"Isn't that how the fae live now?"

"Yes," Tamani said. "But they didn't used to. The Seelie even made treaties with some human kingdoms—including Camelot."

"But that failed, right?" asked Laurel. "That's what you said at the festival last year."

"Well, it worked for a while. In some ways the pact with Camelot was a huge success. With Arthur's help, the Seelie drove the trolls out of Avalon for good and hunted the Unseelie practically to extinction. But eventually, things . . . fell apart."

It pained Tamani to gloss over so much detail, but when it came to the Unseelie, it was hard to decide where one explanation ended and another began. And it would take him hours to explain everything that had gone wrong in Camelot. Especially considering that, even in Avalon, the story was ancient enough for its accuracy to be disputed. Some claimed that the memories collected in the World Tree kept their history pure, but—having conversed with the Silent Ones himself—Tamani did not think it gave answers straight enough to qualify as historical facts.

He would have to do his best with what he had.

"When the trolls overran Camelot, it was taken as final proof that even our most well-intentioned involvement with humans was doomed to end in disaster. The isolationists rose to power. Everyone else was branded Unseelie."

"So part of the Seelie Court became the new Unseelie Court?"

Tamani frowned. "Well, there hasn't been an Unseelie 'Court' in more than a thousand years. But Titania was dethroned, Oberon crowned as rightful king, and the universal decree was that for the good of the human race the fae would leave humans alone forever. Everyone was summoned back to Avalon, Oberon created the gates, and for the most part we've been isolated ever since. But the idea that faeries should meddle in human affairs—as benefactors *or* conquerors—crops up sometimes. If anyone gets too zealous about it, they are exiled."

"To Hokkaido?"

Tamani nodded. "There's a . . . detention camp, not far from the gate. We send them there because we can't have them in Avalon causing unrest, but we don't want them to meddle with humans, either. They aren't really a separate kingdom, but everyone calls them Unseelie."

"When was Shar's mother . . . kicked out?"

"Maybe fifty years ago? Before I sprouted."

"Fifty?" Laurel laughed. "How old is Shar?"

"Eighty-four."

Laurel shook her head with amazement. "I'm never going to get used to that."

"Sure you will," Tamani said, poking her in the side, "about the time *you* turn eighty."

"So why did Shar go see her today? Does he think Yuki is Unseelie? And what did he mean about Glamour?"

Tamani hesitated. They were really getting into shady territory now. "All right, here's the thing about the Glamour: It's total madness. But it's the kind of madness that sounds just plausible enough to suck you in. So what I'm about to tell you, you have to understand—nobody really believes it. Nobody sane, anyway. And just mentioning it in Avalon can make trouble."

When Laurel sat up a little straighter and folded her hands in her lap, Tamani realized his warning had succeeded only in piquing her interest. Sometimes she could be so *human!* "Let me start this way: Have you ever wondered why humans look so much like us?"

"I guess I don't usually put it like that," Laurel said, favoring him with a smile, "but sure. David says it must be convergent evolution—we fill similar, um, ecological niches. Like sharks and dolphins, only . . . closer."

Tamani suppressed a grimace; he hadn't intended to bring David into this. "Well, the Unseelie believe that we did this to ourselves—that before the Glamour, we didn't resemble humans at all. That we looked more like plants."

"What, like green skin and stuff?" Laurel asked.

"Who knows? But the Unseelie think one of their ancient queens, a Winter faerie called Mab, used her power to change our entire race—to make us look more human. Some of them think she was granting our wish to blend in with the human world. Some think it was a punishment, for trying to live like humans, falling in love with them, that sort of thing. But they all agree that a seedling who sprouts near a human settlement will physically resemble the humans who live there."

"So a faerie born, er, sprouted in Japan would look Japanese," Laurel said, and Tamani could almost hear her making connections as she spoke. "Seems like that would be pretty easy to test. All the Unseelie children would look Japanese. So Shar went to see if Yuki escaped from the Unseelie . . . prison?"

"Except the Unseelie are forbidden to Garden, so there's nowhere for a young faerie to come from in the camp. There hasn't been a faerie sprouted outside of Avalon in over a thousand years. And we don't exile seedlings."

"Wait, what does that mean, forbidden to Garden?"

"They are . . . not allowed to reproduce," Tamani said, wishing she hadn't asked.

"And they can stop them how?" Laurel said hotly.

"The Fall faeries give them something," Tamani said. "It destroys the females' ability to blossom. No blossom, no seedlings."

"They cripple them?" Laurel said, her eyes flashing.

"It's not exactly crippling," Tamani said helplessly.

"It doesn't matter!" Laurel exclaimed. "That's not a choice anyone has *any* right to mess with!"

"I don't make the rules," Tamani said. "And I'm not trying to say they're doing the right thing. But look at this from Shar's perspective. Because his mother was always secretly Unseelie, as a seedling Shar was taught about the Glamour. Among other things," Tamani added cryptically. "Then his mother was branded Unseelie and sent to Hokkaido. Today we told him about a faerie who comes from Japan, where we keep the Unseelie. The fact that Yuki claims to have sprouted in Japan and happens to look Japanese doesn't prove that the Glamour is real—you've seen how diverse our appearances are by human standards—but in Shar's mind, it's just one more thing connecting her to the Unseelie."

"So why didn't you mention the Unseelie before—when Yuki first showed up?"

They pulled up to the first red light in Crescent City and Tamani turned to face Laurel. "Because I think Shar is jumping to conclusions. The Unseelie are guarded very closely, and with good reason." Tamani paused, remembering the one time he had accompanied Shar to Hokkaido. It had been terrifying to hear the pure insanity pouring from the mouths of fae whose eyes were so clear and intelligent—conspiracies and secret worlds and tales of dark magic that were clearly impossible. "I've seen the facility—they keep careful records of everyone there. Once you're in that camp, you don't leave until you die."

"So if Yuki's not Unseelie, what is she?"

"That's what we need to find out," Tamani said, looking back at the road. "The idea of a wild faerie, with no allegiance to Seelie or Unseelie . . . that's not something we ever expected to encounter. But I don't see any convincing alternatives."

"So what do we do now?" Laurel asked, looking up at him. Her earnest gaze was so open, so trusting; her pale green eyes blazed in the day's dying light. Tamani didn't realize he had started to lean toward her until he had to catch himself and pull back.

The next step would have to involve Laurel, even though he wished he could keep her out of it entirely. "Klea handed you an opportunity to befriend Yuki. Hopefully you can find out more."

Laurel nodded. "Hopefully. She doesn't seem to like Klea's plan, though. I get the feeling she's avoiding me."

"Well, keep trying," Tamani said, doing his best to sound encouraging. "But be careful. We still don't know what she can do, or whether she intends to hurt you."

Laurel looked down at her lap.

"And work on figuring out her caste," Tamani added. Then, remembering that Laurel didn't like that word— for reasons he suspected he'd never quite understand—he corrected himself. "Season, I mean. Just knowing that would make a huge difference. Then at least we'd know *something*."

"Okay."

Tamani pulled his car into Laurel's driveway and she looked up at her house. She put a hand on the door handle, then paused.

"Is Shar . . . Unseelie?"

Tamani shook his head. "His mother tried to raise him that way, but Shar was never much of a believer. And after he met his companion, Ariana, the last thing he wanted was to get kicked out of Avalon. Ariana and their seedling, Lenore, are his whole world. As far as Shar is concerned, no price is too high for their safety—or the safety of Avalon. Even if it means his own mother has to live and die in exile."

"I just wondered," Laurel said softly.

"Hey, Laurel," Tamani said, catching her wrist just before she was out of reach. He wanted to take that wrist and pull her closer, wrap her in his arms, forget everything else. His hands started to tremble with the wanting and he forced them to still. "Thank you for coming with me today. Without you, we wouldn't have gotten in at all."

"Was it worth it?" she asked, her wrist limp in his hand. "We didn't find anything out. I hoped . . . I thought Jamison would know something." She looked at him, her eyes only now reflecting the disappointment she must have been feeling all evening.

Tamani swallowed; he hated letting her down. "It was for me," he said quietly, his eyes focused on their hands, so close to being joined. He didn't want to let go. But if he didn't, in a few seconds she would subtly tug her hand away, and that was worse. He forced his fingers to open, watched her arm drop to her side. At least this way, it was his choice.

"Besides," he added, trying to sound casual, "it was good for Jamison to find out about Yuki and Klea. Shar is kind of . . . independent. He likes to figure things out on his own before he passes any information on. He's stubborn like that." Tamani leaned back in the driver's seat, one arm resting atop the steering wheel. "I'll say hi to you in the halls next week," he said, smiling. And with a rubber-and-asphalt squeal, he sped away from Laurel's house, resisting the urge to look back.

He drove to his empty apartment and let himself in. He didn't bother to turn on the lights, instead sitting silently in the shadows as the sun set and the room grew dark. He tried not to think too hard about what Laurel would be doing that weekend. Even with the privacy he tried to afford her—and not just to be polite—he had witnessed more soft kisses and intimate embraces than he wanted to think about. He suspected that every weekend would be the same, and he wasn't sure how much more he could take.

Forcing himself back to his feet, Tamani walked over to the window that looked out on the line of trees behind the apartment complex. Jamison had told him to trust himself, and he was going to. A few days ago he'd shadowed Yuki to the small house he could only assume she lived in. The squads who would watch her full time wouldn't arrive for another day or two. It meant he'd get very little sleep tonight, but for now, he would watch her himself.

# TEN

"TOO WEIRD," DAVID SAID AS THEY SAT ON LAUREL'S bed talking about her trip to Avalon and ignoring the textbooks spread out around them.

"I know, right? I sort of assumed being cast out for your beliefs was a human thing. Which I personally find totally ironic."

David laughed. "I was thinking along the lines of breaking the laws of physics by traveling thousands of miles yesterday in, like, two seconds."

"Different strokes," Laurel said, waving his comment away with a smile. "So did you find out anything about the membrane Katya was talking about?"

"I think so," David said. Then, in a teasing tone, "Did you?"

"Maybe? From what I read online, the thylakoid membrane is the place where the chloroplasts are. So all of the conversion from sunlight into energy happens there."

"We got the same answer, then," David said, smiling. "So your friend Katya said that in Summer faeries, the thylakoid is more efficient. I guess that means it gets more energy out of less sunlight."

"Probably because their magic uses light," Laurel said, thinking back on the "fireworks" she'd watched at the Samhain festival last year.

"And Katya discovered this because she and her friends basically drank the equivalent of glow-sticks, right?" David asked, not bothering to contain his amusement.

"Essentially," Laurel said, rolling her eyes.

"Wish I could do something like that."

Laurel raised an eyebrow at him.

"No, seriously," David said. "Can you imagine how cool that would be? Like at Halloween, you could give kids some kind of glow punch before they went trick-or-treating and they would be safer."

"Something tells me the safety of a bunch of kids was not the first thought you had," Laurel said.

"Well, maybe it would also be fun to jump out from behind a tree at night, glowing all funky green."

"That's more like it." Laurel looked down at the scant notes Katya had helped her make. "It seems like if I got a sample of cells and treated them with a phosphorescing substance, I could observe how long the cells kept their glow and could rule out Summer fairly easily."

"I don't think it's going to be quite that simple," David

said, rolling over onto his stomach and bringing his head close to Laurel's. "Katya's friend probably kept glowing because she was still alive, so the thylakoid membrane processed all of the phosphorescent. If you had a sample, the cells wouldn't still be living and growing. You'd have to find a way to keep the sample alive. Or test it right on Yuki's skin."

"Something tells me she's not going to agree to that," Laurel said wryly.

They both sat back, silent for a while.

"You can keep flowers fresh with sugar water, right?"

David shrugged. "Sure, I guess."

"And when we got thrown in the Chetko River by Barnes's trolls, Tamani patched me up and put me under this light that helped me heal. It was like . . . portable sunshine. What if I was able to somehow, without being noticed"— she shook her head, trying not to worry about that hurdle just yet—"get a small sample from Yuki? I could put it in a solution of sugar water and then expose it to that special light. Do you think that would be enough to keep it alive and processing?"

"Maybe. I mean, if it was a regular plant, I would be skeptical, but faeries are the most highly evolved form of plant life, right?"

Laurel nodded.

"And that light is faerie magic stuff, so it might be enough. Can you make the light thing?"

"No, it's really, really advanced. But Tamani can probably get one for me."

"Can you make the glow stuff?"

Laurel nodded. "I think so."

"And will you drink some one of these nights so you glow in the dark?"

Laurel's jaw dropped. "No!"

"Please? It would be awesome." He was raised up on his knees now, his hands clenched excitedly. "*I* would totally do it if I could."

"No."

"Come on!"

"No!"

David poked her ribs. "You'd be pretty. Like a sparkling angel."

"I'd probably just look radioactive. No thanks."

He grabbed her now, pinning her under him and tickling her sides till she gasped for air.

"Stop!"

He pulled his hands away and flopped down beside her. "You're amazing, you know," he said, pushing a lock of hair off her forehead.

"So are you."

He scrunched up his nose and shook his head. "Whatever. One of these days you'll get tired of me and toss me aside."

He was smiling, but there was a tiny note of seriousness in his voice. "I'm never going to get bored of you, David," Laurel said softly.

"I sure hope not," he replied, burying his face in her neck. "Because if you ever do, I'm afraid regular old human life would bore *me* right to death."

★ ★ ★

Laurel looked for Tamani as soon as she got to school on Monday. She wondered what he had been doing all weekend—especially in light of their new discoveries. And she was anxious to find out if he could get her the light globe. It would take a few days to make the phosphorescent, but she was hoping to be able to try out her new theory on herself in the next couple of weeks.

Just in time to use a piece of her blossom.

She had discovered the tiny bump forming when she got out of the shower and felt a familiar tingling where her hair fell against her back. It was fairly early, but summer had been warmer than usual, and Mother Nature seemed anxious to make up for it in the fall. The air had chilled and the leaves were already starting to turn. Fog season had commenced and the early mornings were downright murky. And Laurel was as affected by the weather as every other plant in Crescent City.

Still, Laurel had been expecting her blossom early, but the bump had never started growing in September. She'd stood and looked at her reflection in the mirror. "Here we go again," she whispered.

Not that she had any reason to whisper. Her blossom was a secret she kept from the world, but not from her family. After last year, when her lies had almost cost her life—and Chelsea's—Laurel had adopted honesty as her best policy. And considering how many people she already had to hide from, it was nice to just be herself in her own home. Her parents knew everything—about her and her faerie identity, that Tamani was in school now, even about Yuki.

She hadn't mentioned how she *felt* about Tamani, and she may have downplayed the significance of Yuki being a faerie, but her parents didn't need a detailed analysis of everything that happened in Laurel's life. They were smart people; they could draw their own conclusions.

Laurel didn't see Tamani anywhere among the teeming students, but David was waiting for her at their lockers.

"Fancy meeting you here," she said, pulling him to her in a warm embrace.

He caught her cheek in his hand, his thumb pushing a strand of hair away from her eyes and raising her chin. Laurel smiled, anticipating a kiss.

"Hey, Laurel."

Laurel and David turned to see Tamani waving as he walked past, grinning—probably with satisfaction that he had successfully interrupted their public display of affection. Laurel watched as he walked away and realized that hers and David's were not the only eyes marking his progress.

Yuki, standing across the hall, was also watching, her eyes fixed on him with a strange, almost wistful expression.

"Weird," Laurel said under her breath.

"You're telling me," David grumbled, his eyes on Tamani's back.

"Not him," Laurel said, gripping David's arm firmly. "Yuki."

David's eyes flitted over to Yuki, who had turned back to her locker and was pulling books off the top shelf.

"What about her?"

"I don't know. She looked at him funny." Laurel paused. "I should go talk to her—I'm still supposed to befriend her. A nice, happy word for 'spy on,'" she added in a whisper.

David nodded and Laurel started to walk away. She paused to squeeze his hand, then hurried off toward Yuki. "Hey, Yuki!" Laurel said, cringing at the tinny brightness of her tone.

The shy way Yuki ducked her head told Laurel that she'd heard it too. "Hi," she responded politely.

"We haven't talked much," Laurel said, trying to find something relevant to say. "I just wanted to make sure you're adjusting okay."

"I'm fine," Yuki said, sounding moody.

"Well," Laurel said, feeling like the biggest dork ever, "just let me know if you need anything, all right?"

Something flashed in Yuki's eyes and she stepped to the side of the hallway, away from the stream of students, and pulled Laurel with her. "Listen, just because Klea decided to come to you for help doesn't mean I actually need it."

"I don't mind," Laurel said earnestly, placing one hand on Yuki's shoulder. "I mean, I was so lost when I was a sophomore. I can only imagine you feel the same."

Yuki glared at her now, and Laurel felt her mouth go dry. Yuki shrugged her hand away. "I'm *fine*. I'm a big girl, and I can take care of myself. I don't need your *guidance* and I certainly don't need your pity." Then she spun, her light blue skirt swirling out around her legs, and headed down the hallway.

"Gee," Laurel said to no one in particular, "that went well."

This chain of events played itself out, with hardly any variation, the next day, and again two days later. "I swear, she hates me," Laurel whispered to Tamani later that week as Mrs. Harms droned on about the War of 1812. "I didn't do anything!"

"We need to work on your people skills," Tamani said, grinning.

"Is it really worth it? Do you think she's going to just spill her guts to us?"

"You ever heard that saying about keeping your friends close and your enemies closer?"

"We don't know that she's an enemy."

"No," Tamani agreed, "we absolutely don't. But either way, we should keep her close."

"What am I supposed to do? I offered her my help and I told you how well that went."

"Come on," Tamani said, his voice soft, but a touch chiding. "Wouldn't you hate someone who came up and was all patronizing like that?"

Laurel had to admit he was right. "I don't know what else to do."

He hesitated and glanced at Mrs. Harms, then leaned a little closer. "Why don't you let me try?"

"Try . . . making friends with her?"

"Sure. We have a lot in common. Well, more than she knows—but we're both foreign and new to Crescent City.

And," he said, raising his eyebrows, "you have to admit I'm handsome and charismatic."

Laurel just stared.

"Plus, I'm saying hi to you in the halls now." That was certainly true. About three times a day and usually timed for maximum kiss interruption.

"Indeed you are," Laurel said blandly.

"So I build a friendship with you, and with her, and a few weeks down the line the roads could converge, that's all I'm saying."

"It could work," she agreed, inwardly grateful for the excuse not to have more awkward conversations with Yuki. Her mom always told her you couldn't force someone to like you, and the last several days were definitely proof of that.

"Plus, I'm not connected with Klea—as far as she knows, anyway. I might have more luck working stuff out of her."

Laurel couldn't imagine Tamani not getting exactly the information he wanted out of pretty much anyone. She leaned back and shrugged. "She's all yours."

Tamani pulled his car alongside Yuki, who was on the sidewalk headed toward the little house where she seemed to stay every moment she wasn't in school. When she didn't look up at him, he called out, "You want a ride?"

She turned, eyes wide, books clutched to her chest. Recognition dawned instantly, but she quickly refocused on the ground in front of her and shook her head, almost imperceptibly.

"Aww, come on," Tamani said with a playful grin. "I don't bite . . . hard."

She looked up at him now, concentration in her eyes. "No thanks."

"Okay," he said after a minute. "Suit yourself." He sped up, pulling ahead of her, and then veered off onto the shoulder. He was sliding from his seat as Yuki reached the car, staring at him in confusion.

"What are you doing?"

Tamani swung the door shut. "You didn't want a ride, so I figured it was a nice day for a walk."

She stopped. "Are you kidding me?"

"Well, you don't *have* to walk with me, but if you don't I'll look awfully strange talking to no one." And then he turned and started walking at a leisurely pace. He counted very slowly to ten in his head, and just as he reached nine, he heard the crunch of gravel as she hurried to catch up. *Perfect.*

"I'm sorry," she said as she reached him. "I don't mean to be antisocial, it's just, I don't really know anyone yet. And I *don't* take rides from strangers."

"I'm not a stranger," Tamani said, making sure to meet her hesitant gaze. "I was probably the very first person you met at school." He chuckled. "Other than Robison, I mean."

"You didn't act like you even saw me," Yuki said guardedly.

Tamani shrugged. "I admit I was pretty focused on just understanding people. They talk funny here. Like they all have cotton balls in their mouths."

She laughed openly now and Tamani took the opportunity

to study her. She really was quite pretty, when she wasn't staring at the ground and he could see her lovely green eyes. She had a nice smile too—something else he hadn't seen much of.

"I'm Tam, by the way," he said, extending his hand.

"Yuki." She looked at his hand for a moment before taking it tentatively. He held it a little longer than necessary, trying to coax another smile out of her.

"Don't you have . . . a host student to walk with you?" Tamani asked as they turned and headed down the sidewalk. "Isn't that the 'exchange' part?"

"Um . . ." She nervously tucked her hair behind her ear. "Not really. I'm kind of a special case."

"So who do you live with?"

"I live alone most of the time. Not *alone* alone," she hurriedly corrected. "I mean my host, her name's Klea, she checks on me every day and comes by all the time. She just travels for her job a lot. Don't tell the school, though," she added, looking almost shocked at herself for telling him at all. "They think Klea's around a lot more."

"I won't," Tamani said, deliberately casual. He had watched her house and knew Klea hadn't set foot in the place in more than a week. "How old are you?"

"Sixteen," she replied immediately.

*Not a moment's hesitation.* If she was lying, she was very good at it.

"Is it lonely?"

She paused now, worrying her bottom lip with her teeth.

"Sometimes. But mostly I like it. I mean, no one tells me when to go to bed or what to watch on TV. Most kids would kill for that."

"I know I would," Tamani said. "My uncle's always been pretty strict with me." *To say the least*, he added to himself. "But the older I get, the more freedom he gives me."

Yuki turned up the path to a small house without thought. "Is this it?" Tamani asked.

Not that Tamani actually had to ask. He knew the cottage on sight. It was covered in ivy and had one small bedroom in the back, with a common area behind the front door. He knew her bedspread was purple and that she had pictures of pop stars ripped from magazines hanging on her walls. He also knew she didn't enjoy being alone as much as she claimed and spent a lot of time lying faceup on her bed just staring at the ceiling.

What she didn't know was that as long as she was in Crescent City, she would never be home alone again.

"Um, yeah," she said quickly, startled, as if she hadn't realized how far they'd walked.

"I'll leave you here, then," Tamani said, not wanting to overstay his welcome on their first encounter. He gestured back the way they had come with his thumb. "I kinda left my car a little way up the road."

She smiled again, showing one shallow dimple in her left cheek that caught Tamani off guard. Not that they were exceptionally rare among the fae, but with their inherent symmetry, having one on only one side was quite uncommon. Still Tamani couldn't help smiling back. She did seem like a sweet kid. He hoped it wasn't an act.

"So," he said, already walking slowly backward, "if I say hi to you tomorrow, you going to say hi back?"

His step faltered just a little when she didn't answer.

"Why are you doing this, Tam?" she asked after a long pause.

"Doing what?" Tamani asked, stopping now.

"This," she said, gesturing between the two of them.

He did his best to look both playful and sheepish. "I lied," he said carefully. "I did notice you that first day." He shrugged and looked down at his feet. "I noticed you right away. It just took me a while to get up the guts to approach you, I guess."

He peered up at her, watched the nervous tightening of her neck, and knew, before she responded, that he'd won. "Okay," she said quietly. "I'll say hi."

# ELEVEN

LAUREL STARED AT HERSELF IN THE MIRROR, TRYING to decide if the bump on her back was actually as big as it seemed to her, or if she was blowing it out of proportion. In the end, she had to just drop her hair down across her back and hope for the best. David had gone into school early for a National Honor Society meeting, and Laurel decided she would walk so she could ride home with him after school. She took a glance at the clock, then hurried downstairs so she'd have time. On her way out the door Laurel grabbed an apple from the ever-present fruit basket on the counter, shouted a quick good-bye to her parents, and hurried out into the early morning sunshine.

"Care for a lift?" a voice called as Tamani's convertible pulled up beside her. Laurel hesitated. She was his friend; technically there was nothing wrong with getting a ride from him. On the other hand, he had made his intentions clear, and she didn't want to encourage him, or worse, string him along the way she had inadvertently done last year. Still, riding in a convertible was just as revitalizing as walking, and in some ways, better—she loved the feel of the wind in her face. "Thanks," she said with a smile, pulling open the door and sliding in.

"How's the Mixing coming along?" Tamani asked as the school parking lot came into view.

"I'm almost done curing the second batch of phosphorescent," said Laurel. "It's slow going, but I'm pretty sure I did it right this time."

"Good timing, then. I brought you a present," Tamani said, handing her a small, cloth-wrapped package.

Laurel could tell from the size and shape that it was the light orb she'd asked for. "Thanks! Hopefully I'll bloom tomorrow and we can start figuring things out."

"Anything you need," he said. "I wonder though, should you try out the experiment on living faeries first? I mean, right now, if I understand right, you're going to try to keep the plants cells alive *and* try the phosphorescent on them. Wouldn't it be better to try one thing at a time? Not that I'm trying to tell you how to be a Mixer," Tamani added hastily.

"No, you're right," Laurel said reluctantly, remembering how David had begged her to drink the phosphorescent. "It's just that I can't exactly come to school glowing, you know what I mean?"

"Well, maybe you don't have to. I mean, it's almost the weekend. Didn't Katya say that stuff wears off overnight?

And if you did us both, we could see if there's a difference between Spring and Fall."

"Maybe," Laurel said distractedly. "I'm still not sure it's a good idea to drink that stuff, but maybe it could be applied directly . . . ?" Her voice trailed off as she pondered ways to test her theories.

"Laurel?"

She snapped back to attention. "What?"

He laughed. "I called your name about three times."

They were in the parking lot. A handful of students were making their way through parked cars on their way to the school, weaving around Tamani's car and feeling very close with no roof between her and them.

"Listen," Tamani said, pulling her attention away. "I actually wanted to talk to you about Yuki, too."

"What about her?" Laurel asked.

"I made . . . first contact, I guess. Walked her home the other day."

"Oh. Good, good," Laurel said, feeling strangely exposed, sitting in Tamani's convertible in the school parking lot. She glanced up at the front doors and spotted David, waiting at the top of the steps. His meeting must have gotten out a bit early. He was looking at the car, and after a moment, headed toward them, covering the short distance quickly.

"So I'll keep working on that and hopefully she'll start to warm up to you. . . ." Tamani's voice trailed off and his eyes focused on something above Laurel's head.

Laurel shifted and met David's eyes, his smile a little tight.

"Can I get that for you?" he asked, swinging her car door open.

"Sure, thanks," Laurel said, shouldering her bag and stepping out.

"I didn't know you needed a ride," David said, his eyes darting between her and Tamani. "You could have called me."

"You had a meeting," Laurel said, shrugging. "I figured we could drive home this afternoon, so I walked."

"And I just happened by," Tamani said, his voice very cool and casual.

"I'll bet," David said to Tamani, putting an arm around Laurel's shoulders and leading her away from the car.

"Laurel?" Tamani called. "So, that thing? Maybe this weekend?" He let the words roll out heavy with insinuation. David took the bait.

"What thing?" David asked, his voice decidedly tense now.

"It's nothing," Laurel said quietly, stepping between the two guys, hoping that if they couldn't see each other, they would stop sniping. "He's helping me with . . . that thing we talked about. Testing the . . . stuff."

"Weren't we going to study for the SATs this weekend?" David asked, sounding disappointed.

"I think she has bigger problems than your human exams."

"Oh, come on!" Laurel hissed, her glare taking in both boys now. "What is this?"

David crossed his arms over his chest guiltily, and Tamani

looked like a child caught with one hand in the cookie jar. Laurel glanced between them and lowered her voice. "Listen, we have a *lot* of stuff going on and the last thing I need is to be babysitting you two. So knock it off, okay?" Without another word she slammed the car door and walked quickly toward the school.

"Laurel, wait!" David called.

But she didn't.

He caught up with her at their side-by-side lockers.

"Listen, I'm sorry. I just . . . got mad when I saw you with him. It was dumb."

"Yeah, it was," Laurel replied.

"I just . . . I really don't like him here. Well, he was okay before, but now he always says hi to you when we're together and he's volunteering for study sessions. . . ." He grinned sheepishly. "If you recall, that's how I lured you in once."

"That is not what this is," Laurel said, pushing her locker shut. "This is important and I can't deal with your ego right now."

"It's not ego," David said defensively. "We both know he wants to be more than just your sentry. I think it's completely understandable if I'm a little upset about that."

"You're right," Laurel snapped back. "If you don't trust me, it totally is." She turned and headed for her first class, refusing to look back.

"Boys are impossible!" Laurel huffed, dropping her backpack on the floor by the register in her mom's store.

"Ah, music to my ears," her mom said with a smile.

Laurel couldn't help but smile back, even as she rolled her eyes.

"So I take it you are escaping from said boys?" her mom asked. "Does your escape plan include a little manual labor?"

"I'm always happy to help in here, Mom." Since Laurel and her mom had straightened out their issues last year, Laurel found herself helping in her mom's store even more than at her dad's bookstore next door. Her mom had one part-time employee now, which made talking openly a little more difficult, but on a school day in the middle of the afternoon, the store was all theirs.

"What can I do?" Laurel asked.

"I have two boxes of new stock," her mom said. "If we work together we can sort and talk at the same time."

"Deal."

They worked in silence for a while before her mom finally broached the subject. "So . . . David coming up a little short in the boyfriend department?"

"Kind of," Laurel muttered. "Well, not really, he's just not dealing with things very well. I told you about Tamani, right?"

"You did," her mom said, smiling craftily, "but I suspected there was more to that story."

"Well, sort of. He's started interfering in our relationship a little. And David's jealous."

"Does he have a reason to be jealous?"

Laurel considered this, not completely sure what the

answer was herself. "Maybe?"

"Is that a question?"

They both laughed and it felt like a tangible weight was lifted from Laurel's shoulders as she shared the story with her mother.

"It sounds like you stood up for yourself really well," her mom said. After a pause she added, "Did you guys break up?"

"No!" Laurel said vehemently.

"So you're still happy with him?"

"Yes!" Laurel insisted. "He's great. He just had a bad day. You don't break up with someone because of one bad day. He's on edge because of Tam . . . ani," she tacked on. She'd gotten too used to hearing his shortened name in school.

"But you like Tamani, too?"

"I don't know," Laurel whispered. "I mean, I do, but it's not the same as with David." Laurel leaned her head on her mom's shoulder, feeling more confused than ever. "I love David. He's seen me through *everything*." She laughed. "And when I say everything, you know what I mean."

"Yes, yes I do," her mom said wryly. "But love is something that has to be as selfish as it is unselfish. You can't make yourself love someone because you feel like you should. Just *wanting* to love someone isn't enough."

Laurel looked at her mother in shock. "Are you telling me to break up with David?" The thought almost frightened her.

"No," her mom said. "I'm really not. I like David. I've

never even met Tamani—which you should remedy, by the way." She paused and laid her hand on Laurel's. "All I'm saying is that you shouldn't stay with him for the wrong reasons, even if they are noble ones. No one owes it to someone else to be their girlfriend. It's a choice you remake every day."

Laurel nodded slowly, then paused. "I love him, Mom."

"I know you do. But there are a lot of different kinds of love."

# TWELVE

SPURRED BY HER MOM'S ENCOURAGEMENT, LAUREL decided there was no reason she couldn't have Tamani over. As a friend. So Friday night she called him on his iPhone for the first time and asked if he wanted to come over Saturday to help her with research. And by research, she meant *research*. Her mom wasn't going to be home to actually meet Tamani—Saturdays were her busiest day at the store—but her dad was there. It was a start.

The doorbell rang and Laurel's dad hollered that he would get it. There was no way she could beat him to the door. Delay tactics were her next best bet. She glanced over her shoulder again, staring at her blossom in the mirror. It was as beautiful—and whole—as ever. After a troll ripped out a handful of her petals last year, she'd been concerned it wouldn't grow back the same. Fortunately, the new blossom didn't look like it had been affected by the trauma at all.

It was still a rich, dark blue at its center, fading to almost white at its tips. The petals fanned out in a four-pointed star that—even now that she knew what it was—looked like wings. Sometimes, when it wasn't terrifying or inconveniencing her, Laurel loved her blossom.

And introducing Tamani to her father while she was blooming definitely qualified as inconvenient.

Trying to stifle her nerves, Laurel adjusted her green halter-top and smoothed her capris before walking over to the door and opening it a crack. She listened for a few seconds until she heard Tamani's soft brogue travel up the stairs. It would be worse than a disaster to head down with her blossom out, only to find that the doorbell had simply been a chatty neighbor.

Not for the first time that morning she considered calling David. He'd emailed her last night and apologized again but she hadn't responded yet. Truth was, she didn't know what to say. About an hour earlier she'd actually picked up the phone and started to dial. But the middle of an experiment with Tamani was not the time to work through their issues and she knew she wouldn't be able to concentrate if David came over now and there was still tension. *I'll call him as soon as Tamani leaves*, she promised herself.

She could hear Tamani and her dad talking as she slowly descended the stairs. It was weird to hear them together, and made her feel strangely jealous. For two years now Tamani had been *her* secret—her special person. Except for a few times with David, she hadn't had to share him at all.

Sometimes she wished she could go back to the way things used to be. When he had deep-green eyes and longish hair and didn't wear shoes or jeans. When he was just hers.

She almost didn't notice when the buzz of conversation stopped. All eyes were on her. "Hey," she said with a lame wave.

"Hey is right!" her dad said, his voice loud with excitement. "Look at you! I didn't know you were blossoming."

Laurel shrugged. "It's not a big deal," she said as nonchalantly as she could manage with Tamani standing right there, staring at her blossom, his expression guarded.

Abruptly, he shoved his hands into his pockets.

*Oh, yeah.*

"So," Laurel said, forcing a smile as her dad continued to gawk at her petals and Tamani looked studiously away. "Dad, Tamani. Tamani, Dad."

"Yeah, Tamani was just telling me a little about his life as a sentry. I think it's fascinating."

"You think everything about the fae is fascinating," Laurel said, rolling her eyes.

"And why shouldn't I?" He crossed his arms over her chest and looked at her proudly.

Laurel squirmed at the attention. "Well, we have work to do," Laurel said, inclining her head toward the stairs.

"Homework?" Laurel's dad asked, clearly disbelieving.

"Faerie stuff," Laurel said, shaking her head. "Tamani has generously agreed to donate his body to my research." The words were out of Laurel's mouth before she realized how bad they sounded. "I mean he's helping me," she corrected herself, feeling like an idiot.

"Awesome! Can I watch?" her dad asked, sounding more like a little boy than a grown man.

"Sure, because my dad watching over my shoulder won't be awkward at all," Laurel said cheerfully.

"Fine," he said, moving over to give her a hug. With his mouth close to her ear he whispered, "You look gorgeous. Keep your door open."

"Dad!" Laurel hissed, but he only raised an eyebrow at her. She chanced a glance at Tamani, but he just looked bemused. "Fine," she said, then pulled away and began walking toward the steps. "It's this way," she said to Tamani.

Tamani paused for a second, then walked over to Laurel's dad and stuck out his hand, which Laurel noted was temporarily free of pollen, probably courtesy of Tamani's pocket-lining. "Great to meet you, Mr. Sewell," he said.

"Absolutely, Tam." Laurel cringed. It sounded twice as bizarre coming out of her dad's mouth. "We'll have to talk more one of these days."

"Sure," Tamani said, reaching his other hand up to clasp her dad's shoulder. "But for now, wow, it's Saturday—your store must be really busy."

"Oh, it usually gets busy at about twelve," he said, pointing to the clock that read just after eleven.

"Sure, but school started a few weeks ago and people always want books for school, right? I bet they're really busy down there and could use your help. You should go to the store. Help out. We'll be fine here."

It took Laurel about three seconds to realize what was happening.

"You know, you're right," her dad said, his voice sounding a little far away. "I should go help them."

"Well, it was good to see you for a little while at least. I'm sure I'll see you again."

"Yep, that would be great!" Laurel's dad said, looking a little more like himself. "Well, you two get some good work done. I think I'm going to go down and help Maddie out at the store. It's a Saturday; I bet it's busy." He grabbed his car keys and was out the door.

"Okay," Laurel said, turning to Tamani, "*not* cool."

"What?" Tamani asked, looking genuinely confused. "I got him out of the way."

"Him? That *him* is my dad!"

"Enticement doesn't hurt him," Tamani protested. "Besides, I've been living on my own for years—I don't do well with hovering parents."

"My house, my rules," Laurel said sternly. "Don't do it again."

"All right, fine," Tamani said, raising his hands in front of him. He paused and looked up to where she was standing, a few steps above him. "He was right though, you do look gorgeous."

Her anger evaporated and she found herself staring at the floor, trying to think of something to say.

"Come on," Tamani said, sweeping past her, a picture of

unaffected nonchalance. "Let's get started."

Over the past few years, Laurel's room had gone from a fairly typical teenager's room to a pink, fluffy chemistry lab. Her gauzy curtains and girlish bedspread were the same, and the prisms strung along her window still sparkled in the sun and cast rainbows across her room. But instead of bouncing off CDs, makeup, books, and clothes, the light caught vials, mortars, and reagents—bags of leaves, bottles of oils, and baskets of drying flowers.

At least her room always smelled good.

Laurel sat at her desk chair and gestured to a pink vanity stool for Tamani, trying not to think about how often David had sat in that same chair to watch her work.

"So," Tamani said, talking more to her blossom than her face. "What have you got so far?"

"Uh," Laurel said, trying to ignore the tightening in her chest, "not a whole lot, actually. I made the phosphorescent right, so that's good. I tried to make some Cyoan powder too, but it's just way beyond me."

"Why Cyoan? That won't tell you anything about a faerie."

"But we want something similar. And sometimes, when a Mixing is going really well and I make a mistake, I get this feeling like, well, I don't even know how to describe it. It's like when I'm playing my guitar, and I play a chord and it sounds right, but I know it's wrong because it's not, you know, what I was *going* for. . . ."

Tamani was smiling helplessly. "I have no idea what you're talking about."

Laurel laughed. "Me either! And that's kind of the problem. I think Katya's right, that different kinds of faeries must process light differently. Like, I like sunlight, but I don't really use it in my Mixing. And Spring faeries . . . I think you guys are adaptable. I mean, you stay up all night sometimes, right?"

"Frequently," Tamani said, in a weary tone that suggested that he'd been staying up a lot of nights lately.

"And the sentries in Hokkaido can withstand enormous amounts of cold."

Tamani hesitated. "Well, yes, but they have help from the Fall faeries with that. They make them a special tea from—"

"White Bryony, I remember," Laurel said. "But still, the energy has to come from somewhere. And the Winter faeries use a ton of energy when they . . . what?" she demanded, when Tamani got a strange brightness in his eyes.

"Listen to you," he said, pride creeping into his tone. "You're amazing. You totally get this stuff. I knew you would slip right back into being a Fall faerie."

Laurel hid a smile as she cleared her throat and busied herself meaninglessly with an already-powdered mixture at the bottom of her mortar.

"So what do we do?" Tamani asked.

"I don't know. I still don't think we should drink this stuff. I wondered if it might have an effect on our skin—"

Immediately, Tamani offered her his forearm.

"—but I'm not about to start trying stuff at random. Mixing is pretty hands-on," Laurel said. "I mean touch-dependent," she amended. "I mean—before I try anything,

I want to get a feel for your cellular makeup, which means I need to touch . . . you."

*Could that possibly have come out any worse?* Laurel thought dismally as she watched Tamani try—and fail—to suppress his amusement.

"Okay," he said, again holding out his hand, which was sparkling with pollen and looking more than a little magical.

"Actually," Laurel said slowly, "what I'd really like to do is have you—" Pause. "Take your shirt off and then go to the window and sit in the sunlight. That way your cells can start actively photosynthesizing after having been at rest and I can hopefully feel that activity."

"That almost makes sense," Tamani said with a smirk. He walked over to her window seat and sat, then waited for her to come sit behind him. She was careful not to actually let any part of them touch. Not just because it wasn't a good idea and severely hampered her concentration, but she had learned that if she could keep the rest of her body away from any kind of plant material, her fingers seemed more receptive.

"You ready?" Tamani asked, his voice soft and vaguely suggestive.

Laurel glanced out the window. The sun had just popped out from behind a cloud. "Perfect," she said quietly. "Go ahead."

Tamani stretched his long arms over his head, pulling off his T-shirt.

Laurel struggled for focus. She moved her hands to Tamani's back and splayed her fingers over his skin. Her fingertips pressed in just a little as she closed her eyes and tried to feel, not Tamani in particular, but his cellular dynamics.

She cocked her head to the side as the sun warmed the back of her hands. It took her only a moment to realize her mistake. She was now blocking Tamani's skin from the sun's rays. With a frustrated sigh, she lifted her hands, and placed them back down, this time lower and along one side of his ribs where the sun had just been shining. She felt him shift a little, but she was in concentration mode now, and even Tamani couldn't affect her.

Much.

Laurel had learned from Yeardley how to feel the essential nature of any plant she touched. He assured her that, with study and practice, this feeling would eventually tell her everything she needed to know about a plant—particularly, what it could do if mixed with other plants. She should be able to do the same with Tamani. And if she could find some way to feel the differences between the two of them . . .

But every time she thought she'd felt something, it faded. She wasn't sure whether it was because she kept blocking the sunlight, or because the differences she was looking for simply didn't exist. And the harder she tried, the less she seemed to find. By the time she realized she was squeezing Tamani so hard her fingers were aching, she couldn't feel any difference at all.

She let go of Tamani and tried not to notice the subtle divots her fingers had left in his back.

"Well?" Tamani asked, turning to her and leaning against

the window without making any move to put his shirt back on.

Laurel sighed, frustration washing over her again. "There was . . . something, but it's like it went away."

"Do you want to do it again?" Tamani leaned forward, bringing his face close to hers. He spoke softly, genuinely. No trace of flirting or teasing.

"I don't think it would help." She was still trying to sort out the sensations she felt in her fingertips. Like a word on the tip of her tongue, or an interrupted sneeze, so close that staring at it would only chase it away. She closed her eyes and placed her fingers against her temples, massaging them slowly, sensing the life in her own cells. It was as familiar as ever.

"I wish . . . I wish that I could . . . feel you better," she said, wishing she knew a better way to say it. "I just, I can't quite get at what I'm trying to reach. It's like your skin is in the way. At the Academy I would slice my sample open, but obviously that's not an option right now," she said with a laugh.

"What else do you do when you can't figure out what a plant does? Besides cut it open, I mean," Tamani asked.

"Smell it," Laurel responded automatically. "I can taste the ones that aren't poisonous."

"Taste?"

She looked up at Tamani, at his half smile. "No," she said, instantly knowing what he had in mind. "No, no, no, n—"

Her words were cut off as two pollen-dusted hands cupped Laurel's cheeks and Tamani pressed his mouth against hers, parting her lips with his own.

Stars exploded in Laurel's head, their rainbow ashes coalescing into a torrential pastiche, a rapid-fire flipbook of flower parades and crazy. Through her head, unbidden, fleeting, and difficult to grasp, poured thoughts that made her giddy and queasy at once. *Mix with zantedeschia stamens for a potent antitoxin. Age revitalization in animals if fermented with amrita. Injectable Enticement block, rose petals, photo-resistor, salve daisies balm tincturepoisonnectardeath*—Laurel jerked away from Tamani, too dazed to slap him.

"Laurel? Laurel, are you all right?"

Laurel slumped back into her chair and brought her fingers to her lips.

"Laurel, I—"

"I asked you not to." Laurel could tell that her tone was flat. Distant. But her mind was reeling. She knew she should be furious, but Tamani's presence barely registered at all, blocked out by the sensations that had assaulted her mind.

"You weren't going to do it. I had to at least try. I didn't mean anything by it—"

"Yes, you did," Laurel said. Research was a convenient excuse, but Tamani had seen an opportunity and taken it. Fortunately for him, it had worked. Sort of. She looked up, numbly, at Tamani. Gradually it dawned on her that he had no idea what just happened.

"You want me to apologize? I will, if it's that important to you. I'm—"

Laurel put one finger to his lips, silencing him. At the touch of him the overwhelming flow of information didn't return, but the images were fresh in her memory. *Is that how it always feels, for the other Falls?* she wondered. *Or was that a fluke?*

Her expression must have been perplexing, because Tamani stepped backward, out of Laurel's reach, and held his hands up, palms out, pleading. "Look, I just thought—"

"Shut up," Laurel said. Her tone was still flat, but she wasn't feeling quite so numb anymore. "We'll deal with that later. When you kissed me, I got all these . . . ideas. For potions I've never heard of." She thought of the way the word *poison* had invaded her mind. "I think maybe they're forbidden."

"Why?"

"I've been doing it wrong, Tamani. I don't need to touch you. I might need to test my potions on you, assuming I find the right plants, but touching you won't tell me how to make potions *for* you."

It took him a moment to process what she was saying. "What *did* it tell you, Laurel?"

"It told me how to make potions *from* you."

"Holy Hecate, petals, branches, and breath," Tamani swore, his face lined with concern. "You can *do* that?"

"With study and practice," Laurel said quietly. How many times had Yeardley spoken those words to her? "I . . . I don't think that was something I was supposed to know about," she said softly. "I don't know why."

"That doesn't make any sense. Surely the other Falls know?"

"I don't know. Nobody's ever said anything. Why . . ." She was having trouble forming a coherent thought. Who in their right mind would think to use other fae as *ingredients*?

126

"Why didn't that happen before?" she finally demanded. "It's not like I haven't . . . kissed you before."

Tamani's grin was a little pained now. "Um, I may have bitten down on my tongue pretty hard just before I kissed you."

Laurel's thoughts jerked to a stop. "That's disgusting!"

"Hey," Tamani said with a shrug, "*you* said you cut things open and taste them, and I knew you weren't going to try either of those things on your own."

He was right. Clearly it had made a difference. Casually touching him—or even kissing—wasn't enough. And yet . . .

"You should probably go," Laurel said sternly. The numbness was fading. Tamani had *kissed* her! Without permission. *Again!* She knew she should be furious, but somehow anger couldn't pierce the shock she felt at her new discovery.

"If it makes you feel better, it really hurt," Tamani admitted, his jaw at a funny angle.

"I'm sorry. And at least this time you didn't do it while David was watching," Laurel added. "But you shouldn't have done it at all."

Tamani simply nodded before turning and silently exiting the room.

As he left, Laurel brought her hand once more to her lips and lost herself in thought. Not thoughts of Tamani, for once. Thoughts of potions, powders, and poisons she somehow knew she was never supposed to learn.

# THIRTEEN

THERE WERE FLOWERS IN LAUREL'S LOCKER ON MONDAY. Not big flashy roses. Just hand-picked wild ones tied with a ribbon, which was how she knew they were from David. He wasn't the kind to make a big deal out of gifts—drawing more attention to himself than to the sentiment.

Which was why she found the jealous, possessive David so perplexing.

"I'm sorry," David said, stepping quietly up behind her.

Laurel looked down at the flowers, but said nothing.

"I was totally out of line. I freaked out." He leaned his back against his locker and ran his hands through his hair. "I just don't like him being here. I haven't from the beginning. I've tried to hide it and deal with it, and I guess I snapped last week."

"I didn't do anything wrong," Laurel said, avoiding his eyes as she stacked books in her locker.

"I know," David said. "That's what I'm trying to say and apparently failing. It's not your problem, it's mine." He turned to her now, his blue eyes earnest. "It's just that I know what he wants, and I don't want him to have it. Trust me," he added, trying to laugh away the tension, "if you had a girlfriend as cool as mine you would turn into a freak at the thought of losing her too."

"I had a boyfriend as cool as your girlfriend," Laurel said, not turning around.

"I'll do better," David said, leaning against his locker now so he could see her face. "I promise."

Laurel stared at her locker, not wanting to admit that half of her anger was at herself. She wanted David to trust her, to know that she wasn't going to let Tamani steal her away. But David had every reason to be suspicious of Tamani—and how could she ask David to trust her when she wasn't even sure she trusted herself?

"I should have called sooner," David said, pulling Laurel from her thoughts.

"I should have replied to your email," Laurel admitted. "I was going to. I kinda wimped out."

"So . . . are we okay?" David asked hesitantly.

This was the moment—the moment to tell him everything. To admit that she was in the wrong as much as he was. She opened her mouth, and—

"Hi, Laurel."

Laurel and David both turned to look at Tamani as he delivered his morning greeting. Laurel looked up at David again, and lost her nerve.

"Yeah, we're okay," she said quietly.

David released a sigh and wrapped his arms around her. "Thanks," he said softly. "I really am sorry."

"I know," Laurel said, guilt smoldering in her stomach.

After a pause he added, "So, we didn't get to do SAT stuff this weekend. How about this week?"

Laurel sighed, wishing with all her heart right then that she hadn't agreed to retake them. "Can't we study for something else? I don't even know why you're bothering with them. You scored more than seven hundred on every section last time."

"Yeah, but that was ages ago. I really think I can do better this time." He stopped. "Plus I want to be supportive of you."

Laurel pursed her lips. She didn't particularly enjoy being reminded that her scores from last spring weren't great. Thus actually preparing this time.

"Anyway," David rushed on, "we always study together and I wanted to make sure we could still do that."

"Absolutely," Laurel said, laying a hand on his arm. "I'm not going to stop doing things with you just because you're a jerk." Laurel smiled to let him know she was kidding and, after a tiny hesitation, he laughed.

"So, after school?"

"Sure."

"Okay." He hesitated and then chanced a quick kiss. "I love you," he said.

"I know," Laurel replied, then wondered where that response had come from.

"I'll walk you to class."

As Laurel shouldered her backpack she caught sight of Tamani leaning against Yuki's locker, smiling and chatting with her. As if sensing her watching him, Tamani looked over and met her eyes for the smallest of instants before turning right back to Yuki and smiling again.

Laurel didn't realize she had stopped walking until she felt David's fingers pulling her forward. She quickly caught up. "Well, well, well," she said quietly.

"What?" David asked.

"Tamani's really making . . . progress with Yuki."

David turned a little and looked across the hall where Tamani and Yuki were still chatting, Yuki clearly hanging on Tamani's every word. David shrugged. "Wasn't that the plan?"

"Sort of," Laurel said, wondering why Tamani's friendliness bothered her so much. Was it because he had succeeded in befriending Yuki after Laurel had failed? "I guess I thought he was trying to convince her to be *my* friend."

After kissing David distractedly, Laurel walked into her Government class, took her regular seat, and waited for Tamani to come and sit beside her. She could feel a headache coming on. *Great.* Just the thing to round out her morning.

Tamani came running in and slid into his seat just as the final bell rang. He was wearing a pair of black leather gloves with the fingers all cut off at the first knuckle.

"What are those?" Laurel said, wrinkling her nose. "Fingerless gloves went out of style before . . . mullets. You look like a dork."

"Better a dork than a freak with glitter coming out of his hands," Tamani hissed darkly. "As far as these kids know, they're all the rage in Scotland."

Laurel felt bad for not realizing; after all, it was being around *her* blossom that brought pollen to his hands. "Oh. What are you doing with Yuki? I thought you were supposed to be getting *us* together, not hooking up with her," she whispered as Mrs. Harms called attendance.

"I am *not* 'hooking up' with her," Tamani hissed.

"Could have fooled me," Laurel muttered.

Tamani shrugged. "I have a job to do here," he whispered. "I do what it takes."

"Including taking advantage of a clueless fae?"

"I'm not *taking advantage* of her," Tamani whispered back, a little heat creeping into his tone. "I'm just being friendly. And if it turns out she's completely innocent in all this, then she'll have someone who can answer all the questions she has about herself." After a long pause he added, "It worked pretty well with you."

"Didn't work *that* well," Laurel said caustically. "I'm not exactly *your* girlfriend, am I?" She turned back to the front of her class before Tamani could answer and raised her hand. "I have a massive headache; can I run to my locker real quick?" Laurel asked the teacher. Laurel didn't want to think about Tamani or David right now. It just made her feel worse about everything.

Stupid boys.

"Dendroid," David said, looking up from his SAT prep book.

Laurel groaned. "Aren't we done yet? I think we've reviewed, like, two hundred words already." She wasn't even exaggerating. It had been a good day though. Monday and Tuesday had both been a little awkward, but things had fallen back into their usual rhythm and now Laurel was actually getting something out of her studying again. They quizzed each other, rewarding correct answers with kisses, and for a break, finished up some homework for their individual classes in companionable silence. It felt like things were getting back to normal.

Laurel liked normal.

"Just this last one," David insisted. "It's fitting."

"Dendroid," Laurel said, scrunching up her face. "A machine that lives in the ground?" she said with a grin.

David rolled his eyes. "Funny. No, actually, it's something you are."

"Oh, annoyed. Tired. Burned out. Am I getting warm?"

"Okay," David said, closing his book. "I'll take the hint before you beat me to death with it. We can be done." He paused. "I just want you to do well."

"I really don't think a ton of cramming the day before I take the test is going to help much. No, really," Laurel insisted.

David shrugged. "Can't hurt."

"Easy for you to say," Laurel said, rubbing her eyes. She walked over to the bed, trailing her fingers across David's shoulders, then flopped down next to her own SAT prep workbook.

"You want me to quiz you on anything else? Maybe the math?"

Laurel grimaced. "I hate the math part."

"Which is why you should work on it. Plus," he added, "it was your best score last time even with no prep. I think you have a great chance of improving it. I mean, it didn't help that you weren't even in a math class last semester. Being in Trig should help a lot this time."

Laurel sighed and turned her blossom to the sunny window. "Sometimes I don't even see the point," she said morosely. "It doesn't matter how I do on the SATs. Why am I retaking them?"

It had made sense to take them initially. At David's prompting she'd looked into the nursing program at Berkley, figured out what she needed to score. Even studied, a little. Sort of. But the test hadn't been what she expected; if nothing else, it was more than four hours in a windowless room. She'd done abysmally on the essay and failed to even finish one of the verbal sections. And she'd just guessed on about a third of the math questions. Even before her below-average scores came back she knew she hadn't done well. In some ways, that made her decision easy—especially since she'd mastered a new potion the same day she got her scores.

It was practically a sign. She wasn't going to college; she was going to study at the Academy of Avalon. It was clearly meant to be.

But she knew she *could* do better.

"Laurel," David said, frustration coloring his tone, "you keep saying that and I still don't understand why. Why can't you go to college?"

"It's not that I can't," Laurel said. "I'm just . . . not sure I even want to."

David looked concerned, but he hid it quickly, before Laurel's conscience could prick her too much. "Why not?" he asked.

"I'm getting really good at Mixing," Laurel said. "Seriously. Tama—everyone's impressed with my progress. My practice is really starting to pay off and I'm totally getting this intuition thing. It works. *I* make it work. It's exciting, David!"

"But, are you sure? I mean, it's not like you have to be in Avalon full-time to get better. You can practice here. Look at your room—you've totally out-geeked me," David said with a laugh. "You can keep doing that and still go to college too." He hesitated. "You could do your faerie studies instead of a job, since tuition won't be a problem for you."

"It won't be for you either, Mr. Straight A's."

"Well, that's why my mom finally let me quit *my* job." He grinned. "Financially investing in my future in a whole different way now."

"And the added advantage of getting to spend more time

with your girlfriend is a bit of a plus," Laurel replied, pulling his head down close and kissing him as much to change the subject as because she wanted to. His arms went to her waist, brushing her petals, but not lingering.

They lay on his bed with Laurel's knee resting on David's hip. Just lying together seemed to soften the frustrations of the past few weeks. She snuggled her head against his shoulder and closed her eyes, remembering why she enjoyed being with David so much. He was hers—always had been, if she was honest with herself—right from that first day. And he was always so calm, even in the face of outrageous things like flowers growing out of her back, trolls throwing them in rivers, faerie spies. Things that would surely have sent anyone else running for the hills. And probably to the news stations too. That alone made David one of the most loyal people she'd even known.

She ran her fingers absently over David's ribs and lifted her face so her forehead rested against his cheek.

"Laurel?"

"Hmmm?" Laurel asked, not opening her eyes.

"Can I just say—and let me finish before you say anything—I think you should try really hard on your SATs this time and apply to a few colleges. You've studied a ton the last couple of months anyway. Why throw that away?"

He paused, but Laurel was silent.

"Thing is," he continued, "applying, getting accepted even, doesn't mean you have to go. But when you graduate and—" He hesitated and Laurel bit her lip, knowing this was hard for him to even say. "And you have to start making decisions, I don't . . . want you to ever feel trapped. Options are good."

The minutes slid quietly by as Laurel thought about that. David was right—she didn't *have* to go just because she got accepted. And she knew all too well that feeling one way now didn't mean she'd feel the same way later. Lots of things had changed in her life, as well as in her head, over the past several years. Often for the better. "Okay," she said softly. She knew that when David said, "Options are good," he was really saying, "Don't make a choice that will separate us for sure." It was his way of holding on for as long as he could—keeping open the possibility of forever.

But that didn't make him wrong.

# FOURTEEN

"SHE'S IN THERE ALL THE TIME," TAMANI SAID TO Aaron halfway between Laurel's and Yuki's houses. "She does homework, reads, watches television. I don't see any evidence of plotting at all." It had been more than a fortnight since they'd discovered Yuki was a faerie, and there was still nothing to indicate that she even comprehended what she was, much less had a master plan that involved Laurel's demise.

"All the guards say their most boring shifts are watching her," Aaron replied. "And I don't mean that humorously. Nothing happens. Suspicious or otherwise."

"We can't pull them away," Tamani said, "but it does feel like an inefficient use of resources, doesn't it?"

Aaron raised an eyebrow. "That's how I've felt most of the past year," he said wryly.

Tamani swallowed the retort that sprang to his lips. He

would have thought the same if he were an unaffected observer. But any effort was worth it when you were guarding someone you loved.

"I wonder—" He cut off sharply. Someone was crashing noisily through the forest, headed in their direction. Aaron and Tamani both darted behind trees, hands poised over their weapons, when two misshapen figures came lumbering through the darkness. *What was this?* For months they'd been combing the forest for trolls, only to have two stumble into *them*? With his free hand, he signaled Aaron.

*Mine dies. Yours talks.*

Aaron responded with a single nod.

As the first troll passed within arm's length, Tamani stepped out from behind the tree, unsheathing his knife in a sweeping arc that scored a long, shallow gash across the troll's back. The troll spun to face him, lashing out with one clawed, gnarled hand—a blind, reflexive counterattack. Tamani sidestepped the blow easily, then, with a savage thrust, buried his knife to the hilt in the troll's eye socket. He gave the blade a sharp twist and the creature crumpled to the ground.

A short distance away, Aaron had scored several cuts on the other troll's arms and legs, slowing its movements. Crippling a troll wasn't easy—better to just kill them quickly—but Tamani needed information. Fortunately, two weapons could cripple a troll faster than one. Bracing one foot against the fallen troll's neck, Tamani wrenched his knife from its skull. Rivulets of blood, black in the starlight, pulsed from the wound. He looked up just in time to watch Aaron's back vanish into the darkness; apparently, the other troll had decided it was time to run. Tamani considered going after them, then decided against it. Aaron was more than capable.

Instead, he took the fallen troll under its arms and dragged it away from the path, in case any more came this way. Once he was far enough, he searched the body for any evidence of what it might be doing here. It was unarmed—not that trolls had any real need for weapons—and dressed in a muddy burlap poncho and black coveralls. No clues there, except perhaps that Barnes's trolls had often dressed similarly. The creature's pockets were empty, no hint of where he came from or who he was after.

Kicking at the corpse with his foot, Tamani crept back to the path, then followed the trail Aaron had left, finding him less than a minute later. His knife was sheathed and he looked unharmed, but there were no trolls to be seen, crippled or otherwise.

"I lost him," Aaron said, shaking his head.

"You *lost* him?" Tamani asked incredulously. "He was two feet in front of you!"

"Thanks for that, Tam. Because I wasn't feeling like enough of a failure," Aaron said caustically.

"Tell me what happened."

"He just . . . vanished." He kicked at a tuft of earth. "I've tracked down scores of trolls in my time, and nothing like this ever happened until I came here."

"Did he go to ground?" Tamani asked, scanning the undergrowth for signs of burrowing.

Aaron shook his head. "I was watching for that. I was chasing him and he was in my sight. I went for a throwing knife—I was going to hamstring him—and I looked down for a second. Half a second, even. And he was gone."

"What do you mean, gone?"

"Gone! Gone like summer. Gone like mist. I'm telling you, Tamani, that troll disappeared. There wasn't even a trail!"

Tamani folded his arms over his chest, trying to comprehend this. Aaron was one of the best trackers he'd ever met. If he said there wasn't a trail, there wasn't a trail. But that didn't mean it made any sense.

"I thought I heard footsteps," Aaron continued. "But even those disappeared soon enough."

Tamani swallowed hard, trying to suppress the niggling fear in his stomach.

"Send out scouts," Tamani said quietly. "Try to pick up the trail."

"There is no trail to pick up," Aaron insisted. Then he pulled back and stood a little straighter. "I will follow any order you give me, Tamani. And if you want a dozen scouts crawling over this forest, you shall have them. But they won't find anything new."

"What else can we do?" Tamani asked, failing to keep the desperation from his voice. "I have to keep her safe, Aaron."

Aaron hesitated. "Which one?"

Tamani paused; were they watching Yuki or protecting her? "Both," he said at last. "These trolls could have been headed for either house. Have we seen anything else?"

"Stripped cow carcasses, paths broken through the trees. The same thing we've been seeing for months," he said, staring toward the horizon. "They're out there, even if we can't see them."

"Any chance it's been just these two?" Tamani asked, though he already knew the answer.

"Not unless they're eating for twelve. Or twenty. I think these ones just got sloppy."

"It's more than that," Tamani said, shaking his head. "They seemed almost . . . confused. I'm sure they were surprised to see us, but they weren't even armed. Mine barely put up a fight."

"Mine didn't put up much of a fight either," Aaron agreed.

"I have to go soon," Tamani said quietly after a moment. "Laurel is going to Eureka for some kind of test. I'll be trailing her. You're in charge of the Wildflower. We haven't seen Klea in weeks—she should be coming round any day now. If she does, I need you to listen to everything they say and let me know. Even if it's something you don't think is relevant. I want to know every word they say."

Aaron nodded stoically and Tamani turned, sprinting through the forest toward Laurel's. He slowed to a walk as he approached the tree line behind her house and saw the glow of lights in the kitchen. A wave of warmth washed over him as her face appeared in the window, looking out at the trees. Looking for him.

She didn't know he was there, but it was easy to pretend otherwise as he watched her. Her eyes were still a little sleepy and she was popping berries into her mouth, one at a time, chewing thoughtfully. He could almost imagine they were having a conversation. Something trivial and meaningless, instead of the weighty discussions they were forced to have these days. Something other than trolls and potions and lies.

When he had accepted—practically begged for—this new mission, he'd assumed he would be able to spend more time with Laurel, recapture the friendship and intimacy they'd known in their youth—something he had felt a little last year when he brought her to Avalon. But that all seemed like a joke now. His duties required him to watch her with David every day, and to spend his time trying to charm someone else. Yuki was nice enough, but she wasn't Laurel. Nobody was Laurel.

Tamani smiled as Laurel continued to stare out the window. He wanted to step out from behind his tree, just to see what she would do.

There might be time. One conversation over breakfast, about nothing more complicated than the beauty of the sunrise. He had almost worked up the courage to do it when he heard that familiar engine tick. He cursed under his breath as David's Civic rolled up the driveway. Then he was sprinting again, to the hedge down the street where his own car was parked. He didn't want to see their greeting, the kisses and embraces that David so casually received.

*Someday*, Tamani told himself. *Someday it'll be me.*

"So?" David asked as they exited the classroom, four hours of testing behind them.

"Don't ask me yet," Laurel said, panic creeping into her

voice as she shouldered her backpack and walked down the long hall toward the exit and some much-needed sunshine. They'd driven to a high school in Eureka to take the test—the same classroom with no windows. Laurel had felt every minute of her confinement and intended to make up for them as quickly as possible. As she crossed over the shadow of the threshold, a gentle autumn breeze caressed her face. She breathed deeply and stopped walking, spreading her arms to embrace the sunlight. Then she sank down onto the unfamiliar front steps and just savored being done.

After a minute or so, David sat down beside her. "I brought you something."

He handed her a cold bottle of Sprite he must have just gotten from a vending machine. Even the condensation against her fingertips was revitalizing. "Thanks."

He waited as she opened the bottle and took a long swallow. "You okay?" he finally asked.

"Better now," she said with a smile. "I just had to get out of that room."

"So . . . ," he said, broaching the subject carefully. "How did it go?"

She smiled. "I think I did okay. Better."

"Yeah?"

"How 'bout you?"

He shrugged. "I don't know. Hard to say." He paused. "Boy, I'd like to beat Chelsea though."

"You're so bad. Your GPA is, like, point-oh-two better than hers. Can't you let her win this one?"

David grinned. "We've been competing since junior high.

It's all in good fun—I promise."

"Good," Laurel said, leaning in for a kiss, then letting her head rest against his shoulder.

"So," David said, a little hesitantly, "how about this Sadie Hawkins dance?"

Laurel laughed and shook her head. "Yeah, couldn't they have waited one more week and held it in November? You know, around Sadie Hawkins Day?" She snorted. "They just don't want the anti-Pagan-zealot parents up in arms again, like last year. It's just a Halloween dance without costumes."

"Still," David said, "it could be fun. Not that I'm asking you," he said, touching her nose, "because it's ladies' choice, but *if* you were to ask me, and *if* Chelsea were to ask Ryan, and *if* the two of you decided to go together, maybe we could all go together. That's all I'm saying," he said with a grin and a shrug.

"That's an awful lot of 'ifs' there, buddy," Laurel drawled. "I certainly hope you undertake your venture under propitious circumstances."

"You're awful," David said, leaning forward to kiss her again.

"Yeah," Laurel agreed, "but you love me."

"Yes, I do," David said, his voice low and throaty. "I love you with great profundity."

"You're doin' it wrong," Laurel said, giggling as David's lips tickled her neck.

"It's all I could come up with on the fly," David said, laughing. "I admit to being bested by you." He pulled back, so he could look her in the face. "Again."

Laurel just grinned.

"Laurel, really," David said, then paused. "I'm way proud of you."

"David—"

"Please let me say it," David interrupted. "It's got to be hard to get disappointing scores and then buckle down and study for a test you already took, especially when it might not matter what you get. I think that's really admirable."

"Thank you," Laurel said seriously. Then she grinned. "And you did use *that* word correctly."

"Come here, you!" David said, grabbing her arm and pulling her across his lap, squeezing her as she squealed and laughed.

David dropped Laurel off at her house just as the sun was disappearing over the horizon, setting the sky afire. As she watched him drive away, she wondered what she would do if her scores really did improve.

"Laurel!"

Laurel jumped when the loud whisper sounded from around the side of her house. She looked over and saw Tamani poking his head out from behind the wall.

"Do you have a second?" he said, inclining his head.

After a moment of hesitation she laid her backpack down on the porch and followed him. "What do you need?" she asked, her voice low. "Is there trouble?"

"No, no, not really," Tamani said. "Well, kind of. We . . . we found some trolls this morning."

"You *what*?"

"We took care of it," Tamani said, putting his hands out to calm her. "I just don't want you to think I'm hiding anything from you. Honestly, it's probably better that we've found them now."

"Why?" Laurel asked, hesitant to believe that.

"Because it means we've actually seen one. We hadn't seen any in months."

"But everything's okay?" Laurel said, almost sarcastically.

"It really is. We're still on high alert, but I don't want you to worry. Anyway, that's not what I came here to say," Tamani said apologetically. "I just wanted to talk. It's been a while."

That was true; Laurel had been avoiding him all week. Because he'd kissed her, and she didn't want to talk about it. Because David didn't like him. Because he was looking at Yuki the way he used to look at her.

When she didn't respond, Tamani shoved his hands in his pockets and kicked at the lawn. "So how did everything go today?"

"Fine, I think I did well."

"Good." He paused. "Have you done any more experiments? Maybe with the globe?"

Laurel sighed. "No. I think you're right that I should try the phosphorescent on my skin first. But I keep putting it off because then I won't have any more excuses before I have to clip a bit off my blossom like I originally planned. You probably think I'm a wimp. I mean, you bit your tongue open and I'm scared of clipping my petals."

"No, you're fine. You'll figure something out," Tamani said, sounding distracted.

Laurel nodded. She didn't know what to say. She was about to come right out and ask Tamani what he wanted when he blurted out, "There's a dance at school next Friday."

A twisted sense of déjà vu descended; Laurel was surprised to discover she preferred the tense silence. "You may not know the tradition, but it's girls' choice," she said quickly. "That means you really shouldn't be asking me. The girl is supposed to do the asking."

"I know," Tamani said bluntly. "I wasn't trying to ask you."

"Oh," Laurel said, half wishing the earth would just open up and swallow her whole. "Well, good."

"Yuki asked me."

Laurel couldn't say anything. She shouldn't have been surprised. In fact, Yuki probably only just beat a huge line of girls all waiting to pounce.

"I just—" He was silent for a long moment and Laurel wondered if he would finish his sentence. "I wanted to come and ask you," he finally continued, "if there was any reason I shouldn't accept." Then he looked up at her with pale green eyes that shone in the setting sun.

No—the light in Tamani's eyes was much more than a reflection. It was the fire that melted her anger and devastated her resolve, every single time she saw it. She blinked and forced herself to look away before it blinded her.

"No, of course not," she said, trying to keep her tone light. "You totally should go. I mean, this is what we're supposed to be doing, right? Figuring out Yuki?"

"Yeah, absolutely," he said. The defeat in his voice nearly

brought Laurel to tears. "Actually, I thought it would be great if me and Yuki and you and . . . and David . . . could all go together. Maybe finally bridge that gap between you and Yuki. And it'll be night, so I'd feel better if I could be close to you. In case anything happened." He smiled sadly. "It's my job, you know."

"Yeah, sure," Laurel said, suddenly desperate to get into her house. "Let's all talk Monday. Maybe we can bring Chelsea and Ryan too," she added, tacking on David's original plan.

"The more the merrier; that's what you guys say, right?" Tamani said, laughing weakly.

"That's right," Laurel said. "Hey, I have to go. My parents don't even know I'm home yet," she added with a smile.

"Sure. You better go."

Laurel nodded and turned, heading back to the porch. She pushed the door open and had just stepped in when Tamani called out again.

"Laurel?"

She caught the door before it closed. "Yeah?"

"I'm sorry. About . . . when I came over. That thing I did. I was out of line."

"It's okay," Laurel said, swallowing back her emotions. "I learned something about . . . you know. So that was lucky. We're still friends." She smiled as best she could. "Have a good night, Tamani."

"You too." Tamani smiled back at her. It was not a very convincing smile.

# FIFTEEN

WITH THAT, LAUREL WENT FROM AVOIDING TAMANI because she was mad at him to avoiding him because talking to him was awkward and confusing. But the plan for the dance was made, and Laurel had a job to do. She stopped by Chelsea's house the next week, feeling guilty that she hadn't been making enough time for her best friend lately. She apologized profusely and blamed the SATs.

"So you think you did better?" Chelsea asked brightly.

"I do," Laurel said, still half in awe at just how much easier the test seemed after studying properly. "And I'm going to do it. I'm going to apply to some colleges."

"I think it's really great, Laurel," Chelsea said, her tone strangely off.

"Really?" Laurel said, prodding a little.

Chelsea looked up at her, a smiled pasted on her face. "I do. David's totally right about the options thing."

"Options are good, but it would be easier if I just knew," Laurel said. "You've known exactly what you wanted to do since you were, what, ten?"

Chelsea nodded and then, to Laurel's surprise, burst into tears.

"Chelsea!" Laurel said, rushing over to the bed and hugging her friend, who was hiding her face in her hands as she gulped for air between sobs. "Chelsea," Laurel said more gently. "What's going on?" Empathetic tears sprang to Laurel's own eyes as Chelsea continued to cry. After several minutes she took a deep breath and laughed as she began to scrub the heels of her hands across her eyes, trying to dry them.

"Sorry," she said. "It's stupid."

"What is?"

Chelsea waved aside Laurel's concern. "Man, you have so much to deal with right now, you don't need to hear about my little issues."

Laurel put both of her hands on Chelsea's shoulders and waited for her to look up and meet Laurel's eyes. "If the world was ending tomorrow there would be nothing more important than listening to your problems," Laurel said, her voice steady and strong. "Tell me."

Chelsea's eyes teared up a bit again. She took a deep breath and rubbed at her reddened lids. "Ryan got his SAT scores back a couple weeks ago."

"Oh no, do they suck?"

Chelsea shook her head. "They're pretty good, actually.

Not as good as mine, but even David's aren't *quite* as high as mine."

Laurel smiled and rolled her eyes. "Then what's the problem?"

"I was in his room the other day—he had to go downstairs and talk to his mom—anyway, the printout of his scores was sitting on his desk. And I may have been snooping a little and I looked at his college profile and—" She hesitated. "He didn't send his scores to Harvard."

Harvard was Chelsea's first choice of schools—she'd wanted to go there since she was in grade school. Everyone knew that. Everyone. "Maybe there just weren't enough slots," Laurel said, trying to reassure her friend. "The SAT people only do like, four automatically, right?"

"He put down two," Chelsea said morosely. "UCLA and Berkeley. He didn't even try and send them to Harvard—I mean, I always knew we might not go to the same school, but he said he'd at least apply!"

Laurel wanted to offer some encouragement, but she didn't know what to say. She remembered Chelsea telling her that she and Ryan had agreed that they would both apply to Harvard and UCLA, then wait and see what happened with acceptances. Ryan had apparently changed his mind. "Did you . . . ask him about it?" Laurel finally asked. "Maybe he just didn't want to let his parents know he was planning to apply to Harvard. You know how pushy his dad can be."

"Maybe," she said, shrugging.

"You should ask him," Laurel said. "Come on, you guys

have been dating for more than a year. You should be able to talk about stuff like this."

"Maybe I don't *want* to know." Chelsea refused to meet Laurel's eyes.

"Chelsea!" Laurel said with a grin. "You are the ultimate proponent of brutal honesty!" She paused and giggled. "Proponent. That's an SAT word."

Chelsea raised one eyebrow. "Seriously. If our relationship is going to end soon anyway, maybe I'd rather not know how early he knew. And if he's just doing it to appease his dad, maybe it'll be a good surprise."

"Maybe," Laurel said. "But is it going to eat you up inside if you don't know?"

Chelsea grimaced. "Apparently."

"So ask."

They sat in silence for a while and Laurel marveled at how effectively worrying about someone else's problems stopped her from worrying about her own. Even if only for a little while.

"Hey, Chelsea," Laurel said softly as an idea began to form in her mind. "Are you busy tonight?"

"Now?" Chelsea asked.

Laurel glanced out the window. "We've got an hour if we hurry," she said, slipping into her sandals.

"Um, okay . . ."

They headed down the stairs and Chelsea yelled to her mom that she was leaving for an hour. Her mom yelled back that it was spaghetti night and to please be back in time for dinner. Laurel had rarely seen a conversation take place in Chelsea's house that didn't involve yelling. Not angry yelling, but the kind of yelling that happens when everyone is rushing around and can't take the ten seconds that would be required to stop what they are doing and get close enough to hear the other person talk in a normal tone of voice. Then again, in a household with three boys under the age of twelve, yelling probably *was* a normal tone of voice.

"So where are we going?" Chelsea asked as she pulled her seat belt across her chest.

"Yuki's," Laurel said.

"Yuki's?" And after a pause, "Are we going to spy on her?"

"No!" Laurel said, although she knew the question was entirely rational. "I thought we could go pick her up and take her to Vera's."

"For . . . smoothies?" Chelsea asked. Vera's blessedly nondairy blended fruit drinks had made it Laurel's favorite whole foods store.

"Yeah, sure," Laurel said, flipping on her turn signal as she approached Yuki's street. "Klea wants me to keep an eye on her, Tamani wants me to keep an eye on her. I was thinking we could all go to that autumn dance together."

"So we show up on her porch out of the blue, kidnap her, feed her frozen fruit, and ask her on a date. Genius," Chelsea said sarcastically.

"I'll buy you one of those carob chocolate truffles you like so much," Laurel said with a grin as they pulled up in front of Yuki's house.

Chelsea clapped her hand over her heart, melodramatically. "Using my love of chocolate against me. I have no choice but to crumble like a . . . chocolate cookie. Or whatever," she said when Laurel eyed her. "My metaphors suck. Let's go."

Yuki's house was about the size of Laurel's garage. It was set back from the road and mostly hidden by two shaggy elm trees growing at the front of the walk. According to Aaron, Yuki was almost always there alone, but so far nobody in the neighborhood had made a fuss. It was possible they simply hadn't noticed.

If so, they were a lot less nosy than Laurel's neighbors.

They rang Yuki's doorbell, which could be heard clearly through the flimsy front door and single-pane windows. Despite Klea's claims that Yuki was here for her own protection, security didn't seem to be a major priority.

"I don't think she's home," Chelsea said in a whisper.

Laurel nodded toward the bike Yuki sometimes rode to school. "Her bike's here. And I don't think she has a car."

"That doesn't mean she didn't go for a walk," Chelsea countered. "She is . . . like you."

Laurel sucked in a breath and held it for a moment. "Okay," she said. "Obviously this isn't going to work."

"Do I still have to go to Vera's?" Chelsea asked as they turned.

The click of a deadbolt made Laurel look back. She suppressed the urge to smooth her khaki skirt and straighten her hair. Yuki's face appeared in a narrow crack in the doorway and she stared in obvious surprise for a moment before opening it all the way.

"Hi," Laurel said, trying to not sound too chipper. "Are you busy?"

"Not really," Yuki said warily.

"We were going to Vera's and thought you might like to come along," Laurel said with what she hoped was a welcoming smile.

"The grocery place?" She didn't look any less nervous. If anything, she looked more suspicious.

"They make really great fruit smoothies. Nothing but frozen fruit and fruit juice." Laurel wondered if describing the smoothies in detail was too weird. "They're so good! You should come."

"Um." Yuki hesitated and Laurel could tell she was looking for a way to say no.

"I'll drive," Laurel said helpfully.

"Yeah, okay, I guess," Yuki said, mustering a smile that didn't look entirely fake. Laurel could only imagine how lonely it must be for Yuki, staying here all by herself. Laurel had seen her talking to a lot of different people in the hallways at school, but Aaron assured Laurel that no one ever came to Yuki's house.

"My treat," Laurel said, stretching her arm out toward her car.

Yuki stayed quiet on the drive over as Laurel and Chelsea tried to keep the conversation going, talking about the psychology class they had together—which proved duller than actually sitting through the class. At least once they got to Vera's they would have food to put in their mouths to excuse the silence.

After everyone selected a dessert, they sat outside at a table with an umbrella that did nothing to block the setting sun—just the way Laurel liked it.

"This is really good," Yuki finally said, with a hint of a smile.

"I thought you'd like it," Laurel said, scooping up a small spoonful of her mango-strawberry slush.

"So," Chelsea said, obviously trying to be conversational, "what's school like in Japan?"

Yuki looked suddenly bored. "Pretty much like here, but with uniforms."

"I hear you guys have cram schools and super-long hours and stuff. Your friend, um, June? He's really smart."

"Jun," Yuki corrected, softening the "J" and making Chelsea blush. "I don't really know him. And I never went to *juku*. A lot of us never do."

"Tell us about you, then," Laurel interjected.

Yuki shrugged, glancing away. "Not much to tell. I like to read, I drink way too much green tea, I do *ikebana*, and I listen to music from the seventies that no one has ever heard of."

Laurel laughed. She and Chelsea both knew there was *so* much more to Yuki than that, and Yuki knew it too. But Yuki didn't know how much Laurel knew, and she didn't know that Chelsea knew anything at all. It was like a supernatural "Who's on First?"

"What's *ikebana*?" Chelsea asked, pronouncing each syllable carefully.

"Flower arrangement. Artistic. You'd probably find it dull."

*Flower arranging?* Laurel thought, sitting up straight. She wondered if that could possibly be a euphemism for some kind of faerie magic—but it could just as easily have been a sign that Yuki was as drawn to nature as any other faerie.

"No, it sounds interesting," Chelsea said, but it was clear that she had no idea what to say next.

All three busied themselves with their food.

"Oh, hey," Laurel started. It was now or never. "Tama . . . uh . . . said you asked him to the Sadie Hawkins? Or Autumn Hop? Whatever they decided to call it." The posters going up around campus were confusing, to say the least. Laurel got the impression that someone in student government had looked up Sadie Hawkins on Wikipedia *after* half the posters were printed.

Yuki nodded. "I did. How do you know Tam?" she asked, gazing intently at Laurel.

"He, um, sits near me in Government," Laurel said. "I was telling him how Chelsea and I usually double to stuff like this, and he seemed pretty interested. Maybe we could all go together?"

"Absolutely," Chelsea said, a touch of sarcasm in her voice that Laurel hoped Yuki didn't catch. "I think that would be fascinating."

*Fascinating?* "Great. It's a date, then!" Laurel said. "If that's okay with you, I mean," Laurel added, turning her attention back to Yuki.

"Sure," Yuki said, smiling at Chelsea now. She sounded totally sincere. Enough that it pricked at Laurel's conscience. "I think it would be fun to do a group thing. Less pressure, you know. I mean, I don't even really know Tam very well yet so . . . yeah." Her voice trailed away.

With a pointed glance in Laurel's direction, Chelsea picked up her spoon, licked it, and said, "Well, I think he's hot."

Both faeries looked studiously away.

"Okay, seriously, what was that?" Laurel said, after dropping Yuki off following the rather painfully awkward half hour they'd all just spent together.

"What?"

"The 'Tamani is hot' thing?"

Chelsea shrugged. "He is."

"The last thing I want to talk to Yuki about is Tamani."

"Why?" Chelsea asked, smirking.

"Because she's a faerie and I don't want her getting suspicious," Laurel said, almost nonchalantly.

"Suuure," Chelsea drawled. "What is up with you and Tam, anyway?"

"Please don't call him that," Laurel snapped, knowing it was completely unwarranted. "His name is Tamani, and I know you have to call him Tam at school, but could you please use his whole name when it's just us?"

159

Chelsea sat silently, looking at Laurel.

"What?" Laurel finally asked, exasperated.

"You didn't answer my question," Chelsea said seriously. "What is up with you and Tam*ani*?" she said, stressing his full name.

Laurel gripped the steering wheel. "Nothing," she said. "Befriending Yuki was supposed to be my job. I failed. So Tamani had to do it and I guess I feel guilty. I hate letting him down. He's my friend."

"Friend," Chelsea deadpanned. "That's why David turns into a fire-breathing dragon whenever they're in the same room."

"He does not."

"He does a really good job of hiding it when you're around because he doesn't want to be the jealous boyfriend. But trust me, he tenses up the second Tamani gets anywhere near him."

"Really?" Laurel asked, guilt creeping in.

"Yes. You think that blow-up last week was an isolated occurrence? It's been building since the first day of school. Don't you guys talk about this kind of stuff?"

"How is it always my fault that Tamani is in love with me!" Laurel said, louder than she intended. "I didn't do any-thing!"

"Come on, Laurel," Chelsea said, softly now. "I get that Tamani likes you, but honestly, that doesn't really matter. Half the guys in our class like you. You're gorgeous. I've seen them stare. It doesn't bother David. If anything, I think it makes David *happy*. He's dating the hottest girl in school and everyone knows it."

"I'm not the hottest girl in school," Laurel said stiffly, pulling up to the curb in front of Chelsea's house. She knew she was pretty, but there were a lot of beautiful girls at Del Norte. And Chelsea was one of them.

"You *are* the hottest girl in school," Chelsea repeated, "and Captain Science is your boyfriend. You didn't know David before high school, so let me spell it out for you: The moment you gave him the time of day, you changed David's life. He would do anything for you. And he's not really the jealous type."

"I'm starting to think *all* boys are the jealous type," Laurel grumbled.

"I'm telling you, David isn't mad at Tamani because Tamani's jealous. David's mad at Tamani because *you're* jealous."

Laurel leaned her forehead against the steering wheel in defeat.

"Is he really in love with you?" Chelsea asked after a long, silent moment.

"Yes," Laurel admitted, looking up at Chelsea but leaving her head against the wheel.

Chelsea raised her eyebrows. "Well. Good luck with that."

# SIXTEEN

"I DON'T KNOW WHY THIS THING IS BOTHERING ME so much this year," Laurel said, hiding behind David's much-larger frame to adjust the sash around her blossom in the hallway.

"Maybe it's because you didn't get to keep it free on Saturday," David suggested. "Kinda like muscles being sore if you don't rest them, or something."

"Maybe," Laurel agreed. "And this weekend isn't going to be any different."

"Do you need to skip the dance?" David asked, hiding a smile. "I wouldn't mind." David hadn't been entirely pleased to hear that they were going to the dance with Tamani—though, on hearing that Yuki would be Tamani's date, his attitude had improved. Marginally.

"I know you wouldn't," Laurel said, "but Chelsea would. She needs this. Especially after last week. It will be a good night for her and Ryan."

"You're sure I can't just deck Ryan?" David growled. It was interesting to watch how protective David was of Chelsea. Laurel knew their friendship went back years, but when she'd told David about Ryan's SAT scores, she'd half expected him to come to Ryan's defense—after all, David and Ryan were friends too, and Chelsea still refused to ask Ryan for an explanation.

"There will be no 'decking,' David," Laurel chided. "Of *anyone.*"

"Yes, Mother," David said, rolling his eyes.

"Oh, and Tamani wants us to meet up before the dance—you and me and Chelsea." He'd dropped that on Laurel in Government class, with scant explanation. "Strategy meeting or something, I guess. He says it's important." Laurel rubbed at her temples. The stress of Yuki was almost worse than having trolls lurking. At least with trolls, you knew where you stood. Trolls liked treasure, revenge, and tearing people limb from limb. For all Laurel knew, Yuki and Klea were valuable allies—but then, they might be busy engineering her death, or worse. Laurel suspected it was that uncertainty that had been bringing on these crippling headaches lately.

"Is it bad today?" David asked as he ran his hands over her shoulders and bent a little to touch his forehead to hers.

Laurel nodded, a tiny movement that didn't jostle David's forehead from hers; she liked the feel of his face so close. "I just need to go outside," Laurel said quietly. "Get out of these halls."

"Hey, Laurel."

Laurel looked up to see Yuki. Smiling.

At her.

Her eyes went to Tamani, who was standing just behind Yuki. "Hey," Laurel answered, a little nervously.

"Listen," Yuki said, "I wanted to thank you for coming by the other day."

"Oh," Laurel said, finding herself at a loss for words. "It's fine. I mean, it's got to be weird, being somewhere totally new."

"It can be. And . . ." Her eyes darted up to Tamani and he smiled his encouragement. "I haven't been super-friendly and you were really nice."

"Really," Laurel said, feeling awkward now. "It wasn't a big deal."

"So, do you mind if Tam and I eat lunch with you? You guys always eat outside, right?"

"I like it there," Laurel said, feeling vaguely defensive. "Um, sure you can join us. If you want." *This is what we've been working for*, she reminded herself.

Tamani and Yuki went off to get their lunches and Laurel turned back to her locker. Her headache was getting worse. She was glad it was lunchtime. Getting out of the school for a few minutes usually helped.

"You okay?" David asked, locking his locker, his lunch tucked under his arm.

"She's going to notice how I eat," Laurel said. "Why didn't Tamani stop this?" But she knew why. It was worth the risk. Probably.

David didn't answer, just put an arm around her shoulders as they walked toward the doors.

Chelsea and Ryan and a few of the other regulars were already sitting and pulling out their lunches when Laurel and David arrived, moments ahead of Tamani and Yuki. The group hardly looked up when Tamani and Yuki sat down; they often had people come and go. Yuki sat down right beside Laurel. Tamani sat next to Yuki.

*So much for low-key*, Laurel thought. Three high school students sitting in a row, eating nothing but fruits and vegetables. Perfect. That shouldn't draw any attention *at all*. Laurel hesitated before opening her salad. At least she'd had some extra time this morning to make her lunch; her colorful salad looked more like a meal than the usual half cup of spinach with a couple strawberries, or piece of fruit and small bag of carrots. She pulled out a can of Sprite and made a bit of a show of opening it and taking a long swallow.

Yuki didn't seem the least bit self-conscious as she pulled out her own lunch. Laurel couldn't help but stare at the small Tupperware containing a pale, oblong, sandwich-sized mound with dark green strips tied around it.

"What is that?" Laurel asked, hoping it sounded like a friendly question.

Yuki looked up at her. "Cabbage roll," she said simply.

Laurel knew she should leave it alone, but she had never eaten anything resembling the thing that Yuki was currently biting into and her curiosity overwhelmed her caution. "What's that stuff wrapped around it?"

Yuki looked over at her in surprise. "*Nori*. Um, seaweed, basically. You've probably seen it on sushi."

Laurel turned back to her own lunch before she drew too much attention to their meals. She felt suddenly lonely as she watched Yuki, eating her cabbage roll and drinking her cold green tea. What would it be like to have a faerie friend who lived in the human world? Someone who could swap camouflage secrets and lunch recipes? She realized just how well she and Yuki could get along. If only she could know Yuki wasn't a threat—to herself or Avalon.

"Aren't you eating?" Yuki asked.

Laurel looked up, but Yuki wasn't talking to her—she was talking to Tamani, who was sprawled casually on the grass. He shrugged. "I'm fine. I usually go out, but I wanted to keep you company today," he said with a winning smile, touching her knee.

Laurel turned away from Yuki, her warm feelings melting away.

"Do you want some of mine?" Yuki asked.

Laurel didn't turn, but she listened, wondering how Tamani was going to get out of this one.

"Oh, no thanks. I'll be all right. I don't really like green stuff."

Laurel almost choked on her Sprite. She saw that Tamani was watching her with laughter in his eyes. She placed one hand on David's thigh and looked pointedly away from her impish guardian.

★ ★ ★

Tamani felt uncomfortably like a teacher as he stood in front of Laurel and her friends before the dance. He'd asked them to come to Laurel's house early, while Ryan was still at work, so that they could all talk freely. "First, I wanted to warn you guys about the troll we found—"

"Laurel said it was a *dead* troll," Chelsea interrupted, her face paling a little.

Tamani still wasn't quite sure what to make of Chelsea, but she seemed to have her heart in the right place. "By the time I was done with him he was dead, yes," Tamani confirmed.

He nearly smiled at Chelsea's satisfied head-nod. He'd never talked to her specifically about her experience last fall, but he suspected being kidnapped by trolls was a pretty traumatic introduction to the supernatural.

"But there was one that got away. And the fact that we found them at all is a clear sign they are either getting sloppy, or bold. Either way, we need to be very careful tonight. Especially with Yuki and Ryan along."

"Have you seen Klea yet?" Laurel asked.

Tamani pursed his lips and shook his head. "No, but Yuki mentioned seeing her the other day. So there's a possibility that either Yuki is slipping away from her sentries—which doesn't seem likely—or Klea is sneaking past them—which seems even less likely. Probably Yuki is just lying, but I don't know why. I don't know what to think there."

"Forgive me for pointing out the obvious," David said in a tone Tamani didn't much like, "but couldn't we just call

Klea? I mean, Laurel's got her number. Hell, *I've* got her number."

"And say what?" Tamani asked, admittedly glaring a little. "That she should come join us for tea?"

"We could make something up. Pretend Yuki needs her."

"And then she would arrive, discover that Yuki is not in need of assistance, and ask why we lied. Then what?" He paused only long enough to highlight that David didn't have an answer before continuing. "As concerned as I am about Klea, I'm more concerned about Yuki at the moment. Once we discover how dangerous she is or isn't, Klea goes instantly back to first priority."

"I'm working on it," Laurel said, sounding forlorn. "I cut off a little piece of my blossom and put it under the globe in some sugar water. When I added the phosphorescent it lasted a couple hours, so I think the globe is working."

"And that's what you wanted it to do, right?" Tamani asked. Much of Laurel's Mixer work confused him, but he loved watching her thrive in her fae role.

"Yeah, but I don't know how much that helps us. I've tried it on my skin and it does react and glow for a while, but it could be different on hair or some drops of sap, or something else entirely. What I need is some kind of sample from Yuki so I can use the same sample from myself and really compare apples to apples."

"I'll do my best to get that from her," Tamani said, trying to think of a way.

"I'll bet you will," David said under his breath.

Tamani just glared.

"Guys . . ." Laurel said in a warning tone.

"Sorry," David muttered.

Laurel looked pointedly at Tamani, but he said nothing. He hadn't done anything wrong.

"I also wanted to talk about security," Tamani said, turning away from Laurel. "I want to keep us all together whenever possible. Trolls have tracked Laurel by scenting her blossom before, and we'll be out after sundown, so we need to stay alert and stick close. Hopefully it will be a very uneventful evening."

"Cheers," Chelsea said, rolling her eyes.

"*Good* uneventful," Tamani said, cracking a smile. He was starting to like the human girl. He pulled out his phone, checking the time. "I have to go pick up Yuki in about fifteen minutes."

"And my mom will be home any time to help me put together some fae-friendly appetizers," Laurel added.

"Then we're all ready," David said, stretching his arm across the back of the couch and settling it around Laurel's shoulders.

"Do we get to play twenty questions now?" Chelsea asked.

All eyes turned to her.

"Not you," Chelsea said, then pointed at Tamani. "Him."

Tamani stared at her for a long, silent moment. "I'm afraid I don't know that game."

"Oh, it's easy," Chelsea said. "You play it with Laurel all the time, but she never asks you fun questions. Although she did tell me about a bunch of Shakespearean plays being faerie legends. I've been waiting for *ages* to ask you the really good stuff!"

"Um, okay," Tamani said, not sure what Chelsea considered "good stuff."

"So is it only Shakespeare, or are there more stories that exist in both cultures?"

"Oh!" Tamani said with a laugh. He sank into an armchair close to Chelsea. "There are lots. In Avalon, we love stories. The Summer fae dedicate their lives to telling stories, through dance or music or painting. But humans are endlessly inventive, always coming up with new ways to make the story interesting by telling it wrong. Nonetheless, a lot of your stories have faerie roots."

Chelsea was undeterred. *"Cinderella."*

"No," said Tamani. "I mean, faeries don't even wear shoes most of the time. And finding someone based solely on shoe size? That doesn't make sense for humans *or* faeries."

"What about the faerie godmother?" Chelsea asked.

"Unnecessary. We can make pumpkins grow that big without magic. And even a Winter faerie couldn't turn a mouse into a horse."

*"Beauty and the Beast."*

"Story of a faerie who fell in love with a troll. Scares the wits out of most seedlings. The troll never turns out to be a handsome prince, though."

*"Rapunzel."*

"Growth tonic gone terribly wrong."

Chelsea squealed. *"Thumbelina."*

"That's just basic anatomy misinterpreted. We *are* born from flowers, but we're never that small. Mischievous Sparklers were known to have encouraged tiny-faerie misconceptions, though."

"Tell me one that would surprise me."

Tamani thought for a moment. "Do you know *The Pied Piper of Hameln?*"

Chelsea looked blank for a minute. "You mean Hamelin?"

"That sounds right. That one's not a story, it's true," Tamani said, very seriously. "And it has scarcely been distorted at all. The Piper was a very powerful Spring faerie. Most of us can only Entice one or two animals at a time, but the Piper could Entice a whole city. He was eventually executed for that stunt."

"What did he do with the children?" Chelsea asked.

"It's kind of a long story. Ultimately, though, he marched them off a cliff. Killed them all."

Chelsea and Laurel were both silent, staring at Tamani in horror.

"Perhaps not our happiest story," Tamani said awkwardly.

"What about the Camelot legends?" Chelsea said, recovering first. Her eyes twinkled in a way that told Tamani this was really what she'd wanted to ask all along.

"What about them?"

"Laurel told me the parts that you told her, and that King Arthur was real and everything. But what about the rest?

Lancelot? Guinevere? The Round Table?"

Tamani hesitated—he wasn't sure he wanted to tell this story, especially not with David around. But it would look even stranger *not* to tell it now that Chelsea had him on a roll. "Laurel told you about the Unseelie, right?"

"Yeah," Chelsea said, rapt.

"So you know the Seelie allied with King Arthur?"

"Queen Titania arranged it."

"Yes. And in human fashion, the alliance was sealed with a marriage."

"What, like a human and a faerie?" Chelsea asked.

"Yes, just like that," Tamani chuckled. "Guinevere was a Spring faerie, like me."

Chelsea's eyes widened. "But I thought the point of alliance by marriage was to produce an heir who could rule both kingdoms—"

"It's not clear if the Seelie knew that Guinevere couldn't have Arthur's children. We were all a lot less sophisticated, in those days—but it's possible they did know, and simply . . . neglected to mention it to Arthur."

Chelsea's jaw dropped.

"There were many fae in Arthur's court, including Nimue and her son, Lancelot. Lancelot was Arthur's friend, but he was also Guinevere's *Fear-gleidhidh*."

"Her what?"

Tamani felt a strange sense of pride that Laurel had not shared that phrase with her friends. "It means watchman. Guardian." It meant more than that, but Tamani was already feeling a little exposed.

"So Guinevere married Arthur, and when her faerie guardian stuck his nose into things and stole her away, that was the end of Camelot?" Everyone looked up as David spoke.

"Twist it how you want," Tamani said, his voice steady, "but Lancelot was the least of Arthur's worries. When it became obvious that King Arthur and Guinevere could not produce a child, many of the human knights cried witchcraft. Guinevere turned to Lancelot for both love and safety. But things in Camelot were already going badly, and let's just say Guinevere was almost burned at the stake before Lancelot rescued her and took her back to Avalon."

"So what if Lancelot hadn't been around at all?" asked David. "What if Guinevere had really had a chance to make it work with Arthur? It still sounds like Lancelot was to blame for the whole thing."

Tamani saw Laurel and Chelsea exchange glances. It was obvious that no one was talking about Lancelot and Guinevere anymore. Not wanting to distress Laurel, Tamani pretended to check his phone and stood. "Maybe," he said. "But Arthur was a great king, especially for a human, and if you ask me, he'd rather lose a challenge than be handed an easy victory." He gave David a long look then smiled. "I'll be back soon," he said, spinning his keys on the end of his index finger. He left the room, closing the door behind him without looking back.

# SEVENTEEN

LAUREL TOOK A SHORT BREAK FROM THE HOT, HUMID dance floor and walked into the slightly less hot—though heavily perfumed—bathroom. She checked under the doors of the stalls, but no one was there. Alone for a moment, Laurel carefully stretched and adjusted her shirt over her blossom—a little achy from being bound so many days in a row—then sighed and leaned her head against the cool mirror.

She really did like dances. For the first hour, anyway. But after a while the room felt too dark, and there were no sunlit windows to give her a dash of rejuvenation. On top of that, the music seemed extra loud tonight and her headache was back with a vengeance.

*Teach me to stay up so long past sunset, I guess.*

Still, there was only half an hour left. Laurel leaned over the sink and splashed icy water on her face. Blotting it dry with a paper towel, Laurel studied her light complexion in the mirror and—even if it was just wishful thinking—decided her head felt a little better. She was glad it was a casual dance; T-shirts all the way. She didn't think she would have been up for a formal tonight.

The three couples had all started the evening in Laurel's kitchen with Laurel's mom's homemade appetizers. It was interesting to watch Yuki out of the corner of her eye. She had lifted the appetizers carefully to her nose, trying to figure out what was in them before taking that first tentative bite. She was actually pretty nice. Very shy, but Laurel sensed there was more she couldn't see. It was fun to have her around, as long as Laurel didn't think too hard about the fact that the only reason they were all together was because Yuki was on a *date* with Tamani.

After the snacks everyone piled into the convertible— Tamani's idea, to keep them all together. Thank goodness for bench seats. There weren't quite enough seat belts, but as long as the person sitting in the middle of the front seat— Yuki, squeezed in close between Tamani and Laurel—had a jacket or something sitting on her lap, you really couldn't tell. Not that there was a police officer alive who could give Tamani a ticket.

Laurel was letting the water run idly over her fingertips when she heard one of her favorite songs start. Feeling a bit of a second wind, she returned to the dance floor and found David. With a playful growl, she jumped on him from behind. He grabbed her arms and bent forward, lifting her off her feet and making her squeal. Then he swung her around and pulled her to his chest, his nose resting against hers. "Dance?" he whispered.

She smiled and nodded.

David took her hand and pulled her toward the middle of the dance floor. Laurel snuggled up to his chest and David held her close, his arms wrapped around her back, one above her blossom and one below.

As the song wound down, David grinned and twirled Laurel around. She laughed, enjoying the way the lights swirled when she looked up. She was in her third spin when Laurel caught Tamani out of the corner of her eye. He was several feet away, dancing with Yuki.

For most of the night they had danced cautiously—typical first-date awkwardness—their bodies a few inches apart. Now Yuki had pulled herself closer, her temple resting against Tamani's cheek. Tamani's arms were loose around her back, and his brow was furrowed, but he didn't put any distance between them. Didn't push her away. As Laurel watched, he sighed and leaned his head against Yuki's.

The faerie couple was circling, slowly, and suddenly Tamani's eyes met Laurel's. She expected him to look guilty, to push back and make Yuki stop hugging him. But he didn't. His gaze was level, calm, emotionless. Then, very deliberately, he closed his eyes and laid his cheek back against Yuki's forehead. Something inside Laurel froze.

Then David was pulling her back around to face him. When she looked up he was smiling warmly at her. He hadn't witnessed that moment—that awful, terrible moment—at all. She made herself smile up at him as the slow song faded out and a loud, bouncing song crashed in.

David's fingers twined through hers and they walked to the edge of the dance floor, Laurel forcing herself not to turn and look around. When they stopped, and she could turn without making David suspicious, Laurel did, her eyes scanning the crowded room, searching for Tamani. She finally spotted him on the far side of the gym, laughing at something Yuki was saying.

"Hey, David," Laurel said, hardly able to smile over the lump in her throat. "There's only, like, fifteen minutes left of the dance, do you think we could cut out a little early?"

David looked down at her, concern in his eyes. "You okay?"

"Yeah," Laurel said, still keeping her smile. "I just have a headache. Have most of the night, actually." She laughed shortly. "I swear I'm allergic to this school. The loud music doesn't help."

"Sure," David said. Then, pulling her close, he whispered in her ear, "After that last dance I think it's all downhill anyway. I'll go get *Tam*," he said with a laugh. "I imagine he and Yuki are both ready to go too, whether they'll admit it or not." He turned away and Laurel reached out for his hand, pulling him back.

"Can't we just walk?" she asked. "It's only half a mile to my house. We used to walk all the time, before we both got cars."

David's face turned serious. "Are you sure? I thought we were all supposed to stay together."

"Yeah, but . . ." Her eyes darted to Tamani. He still hadn't seen them, but it was only a matter of time. "There hasn't been any real *danger* for months and months. There's probably, like, a million sentries in town by now."

"And at least one troll," David noted.

"Besides," Laurel said, ignoring that, "I never go anywhere without my trusty kit," she said, edging toward the coat rack and grabbing her purse. "We'll be safe. Please? We haven't been alone all night. I just want some quiet."

"It's cold."

Laurel grinned. "I'll keep you warm."

"You will not, you're practically cold-blooded," he said, laughing. But he grabbed his jacket from a hook and placed a hand at her back, guiding her toward the double doors that led out of the gym.

It was a huge relief to get out of the gym and enter the quiet atrium where only a few people were mingling.

"Thanks," Laurel said, then pointed toward the rear doors. "Let's go this way."

They had only gone a few steps before the doors of the gym flew open, cracking against the walls behind them. Laurel and David both turned and saw Tamani burst from the gym, his eyes scanning the room until they lit upon Laurel.

"There you are," he said as soon as he was in earshot. "Where are you going?"

"I'm going home," Laurel said, not meeting his eyes. "*We're* going home. It's not that far; you guys can stay and finish the dance."

"Like hell," Tamani said, his voice tight.

"Hey!" David said. "Back off."

Tamani sighed and lowered his tone. "Laurel, please just wait. It's my job to protect you and I can't do that if you're running off alone in the middle of the night."

"She's not alone," David countered.

"She may as well be. You can't protect her."

"I—"

"Don't even try to pretend you have your gun tonight," Tamani said, cutting David off. "I scoped you out earlier."

David's mouth closed. *How often does David still carry his gun?* Surely she would have noticed—it couldn't be *that* often. Could it?

Tamani clenched and unclenched his fists, then raised his head, looking remarkably calm. "I'm not trying to get in your way, David. We just need to stick to the plan, no matter how safe things seem. Please just wait while I get the others so I can drive you home. Then I'll leave and you . . . you can do whatever. But let me get you home safely. Please?"

Laurel looked up at David, but she knew he would be on Tamani's side. He hadn't really wanted her to walk home either.

"Fine," Laurel said in a small voice.

"Thank you." Tamani turned and hurried back into the gym. As soon as the doors swung shut behind him, she felt

David's hand on her shoulder.

"I'm sorry I didn't get us away fast enough," David said. Then, after a moment of hesitation: "But I do feel better this way."

"Nothing is going to happen!" Laurel said, exasperated. "Nothing has happened for months; nothing's going to happen tonight!"

"I know," David said, holding both of her hands. "But it doesn't hurt to be safe. Once we get there we can send everyone home and you and I can watch a movie and forget about everything else, okay? Ten more minutes, and it's just you and me, all right?"

Laurel nodded, not trusting herself to speak. That was exactly what she wanted. Exactly what she needed. A night of David.

Soon Tamani led the other three out of the gym.

Laurel forced a smile and looked at them. "Sorry to be such a spoilsport," she said brightly. "I have this major headache and the music is just making it worse."

"No problem," Chelsea said, linking one arm with her. "The dance is basically over anyway."

After a moment of silent communication with Chelsea, Laurel climbed into the back of the car to sit between the two guys, and Chelsea sat up front with Yuki and Tamani. After giving her a long, questioning look, Tamani faced front and started the car.

Laurel watched dark houses roll by, thinking how absurd it was that Tamani thought she needed protection from this.

Never mind what Jamison had said to her, so long ago, about flytraps. Barnes was dead. Barnes had been smart; it made sense that he would lay in wait, planning and scheming until Laurel dropped her guard. Whatever was left of his horde didn't seem to be doing anything but hiding and, failing that, dying.

Halfway down an empty stretch of road, a large shadow registered at the corner of Laurel's vision, then darted in front of Tamani's car. Laurel didn't even have time to scream before Tamani's brakes squealed—too late. The car smashed into something with a sickening thud and Laurel was thrown hard against her seat belt, the strap biting into her shoulder before pulling her back and slamming her against the seat.

Beside her David swore and yanked at his seat belt. Laurel could see the white of the deflated airbags in front of Tamani and Chelsea.

Airbags.

Seat belts.

*Yuki.*

Doors were opening and everyone was detangling themselves from their restraints, but Laurel only saw Yuki, slumped against the dash. She groaned and started to push herself up, and clear drops of sap dripped down her forehead. None of the guys were paying attention; they had all run to see what Tamani had hit. Laurel had to do something; it was too dangerous for Ryan to see this.

"Chelsea, give me your shirt!" Laurel hissed as she crawled over the seat.

"But—"

"Now!" Laurel yelled, wishing that she could explain that she couldn't use her own because of her blossom.

Chelsea hesitated, then yanked her shirt over her head to reveal a lacy black demi-bra. Apologetically, Laurel took the shirt and leaned forward, pressing it against Yuki's head.

"Wha?" Yuki muttered, blinking.

"Stay still," Laurel said, her voice low. "We hit something—you cut your head—you have to hold still or they are *all going to find out*," she said, injecting as much meaning as possible into her last few words.

Yuki's eyes widened and she nodded, then cringed. "Ow," she said through gritted teeth, as the pain cut through her disorientation.

Laurel looked up when she heard shouts from the front of the car. Illuminated by the convertible's high-beams were three figures in faded navy jumpsuits, their uneven, snarling faces marking them instantly.

Trolls.

Then suddenly someone was flying through the air, smashing against the hood of the car. His head bounced hard against the windshield, adding a star-shaped crack to the webbing of fractures Yuki had already created. "Ryan!" Chelsea screamed, but Ryan's head lolled to the side and his eyes fluttered before closing.

"Give us the girl," growled one of the trolls, "and no one else has to get hurt."

Tamani leaped forward, snapping one leg out with a

resounding *crack!* against the side of one troll's head. The troll stumbled back slightly as Tamani sprang away, evading another troll's clumsy punch.

"Chelsea!" Laurel said sharply. "Take the shirt—hold it against Yuki."

"I can't," Chelsea said, trying to climb past her. "I have to—Ryan—I have to go—"

Laurel grabbed Chelsea's arm. "Chelsea, if you climb up there you will just draw their attention to him. You need to stay here and help me. That's the best way to help *him*."

Chelsea's eyes were wide and panicked, but she nodded. "Okay."

"Now take over here for me."

Chelsea's warm hands slid on top of Laurel's to take their place.

"Yuki!" Laurel held Yuki's face in her hands, trying to get her to concentrate, but her eyes were still vaguely unfocused. "Use your phone. Call Klea!" There was no way to hide this from her—may as well get her help.

Laurel jumped to the backseat and grabbed her purse, sifting through it for a sugar-glass globe the size of a large marble. Wrapping her fist around it, she burst out the passenger-side door and ran to the front of the car. Just as she rounded the headlights, someone tackled her at the waist, bringing her to the ground. As she fell, she threw the ball at Tamani's feet and heard it shatter.

Thick smoke rolled up from the pavement, engulfing the fighters in a haze that refracted the beams from the headlights.

As soon as she saw the smoke start to billow Laurel turned her shoulder and threw an elbow hard at her assailant.

David grunted and grabbed her arm, shielding himself from a second blow. "It's me!" he said in a strangled voice. "I couldn't let them see you."

"Sorry!" Laurel whispered, turning her attention back to the smoke. It was so dense she couldn't see any movement in it. She stared hard, willing the potion to work.

Something staggered out of the cloud. A troll? Laurel clenched her hands together, hoping. But after a misstep the figure stood tall again. It was Tamani. He braced himself against the hood of the car and lifted both legs to kick out hard against the two trolls that followed him. They fell back, giving him enough time to raise two knives in front of him and swing one in a wide arc that left a spray of blood in its wake. The troll in front of him vanished back into the smoke and Tamani turned his attention to the others.

"They shouldn't be able to fight!" Laurel said, panic gripping her chest. The globe contained a serum that attacked animal irises, temporarily blinding them—but had no effect on faeries. "They should be helpless! David, I have to do something." She tried to rise from the pavement, but David's arms held her like a vise.

"What? Get yourself killed?" David whispered. "Believe me, the best thing you can do for him right now is to stay put."

He was right, but Laurel felt like a complete traitor as she hunched back down, safely hidden in David's arms, watching Tamani fight for his life. For all their lives. She saw him whirl, turn, and feint; heard the whistle of the knives as they cut through the air, the groans of the trolls as Tamani's blades bit into their flesh. He was fast, but Laurel knew he had to be—one or two hits from a troll and it would all be over. The fight couldn't have taken more than thirty seconds, but it felt like hours before one of the trolls let out a high-pitched whine and collapsed to the ground. The other two ran away from the car, heading for the woods.

Laurel peeked around the tire, waiting for the next wave of trolls, but everything was silent.

She glanced over the door into the car where Chelsea sat with her shirt still pressed against Yuki, her eyes locked on Ryan, who lay motionless on the hood. Tamani was bent over, hands on his knees, bracing himself as he tried to catch his breath.

"Tam!" Laurel said desperately, her voice cracking as she stood.

Tamani's eyes darted to her, but only for an instant. "David," he called, pushing his arms under the fallen troll, "help me! Quickly!"

David ran to help lift the heavy troll and they pulled him off to the side of the road and stashed him behind a fence.

"I'll deal with him later," Tamani said, running back to the car. "Now this one."

It was the first time Laurel had actually gotten a good look at what had jumped in front of the car. It was definitely a body. Its lifeless eyes, bulbous nose, and thin, patchy hair sent shivers down her spine. It wore only rags and looked more animal than human—like Bess, the troll Barnes had kept chained like a dog.

"A lower," Tamani said. "A sacrifice. They knew it would die and tossed it out here anyway. Help me, David." He grasped the dead troll under its arms and David grabbed its short, thick legs, turning his head to the side to avoid the sight, or perhaps the smell.

They jogged back to the car as Ryan let out a moan and tried to roll over. "He's waking up," Laurel said, clutching David's arm. "We need to get him back in the car or he'll figure it out."

David grabbed Ryan around the chest and dragged him off the hood, dumping him rather awkwardly into the backseat of the convertible.

"What happened?" Ryan asked, his hand clutched to the back of his head.

Laurel could almost feel everyone holding their breath. "Car accident," Laurel said hesitantly. "You hit your head."

Ryan moaned and said, "I'm going to have a bruise tomorrow, huh?" He closed his eyes and mumbled something else, but he appeared to be losing consciousness again.

That sent everyone back into action. Tamani gave Chelsea and Yuki a once-over. "You okay?" he asked Yuki, his tone rushed.

"She's fine," Chelsea said. "She called Klea. But she seems pretty out of it."

Tamani sighed. "David," he said, turning.

David stood transfixed, eyeing Chelsea's state of undress.

He looked completely mortified.

"David!" Tamani said louder, touching his shoulder. David looked up with a start, his cheeks flushing red.

"You guys have to get out of here now, before anyone comes out to see what happened," Tamani said, whispering so Yuki wouldn't hear him.

"Where are you going?" Laurel asked.

"I have to track them. *You* have to get to your house."

"But the car—"

"Still works," he said, pressing his keys into her hands. "Please go. Take them to your house. You'll all be safe there." He started to turn and Laurel grabbed his arm.

"Tam, I—"

Lightning burst in Laurel's head. She slumped to her knees and threw her hands to her temples as knives of pain shredded her consciousness. She wanted to scream, tried to scream. Was she screaming? She couldn't tell. All she could hear was blaring, meaningless noise.

And as soon as it had started, it was over.

She collapsed onto the street, overwhelmed by the shockingly abrupt absence of pain. Her limbs shook and it took her a few seconds to realize she was damp all over because her entire body had broken out in sweat—something she had never experienced before. Someone was calling her name. David? Tamani? She wasn't sure. She tried to open her lips to answer, but they wouldn't move. Blackness crept in at the edges of her vision and she welcomed it. She felt arms curl beneath her, lifting her, then her eyelids fluttered and the darkness embraced her.

# EIGHTEEN

TAMANI WATCHED IN HORROR AS LAUREL FELL. HE
scanned her body for an injury, but saw nothing. "David,"
he said, urgently running to the trunk and jamming his key
in, "pick her up, put her in the backseat."

"We shouldn't move her," David said, crouching beside
her.

"What are you going to do?" Tamani said, his temper flar-
ing. "Call an ambulance? The most important thing right
now is that we get her away from here. Put her in the car."

David lifted her tentatively and put her beside Ryan, who
was still out. "What now?" he asked, looking at Tamani.

Tamani stared at his supply belt, sitting, waiting for him,
in the trunk. He could hear Shar in his head, urging him to
pick it up, to follow the trolls. It was what his training dic-
tated. But even as he reached out his hand to take it, he knew
he couldn't. Laurel was unconscious in the back of his car.

He could no more leave her in this condition than he could tear off his own arm. With a growl he slammed the trunk closed. "Get in," Tamani snapped at David.

He slipped into the driver's seat and held his breath as he clicked the ignition. The second the engine caught, Tamani pressed on the gas, wanting Laurel safe in her home as soon as possible.

"When we get there I want everyone in," Tamani said sharply, only moments away from Laurel's driveway. "We'll figure things out from there. I'll take Yuki," he added in a softer voice, remembering that although her eyes were closed, she could still be listening.

He bumped up on the curb and killed the engine. Chelsea carefully shifted Yuki over to Tamani and ran to open the front door. Tamani slipped Yuki into his arms, curling her against his chest, watching David out of the corner of his eye with more than a little jealousy as he did the same with Laurel. Chelsea had managed to tie her shirt around Yuki's head in such a way that it wouldn't slip off and Yuki would be allowed to believe that her secret was still safe.

By the time they reached the door Chelsea was already leading Laurel's dad, clad only in a pair of drawstring pants and a T-shirt, out toward the wrecked car, presumably to help with Ryan.

"What happened?" Laurel's mother asked in a panicky tone from the doorway.

"We hit a deer," Tamani said before anyone else could answer. He stared meaningfully at Laurel's mom until her look of skepticism melted away, and she nodded at him in understanding. She gestured to an armchair where Tamani set Yuki while David laid Laurel on the couch. Laurel's mom immediately crouched down next to her, stroking her hair.

Laurel's dad and Chelsea showed up in the doorway, steadying Ryan between them. He was awake again, but still quite disoriented. "Do you have a car?" Tamani asked Chelsea.

She shook her head. "David picked me up earlier."

"What about Ryan?"

She nodded, almost convulsively. "His truck is here."

"Get his keys; take him home."

He started to turn, but her hand closed firmly around his upper arm. "What am I supposed to tell his parents?"

"We hit a deer."

"We really shouldn't be moving him around after a car accident. We should go to the hospital. He may have a concussion."

"Whatever you need to do," Tamani said, leaning in close to her ear, "as long as they all know *we hit a deer*." He paused to slip out of his button-down shirt, which he draped around Chelsea's bare shoulders as he looked her in the eye. "Any girl who has done as much as you have tonight can pull off one more thing for me."

A smile started to spread across her face and Tamani knew he had said the right thing.

"And I'll make sure you get completely filled in," he added, knowing it was the last thing holding her back.

Chelsea nodded, then let Laurel's dad hold on to Ryan while she pushed her arms through the sleeves of Tamani's shirt and hurriedly buttoned up. As they helped Ryan out to his truck, Tamani turned to the remaining people and tried to assess the damage. Laurel was still unconscious, but Yuki was surveying the room from beneath lowered lids.

Tamani stared at her while she was distracted. The moment after Laurel had fallen, Tamani had glanced up at Yuki, and she had been staring at Laurel. There had been a gleam in Yuki's eyes, something Tamani didn't like. Maybe he was being paranoid, but it seemed like coincidence followed Yuki the same way it followed Klea. And coincidence was never something Tamani trusted.

The trolls had demanded "the girl." But which one did they mean? Not for the first time, he wished he could just work his Enticement on Yuki and ask his questions. But his secret identity was one of the few advantages they had over her—assuming it was still secret at all. Tonight had certainly given him reason to doubt. Still, just in case, he couldn't risk losing that advantage in exchange for a few minutes of question-and-answer that might not even lead anywhere.

When Yuki glanced up at him, Tamani immediately put on a mask of concern and dropped to the ground by her side. "Are you okay?"

Yuki smiled and Tamani forced himself to smile back. "Better now," she said, her voice a little scratchy. She placed a hand to her head, still wrapped in Chelsea's shirt. "What happened?"

Tamani was hesitant to answer. "I ran into a deer," he said finally. "You hit your head." He leaned forward, determined to push her a little while she was still disoriented. "Chelsea wrapped it up—do you want me to look at it?"

"No," she said quickly, her eyes wide. Then her expression went neutral. *Back on guard.* "It's okay," she said, her voice calm again. "Klea will be here soon; she'll take care of it."

Tamani forced himself to nod. Having Yuki summon Klea presented an opportunity to follow her, but Laurel was still unconscious, and then there were those two trolls to track . . . not to mention Ryan—he didn't seem to remember confronting the trolls, but Laurel would surely forbid Tamani from using a memory elixir on the boy, so if he remembered anything at all, Tamani would have one more human to keep an eye on. He grimaced; he had his work cut out for him.

"Laurel told me to call," Yuki continued, seeming to misread his expression. "I don't really remember what I said, but she's coming."

"We should get you some paper towels or something," David said, piping up rather suddenly.

Yuki's hand went immediately to her head. "That's okay," she said shortly. "This is good."

"Yeah, but Chelsea will want that shirt back," David pressed. With a look at Tamani, he leaned down close to Yuki and whispered softly near her ear. After a moment, Yuki nodded, and he left the room.

"What about Laurel, did she hit her head too?" Yuki asked after a moment of awkward silence.

"You don't remember?"

Yuki shook her head slowly. "Not really. I just remember smoke, and voices, and . . ." She paused. "Laurel fainted or something."

"Yeah, I think she hurt something in the crash and just didn't feel it till it was all over. Adrenaline, you know," he said with a dark laugh. But Yuki didn't respond.

David came back from the kitchen with a roll of paper towels. "Can I get some space?" he said pointedly to Tamani.

Tamani backed away, not sure what David was trying to pull here. Clearly he'd said something to Yuki to let her know he knew about her. Or at least about her non-human blood. And that was information Tamani had *not* been ready to share.

"Look who I found," Laurel's dad said from the doorway, clearly trying to sound cheerful in the face of having so much thrown at him. "She pulled up just as Chelsea and Ryan were leaving. Klea, right? Laurel's told us, um, so much about you."

Tamani wasn't sure whether fear or intrigue was stronger as he turned to greet Klea for the first time. She looked exactly as Laurel had always described her; dressed all in black—mostly tight leather tonight—with cropped auburn hair and sunglasses. She exuded an aura of intimidation and Tamani imagined he could feel Laurel's sentries moving in closer.

Tamani watched Klea and Yuki as inconspicuously as he could. In the two or three seconds before Klea softly said, "Are you okay?" there was a silent conversation between the two that he wished he could interpret.

"I think so," Yuki said, nodding slowly. Tamani studied her downcast eyes, her tense shoulders. He had just spent three hours with Yuki—which included a car accident and troll attack—and she had never looked as frightened as she did right now. Because Yuki spent so much time on her own, Tamani had never considered the possibility that she could be Klea's prisoner. Pawn, perhaps, but never prisoner. But watching her now . . . ?

"She cut her head," David said, and Tamani noticed that he was holding the soiled T-shirt carefully, but casually, behind his back. "Chelsea and I helped her clean it up," he said, meeting Klea's eyes and injecting a hint of purpose into his words.

Tamani watched Klea's eyebrows raise just barely over the rims of her sunglasses, then she nodded. "Okay," she said, clearly not responding to the words David had actually spoken.

As if feeling Tamani's eyes on her, Klea turned to Tamani. "And who are you?" Klea asked, not bothering to hide her suspicion.

"I'm Tam," Tamani said quickly, holding out his glove-clad hand. "Yuki's date. You must be her host, uh, family?"

Klea looked at his hand for a long moment before shaking it as briefly as possible.

"I'm from Scotland," Tamani added, letting his accent deepen just a little. "Yuki and I, we're both foreign. Met on the first day. I . . ." He dropped his gaze, donning a sheepish expression. "I was driving. I'm so sorry."

"Things happen," Klea said dismissively. "I do need to get Yuki home though." She started toward the armchair, but stopped as she passed Laurel. "Is she all right?" Klea asked, real concern in her voice.

"We were just waiting for you to come get Yuki before taking her to the hospital," Laurel's dad said quickly, his lie easy and natural.

"Of course," Klea said brusquely. "I won't keep you." She helped Yuki up from the couch, one hand covering Yuki's, pressing the paper towels to her forehead. "I'll call and see how Laurel is in the next couple days," she said, vaguely addressing the whole room.

"Sure," Laurel's mom murmured. "We do need to get her to a doctor, though."

"Absolutely," Klea said, prodding Yuki toward the door.

The door closed behind her and everyone in the room let out a soft sigh.

Except Tamani.

He ran to the front window and peeked out, carefully, watching Klea load Yuki into her car—a sleek black two-door model that looked, even to Tamani's unaccustomed eye, *extremely fast*—and then drive off. Only when he saw dark, agile shapes whip under the streetlight, following them, did he turn his attention back to the rest of the room.

"David, what were you thinking?" Tamani demanded. "You totally tipped our hand!"

"It was worth it," David said, pulling the shirt out from behind his back. "I got this."

"I somehow think Chelsea would have survived without her shirt," Tamani said. "Quite frankly, with the way she collects faerie souvenirs, I don't expect to get *my* shirt back."

"You don't get it," David shot back. "We've been trying to get a sample, right? This is covered in her sap!"

Tamani was speechless for a second. It was so simple, so obvious, so . . .

"Brilliant," Tamani allowed grudgingly.

David just grinned.

"Mom?" Laurel's voice was scratchy and weak, but they all heard her.

Her parents rushed to the couch and David leaned over the back of it, his face close to Laurel's. Tamani forced himself to remain where he was, feeling even more an outsider than he had at the dance, watching Laurel spin in David's arms.

"How did I get here?" she asked, disoriented.

"We brought you here after the accident," David said softly.

Laurel lay back, looking a little confused. Her mom squeezed her hand and turned to Tamani. "What *exactly* happened?" her mom asked. "And none of this 'we hit a deer' stuff."

David looked at Tamani, allowing him to make the call.

But Tamani knew it didn't matter; Laurel would tell them everything anyway. So he took a deep breath and told them the whole story, not leaving anything out.

"And she just collapsed?" Laurel's mom asked when he finished, her hand soft on Laurel's face. "Why?"

"I'm not sure," Laurel answered, her words slow and deliberate. "Everything was over, and I was standing there, and then I had the most excruciating headache ever. I . . . I guess I blacked out."

"Are you sure you didn't hit your head in the wreck?"

"I don't think so," Laurel said. "It didn't feel like that. For a second, it was just . . . pain. And a roaring sound in my head. And pressure. Then nothing."

Her dad looked up at Tamani. "Can trolls do that?"

All Tamani could do was shrug. "I don't know. It's never happened before, but I seem to be running into that problem a lot lately."

"My potion didn't work on them," Laurel said. "It should have worked."

After a moment's hesitation, David asked, "Did you make it?"

Laurel rolled her eyes. "No," she said dryly, "*I* didn't make it. One of the advanced Fall students made it. I don't know who."

"Still, it could have just gone wrong, right?" David pressed.

"Fall potions can always go wrong," Laurel admitted. She paused, remembering. "Yuki, she was hurt." She spoke slowly, like even that was effort.

"Yeah," David said. "Klea came and got her just a couple minutes ago."

"Klea came here?" Laurel asked, trying to sit up. Her mom helped her, placing an arm around her shoulders. Laurel's eyes closed for a second, as if she was in danger of losing consciousness again, and Tamani took an involuntary step forward before they opened again.

"There was nothing I could do about that," David said. "But we gave her as quick an explanation as we could and got them both out of here. She . . . she knows that Chelsea and I know about Yuki. I'm sorry, I didn't know what else to say."

"It's okay. Klea didn't *tell* me not to tell you two. What about Ryan and Chelsea? Where are they?"

David hesitated. "They drove home. Or maybe to the hospital. Well, Chelsea drove Ryan. Wherever they go, his dad will probably check him for a concussion. And we're probably going to get a lecture for not calling nine-one-one."

Laurel shrugged. "I can handle a lecture from Ryan's dad. It's better than him finding out. So . . . Ryan doesn't remember anything?"

"Doesn't seem to." David sighed. "Lucky for us, he was really disoriented."

"And for sure he doesn't remember the trolls?" asked Tamani.

"Not as far as I can tell," David replied.

"Thank goodness for that. What about Yuki?" Laurel asked.

David looked at Tamani.

"I don't know," Tamani admitted. "She seemed pretty disoriented too. I'm not even sure she saw the trolls. But she could easily have been lying for *my* benefit. Either way, she's *acting* like she knows nothing. At least to me."

"But what—"

"That's enough now," Laurel's mom said, laying her back down again. "You've got to stop thinking about everyone else and worry about yourself for a moment. Are you feeling okay?"

Laurel nodded. "Yeah, I am," she said, and she did look better. She stifled a yawn. "I'm totally exhausted though. I mean, that was the reason we came home in the first place, right?" She laughed shallowly, and even that faded away when no one joined in.

"All right," her mom said cheerily, "let's get our girl to bed."

"There's one more thing," Tamani said quickly.

"Not tonight," David said.

"It might be too late tomorrow," Tamani hissed.

"Don't fight!" Laurel said, her tone making Tamani freeze mid-step. He muttered a quick apology and backed away from David.

"What are you guys talking about?" Laurel said weakly. The weariness in her voice made Tamani want to run over and take her in his arms and away from everything. Back to Avalon where no one, none of this, could hurt her again. For the millionth time he wondered what about this world— about this human boy—made her so determined to stay.

199

To put herself in constant danger to protect them, when all Tamani wanted was for her to be safe. She was strong—so strong—but he had seen bigger trees than Laurel break when the wind blew hard enough.

"I got Chelsea's shirt," David said. "The one she wrapped Yuki's cut with. I . . . I thought you could use it as a sample for your experiment."

Laurel's eyes widened. "Yes! David, that's perfect!" She tried to get up, but collapsed back onto the couch. David and Tamani both stepped forward, extending a hand. David scowled at Tamani. Tamani scowled right back.

"I'm okay," Laurel said. "I just stood up too fast. I need the sample," she said, and Tamani could tell she was straining to keep her voice even. "I have to prepare it tonight or it'll be too late."

David held up the shirt. "I'll bring it upstairs," he said.

"I'll help you up," Tamani offered at the same time. A tense moment passed before Laurel's mom stood and helped Laurel get up from the couch.

"*I* will take Laurel," she said in a very gentle voice, "and Mark will bring the shirt." David handed the shirt reluctantly to Laurel's dad. Laurel leaned against her mom's shoulder and avoided looking at either of them, but Laurel's mom took David and Tamani in with a glance that reminded Tamani all too vividly of his own mother. "I think you've both had plenty of excitement for one night. I'll help Laurel prepare her sample and then she needs to sleep. Everything else can wait till tomorrow. David, you're welcome to crash on the couch if you want. I'm not sure you should go back out there tonight." Then, almost as an afterthought, she added, "You're welcome to stay as well, Tamani, but . . ."

"Thank you, but no," Tamani said. "There is still work to be done tonight, I'm afraid."

"I assume you can let yourself out," Laurel's mom said, and Tamani was almost certain there was a touch of laughter in her voice as she said it. But he just nodded and watched as Laurel and her mom slowly mounted the stairs.

"Well," David said, turning his eyes to Tamani.

Tamani said nothing, simply turned and slipped silently out the back door. He had no patience left for David tonight.

Aaron fell into step next to Tamani the instant Tamani stepped off the back porch. "Would you like to explain what just happened?" he asked, a definite edge to his voice.

"We were attacked by trolls," Tamani retorted, tired of holding his temper. "But then, if you didn't know that already, you are seriously failing in your job."

"We arrived seconds after you drove away, but it was too late. We had a trail to follow, but nothing else."

"I hope you followed it."

"Of course we did," Aaron said sharply. "But it disappeared. Again. What I want to know is why *you* didn't follow it. You had them in visual range!"

Guilt welled up at Tamani's core, but he pushed it away. "I had to stay with Laurel."

"We could have made sure she got home safely."

"I didn't know that. All I knew was that you weren't there."

Aaron sighed. "Tracking you while you're driving that vehicle is exactly as difficult as you'd imagine."

"What about our life *isn't* difficult, Aaron?"

"You should have followed them, Tamani. That is your job!"

"That is *your* job!" Tamani snapped back, louder than he should have. "*My* job is to protect Laurel, and that is what I did." He turned away and laced his fingers behind his neck, letting his elbows hang limply by his face as he drew in short, fast breaths, trying to regain control. "I'll find them," he said after a long pause.

"The trail is long-cold," Aaron said, refusing to yield.

"I don't care. I'll find them. I'll put in extra shifts after Laurel is in for the night. I'll make this right," he promised, more to himself than to Aaron. He listened for Aaron's reply, but heard nothing. After a long minute he dropped his arms and turned, but he was alone in the trees.

# NINETEEN

"WE NEED TO TALK," CHELSEA SAID, SEIZING LAUREL'S arm as she walked into the hall at school.

Laurel grinned. "Oh, I'm all right, Chelsea, thanks for asking. How about you? Did you develop any whiplash over the weekend?"

"I'm serious," Chelsea hissed. "We need to talk. Now," she added, her voice catching a little.

"Okay," Laurel said, realizing this was not a time for jokes. "Absolutely. I'm sorry, um . . . let's go down here." She pointed Chelsea down the hall toward the janitorial closet that was always hanging open. No one hung out there. "What's going on?" she said, sliding down the wall and patting the floor beside her.

Chelsea joined her, leaning her head close to Laurel's. "It's Ryan. He doesn't remember what happened Friday night."

Laurel looked confused. "That's normal with head injuries, isn't it?"

"He doesn't remember *anything*. Not the crash, not me taking him home, he doesn't remember about half of the dance, Laurel."

"Will that wear off?"

Chelsea raised an eyebrow. "Somehow I don't think it will."

In a panicky moment, Laurel understood. "You think I gave him something?" Laurel said, as loud as she dared.

Chelsea's face immediately softened. "No, of course not!" She hesitated. "But I think *someone* gave him something. And let's just say I don't think it was his parents."

"You really think his memory loss is . . . unnatural?" Laurel asked.

"It doesn't make sense for it to be anything else. Saturday night on the drive home he was coherent and answering questions. He knows less today than he did an hour after it happened."

"Why didn't you tell me this yesterday?"

"I wasn't sure at first. But we were talking on the phone last night and he seriously doesn't remember anything from about ten o'clock Friday night till Saturday morning. It's too big a window of time. My brother Danny got a major concussion last year and there are only a few minutes that he doesn't remember. Nothing like this."

Laurel sighed. She didn't know which would be worse—if it was Tamani who did this, or if it was Yuki.

"Laurel?" Chelsea's voice was quiet now.

"Yeah?"

"You told me last year you'd do everything you could to protect Ryan. I'm calling in that promise now."

"I can't undo it," Laurel said. "But you have my word I will do everything in my power to make sure it doesn't happen again."

They both got to their feet and headed back toward the main hall, which was filling with students. Laurel stood in front of her locker, trying to decide what to do. She caught Tamani's slender profile out of the corner of her eye and carefully tracked him through the halls, trying not to make it too obvious she was watching him.

Instead of stopping at his own locker, Tamani paused in front of Yuki's, stepping in close to her. Laurel managed a quick peek at Yuki's wound, but there wasn't much to see. The cut had been right at her hairline, so it was mostly hidden anyway. On top of that, she—or Klea—had applied some kind of makeup to the wound that made it look like a regular human scar. Laurel had to admit, it was clever. The Mixer in her wanted to take a closer look, but . . . it just wasn't possible right now. Especially with Tamani blocking her view.

He reached out and touched Yuki's head, just below her cut, and then traced his finger down her face. Anger roiled in her stomach and Laurel had to turn away. She didn't know for sure which one had given Ryan a memory elixir, but it *had* to have been one of them.

Laurel felt strong hands slide up her hips and David's barely scruffy cheek pressed against hers.

"Good morning," she said with a smile.

"Are you—"

"Please don't ask if I'm okay," Laurel interrupted. "I'm fine."

"I was going to ask if you were . . . hungry," David said, grinning.

Laurel rolled her eyes and Chelsea smacked David's shoulder good-naturedly.

"Did Klea stop by again?" David asked, opening his locker.

"Not since eight o'clock yesterday when you asked last," Laurel replied.

"That's weird, isn't it?" David asked.

Laurel had to admit it was. Klea was being way too hands-off about the whole thing. "We have a problem," Laurel said, sobering. They all looked up as the five-minute bell rang. "Abbreviated version," Laurel amended. "Somebody gave Ryan a memory elixir, and it wasn't me, so I'm either angry or afraid, and maybe a little of both."

"You want me to talk to him?" David said, folding his arms across his chest and shooting Tamani a glare.

"No," Laurel hissed, pulling him back around, knowing Tamani would already have noticed anyway. "I can talk to him myself, thank you."

"Fine," David said darkly.

"Besides, we don't know it was him," Laurel said.

206

"Oh, please," David argued. "What was it he said right before he left?" David affected a Scottish accent. "There is still work to be done tonight.'"

"He could have meant anything," Laurel said, running her hand down David's arm. "Please don't jump to conclusions."

David pursed his lips. "Fine," he said. "But if you change your mind, just let me know."

"I will," Laurel said sincerely, tugging at the front of his shirt for a kiss. "We'll talk later."

David turned and headed down the hall just as Tamani said good-bye to Yuki and started walking toward Laurel. At the last second, Tamani looked over his shoulder, as though he were glancing back at Yuki—but this move changed his trajectory just enough for his shoulder to slam into David's. David snapped around, hands spread wide.

"Hey!"

Everyone in the hallway stopped and stared.

Everyone but Tamani, who continued walking. But he held up one hand, still clad in his black, fingerless glove. "Sorry, bro," he said, his accent sounding strangely American. "My bad." He neither stopped nor met Laurel's eyes as he strode past her, on his way toward their classroom.

Tamani couldn't look at Laurel as she took her seat beside him in Government. He was wrong to shove David and he knew it, but after spending the whole weekend stewing, his temper had gotten away from him.

And it *could* have been an accident.

From her stiff posture, Tamani could see Laurel knew better. She was mad at him and he was tired of apologizing.

He had to admit, seeing her with David day in and day out had proven harder to handle than he expected. If he was honest with himself, he had kind of expected Laurel to be his by now. He always assumed that if he could just be in the same place as Laurel for long enough, he would win her over—awaken the chemistry that had sparked between them so many times in the past. But he'd been in Crescent City for more than two months and clearly that wasn't happening.

He was essentially failing on all fronts. He had lost the trolls—and hadn't found a single sign of them all weekend— he still had no idea what to do with Yuki, and the one time Klea had shown herself, he hadn't been able to do anything at all.

Maybe Shar was right. Maybe this *was* a bad idea. Maybe it had always been a bad idea. But he couldn't give up now— it just wasn't in his nature. He tried to catch Laurel's eye one more time, but she had her head down over her notebook and was scribbling furiously on the pages, taking down Mrs. Harms's every word.

*Fine*, Tamani thought stubbornly. *I don't want to talk to you, either.*

When class ended Tamani saw Laurel turn to him, but before she could speak, he presented his back, slid his books into his backpack, and hefted it onto his shoulder. He gave her one quick glance, met her narrowed gaze, then stormed out of the classroom.

He tried to look over the heads of the students around him, cursing his stature. But he managed to glimpse Yuki heading toward her locker and pushed through the crowd to get to her.

"Hey," he said, a little breathless.

Her eyes widened and then she looked at the floor, trying to hide her smile. "Hi."

"I *so* don't want to go to class. Any interest in ditching with me?"

Her eyes swung to both sides before she stepped closer and whispered, "Ditching?" in a voice so mortified you'd have thought he suggested murder.

"Sure. You've never done it?"

She shook her head sharply from side to side.

He held out a hand. "Want to?"

She stared at his hand for a long moment, as if it might jump up and bite her. *Or, more likely,* Tamani thought, *that it might be a trap.*

"Okay," she said, a smile crossing her face now as she put her hand in his.

"See," Tamani said, kind of enjoying himself now. "That wasn't so bad." He grinned as he pulled her with him, through the sea of warm bodies, toward the front doors. He had skipped class enough times that he knew there was no one standing in the parking lot waiting to pick off truants, but Yuki's gaze was darting all over the place as if waiting for someone to jump out from behind a bush to catch her.

Tamani opened the passenger side door for her and said, "I'll keep the top up till we're off school property," before slipping in the other side.

Yuki was staring at the windshield. "It's fixed," she said in surprise. "The hood too."

"Yeah," Tamani said casually. "I know a guy."

*Know a guy who likes money, more like.* It was comical how quickly a little money could get something fixed in the human world. The mechanic had insisted it wasn't possible in such a short time, but when Tamani dropped a stack of hundreds on the counter the mechanic had explained that by *impossible*, he really just meant *outrageously expensive*.

Yuki slumped down in the seat beside him so as not to be seen through her window and Tamani had to stifle a laugh. Faerie or not, she was clearly intimidated by the human school's authority; she really felt like she was doing something bad. Once they were off school grounds and out of sight, Tamani pushed the button that opened up the top of the car and Yuki visibly relaxed, pulling her hair out of its ponytail and letting the wind flutter through it.

"So where are we going?" Yuki asked, her head lolling against the headrest.

"I don't know. You have a favorite place?"

Yuki grimaced. "I don't have a car. I can't go too far."

Tamani didn't want to admit that his range was limited too. He couldn't get very far from Laurel. Even though there had never been a troll attack at her school, there was no point tempting fate.

He saw a park off to his right and pulled over behind a

bush so the car was hidden from the main road. "How's this?"

"For what?" Yuki asked shyly, not raising her eyes to his.

It was obvious what she was thinking. And he *had* come on a little strong today. But he didn't want to follow through on his false intentions quite so soon. "Thought we could just chat," he said, his tone deliberately casual. "I haven't been by your house lately and at school . . . there's just so much pressure. Conversations are better out of school."

"In a park?" she asked with a smile.

"I don't see why not," he said, leaning his head close. "You got something against parks?" Without waiting for a response he slipped out of the car, knowing she would follow. Sure enough, within seconds he heard the passenger door slam shut. Yuki caught up quickly.

"So are you tired of everyone asking you to say things in Japanese?" he asked, starting off on a nice, neutral topic.

She rolled her eyes. "Am I ever! Everyone wants me to tell them how to say their name. And when I tell them their name would be the same in Japan, they want a Japanese name. And then they butcher the pronunciation. At least you speak English."

"Aye, but they still all want to hear me say 'Top o' the morning!' I don't have the heart to tell them that's Irish, not Scottish." Not that Tamani knew *that* before he'd looked it up on the internet after the tenth time someone said it to him.

"And they want to know if I watch anime."

"Do you?" Tamani asked, wondering what anime was.

He'd have to ask Laurel later. If she'd speak to him.

She snorted. "No. I watch regular shows. HBO"—she ducked her head—"and, I admit, some Disney Channel."

Tamani chuckled because it seemed like the right thing to do. He had no idea what he was laughing about. He'd learned about television, but had never really watched any. Without context it was hard to apply many of the terms he'd picked up at the Manor. And he'd never been able to keep all those acronyms straight.

"So how have you been?" he asked, serious now as he leaned on a set of monkey bars and studied her.

"I've been pretty good. Nothing exciting."

"You don't call last weekend exciting?" he said, smiling.

"Oh, um, yeah," she said, flustered now. "That was exciting. I meant besides that."

"Is Klea okay with it all?" Tamani prodded. "She didn't seem too worried about the accident."

"Yeah, well," Yuki started, walking away from Tamani and stepping up onto a swing, grasping the chains to steady herself. "She's in law enforcement and sees a lot of stuff like that. Even when she is worried, she doesn't show it."

"Are you happy living with her? Well, kind of living with her, like you said."

"Sure. I don't see her much, but it's fine."

Tamani went out on a limb now, knowing she wouldn't show her cards unless he tipped his hand a little too. "You seemed . . . nervous when she came by. Scared, almost."

Yuki grimaced, almost imperceptibly. "I wasn't scared,"

she said, lifting her chin a tiny bit. She'd coaxed the swing into swaying side to side. "I hate calling her off a job. She doesn't like it. It's not that she's mean or anything, she's just not the nurturing type. She expects things of me, and one of them is to stay out of trouble. It's not a bad thing; she has big plans and doesn't let anyone or anything stand in her way." There was a small hesitation. "I want to be like that some-day," she added quietly.

"I think you're already like that," Tamani said. He got behind her and grabbed the chains of her swing, pulling her carefully to a stop. Then he put one foot on the seat, wedging it between Yuki's small sandals. Pushing off with his other foot, he stood and started them swinging, press-ing his chest against her back. He felt her breath catch. "I worry about you being alone all the time. Dealing with her. She kinda scared *me*. I didn't want to tell her I was the one driving."

Yuki smiled up at him over her shoulder, clearly amused.

He hesitated, trying to time it for best effect. "If anything happens, if you get into trouble—with her, with anyone— will you tell me?"

She looked at him for a long time, their faces only inches apart, before she nodded slowly. "I will," she whispered.

And for once, Tamani believed her.

# TWENTY

AFTER TAMANI DISAPPEARED HALF THE DAY AND ignored her the rest, Laurel got sick of trying to pretend that everything was fine and begged out of her usual study session at David's house, telling him she needed some alone time. David accepted this stoically and without comment. Perhaps because they had spent the entire weekend either together or on the phone. Or maybe because once Tamani finally *did* get back, he spent the afternoon fawning over Yuki.

Once home, Laurel dragged her backpack behind her as she climbed the stairs, enjoying the way it thumped, sounding like a petulant child stomping up the steps. Come to think of it, she *was* feeling a little petulant. Tamani must have doped Ryan, even though he knew Laurel wouldn't approve. And he had to know she knew. It was the only logical reason for him to ignore her like he had today.

She was *not* mad that Yuki had a crush on Tamani. That was *his* problem.

Laurel swung her bedroom door open and bit off a scream. Tamani was sitting on her window seat, a silver knife dancing an elaborate jig across his fingers.

"You scared me!" she said accusingly.

Tamani shrugged. "Sorry," he said, the knife disappearing into his clothes somewhere.

Laurel pursed her lips and turned away, pretending to dig through her backpack. She heard him sigh as he stood.

"I *am* sorry," he said, standing close behind her. "I didn't mean to scare you. You weren't here when I arrived. So . . . I let myself in."

"It was locked!" Laurel said. She had turned her key into the deadbolt not thirty seconds ago.

"Human locks? Please," Tamani said. "May as well leave the door open."

"You really shouldn't be in here without permission," she muttered, refusing to give up her anger so easily.

"I apologize. Again," he said, the tiniest hint of tension entering his tone. "I hardly ever come in here unless I need to deliver something like"—he gestured almost aimlessly toward her table—"you know. It's not like I stalk you or peek in your windows or anything."

"Good." But she couldn't think of anything else to say. So she grabbed the only homework she had—a Speech assignment she hadn't planned on even looking at until after dinner—and sat at her desk, pretending to read it.

"Are you upset?" Tamani asked.

"Am I *upset*?" Laurel asked, slamming her hands down on the desk and turning to face him. "Are you kidding me? You ignored me all weekend, picked a fight with David in the hall, drugged Ryan, and had stupid Yuki hanging all over you every chance she got. I'm not 'upset,' Tamani, I'm mad!"

"Drugged Ryan? What happened to Ryan?"

Laurel held up a hand. "Don't even try the innocent act on me. I am so sick of it."

"What happened to Ryan?" Tamani repeated.

Now Laurel threw both hands in the air. "Someone hit him with a memory potion. There's a twelve-hour block he just simply doesn't remember. Convenient, isn't it?"

"Actually, yes," Tamani said.

"I knew it," Laurel said. "I *knew* it! I told you never to use those potions on my family and friends again. I was very specific!"

Tamani just stood silently, looking at her.

"But no," Laurel ranted on, feeling as though something had burst inside her and now that everything had started coming out, she couldn't stop it. "No, you have to be Tamani with the plan. Tamani manipulating the stupid worthless humans. Tamani going behind my back and lying to me!"

He met her gaze and held it until it was she who had to look away. "You're not even going to ask?"

"Ask what?"

"If I did it."

Laurel rolled her eyes. "Did you do it?" she asked, more to placate him than anything.

"No."

She hesitated only a moment. "Did one of your sentries do it?"

"Not as far as I know. And if they did, it was a violation of a direct order and I will see them relieved of their position here and sent right back to Orick."

She looked up at him in shock now. His voice was too firm, too steady. He wasn't lying. Mortification washed over her. "Really?" she asked softly.

"Really."

She sank down into her chair, feeling the grudge she'd been nursing all day start to melt.

"I suppose I should be used to it by now," he said quietly.

"What?" Laurel asked, not sure she wanted to hear the answer.

"The way you still don't trust me."

"I trust you," Laurel countered, but Tamani just shook his head.

"No, you don't," he said, laughing bitterly. "You have *confidence* in me; in my abilities. If you're in trouble, you know I'll save you. That's not the same as trust. If you trusted me you'd have at least asked me before assuming I was guilty."

"I should have asked," Laurel blurted, feeling unbearably small. But he wasn't looking at her now; he was staring out the window. "I was going to ask, but you were avoiding me! What was I supposed to think?" She stood and walked over

217

to him, willing him to turn around and look at her. "I'm sorry," she finally whispered to his back.

"I know," he said with a heavy sigh. Nothing more.

She laid a hand on his shoulder and tugged. "Look at me."

He turned and when he met her gaze, she wished he hadn't. Pain radiated from his face—pain and betrayal. He placed his hand over hers and the pain turned to longing.

Desperate to be looking anywhere but Tamani's eyes, Laurel studied the hand covering hers, at once so familiar and so foreign. Tamani's hands weren't like David's, thick and strong. They weren't much bigger than Laurel's own, with long, slender fingers and perfectly shaped nails. She spread her hand under his, moving ever so slightly to allow his fingers to fall into the hollows between hers. She could feel Tamani's eyes on her as she stared at their hands, wanting this so badly.

And knowing she couldn't have it.

Unwilling to go forward, unsure how to go back, Laurel looked desperately up at Tamani. He seemed to understand her silent plea. Disappointment clouded his expression, but with it, determination. He lifted his hand from hers, leaving a glittering print on her skin. Then he slid her hand slowly down his arm, pushing it from him until it once again hung by her side.

"I'm sorry," Laurel whispered again, and she was. She didn't want to hurt him. But she couldn't give him what he wanted. Too many people needed her now, and sometimes it felt like she was letting them all down.

After a long look Tamani cleared his throat and turned back to the window. "So we know *I* didn't give Ryan anything," Tamani said, a little stiffly. "And I'll make sure none of the other sentries did either. But if that's the case, what are we left with?"

"Yuki seems like the most obvious answer." Laurel went over to her bed and sat with her elbows on her knees, her chin in her hands. "And *if* she can make memory elixirs, she must be a Fall."

"Yes. *If.*" Tamani paused thoughtfully. "But why give him the memory elixir at all? He didn't remember anything."

"But he did see the trolls, at least for a second. Maybe it was a precaution? In case he remembered later?"

"It just seems . . . sloppy. She had to know we'd notice his memory loss."

"Unless . . ." Laurel hesitated. "Unless she *doesn't* think we would notice. If she doesn't realize I'm a faerie, she might assume I wouldn't know about things like this."

"Which takes us back to 'if Klea's actually telling the truth,' which none of us really believe," Tamani said, shaking his head.

"I don't trust Klea, but other than giving us guns and showing up at convenient moments, she's never done anything suspicious. She's saved my life almost as often as you have. Maybe we should stop being paranoid and just . . . trust her," Laurel said, trying to put some enthusiasm behind it.

Tamani shrugged. "Maybe. But I doubt it." Circumstantial evidence wasn't enough—if only they could know for certain that Yuki was a Mixer. "What about your experiment this weekend? Did it work?"

Laurel flopped backward onto her mattress, arms flung wide. "Depends. Did the cells stay alive under the globe long enough to process the phosphorescent? Yes. Did I learn anything useful? No."

"What happened?"

Laurel stood and walked over to the experiment she still had set up at her desk—two small glass dishes with clear, sticky residue in them and a closed light globe sitting nearby. "This is Yuki's sap. This is a little of mine. I didn't want to dilute it in sugar water . . . I wasn't even sure it would work with the phosphorescent. But it did, and both samples glowed. Mine only glowed for half an hour. Yuki's glowed for forty-five minutes."

"But Katya said she glowed for a whole night!"

Laurel nodded. "But she also said they would drink whole vials of this stuff, and it makes sense that most photosynthesis would take place in our skin. I'm not sure a difference of fifteen minutes rules out the possibility that Yuki's a Fall."

"Did you want to try some of my sap? Maybe there will be a bigger difference."

"Do you mind?"

Tamani produced his silver knife and made a shallow cut across his thumb before Laurel could protest. He squeezed a few drops of sap into an empty dish. Laurel reopened the golden light globe and set it next to the fresh sample. She hated that he was so willing to hurt himself for her, but now that he had, she should at least do something to make it worthwhile. With a small dropper she added some phosphorescent to Tamani's sap, which immediately glowed a gentle white.

"I better go," Tamani said without looking at her, moving toward her bedroom door as he wound a small bit of cloth around his thumb.

"Don't you want to see how long it takes?" Laurel asked, suddenly hesitant to have him leave her.

"I'm sure you'll let me know how it turns out."

"I'll walk you to the door," Laurel said, scrambling to her feet, desperate to be some kind of passable hostess.

They walked downstairs to the front door in silence. Tamani laid one hand on the doorknob and opened it a crack before stopping. "Laurel, I . . . I don't think I can . . ." He licked his lips and there was a blazing determination in his eyes that made Laurel's breath quicken.

But even as she saw that fire, it was gone. "Never mind," he mumbled, throwing the door all the way open.

David was standing on the porch, looking as surprised as Laurel felt. "I found your notebook in my backpack," he said, holding up a green spiral-bound book. "I must have grabbed them both. I just wanted to return . . ." His voice trailed off.

There was a beaten expression on Tamani's face that even David couldn't have missed. He ducked his head and slid between David and the door frame without a backward glance.

David watched Tamani disappear around the corner, then turned back to Laurel.

"Thank you," Laurel said, taking her notebook from him.

He continued to stare silently at her.

"I'll see you tomorrow," Laurel said firmly.

"But—"

"I don't have the energy to have this conversation—again," Laurel insisted. "If you're still bothered by it tomorrow, we can talk about it. But if you come to your senses before then, it would be greatly appreciated," she said and shot him a tense smile as she closed the door between them.

# TWENTY-ONE

TAMANI WATCHED DAVID RUSH AROUND TO THE driver's side of Laurel's car and open the door for her. After they walked hand in hand through the front doors of the school, Tamani grabbed his gloves out of his backpack. He was so tired of them. Still, another week, maybe less, and he could throw them away, hopefully forever.

He fastened the Velcro strip at his wrist and stared at his hand. He could still feel her fingers on his shoulder, her hand beneath his. Maybe he should have pushed for more. Maybe he would have gotten more. But for how long? A day? Maybe a week, before she started feeling guilty and cut things off again—cut *him* off again?

He followed David and Laurel inside. His eyes found her the instant he passed through the doors. She was standing with David, as usual, and hadn't noticed him yet. David's arm was draped casually over her shoulders and Tamani wrangled with his jealousy. He knew that, for humans and faeries alike, romance was often impermanent, especially between young lovers. Laurel had even told him, once, that she wasn't looking for her "one true love." Tamani clung to those words, though her behavior since that time seemed at odds with her claim.

A cool hand caught his wrist and pulled Tamani back to reality.

"I called your name, but you didn't hear me," Yuki said in her perfect, unaccented American English.

"Sorry." Being alert was central to Tamani's job. One moment of distraction could be the end of Laurel. This was why Shar had been reluctant to send Tamani in the first place. Chastising himself for letting his feelings for Laurel endanger her, however slightly, however briefly, Tamani turned and smiled at Yuki, though he kept one ear tuned to Laurel's conversation.

Yuki returned his smile, then asked if he had watched some television program he'd never heard of before. He shook his head and invited her to tell him about it. After that it was pretty easy. She tended to prattle on about human musicians, internet gossip, and television programs with ludicrous or demeaning premises, but this made it easy to nod amicably at everything she said.

Laurel had turned and was walking toward her first class. Yuki was in the middle of explaining how Japanese *aidoru* differed from American starlets, so Tamani just shifted a little, to better keep an eye on Laurel as she navigated the sea of students. He didn't even see David until a shoulder slammed into him, swinging him around and wrenching Yuki's arm away.

"Watch it!" Tamani said, suppressing the urge to break David's nose. Or his neck.

But David just looked back with a satisfied grin on his face before continuing down the hall. "Sorry, bro," he said, mimicking Tamani's brogue. "My bad."

"I don't know what Laurel sees in that guy," Yuki said disapprovingly. "She seems nice, I guess. But he's kind of . . . intense."

Tamani nodded. His eyes searched for Laurel again as Yuki touched his shoulder tentatively and asked if he was okay. He opened his mouth to reassure her when his eyes found Laurel's face.

She was looking back, her hands gripping the straps of her backpack, glaring. Tamani had to look twice to make sure, but it was true! She wasn't glaring at him.

She was glaring at David.

It was a nice change of pace.

But this did little to dissipate Tamani's anger. He hated that he couldn't go all out with his rival. Couldn't fight David, couldn't steal Laurel, couldn't court her the way a faerie should be courted—not without giving them both away. He sat and fumed through Government. Laurel sat so close—just inches away, in the next desk over—but what did it matter? She may as well be a hundred miles away. A thousand. A million.

And, of course, she was a Fall faerie, which limited him in other ways. But he didn't like to think about that.

About halfway through class Laurel passed him a note. He glanced at it—the results of the phosphorescent test on his sap. Thirty-seven minutes. Right between Laurel and Yuki. Tamani had to admit he didn't really know what that meant—if anything. He took out a pen and started to write a response. Scratched it out and tried again. But they were the wrong words. Were there any right words with her anymore? With a sigh he shoved the note into his backpack with all his writing scribbled out. He didn't look at Laurel; didn't know if she even noticed.

Laurel waved at him as she left the classroom—concern in her eyes—but even that felt like mockery as Tamani dragged himself out of his chair, collected his meaningless, stage-prop pile of books and supplies, and headed to his next class.

By the time he'd finished second hour, he'd had enough. He escorted Yuki to her third-period class, but couldn't bear to go to his own. After wandering the school grounds for a while, he walked out to the parking lot instead and slumped into the driver's seat. With the top down and his shirt unbuttoned, he enjoyed the sunlight that filtered down through the autumn clouds.

A few minutes before the lunch bell, Tamani forced himself to return to the school, having made the same decision he made about twice a week. All of the heartache, the anger, the fear that this was as good as it was ever going to get, was worth it. Here, he could see her eyes and bask in her smiles—even when she wasn't smiling for him. Every day was worth the pain.

But he didn't have to like it.

The hall was empty. There were a few more minutes before the flood of humans would be released, and they would pour out of their classrooms, half climbing over each other to get to their meals, ravenous beasts all. He spun the sticky dial on his locker—not that he would care if someone made off with anything he kept in there—and yanked on the latch. He casually tossed his backpack in and tried to decide what to do for the lunch break. Would Yuki want to have lunch with Laurel's group? He wanted to see Laurel, but he didn't know if he could bear the sight of David. Not today.

Tamani heard footsteps and turned to see David walking along the opposite side of the hallway, glaring. A few other kids were milling about—they must have gotten out of class early. What was that saying humans had about speaking of devils?

Tamani knew he should turn away, ignore the boy's dirty looks and petty one-upmanship. He knew better than to feud with a human. He had a job to do.

Instead, he returned David's glare, measure for measure.

David slowed down, then stopped in front of Tamani, the air between them cooling tangibly.

"You got a problem, Lawson?" Tamani asked.

David hesitated. He was clearly out of his element. But Tamani knew from two years of experience just how stubborn and persistent this human boy could be. He wouldn't back down. "You know what my problem is," David replied.

"Let me rephrase," Tamani said, taking two steps forward. "You have a problem with *me*?"

"I have nothing *but* problems with you," David said, matching Tamani with two steps of his own, bringing him within arm's reach.

Tamani took one more step forward, halving the gap, and felt, rather than saw, eyes turn toward them. "Tell me how you really feel," Tamani said, so quietly he doubted anyone else even heard.

"Even my vocabulary couldn't quite describe it," David said, crossing his arms over his chest.

It wasn't exactly trash talk—maybe nerd trash talk—but Tamani had to admit it was clever. "Luckily," Tamani said, a malicious grin playing at the corners of his mouth, "I know a lot more words than you, *òinseach*." He threw the Gaelic word at David with more scorn than the literal translation probably warranted. The lunch bell rang, but Tamani scarcely heard it.

"You're just baiting me," David said, but he sounded unsure. Hesitant. "You want me to make Laurel mad. You want her to feel sorry for you." More students were gathering around them, hopeful for some entertainment.

"Not at all," Tamani said, placing the fingertips of one hand against David's chest. "I want to put you in your place, *burraidh*." He pushed just hard enough that David had to take one small step backward to keep his balance.

The combination of confusion and anger had just the

right effect. David stepped forward and pushed Tamani back. He could have kept himself upright, or taken David to the ground with his own momentum, but instead Tamani staggered back, then came forward with both hands outstretched. He put a lot of show into the push, but little effort; still David had to take two steps back this time. Before he could recover, Tamani moved in close and shoved him one more time, so David's back hit the lockers with a rickety metal *clang*.

"Fight!" an anonymous student shouted from the crowd. Others took up the chant. "Fight! Fight! Fight!"

*Oh yes*, Tamani thought. *A cornered animal will* always *fight*.

As David's fist slammed into Tamani's jaw, he was forced to admit that the boy had a good arm. But Tamani's pain was swallowed up in satisfaction; David had thrown the first punch. He was fair game.

# TWENTY-TWO

LAUREL WAITED OUTSIDE CHELSEA'S CLASSROOM AND grabbed her arm as she walked out. "Are you and Ryan eating lunch with us today?" Laurel asked.

"I think so," Chelsea said. "Why?"

"You just sneak off together sometimes," Laurel said—though they seemed to be sneaking off a good deal less than usual these days. Chelsea steadfastly refused to confront Ryan about Harvard, and keeping her mouth shut about it seemed to be taking its toll. "I wanted to check." The truth was, she didn't want to face David alone. Not yet. She was still mad that he'd "bumped" into Tamani that morning. She didn't think she had the patience to head off both guys' bad behavior today.

Laurel heard the commotion before she saw it. She and Chelsea rounded the corner just in time to see David slam his fist into Tamani's face. In the time it took her to blink,

Tamani had David by the shirt. David took one lightning-quick blow to the stomach and doubled over, gasping for breath. Tamani held on and raised his free hand to strike again.

"Tamani!" She ran forward, shoving people out of her way to get to them.

Tamani held on to David's shirt a moment longer, but when Laurel emerged from the crowd, he shoved David back, releasing his T-shirt and leaving a wrinkled circle where his hand had clenched it.

"What the *hell* do you think you're doing?" Laurel yelled, looking back and forth between them.

"He started it!" David shouted, looking like he was about to attack Tamani again.

"He *hit* me," Tamani said calmly, addressing his complaint to Laurel with his hands resting easily on his hips. "What was I supposed to do? Let him?"

"You wanted me to hit you and you know it," David said, lunging forward. Ryan grabbed David by the shoulder and pulled him back. David shoved Ryan's arm away, but he didn't try to go for Tamani again.

"Oh, please," Tamani argued, looking at David. "You've been wanting to take a shot at me since day one, admit it."

"With pleasure," David growled.

"That's enough!" Laurel yelled. "I can't believe . . . what the . . . forget it!" she said, raising her hands sharply to cut off all protests. "You want me to choose? Fine, I'll choose. I choose to walk away from you both! I don't want either of you if you're going to act like this. I'm through." She spun on her heel and started shoving her way toward the front doors.

"Laurel!" The desperation in David's voice made Laurel stop and turn.

"No," she said levelly. "I'm not going to do this again. We're done." She didn't look back as she broke into a run. She heard footsteps behind her, but she couldn't stop—wouldn't stop.

"Mr. Lawson! What is the meaning of this!" She'd recognize his voice anywhere; it was Mr. Roster, the vice principal. "Mr. Collins! Tam Collins, come back here this instant!"

Laurel kept going and no one called after her. She shot through the front doors, grateful she'd driven that morning instead of riding with David—or Tamani. She jammed the keys in the ignition and for the first time she could remember, peeled out of her parking spot. The asphalt lot was not yet thick with milling students and Laurel didn't touch her brakes until she pulled up to the first stop sign.

Her hands naturally steered her to the 101 and it wasn't until she was halfway there that she realized she was heading to her old house. She found it rather ironic that since moving away from Orick, she'd mostly gone there to see Tamani. Now she was running away from him.

And David.

She didn't want to think about that.

There was some light rain on the way down, but Laurel

didn't bother to close her windows. Her windshield was spotted and her hair a little damp, but she just pushed it away from her face. It began raining in earnest as she pulled into the unpaved driveway, and the clatter of raindrops tumbling through the canopy grew almost deafening. Laurel rolled up her windows, pushed open her door, and decided to take shelter in the cabin instead of the forest.

Besides, she was in no mood for lectures from Shar. He *might* follow her into the house, but in the forest he would be unavoidable.

Absently, Laurel fiddled with the knotted sash that kept her blossom bound. Her wilting petals didn't spring up so much as sag out, shifting gradually into place as she walked toward the cabin door with her shirt hiked to the bottom of her ribs. She jiggled her key in the deadbolt—sticky from disuse—and finally managed to make it turn. She had just laid a hand on the doorknob when she heard another vehicle crunch down the long driveway. She glanced around for something she could use as a weapon, then realized if it was anyone hostile, the sentries would handle them.

But when Tamani's convertible appeared around the bend, a whole new kind of fear set in.

His top was down and he was soaking wet. "Laurel!" he called, springing out of the seat almost before his car stopped rolling.

"No!" Laurel called over the rain, which drummed heavily on the tin roof of the cabin's small porch. She pressed her back against the door, her hand still tight around the doorknob. "I came here to get *away* from you!"

Tamani paused at the small wooden gate, his hand resting on the fence post. Then he strode forward, his eyes filled with purpose.

"I don't want you here," Laurel said as he drew closer.

"I'm already here," he said softly. He was just inches away from her, but he didn't touch her. Didn't even try. "The question now is whether you want me to *leave*."

"I do," Laurel said, her voice barely loud enough to be heard over the rain.

"Why?"

"You . . . you make everything confusing," she said, her emotions overflowing into stinging tears that she swiped at with angry hands.

"I could say the same about you," Tamani said, his eyes boring into hers.

"So why are you here?"

He lifted his hands and made as if to lay them on her arms, but just before they touched he stopped and let them fall. Then, simply, as though it were all the explanation she could ever need, he said, "Because I love you."

"You have a funny way of showing it."

A heavy sigh escaped Tamani's lips. "Look, not my finest moment, obviously. I was mad. I'm sorry."

"What about Yuki?"

"Yuki? I—" Tamani frowned, his brow furrowed in thought. Then his eyes widened as realization dawned. "Oh, Laurel, you don't think—"

"She really likes you."

"And I would trade every minute I have ever spent with her for one second with you. Every instant I'm with Yuki is an act, a game. I have to find out what she is, what she knows, to keep *you* safe!"

Laurel swallowed hard. His words *sounded* like truth. For a moment she pondered whether this truly *was* all the explanation she ever needed. But she mustered her resolve; he had only answered half of the question she really needed to know. And as he could not read her mind, if she wanted an answer she was going to have to ask.

"Would it hurt you more if I was with David because I loved him, or if I was with David because I wanted to make you jealous?"

"Hurt—?" Tamani started immediately, before the analogy could sink in. Then he stopped and studied her, as they stood beneath the cabin's porch, the rainfall settling into a steady liquid hiss against rooftop and treetop alike. And though it was the only sound for miles, she couldn't hear it over the sound of her own ragged breath.

Quietly, almost too quietly to hear, Tamani spoke. "I would never do something just to hurt you."

"No?" Laurel asked, much louder than Tamani, her voice rising louder with every word as she finally asked the question that felt like it had torn deeper into her every day. "What about at the dance? You were dancing with Yuki and I looked at you. And you turned away and held her closer. Why did you do that? If you didn't want to hurt me, then why?"

He looked away, as though slapped, but he didn't look guilty. He looked *pained*. "I closed my eyes," he said, his voice so low and strangled she could hardly hear him.

"What?" she asked, not understanding.

Tamani held up a hand and Laurel realized he hadn't finished—he was having trouble speaking at all. "I closed my eyes," he repeated after a few shallow breaths, "and imagined she was you." He looked at her, his face open, his eyes honest, his voice a song of anguish.

Without thinking, Laurel pulled him to her and her mouth met his with a passion, a hunger, she felt powerless to fight. He braced himself against the door frame with both hands, as though he were afraid to touch her. She tasted the sweetness of his mouth, felt the strength of his body against hers. She still had one hand on the doorknob, so she turned it. Their combined weight sent the door flying open and, stumbling backward, her fist tangled in his hair, Laurel pulled Tamani in after her.

# TWENTY-THREE

THEY REALLY HAD STAYED TOO LONG—IT WOULD BE nearly dark when they got back—but they'd kept finding reasons to stay. To linger in the empty cabin, holding hands, or laughing at memories of Laurel's childhood, or stealing just one more kiss—one kiss that turned into two, then ten, then twenty. She knew that once they left the cabin, everything would get complicated again. But for those few hours, in the empty house with no electricity, phone, internet, or television, the world was theirs alone.

But they couldn't keep night from falling. She had considered just staying—she was safe at the cabin, maybe even safer than at home. But though it was Tamani's job to keep *her* safe, it was her job to keep her family safe. And she couldn't do that from fifty miles away. Besides, her parents were probably worried. By the time she had collected herself enough to remember that Tamani had a cell phone, they were in separate cars, headed back to Crescent City.

The drive went much too quickly and soon she was within a few blocks of her house. She looked in her rearview mirror and waved at Tamani as he peeled off and headed to his apartment, watching his taillights until they disappeared. It was only when someone honked behind her that she realized she'd been sitting at a green light.

Stars were peeking out behind the clouds by the time Laurel pulled into her driveway. She was going to be in so much trouble. Her mom's car was in the garage, though it didn't look like her dad was home yet. Pocketing her keys, Laurel attempted to sneak into the house and was immediately foiled by her mother sitting in the front room sipping a cup of tea and reading a gardening magazine.

Laurel shut the door behind her. "Um, hi," Laurel finally said.

Her mom studied her for a minute. "I got an interesting call from the school's attendance office today."

Laurel cringed on the inside. She busied herself with loosening her petals from their silken bonds.

"You were absent from all your afternoon classes."

The speech she'd planned all the way home evaporated. So she remained silent. A single petal came free with her scarf, and Laurel wondered if she would lose them all tonight, or if this one had been jarred loose by the day's activities.

"And then you walk in after seven o'clock on a school night—with no word whatsoever—and your eyes are sparkling like I haven't seen them in weeks," she finished, her voice soft.

"I'm sorry I worried you," Laurel said, trying to sound sincere while suppressing a smile. Her apology *was* sincere, but a guilty smile would undermine that.

"I wasn't worried for long," her mom said, swinging her legs over the side of the couch. "I'm a quick learner. I went out to the backyard and talked to your sentry friend, Aaron."

Laurel's eyes widened. "You talked to Aaron?"

"He told me Tamani checked in at about noon and told them you were safe with him. So I stopped worrying."

"That was enough to make you stop worrying?"

"Well, I stopped worrying about your *safety*, anyway. I saw the look in that boy's eyes the other night. There's no way he would let anything happen to you."

That grin she just couldn't stop curled back onto her face.

"Don't think that gets you off the hook though; you're still in trouble. We'll talk punishment when your father gets home." She sobered now. "Seriously, Laurel. What were you thinking? Does David know where you are?"

Laurel's face fell and she shook her head.

"Is he at home worried sick?"

"Probably." She felt awful.

"Did you want to call him?"

She shook her head in a stiff, jerky way.

"Oh." Then a long pause. "Come in the kitchen," she said finally, pulling gently on Laurel's arm. "I'll make you a cup of tea."

As far as her mom was concerned, tea fixed everything. Have a cold? Have some tea. Broken bones? There's tea for that too. Somewhere in her mother's pantry, Laurel suspected, was a box of tea that said, *In case of Armageddon, steep three to five minutes.*

Laurel sat on a barstool and watched as her mom fixed her a cup of tea, then stirred in ice cubes until it was cool.

"I noticed you losing a petal there," her mom said conversationally. "Would you mind if I preserved a few? They really smell fantastic. I bet I could make a killer potpourri."

"Um, sure," Laurel said, trying not to feel too weird about her mom making something out of her petals.

"You get rained on much today?"

"A bit."

"Well," Laurel's mom said after spooning some sugar into the tea, just the way Laurel liked it, "that's all the small talk I've got. Are you going to tell me what happened?"

Laurel put it off just a few more seconds as she sipped her tea. "David and Tamani got in a fight at lunch. A fistfight. Over me," she finally said.

"David? Really?"

"I know, right? But they've been angry and mopey lately. And there have been little confrontations the last couple weeks. I guess they just blew up today."

Her mom was smiling now. "I never had two boys fight over me."

"You say that like it's fun. It's *not* fun!" Laurel protested. "It was awful. I broke up the fight, but it was just too much. So I left."

"And . . . Tamani followed you?"

Laurel nodded.

"Where did you go?"

"To the cabin in Orick."

"And Tamani joined you?"

"I didn't ask him to," Laurel said defensively.

"But he did."

Laurel nodded.

"And you let him."

Another nod.

"And then . . ." Her mom let the question hang in the air.

"And then we went to the cabin. And hung out," she tacked on, feeling like a moron.

"Hung out," her mom said wryly. "Is that what the cool kids are calling it these days?"

Laurel rested her face against her palms. "It wasn't . . . like that," she muttered through her fingers.

"Oh, really?"

"Okay, fine. It was kind of like that," Laurel said.

"Laurel." Her mom walked around the counter and put her arms around Laurel, leaning her cheek against the top of her head. "It's all right. You don't have to defend yourself to me. I'd be lying if I told you I was surprised."

"Am I really so predictable?"

"Only to a mother," her mom said, kissing the top of her head. "I have an idea. Why don't you call Chelsea and tell her everything's okay, and she can pass the word on to David. He's called here twice already."

"Good idea." Laurel smiled up at her mom, if a little weakly. In truth Chelsea wasn't a lot easier to face than David, but after today she'd take what she could get.

★ ★ ★

"Homigosh," Chelsea said breathlessly before Laurel even said hello. *Thank you, caller ID.* "You broke up with David!"

Laurel winced. "Yeah, I guess I kind of did," she admitted.

"In front of the whole school!"

"I didn't mean for it to happen in front of the whole school."

"So you meant for it to happen?"

Laurel sighed, glad she'd decided to call Chelsea from the privacy of her room instead of downstairs in front of her mom. "No, I didn't mean for it to happen."

"So are you taking it back?"

"No," Laurel said, strangely sure of her answer, "I'm not taking it back."

"Seriously?"

"Yes. At least . . . for now."

"So what does that mean? Are you with Tamani now?"

*After this afternoon?* "I—I don't know," she admitted.

"But maybe?"

"Maybe."

"Whoa."

"I know." Laurel toyed with a sugar-glass vial on her desk. She had no idea what to say. "I, um, I called to tell you I'm okay since I disappeared kinda fast today. And in case you were worried . . ." Her voice trailed off as she heard a soft tap and spun around to catch a hint of movement outside her bedroom window. Tamani raised his head and smiled. Laurel smiled back and almost let go of the phone. "Hey,

Chelsea, I gotta go," she said breathlessly. "Dinner."

"At eight o'clock?"

"Yeah," Laurel said, remembering the whole reason for calling in the first place. "Could you . . . would you mind calling him and telling him I'm safe?"

"Him? Like, David?"

"Yeah. Please?"

She heard Chelsea sigh and mutter something about shooting the messenger. "You want me to tell him anything else?"

"No. Just that I'm safe. I gotta go. Thanks, Chelsea, bye," she said in a rush before hitting END and tossing the cordless onto her bed. She hurried over to the window seat and unlatched her window.

"May I come in?" Tamani asked, his smile gentle, eyes warm.

"Sure," Laurel said, returning his smile. "But you'll have to be quiet; my mom's downstairs and my dad should be home any minute."

"I'm good at quiet," Tamani said, stepping silently over the windowsill in bare feet.

Laurel left the window open, enjoying the lingering scent of rain. She stared down at her carpet. Then Tamani reached over and curled his fingers around hers. He pulled her gently toward him and twined his arms around her waist. "I missed you," he whispered in her ear.

She pulled her head back and looked up at him. "I didn't think I'd see you till tomorrow."

243

He reached up and covered her hand with his, then lifted it to his lips and slowly kissed each fingertip. "Did you really think I could stay away?"

He let go of her hand and lifted her chin. He kissed her eyelids first, one then the other, and Laurel stood very still, her breath shallow, as he kissed each cheek, then her chin, then her nose. She wanted to grab him, to pull him in and reignite the sparks that had blazed between them this afternoon, but she forced herself to hold still as he lowered his lips to hers, the sweetness of his mouth enveloping hers. So slowly, so gently.

She lifted her hands to the sides of his face when he started to pull away. She couldn't bear for this sweet kiss to end. His arms tightened around her in response and Laurel pressed her body against him, wishing—for a moment—that she could be part of him.

She turned when a knock sounded on her door. "Yeah?" she asked, hoping she didn't sound as breathless as she felt. The knob turned and before Laurel could say anything, the door opened.

"Your dad's home," her mom said. "Come on down and face the music."

Laurel turned very slightly and looked out from the corner of her eye.

No Tamani.

She nodded and followed her mom out the door, hardly daring to look back.

★ ★ ★

244

"So what's the damage?" Tamani was sprawled on Laurel's bed, startling her as she closed her bedroom door.

"Where were you?" Laurel asked in a whisper.

"When in doubt, head under the bed," Tamani said with a grin.

"But there wasn't time," Laurel protested.

"Time enough for me."

Laurel shook her head. "I thought we were busted."

"Are *you* busted?" Tamani asked. Laurel wondered if he'd ever said *busted* before in his life.

"I'm grounded for a week," she said, shrugging as she sat beside Tamani. It still felt strange, having him here. It was one thing to lose herself in a kiss, but having a mundane conversation with Tamani felt awkward. It wasn't like talking to David, who was a fixture in her life—comfortably familiar, like a favorite pair of slippers. Could Tamani replace that, now that he lived close by? Now that she saw him every day?

"Does that mean I should leave you alone this week, so you can feel the full weight of your punishment?" Tamani said, his face serious.

Laurel's eyes widened, but Tamani's mouth twitched into a grin and she whacked his arm.

He caught her hand and held it for a moment before tucking his fingers between hers and pulling her down against his chest. "Does that mean it's okay if I come keep you company?" he asked quietly, before turning to look at her with his pale, intense eyes.

Laurel hesitated. She'd been with David for almost two

years, had loved him every day. And even though she'd broken up with him, just having Tamani here felt a little like cheating. She was tired of David's jealousy, of his mood swings, but did that mean she wasn't in love with him anymore? Besides, David wasn't the only one she'd told off today. She had little doubt that Tamani had picked that fight, but here she was, rewarding his efforts. His virtues shined too brightly for her to focus on his flaws. Did that mean she *was* in love with Tamani?

Was it possible to be in love with two people at the same time?

"You going to sleep?" Tamani whispered.

"Mmm?" Laurel replied, her eyes fluttering open.

Tamani bent his head a little closer to her ear. "Can I stay?" he whispered.

Laurel opened her eyes all the way now. "Here?"

He nodded.

"Like, all night?"

His arms pushed a little farther around her. "Please? Just to sleep."

She tilted her head up, kissing him quickly to soften her answer. "No."

"Why not?"

"It's just weird." She shrugged. "Plus, my parents would hate it."

"They don't have to know," Tamani said with a grin.

"I know," Laurel said seriously, putting a hand on Tamani's chest. "But *I* would know. I don't like lying to them. Things have been way better since I started telling them the truth. Waaaay better."

"You didn't tell them I was up here before, or that I'm planning on being around this week."

"No, but those are small things. This feels like a big thing."

"Okay," Tamani responded, leaning forward to kiss her one more time. He smiled as their foreheads and the tips of their noses touched. "I don't want to go, but I will if you say so."

Laurel smiled. "I say so," she answered, yawning.

The next morning, Laurel couldn't remember how he'd left, or when. But he was gone, and a single wildflower lay beside her pillow.

# TWENTY-FOUR

LAUREL SAT IN HER CAR, STALLING, FEAR BUILDING up in her stomach. It was almost worse than that first day of school, more than two years ago. Back then she had been paranoid about embarrassing herself in front of a bunch of complete strangers. Now she had to go in and face the fact that she had embarrassed herself in front of a bunch of people she knew.

Among them, David.

She didn't think she'd ever been afraid to see David. Feelings warred within her—part of her missed him and didn't want to admit it. Part of her was glad she'd broken up with him and shown him for once that she was serious. And yet another part of her wanted to run to him in tears and beg his forgiveness.

She locked her car, wondering if she could just linger in the parking lot and be late. But after ditching yesterday, she couldn't risk it. Her parents had agreed that, under the circumstances, Laurel's punishment belonged at home, not in the school system, so her mom had called in and excused her absences. But Laurel knew she would be expected to follow *all* the rules at school for a while.

With a sigh, Laurel forced herself to head for her locker.

As she approached the double doors at the front of the school, one swung open, revealing David. Laurel stopped in her tracks and stared. He looked so sad. It wasn't that he was frowning—in fact he had mustered a reasonably convincing smile. But his eyes were deep-blue pools of sorrow so intense, it took her breath away.

"Hi, Laurel," he said, his voice barely more than a whisper.

The part of her that wanted to run to him and throw herself into his arms got a boost from that.

And then Tamani was there, holding the other door open. "Hi, Laurel," he said, his smile brash, cocky.

Laurel's legs felt shaky. "Don't do this." A strangled plea.

David turned on his heel and strode away without another word. But Tamani looked confused.

"I just didn't want him pestering—"

Laurel grabbed the front of Tamani's shirt and dragged him around the side of the building.

"Hey, if you wanted to sneak off with me you only had to ask," Tamani said with a laugh. But his smile melted away when he saw Laurel's face. "What's the matter?" he asked earnestly.

"I'm not your girlfriend, Tam."

"Well, obviously I can't kiss you in front of Yuki, but—"

"No. I care about you. And I don't regret what happened yesterday, but I don't know what it means. I'm still trying to figure things out. Breaking up with David doesn't make you my boyfriend by default."

Tamani hesitated, then asked, "So I'm back to waiting again?"

"Kind of. Maybe. I don't know! But no matter what, I'm not a weapon. I will not let you use me to get back at him."

"He did. All the time," Tamani said hotly.

"Yes," Laurel agreed, "and then he got dumped. Is that what you want?"

Tamani finally started to look cowed.

"I don't *want* a boyfriend right now, and if you want me to ever reconsider that, I expect you to behave." She gave him the sternest glare she could and he looked away.

"So are you and David really over?" Tamani finally asked.

"I don't know," Laurel said. It was the only answer she could give. "For now, yes. I need some time. Some time to just be myself. By myself. And it's for your sake too," Laurel continued before Tamani could respond. "You don't just stop loving someone in one day. It's not that simple."

"The best things in life rarely are." Tamani sighed shakily as the warning bell sounded, startling Laurel.

"We should get to class. I really can't be late."

Tamani nodded. His smile was tight, but he seemed to be okay. As okay as he was going to get, under the circumstances.

Impulsively, Laurel threw her arms around him and pressed herself against his chest. He didn't try to kiss her, and she didn't offer, but it was enough just to feel his arms around her. To know that somehow, everything would work out.

With one last squeeze Laurel turned back toward the front entrance and nearly dropped her backpack when she saw Shar approaching them through the parking lot, dressed in jeans and a loose T-shirt, his hair pulled into a simple ponytail that hung at the nape of his neck.

"What's he doing here?"

"Oh," Tamani said, as if only just remembering, "the vice principal wants to talk to me and my 'uncle.' About, um, yesterday." Tamani shrugged.

Laurel raised an eyebrow as Shar got closer, his steely eyes taking everything in. "Well, despite the fact that this is a sight I would love to see, I have to go." And with that, she pivoted toward the front doors, breaking into a jog as she tried to beat the final bell.

"Mr. Collins," Vice Principal Roster said, opening a file and placing it on his desk before sitting in his squeaking chair.

*Hate him*, thought Tamani.

"Thank you for coming," the vice principal said, looking up at Shar.

As Tamani had expected, Shar refused to sit at all. He just stood with his arms folded across his chest, looking down at the human with an unmistakable air of superiority. Tamani rarely saw him look any other way and contemplated briefly how often Shar must have looked at his companion, Ariana, that way, and what she'd done to break him of the habit. He had to cough to cover the chuckle that escaped his throat.

Shar's eyes darted between Tamani and the principal. "Of course," he said smoothly. "What seems to be the problem?"

"Tam was in a fight yesterday," the vice principal said, looking sternly at Tamani.

Shar didn't even blink. "My understanding is that Tam was assaulted and defended himself."

Mr. Roster stuttered. "Um, yes, well, but there was a great deal of pushing before that, provoking an outburst from—"

"So because this other boy lacked self-control, my"—he hesitated—"nephew is to be punished?"

"Both boys were fully involved in the exchange of blows, and both boys will be punished, per our policy," Mr. Roster said, his voice firm now. "As this is Tam's first offense, of course we hope this incident won't be repeated—"

"It won't," Shar said, raising an eyebrow at Tam. And indeed, Tamani had been taken to task about letting his temper get the better of him, particularly when it came to David, who with his knowledge of Avalon could make a lot of trouble for them if ever he felt so inclined. The tongue-lashing Tamani had gotten from his superior was far worse than anything this human administrator could hope to dole out.

"I'm happy to hear that. Now, Mr. Collins, I wanted to take this opportunity to discuss something else. You may not realize that your nephew is failing almost every class he is currently enrolled in. His attendance is abysmal, and he is, in general, disruptive to the classroom environment."

Tamani knew that last part was a blatant lie. He was never a disruption. He never raised his hand to answer a question, either, but for the most part, he simply sat in his classes and listened for any sign that something had entered the school intent on harming Laurel. If you didn't take his grades and occasional disappearances into account, he was a model pupil.

"What does that mean?" Shar's voice was flat and Vice Principal Roster was clearly unnerved.

"Er, well, we typically suspend students for fighting, but with three F's, one D, and one B, we thought some alternative discipline might be in order. To encourage . . . improvement."

Shar stared at Mr. Roster blankly for a moment and Tamani tried not to smirk. For all his training at the manor, Shar had never had reason to learn the intricacies of the human grading system. But he was unfazed.

"What can be done?" Tamani noticed for the first time just how anachronistic Shar sounded, especially compared to the teenagers Tamani conversed with every day. It really was a good thing their English was accented—a good accent seemed to cover all kinds of quirks in grammar.

"Well, if he wants to graduate with his classmates, he's got to pull his grades up." The vice principal folded his hands on top of the desk in front of him. "I thought perhaps some tutoring?"

"Of course. If that's what it takes." He clapped Tamani on the shoulder in a move that Tamani knew looked friendly to the untrained eye—but he'd have a bruise there later. "We want Tam to graduate, naturally." The vice principal would hear earnestness in those words, but only because Shar had grown weary of this meeting; a light warmth in Tamani's chest told him Enticement was at work. Shar and Tamani had agreed there were too many anonymous witnesses to effectively erase the fight, so in order to maintain perfect cover, no memory potions would be administered and Tamani would accept whatever punishment the school assigned him—assuming it didn't compromise his mission. But Shar had also allowed that, as long as Yuki wasn't close enough to potentially sense it, Enticement could be used to ease the process.

It would be Shar's job rather than Tamani's, though. Shar was extremely talented and could work his Enticement without physical contact—something Tamani had always been jealous of.

"Naturally," Vice Principal Roster said, smiling now. "Now, David Lawson—that's the boy Tam was fighting—is one of our finest students. We're giving both David and Tam three days in-school suspension and we thought perhaps David could spend those days tutoring your nephew. I think you'll agree this is very lenient, and will hopefully give the boys an opportunity to work through their differences."

Tamani bit back a sigh. What a colossal waste of time.

"They will be supervised, of course," the vice principal

continued, as if Shar cared. "Now if I can have you sign some paperwork," he said, sliding a piece of paper forward.

Tamani shot a look at Shar, but Shar either didn't see or chose to ignore it. "That's fine," he said. He took the pen and managed an illegible scrawl across the signature line.

"Excellent," Vice Principal Roster said, rising from his chair and shaking hands with Shar. "We want nothing more than for our students to succeed, and parents, or uncles in your case, are the biggest factor in that."

"We will make sure things improve," Shar said. "I'll take Tam out to the parking lot and chat for a while before I send him back into class."

"Good, good," the vice principal said proudly, surely assuming Tamani was about to receive further discipline. He opened the door and gestured to the hallway.

Tamani felt the human's eyes on them all the way down the hallway and out the front doors. They walked silently to Tamani's convertible, where Shar stopped and leaned against it, turning to face Tamani.

"Well, young man," he said, his face serious, "what do you have to say for yourself?"

They stared at each other for a moment longer. Tamani broke first, a quick chuckle escaping his lips, and then both faeries burst out laughing.

# TWENTY-FIVE

SPEECH CLASS WAS PAINFUL.

Laurel could feel the tension in the room and knew there was no way anyone else missed it. Especially with the way everyone kept glancing at David and Tamani, who very carefully avoided even looking at each other. She'd overheard Tamani telling Yuki that he had to serve three days of in-school suspension with David, but she hadn't had a chance to talk to either of them about it. David had spent his lunch hour in the office with his mom and the vice principal, and Tamani had spent his lunch hour with Yuki. Chelsea was away at a cross-country meet, so Laurel had spent her lunch hour fretting. Alone.

"Okay," Mr. Petersen said, finally starting the class about a minute after the bell rang. Longest minute of Laurel's life. "You've all had a chance to present your own speeches. But giving a speech sometimes has very little to do with the words you are actually saying. Today you will all be giving someone else's speech."

He waited, as if expecting a reaction. What he got was silence.

"Each of you will be handed a personal ad; you will have sixty seconds to read it over, and thirty seconds to present it."

Now the murmurs started.

"Your goal," Mr. Petersen said above the buzz, "as a persuasive speaker, is to convince the members of this class that they should meet you. Over nonalcoholic drinks, of course," he added, chuckling at his own lame joke. After another moment of silence, he cleared his throat and continued. "I spent a long time preparing these materials. I think I'll make it ten percent of your presentation grade this month," he declared. "Don't take it lightly!" The class groaned and Mr. Petersen raised both hands in the air. "The assignments will be random. Just give it a chance! You might be surprised how fun this can be."

No one seemed convinced.

Laurel spent the next fifteen minutes completely mortified on behalf of her classmates and dreading her turn at the front of the classroom. Mostly it was a lot of pretend puppy eyes and exaggerated poses as people read Mr. Petersen's hokey personals. Laurel wondered if adults really wrote things about themselves like *I'm a sweet Romeo without a Juliet* or *I'm sassy, sultry, and super-fun*, and how serious they could possibly be if they did.

"Tam Collins."

Several of the girls sitting near Laurel began whispering excitedly. Clearly, they hadn't lost hope. Laurel wanted to sink into her chair and die.

Tamani took the small piece of paper from Mr. Petersen and stood at the front of the classroom, studying it for his sixty seconds.

"And begin . . . now," Mr. Petersen said, leaning back in his chair and crossing his arms over his chest.

Tamani looked up from his paper and, instead of starting to speak, he took a few seconds to lock eyes with several of the girls in the class.

"Single Scottish male," he said, his voice low, his accent more pronounced, "seeks beautiful woman."

Every human girl in the classroom sighed as one. Laurel wondered how many other liberties Tamani would take with the assigned speech.

"I'm looking for that special person, the one who can complete me. I need someone to share my life and my heart. More than just a fun time, I'm looking for commitment and . . . intimacy." At that point, if anyone else had been speaking, there would have been whistles and catcalls. Coming from Tamani's lips, the phrase actually sounded inviting, sexy.

"I am a twentysomething who likes loud music, fine food, and"—he paused dramatically—"physical activity. I'm looking for someone creative, artistic"—his eyes flitted to Laurel's, for just a second—"musical, to share my love of beautiful things. Are you looking for something real in this world of illusions? Call me. Casual flings need not apply. *I am looking for love.*"

Without another word, Tamani crumpled his ad in his hand, shoved it in his pocket, and took his seat.

Every girl in the room burst into applause and a few shrill whistles.

Laurel cringed and dropped her head to her desk. There was no digging out of this hole.

After school, Laurel practically ran to her car. She knew she'd done poorly on her own personal ad speech, but seriously, who could expect anything else today?

She had managed to go the whole day without speaking to David, but she couldn't put it off forever. She had no idea what to say. That she still loved him, she just didn't know if she loved him like that? Or that she wasn't sure she could live the rest of her life without getting a chance to be with Tamani—really be with him—with a clear conscience, to see if it was as good as she dreamed? That she had made a snap decision, it had been a mistake, and she wanted him back? That she needed space—from both of them, maybe— to decide *what* she wanted?

It hadn't felt like a mistake, back at the land. But this morning, seeing David's face—it made her ache for him. She wanted to make everything better. Was that because she loved him as a friend, or because she wanted him back?

Did he want *her* back?

That was something she couldn't consider as she locked

her car and walked into the very empty house where, she had been reminded by her mom that morning, she was to stay. Easy enough—she had plenty of homework to do. And she could work on figuring out what kind of faerie Yuki was. Laurel could hardly believe it had been two weeks since the troll attack. It felt like ages. Time was like that, though—racing forward when she wanted it to slow down, then crawling to a stop when she could least bear it.

But rather than heading straight for her room, Laurel flipped idly through a stack of mail on the counter. She was still frustrated by not finding out anything conclusive from the phosphorescent tests. Tamani's sap had glowed for just under forty minutes—a little longer than Laurel's. She had hoped to find a substantial difference between the kinds of fae, but apparently sap wasn't going to do it—at least not without samples from a lot more faeries. She wished she could just assume Yuki was a Spring based on probability, but assumptions were a luxury she couldn't afford.

Beneath a Publishers Clearing House postcard Laurel encountered a large envelope with her name on it. Her SAT scores! She'd all but forgotten about them; she'd taken the test so long ago. When she and David were together. When they'd studied every day to improve her scores. They had both planned on checking online, to get their scores early, but Laurel was clearly not the only one who had forgotten. She grabbed the letter opener from the mail rack and sliced open the top of the envelope, then stood clutching it in both hands for a long moment before she reached in and pulled out the small stack of papers.

When she finally managed to locate her scores, Laurel squealed.

Mid six-hundreds and a 580. A *huge* improvement. Laurel ran to the phone and dialed half of David's number before she realized what she was doing. This was never what she intended. No matter what happened, she at least wanted them to be friends. It wasn't until that very moment that she realized it simply might not be possible.

*No.*

She would never know if she didn't try. She finished dialing his number.

"Hello?"

"David?"

"Hello?"

It was David's voice mail. He thought it was clever to pretend he was really answering the phone. Laurel found it irritating, but she hadn't left him a voice mail in months.

"You know what? Just leave a message."

Laurel hung up. He would see the missed call and who it was from. If he'd gotten his envelope today, he'd probably be able to guess why she was calling.

Laurel sank down onto a barstool, her scores held loosely in her hand, feeling deflated. Obviously, breaking up with David wasn't the answer to all of her problems. It was its own problem. And the longer she waited to solve it, the more likely it was that David would move on, making the decision for her.

David moving on. It was a horrifying thought.

She grabbed her scores and her backpack and started up the stairs. She had to cool things off with Tamani and decide what she really wanted. She had chosen David before, one hundred percent, and for a long time it had been wonderful. She wanted that feeling again, but first she had to figure out who she wanted it *with*. And maybe that was going to require no kissing for a while. No kissing anyone. She needed a clear head.

Laurel startled when someone rapped quietly on her door.

"Can I come in?"

Tamani.

Laurel shoved her scores under her backpack and went to her bedroom door, hesitating a moment before letting him in.

"Sorry for not waiting at the front door," he said apologetically. "But with you being grounded I figure it's better if no one sees you let me in."

"You've finally learned about my spying neighbors," Laurel said, forcing a laugh.

Tamani studied his shoes for a moment. Then he looked up, smiled, and stepped forward, arms open.

Every resolve, every promise she had made to herself about taking time to clear her head, crumbled as she folded herself into his arms. She clung to him and even when he pulled back, ever so gently, she held him harder. One more second and she would let him go.

One more.

Or two more.

Finally she made her arms drop and forced herself not to look up at him. If she did, there would be nothing to stop her from kissing him, and once that happened, it would be over. She would want nothing but him for the rest of the afternoon.

"So," Laurel said as she sat down on her desk chair—where he definitely couldn't sit beside her—"how was your chat with Roster?"

"Ridiculous. Pointless." Tamani rolled his eyes. He sat on her bed and lounged on one elbow. She had to grip the arms of her chair to remain seated—every ounce of her wanted to join him. To snuggle against his chest with her head tucked under his chin, feeling the vibrations in his throat when he talked and—

*Focus!*

"What's your punishment?" Laurel asked, not wanting to admit she'd been eavesdropping on the school gossip and had a pretty good idea already.

"Three days in-school suspension. *David*"—he said David's name like it was a bad word—"is going to tutor me, to save my grades."

"Are you serious?" Laurel asked, louder than she had intended. None of her sources had told her they would be working together. This was bad.

Tamani scoffed.

"Well." Laurel was silent for a few seconds. "He actually *is* a really great tutor." She knew it put Tamani on edge when she praised David, but how could she not? After years of homeschooling, it was David who'd taught her how to cope with the public school system.

"I don't doubt it. But the whole concept of grades is pretty insulting. I've never seen a more arbitrary, uninformative metric. The way humans measure their differences is—"

"Worse than the way you do it in Avalon?"

Tamani pursed his lips. "Well, anyway, it's just a good thing I'm not really a student. I'd have to do something drastic. I don't know what I'm going to do with David for three days."

"Be nice to him," Laurel said.

"We're going to be supervised, Laurel."

"I mean it. No bragging, no taunting, nothing. Be nice."

"No taunting, I promise."

Laurel nodded approvingly, but she wasn't sure what else to say. Finally she decided to just change the subject. "So Shar's here now?"

Tamani shook his head. "Just for a few days. He has duties back at the land."

"How does he get here? Does he have a car too?" The idea of the faeries all driving around in cars made Laurel laugh.

But Tamani looked a little chagrined. "Tamani de Rhoslyn, sentry, *Fear-gleidhidh*, and chauffeur, at your service."

"When? I thought you watched me, like, all the time."

"Less when I know you're at home. And in for the night. And don't forget," he added with a grin, "I have a cell phone—Aaron can call me if anything goes wrong." He leaned forward, his partially unbuttoned shirt affording her a splendid view. "And then I come rushing back to save you."

Laurel quelled the giddy warmth that was spreading through her limbs. "That's good," she said. Then, realizing that maybe—maybe—her chest wouldn't feel quite so tight if her ribs weren't bound with a sash, she untied the knot and let her limp petals go free. What was left of them. They'd been falling out all day. By tomorrow morning she could stop hiding entirely. That was going to be a relief.

She was momentarily frozen in place by the realization that this might be the last time she would ever have to hide it. If she were in Avalon, it wouldn't be necessary. College, on the other hand, meant at least four more years of binding down her blossom. Her SAT scores were still hidden underneath her backpack. They were high enough to get into a good college. They even gave her a reasonable shot at Berkeley. Last spring Laurel's below-average scores had pretty much made up her mind for her—especially since they'd been followed by a stellar summer at the Academy. But now? There was a whole new road she could take, if she wanted.

Options were beginning to feel more like a burden than a blessing.

# TWENTY-SIX

THREE WHOLE DAYS, LOCKED IN A ROOM WITH MR. Robison and David.

Doing homework.

Pretending to do homework.

And trading glares.

The first day, David had done more glaring than Tamani. But then, considering Tamani was the winner, it was only fitting.

Well, kind of the winner.

For one perfect day Tamani had actually wondered if he could perish of happiness. Being with Laurel, really with her, holding her in his arms as she smiled up at him—it was better than he had ever dreamed. Everything else in his life paled in comparison. Becoming the youngest commanding sentry in three generations? A minor success. Training as the leading expert on applied human interaction? Nothing more than a means to an end. But being with Laurel? This was his crowning achievement, and he had surprised himself with how easily he slipped into the role. How perfectly she fit in his arms. The complete joy he felt when she smiled at him. Nothing else mattered.

He would get that back. He'd thought himself determined before, but he'd only been chasing a dream. Now he knew what he was missing and he could do anything if it meant one more day like the one they'd shared at the cabin.

When Tamani realized he was smiling, he cleared his throat and forced himself to look dour again and pretend to focus on David's explanation of the Pythagorean theorem. *What a waste of time.*

"Boys, if you'll excuse me, you seem to be doing fine on that assignment. I need to step out for a moment."

Tamani suppressed a chuckle. Their "supervision" was a joke. Mr. Robison had left the room fourteen times today—twice as many as yesterday. And whenever he did, David would just shut down. He wouldn't respond to anything Tamani said. He'd just sit and stare at the whiteboards hung at the front of the room. When Mr. Robison returned, David would launch back into whatever halfhearted tutorial they'd been on before. It was uncanny, really—he'd just start up exactly where he'd left off. Mr. Robison didn't seem to notice.

What got Tamani was the way David seemed to be brooding almost as much over this punishment as over losing Laurel. As far as Tamani was concerned, punishments were just part of life. You suffered them and went on your way—there was no reason to stop and regret.

Tamani sure didn't.

He wondered if humans couldn't escape their anxieties because they were always cooped up. It must be hard to cope when a person couldn't breathe fresh air and work things out constructively, with some honest physical labor. Before Tamani was ten years old, he had spent several years out in the field with his father, maintaining dams with his sister's companion, or running errands for his mother at the Academy. Humans, on the other hand, were lined up and put in pens like cattle. Perhaps it worked for them—maybe animals liked being boxed up. But Tamani had his doubts.

Mr. Robison had been gone for five minutes. There was only an hour left before the final bell. Tamani wondered if they'd be seeing him again before tomorrow.

"You're fighting a losing battle, you know," Tamani said. "Always were."

Predictably, David said nothing.

"Faeries and humans, they just can't be together. You've had a good run and, quite frankly, I'm glad you were there for her when I couldn't be. But it just won't work. You're too different. We might look the same, but faeries and humans have very little in common."

Still no response.

"You can't have children."

At that, David turned and looked at Tamani. It was the first real response he'd gotten from David since the start of their "suspension." He even opened his mouth to say something, then clamped it shut again and turned away.

"You may as well say it. We're supposed to be working out our differences, right?" Tamani chuckled. "Though maybe these aren't the differences they had in mind."

David eyed Tamani, ignoring the jest.

Tamani was suddenly struck by just how *young* David looked. He forgot, sometimes, that David, Laurel, and their friends were younger, in some ways *much* younger, than Tamani. He was posing as a school-age human, but in truth he was an officer in the Guard. He knew his place, he knew his role, with a certainty some humans never achieved. The amount of freedom human children had must be paralyzing. No wonder they took so long to become adults.

"I'm just trying to help you understand, that's all," Tamani said.

"I don't need your help."

Tamani nodded. He wasn't fond of David, but it was hard to hate him when he was no longer an obstacle to be overcome. In many ways, Tamani could sympathize. And he certainly couldn't fault David's taste.

Fifteen minutes passed in total silence. Then half an hour. Tamani was wondering if he could get away with just disappearing for the last half hour when David spoke.

"A lot of people can't have children—Laurel's parents, for example."

Tamani had already forgotten he'd even mentioned children. It seemed odd that, after almost two whole days of silence, David would latch on to this particular point. "Granted, but—"

"So they adopt. Or they just stay together the two of them. You don't have to have children to be happy."

"Maybe not," Tamani allowed. "But she's also going to live a hundred years longer than you. You really want to make her watch you die? You want to adopt children and make her watch *them* die, of old age, while she still looks forty?"

"You think I haven't thought about that? Life is like that. I mean, not for you, since you have your perfect medicines or whatever." He said the words mockingly and Tamani suppressed his anger—hadn't David benefited from faerie elixirs himself? "But that's how it is here. You don't know if you're going to die next month or next week or in eighty years. It's a chance you take and it's worth it if you really love each other."

"Sometimes love isn't enough."

"That's just something you tell yourself," David said, looking Tamani full in the face. "It makes you sure you'll win in the end."

That stung a little; it *was* something he had told himself, frequently, over the last few years. "I've always been sure I was going to win," Tamani said softly. "I only wanted to know *when*."

David made a soft scoffing sound and looked away.

"Do you remember what I said, about Lancelot?"

"He was Guinevere's faerie guardian," David said, "at least

according to *your* version of the story."

Tamani sighed. The boy was being difficult, but at least he was listening. "*Fear-gleidhidh* does mean 'guardian,' but maybe not in the sense you're thinking. *Fear-gleidhidh* is as much a . . . an overseer as a protector. Lancelot's job included protecting Guinevere's life, but it was also his job to protect Avalon—to do whatever he had to do so that Guinevere could succeed in her mission. To see to it that she didn't back out."

"And you're Laurel's *Fear-gleidhidh.*"

"I don't know how much Laurel has told you about this, but I knew her . . . before. From the day Laurel left Avalon, I did everything I could to become her appointed guardian. Every choice I've made in life—every minute of training— was in pursuit of that position. Because I wanted whoever was out here watching her to be someone who loved her— not some indifferent taskmaster. Who better to guide and protect her than someone who loved her as much as I do?"

David shook his head ruefully and started to speak.

Tamani cut him off. "But I was wrong."

Interest and suspicion showed in David's eyes. "What do you mean?"

"Love clouded my judgment. I knew she valued her privacy, so even though she never knew she was being watched, I scaled down observation at the cabin. Her family moved away while I wasn't looking. Until she came back, I was afraid I'd failed Avalon and Laurel both. We posted sentries here, and I wanted to come—but I wanted to be near Laurel as much as I wanted to protect her—maybe more. So I stayed away because I wanted to come for the wrong reason, and I convinced myself that a bad reason was the same as a bad choice. And now I'm here, and I have to say, watching her with you has been misery. Loving her so much has made me very bad at my job. Like that night with the trolls. I should have gone after them. But I couldn't leave her."

"What if there had been trolls waiting around the corner? What if the first group had been there to simply lure you away?"

Tamani shook his head. "I should have trusted my backups. Don't get me wrong, I intend to do my job. But my reasons for being here are different than the faux-noble ideals I once had. I would die to keep her safe, and I used to think that made me special. But the fact is, so would any of the sentries. And sometimes I wonder if Laurel would be safer with someone else as her *Fear-gleidhidh*."

"So why don't you quit?" David asked.

Tamani laughed and shook his head. "I can't quit."

"No, really. If you think she's safer, wouldn't it be your duty to quit?"

"It doesn't work like that. I took a life oath that bound me to Laurel. This is my job until I die."

"Forever?"

Tamani nodded. "If Laurel is outside Avalon, at any time, she is my responsibility. So if she decides to stay with you and the two of you go traipsing off to college, guess who's coming along?" Tamani pointed an index finger at the ceiling, then spun it to point at himself.

"What!"

"One way or another. I'll watch her from a distance, silently and without her knowledge, if that's what it takes. And no matter how long you live—I'll be around when you're gone. I get to spend my entire life either with Laurel, or watching over her while she's with someone else. Bliss or torture—there's really no middle ground."

"Forgive me for saying I hope it's torture," David said wryly.

"Oh, I understand," Tamani said. "And I don't begrudge you your feelings. But in all that time I worked to become her *Fear-gleidhidh*, I never imagined that my feelings for Laurel would make me a poor protector. And sometimes it gets the better of me and I do things I know I shouldn't." He hesitated. "Like hitting innocent bystanders just to make myself feel better. That was very unprofessional of me and I apologize."

David raised an eyebrow. "Unprofessional?"

"Yes," Tamani replied.

David snickered, coughed, then laughed full-out. "Unprofessional," he muttered.

*Humans have the strangest sense of humor.*

"Well, I'm not sorry," David said, but his grin was good-natured. "*I* wanted to hit you, *you* wanted me to hit you—I'd say we both got what we wanted."

"Can't argue with that."

The two sat looking at each other for a few seconds before they both started laughing.

"Look at us," said David. "We're so pathetic. Our lives

revolve around her. I—" He paused and looked down at the floor, obviously a little embarrassed. "I thought I was going to die when she broke up with me."

Sincerely, Tamani nodded. "I know the feeling."

"Thing is, even when you were gone, you were never really gone," David said. "She missed you, all the time. Sometimes I'd catch her staring off into space and ask her what she was thinking about, and she would smile and say 'nothing,' but I knew she was thinking about you." He leaned forward. "When you showed up in September, I think I hated you more at that moment than anything in my whole life."

"A bit of your own medicine, if you ask me," Tamani said, trying not to show just how pleased he was. "Laurel carried a picture of you in her pocket—she had it when I saw her in Avalon two summers back. And I hated that even those few times when I had her to myself—completely to myself—you were there too."

"Do you think she knows we know?"

"If she didn't before, she does now," Tamani said, the melancholy slipping in again. "That's why she's not with either of us. I've wondered if it's as much to keep the peace between us as to give her the space she needs." Tamani hesitated then added, "You should go make up with her."

"Are you serious?"

"I said make up, not get back together," Tamani said, working to keep the edge from his voice. "She would be happy if the two of you were friends again. I want her to be happy. I'm going out tracking with Shar after school and into the night—I'll stay away; you go make nice."

David was silent for a minute. "What do you get out of this?"

"I want you to tell her I sent you."

"Ah, so Laurel is happy *and* you get brownie points for making peace."

"You're pretty sharp. For a human," Tamani said, not hiding his grin.

David just shook his head. "You know what I hate almost as much as the thought of losing Laurel to you?" David asked.

"What?" Tamani braced himself for whatever David had to say.

"That this lame-ass work-your-problems-out thing actually worked."

Tamani chuckled as the final bell rang. "I wouldn't go that far, mate," he said. "I still don't like you." But he couldn't help but smile as he said it.

Laurel cautiously opened the front door to find David with a single zinnia in his hand.

"Hi," he said awkwardly. Then he thrust the flower in her direction. "I'm sorry," he said. "I was a jerk, and I really let my temper run away with me and it was so completely inappropriate and I would break up with me too."

Laurel stood there staring at the proffered flower for a long moment before taking it with a sigh. "I'm sorry too," she said softly.

"You? What do you have to be sorry for?" David asked.

"I should have listened to Chelsea. She told me you were having a hard time with Tamani and I just figured you would get over it. I should have taken her seriously. Taken *you* seriously. I'm sorry I let it get this far."

David rubbed at the back of his neck. "It was never that big of a deal. Chelsea lets me vent to her. And that's what it was, most of the time. Venting."

"Yeah, but you should have been able to vent to *me*. I totally cut off any kind of negative talk and I should have asked you how you really felt and then listened. That's what a good girlfriend does." Laurel looked down at her feet. "Forget girlfriend, that's what a good *friend* does."

"I don't think you owe me an apology, but I appreciate it anyway," David said. "And, well, I hope that we can get past this and put it behind us." He hesitated. "Together."

"David," Laurel said, and she saw from the crestfallen expression on his face that he knew what she was going to say. "I don't think I'm ready to be 'us' again."

"Are you with Tamani, then?" David asked, eyes downcast.

"I'm not with anyone," Laurel said, shaking her head. "We're seventeen, David. I like you, and I like Tamani, and I think maybe I need to stop worrying about 'forever' for a little while. I'm having a hard enough time deciding if I'm going to go to college next year, never mind who I should be with for the rest of my life."

David had a strange look on his face, but Laurel rushed on.

"Between Yuki and Klea and trolls and finals and colleges and—" She groaned. "I just can't do it right now."

"It sounds like you need a friend," David murmured, his eyes fixed on the doormat.

Laurel was surprised by the relief that surged through her. The tears were on her cheeks before she even realized it. "Oh, man," she said, trying to wipe them away subtly, "I need a friend so badly right now."

David stepped forward, wrapping his arms around her and pulling her to him, his cheek pressed against the top of her head. Laurel felt every worry of the day seep away as she absorbed the warmth from his chest, listening to his steady heartbeat, scared now at how close she had come to losing his friendship. "Thank you," she whispered.

"I want you to know that I have every intention of convincing you to be my girlfriend again," David said, releasing her and taking a step back. "I'm trying to be honest, you know."

Laurel rolled her eyes and laughed.

"But until then," he said, more serious now, "I'll be your friend, and I'll wait."

"I was beginning to think you would never speak to me again." She watched, confused, as David's face flushed red.

"I . . . had some encouragement. Tamani sent me," he finally said.

"Tamani?" Laurel asked, certain she hadn't heard right.

"We actually had a good talk today and he said he'd stay away so I could come apologize."

Laurel contemplated this. "Why would he do that?"

"Why else? To score points with you," David said with a snort.

Laurel shook her head, but she had to give him credit; it had worked. "I called you the other day," Laurel admitted.

"I saw that. You didn't leave a message."

"I got mad at your voice mail."

David chuckled.

"I got my SAT scores."

He nodded shortly. This was almost as important to him as it was to her. "Me too. I still didn't beat Chelsea, though. How about you?"

Laurel smiled as she told him about her vastly improved scores and the possibilities they brought with them. And for a few moments, it was like nothing had changed—because, Laurel realized, David had always been her friend first. And maybe that was the biggest difference between him and Tamani. With David the friendship had come first—with Tamani, it had always been the heat. She wasn't sure she could imagine life without either extreme. Did choosing between them mean leaving one of those behind forever? It wasn't a thought that made her happy, so for the moment she pushed it to the side and enjoyed the one she had here in front of her.

"You want to come in?"

# TWENTY-SEVEN

TAMANI SAT VERY STILL, HIS EYES SCANNING THE forest for movement as the sun disappeared behind the horizon. This was the ideal time to spot trolls—as their "day" was just beginning and the long shadows offered plenty of places to lurk. Wherever they were hiding, it had to be nearby—the trolls they'd wounded always seemed to head in this direction. But the few square miles of forest sandwiched between two human neighborhoods had yielded nothing but frustration. Tamani ground his teeth. He had promised Aaron he would make things right and, eye of the Goddess, he was going to!

"Please, Tam, for all your training in stealth, even a half-deaf troll would hear those teeth grinding," came a flat, almost bored-sounding voice from lower down the conifer Tamani had climbed for a better view.

Tamani sighed.

"You're spreading yourself too thin," Shar added, sounding more concerned now. "Three nights in a row. I worry for you."

"I don't normally go for so long," Tamani said. "I just want to make use of you while you're here. Normally I do one night on, one night off."

"That still has you not sleeping half of your nights."

"I sleep a little while on watch."

"Very little, I imagine. You know catching trolls isn't your job," Shar went on, his voice so low Tamani could barely hear him. He'd said the same thing the last two nights as well.

"How better to protect Laurel?" Tamani asked hotly.

"That's an excellent question," Shar said. He had climbed almost as high as Tamani now. "Do you intend to harrow yourself to death with it?"

"What do you mean?"

"You had a choice. Follow the trolls, or stay with Laurel. You stayed with Laurel. I don't know if you made the best possible choice, but you made a *defensible* choice, particularly with Laurel unconscious and unable to defend herself. If you'd made a different choice, maybe you could have followed those trolls back to their lair. Or maybe the chase would be fruitless, as it has been so far. I'm sorry that Aaron disagreed with your decision, but you can't let it take root in you like this. You have to move on."

Tamani shook his head. "Aaron was almost there. Laurel would have made it home fine. And I could have been one step closer to eliminating the ultimate threat against her."

"It's easy to think that, because she *did* make it safely home. But who's to say there weren't more trolls waiting for you to leave Laurel alone? Or that Yuki or Klea weren't waiting for the same thing?"

"That seems remarkably unlikely," Tamani muttered.

"Aye. But you're *Fear-gleidhidh*. Your job is to anticipate even the most unlikely threat. Above all else, your job is to keep Laurel alive and on task."

"I would leave everything and join the World Tree tomorrow if she died," Tamani said.

"I know," Shar whispered through the darkness.

An hour passed, then two, and the fae said nothing as they scanned the forest. Tamani felt his eyes start to droop, a weariness settling into him that seemed to reach all the way to his core. He'd stayed out two nights in a row often enough, but three was pushing it. Shar had slept during the day, but aside from a brief nap at school while Mr. Robison was out of the room, and a few short stints in the tree, Tamani had not slept since the night he'd forced himself to leave Laurel's bed—obeying her request even though he knew that as long as he left before dawn, she would never know. He closed his eyes now, thinking of that last sight of her, her blond hair spilling out over her pillowcase like the softest of corn silk, her mouth, even in sleep, turned up ever so slightly at the corners.

His eyes fluttered open at the crunch of dry leaves. At first he thought it was only another deer. But the sound came again, and again. Those footsteps were too heavy to be made by anything so graceful.

Tamani held his breath, willing it to happen, almost doubting his own eyes when two trolls came lumbering into sight, reeking of blood, one dragging a full-grown buck. If they kept going straight, they would pass right under the tree where he and Shar were perched.

Quickly and silently, Tamani and Shar descended. The trolls didn't seem to be in any hurry, so it was easy to keep them in view. Tamani was tempted to ambush them, to finish them off, but tonight's mission was far more important than simply eliminating a few trolls. It was time to find out where they were hiding. *All* of them.

He and Shar tracked them at an almost leisurely pace, traveling alongside the path in short sprints. The trolls paused, and Tamani crouched low, knowing Shar was doing the same behind him. He knew they couldn't smell him—he carried neither blood nor brimstone to tickle their noses. But some trolls could sense danger, or so Shar claimed from time to time.

The troll with the deer carcass lifted it off the ground, as though to examine the quality of the meal. Then, both trolls vanished.

Tamani suppressed a gasp. They had disappeared right in front of his eyes! Forcing himself to remain hidden, Tamani held his breath, listening. There was a distant shuffling, a creak, the slam of wood against wood. Then silence. A minute passed. Two. Three. There were no more sounds.

Tamani rose to his feet, every stem in his body ready to run, to fight.

"Did you see that?" Shar whispered.

"Aye," Tamani said, half expecting the trolls to jump out from behind a tree. But the forest remained quiet and empty. He stared at the place where the trolls had just been standing. The messy one had left several drops of blood from his kill-trophy splattered on the fallen leaves. Tamani followed the blood droplets to where the trolls had paused, at the edge of a smallish clearing. The crimson trail ended where they had disappeared.

Crouching to get a closer look, Tamani studied the blood. He stood over it and walked forward, fixing his eyes on the tree in front of him. When he had reached about half the distance to the tree, he turned.

The blood drop was not behind him. It was off to his left.

But he'd walked a direct route.

"What are you doing?" Shar asked.

"Just a second," Tamani said, confused. He went back to the blood drop and tried it again. He focused on another tree and walked halfway to it. When he turned, the drop was behind him and to his right.

Tamani knelt down, studying the trees that appeared to be in front of him, but apparently weren't. "Shar," Tamani said, making sure he was standing over the blood drop, his back to the trail he had followed. "Come stand in front of me."

As he stepped forward, Shar's feet seemed to reset themselves on a diagonal path. He took two more steps, then stopped and turned, eyes wide.

"Understand now?" Tamani asked, the confusion on his mentor's face making him smile a little in spite of their predicament.

As Shar stood staring at the spot where he had just been standing, Tamani braced his feet and reached out with his hands. He didn't feel anything, but the farther out he reached, the farther apart his hands spread. When he tried to bring his hands together, he found himself bringing them back toward his chest. "Shar!" Tamani whispered breathlessly. "Come do what I'm doing."

It took Shar a few moments, but soon he too stood with his hands held in front of himself, tracing the intangible contours of the barrier that seemed to bend the space around them. It was as though someone had cut a very small circle in the universe. A dome they could not perceive, let alone enter.

But it *could* be entered, somehow, Tamani was certain. That must be where the trolls had gone.

"If I hadn't seen the trolls vanish, I wouldn't know anything was amiss," Tamani said, dropping his hands to his sides.

"But we can't see it, and can only feel it indirectly," Shar said, his arms folded across his chest as he stared into the darkness. "How do we breach a wall we cannot touch?"

"The trolls went right through it," Tamani replied. "So it's not really a wall."

Shar silently stepped away from Tamani and picked up a

small rock. He stood a few feet away and gave it an under-hand toss. It arced toward the barrier and then, without the slightest interruption, vanished.

Encouraged, Tamani bent down to grab a small stick. He walked forward, just to the point where he found himself turning, and reached out with the stick. There was no physical sensation, nothing stopped him from moving freely—but when he thought he was thrusting it forward, he found the stick pointing sideways. He started to pull back, confused, when a new idea struck him.

*Maybe it's attuned to plants.*

He tossed the stick at the barrier instead, expecting it to bounce back. The stick vanished, just like the rock.

*Guess not.*

"That's some warding," Tamani breathed.

"Since when do trolls work this kind of magic?" Shar asked.

"Since never," Tamani responded darkly. "So it ought to be easily overcome."

"Oh, aye, clearly," Shar said, sarcasm heavy in his tone.

Tamani studied the mysterious nothingness. "I can throw things through it, but I can't poke through it with a stick. Think you could throw *me* through it?"

Shar looked at him for a long time, then arched one eyebrow and nodded. "I can certainly try." He knelt with his fingers laced together and Tamani placed one foot into his open palms.

"*A haon, a dó, a trí!*" Shar heaved, and Tamani made a

flying leap, directly toward the barrier.

He was airborne, and then he had the excruciatingly distinct impression that something was turning him inside out. But the pain passed quickly, and his back hit the ground, forcing the air from his chest. There were too many stars in the sky, he thought, trying to focus. Shar was looking down at him, vaguely amused.

"What happened?" Tamani asked.

"You . . . bounced."

Tamani sat up and stared at the space before him. "It must be very specifically attuned to fae. That shouldn't even be possible." He glared at the ground for a moment. "Maybe we can dig under it?"

"Maybe," Shar said, but he didn't sound confident.

"What can we do, then?"

Shar didn't respond immediately. He was studying the small clearing with a look of consternation, tilting his head this way and that, as if in search of an angle that would allow him to see the secret. Then he stopped and straightened.

"I wonder . . ." Shar reached his hands forward, dragging his toe along the invisible barrier, marking its perimeter. From his pack, he produced a small drawstring pouch. "Stand back."

Automatically, Tamani took a few steps backward, wondering what Shar was up to.

After loosening the strings that held it closed, Shar pinched the bottom corner of the little pouch between his thumb and forefinger. Then he crouched on the ground, carefully scattering its pale, granular contents around himself, completing the circle by dropping an arc from overhead that disappeared as it passed the invisible wall.

Tamani jumped back in alarm as the small clearing where they stood swelled to triple its size in the blink of an eye. His breath caught in his throat as he surveyed the expanse that materialized before them from the vaguest hint of a shadow. In the center of the clearing was a dilapidated cabin, its windows tightly boarded. It practically glowed in the full moonlight.

Realizing at once how vulnerable they were—how vulnerable they had been the whole time—Tamani dropped to his stomach and scrambled for cover behind a scrub oak. When nothing moved in the moonlit clearing, Tamani crept out slowly, though part of him suspected it didn't matter. If anyone had been watching them for the last quarter of an hour, the time for hiding was long past. Still, his training didn't allow him to do anything but proceed as carefully as possible.

Shar hadn't moved. He was standing in the middle of his improvised circle, staring at the now-empty pouch that rested in his upturned palm. The look on his face was a mixture of awestruck horror and giddy delight. Whatever he had done, he hadn't expected it to work.

"What was that?" Tamani said appreciatively.

"Salt," Shar replied, his voice hollow. He didn't take his eyes off the pouch in his hand. Tamani laughed, but Shar did not.

"Wait, you're serious?"

"Look there."

Tamani looked at the ground where Shar was pointing. The white line of salt Shar had made around himself overlapped a thick arc of dark blue powder that appeared to encircle the entire clearing.

"That's Mixer's work," Shar said, frowning.

"It looks that way, but this is Winter-class enchantment. They've hidden half an acre just by drawing a circle around it!"

"Benders don't use powders," Shar replied. Tamani suppressed a grimace; referring to Winter faeries as *Benders* was vulgar even by sentry standards. "The powder makes it a Mixing for sure."

"Or maybe we're dealing with a new kind of troll. Laurel hit those trolls with caesafum and they didn't even blink. Tracking serums don't work, either. And it seems like Barnes was immune to everything but lead. Specifically, lead shot into his brain."

Shar ruminated on that. "Maybe. But there *have* been some very, very strong Mixers in our history."

"Not outside Avalon. Except the one exile, and she burned, what, forty, fifty years ago?"

"Indeed. I saw it happen with my own eyes. But perhaps an apprentice?" Shar hesitated. "There is the young faerie."

"I don't think it's possible. Even on the off-chance that the Wildflower is a Fall, she's *too* young. An Academy-trained Mixer would be a hundred before they could do something like this, never mind a wild one."

"Anything is possible."

"So I see," Tamani said, gesturing at the powder. "Both this blue powder and whatever you did," he added. "Why salt?"

"Testing a theory," Shar said. "So far, I'm encouraged by the results."

Sensing that Shar was not going to say more on the subject, Tamani knelt and examined the blue powder. "Can I have that pouch?"

Wordlessly, Shar dropped the small burlap sack into Tamani's outstretched hand. Tamani scooped some of the powder onto the blade of his knife and poured it into the pouch. Then, as an afterthought, he used his knife to draw a line in the dirt, breaking the blue circle.

"What are you doing?" asked Shar.

"I'm guessing a broken circle won't work," Tamani said. "If the trolls inside didn't see us, they may not know the circle is broken—but they might find your salt. If we scatter the salt, and cover this break, maybe they won't notice their lair is exposed."

"I want this place watched day and night from now on."

"I'll need to call reinforcements," Tamani said, the weight of his weariness bearing down on him as the excitement of discovery waned. He ducked behind a thick tree to turn on his iPhone, wishing the screen didn't light up quite so brightly. Hoping Aaron remembered how to use the GPS, Tamani sent his location to the other sentry's phone.

By the time Tamani returned, Shar had eradicated his salt circle and scattered leaves over the break Tamani had made with his knife. There was still no light or sound coming from the cabin, which seemed odd; it wasn't like trolls to sleep at night.

"Maybe we should just storm the place and get it over with," said Tamani.

"You're in no condition for a fight," said Shar. "Besides, I'd like to keep them under observation for a bit, get a feel for their numbers. For all we know, there are thirty trolls in there, just waiting for us to knock."

It wasn't much longer before Tamani heard the telltale whisper of leaves all around him, heralding the arrival of at least ten sentries.

"Can you take it from here?" he asked Shar.

"If you like. Where are you off to?"

Tamani held up Shar's burlap pouch, then tucked it into his pack. "I have to get this back to Laurel. She may be able to figure out what it is."

"I hope so," Shar said, staring at the moonlit cabin.

With that, Tamani turned and ran, his bare feet whispering through the blanket of autumn leaves. He felt like he could have made the run with his eyes closed—as though all paths led to Laurel.

Tamani shook his head, realizing it was starting to swim—blackness encroaching on the edges of his vision. He blinked hard and forced himself to run faster, trying to push away the weariness that threatened to overwhelm him. Maybe

Shar was right—maybe he *was* spreading himself too thin. *After this*, he told himself. *After I deliver this, I can sleep.*

He braced himself against Laurel's back door and knocked, feeling his eyes close even as she came into sight. She opened the door in wordless surprise and he only managed one step into the kitchen before the ground rushed up to meet him.

# TWENTY-EIGHT

LAUREL HAD SET HER ALARM FOR HALF AN HOUR
before sunrise so she could go downstairs and check on
Tamani, but she was already awake when it sounded. Her
whole night had felt more like a restless dream than actual
sleep. Once she'd convinced herself he was okay, Laurel
draped a blanket over Tamani and went to bed. She considered trying to move him—the kitchen floor didn't look very
comfortable—but in the end, decided to leave him in peace.
He'd probably slept on worse out at the land.

Glancing at the mirror and finger-combing her hair a
little, Laurel crept downstairs as silently as she could. He
was still there—he hadn't so much as stirred. The morning light was gray and soft, and Laurel tiptoed over to sit
where she could see Tamani's face. It was strange to see him
sleeping—completely relaxed, his expression unguarded.
In some ways, it was weird to think of him sleeping at all.

He was a constant in her life—someone who was always there when she needed him, day or night. She had never seen him when he wasn't alert and ready.

She watched him as the kitchen brightened to purple, then pink. Finally, a square of yellow sunlight started crawling across the kitchen floor. Tamani's eyelashes fluttered, catching the light and casting narrow shadows over his bronze cheeks. Then his eyes snapped open and focused on Laurel. Instantly, he rolled away from her, coming up on his feet, hands held defensively in front of him.

"Tam!" Laurel said.

He looked at her, seeing her clearly for the first time, then straightened, dropping his hands. "Sorry," he said, his voice rough and scratchy. He looked around the kitchen in confusion. "What happened?"

"You burst in here last night around ten. And then you collapsed. I checked with Aaron out back. All he would say was that I was safe and he didn't know why you were here. Is everything okay?"

Tamani sat carefully on a barstool and rubbed his eyes. "Yeah, more or less. I just pushed myself a little too hard."

"A *little*?" Laurel said, scolding him with a smile.

"Maybe more than a little," Tamani admitted, grinning wryly. "I should have just bunked out and waited till morning. Hey, can I steal something to eat, please?"

"Sure," Laurel said, going to the refrigerator. "What do you want? Peaches? Strawberries? I have some mango."

"Do you have vegetables? I would kill for some broccoli

right now. No," he amended. "I really shouldn't have broccoli. I eat too much green stuff as it is—don't want my hair to change."

Laurel scrutinized the fridge. "Jicama?" she asked. "It's white."

"Actually that sounds really good, thank you."

Laurel pulled out a dish of jicama her mother had chopped up last night and set the whole thing in front of Tamani. It was way more than she could have eaten, but after last night, Tamani might need it all. Laurel watched him down several slices. "So what happened?" she asked, snagging a piece of the white veggie for herself.

Instead of answering, Tamani pulled a small pouch from his pocket and handed it to her. "Be very careful with that," he said, curling her fingers around the bag. "I'm not sure I can get more."

"What is it?"

Between the sunlight and the food, Tamani was growing more animated. He related his adventures from the previous night. "This powder . . . it's like it slices out a piece of space and folds it in on itself. It was the strangest thing I've ever seen."

Laurel peered into the pouch, unsure she knew how to begin testing such an unusual mixture. "You think this is fae magic?" she asked.

"Possibly. It could be some new troll magic. Or old human magic, for all I know. But we seem to be accumulating a lot of evidence of a rogue Mixer."

"Are you still thinking it could be Yuki?" Laurel asked quietly.

Tamani hesitated, his brows knit. "I'm not sure. I never, ever discount a possibility, but she's so young. Could *you* make anything like this?"

Laurel shook her head. "I seriously doubt it. It sounds incredibly complicated."

"But who else could it be?"

They both sat silently, Tamani munching and thinking, Laurel absently sifting through the powder with her fingertips.

"You know, everyone seems to think Yuki is some huge anomaly," Laurel said. "But if there's one wild faerie, why not two? Or ten? Or a hundred? What if Yuki is just some kind of . . . diversion?"

Tamani pondered this for a moment. "It's something to consider," he said. "But we didn't chase faeries to that cabin. Just trolls. And we don't even know if they're after you, or Yuki."

Laurel nodded.

"Speaking of Yuki, I haven't seen her in three days, and since we have a holiday next week, I had better go make amends while I can."

Laurel suppressed a wave of jealousy. It was his job!

Tamani walked over to the back door and swung it open, taking a deep breath of fresh morning air. "Thank you for the exquisite comfort of your kitchen floor," he said with a chuckle, though she knew he must be rather chagrined over the whole experience, "and for the excellent breakfast. I'm off."

Tamani sprinted to his apartment, trying not to be seen. In his handmade breeches and bare feet he would probably look like a wild man to any humans who spied him. After taking a quick shower—an indulgence he was really starting to get used to—and throwing on new clothes for the day, Tamani dashed out of the apartment and toward Yuki's house, hoping to catch her on her way to school.

He speed-walked up her driveway just as she was unlocking her bike from the porch rail. "Hey there," he said, turning on his flirtatious grin.

Yuki's eyes widened, then sparkled. "Hey, Tam," she said shyly.

Tamani smiled back. He hated going from Laurel's house to Yuki's house. He felt like a traitor to both of them. He was beginning to understand why Sparklers avoided sentry duty whenever possible. Their abilities made them excellent spies, and Marion's court used them extensively in the United Kingdom and in Egypt, where human proximity made intelligence and espionage almost as important as posting guards at the gates. But pretending to be someone else on the stage could not be nearly so taxing as pretending to be someone else every single day.

Nevertheless, Tamani had his orders. Yuki seemed to have grown quite attached to him, and if he could just get her to lower her defenses, maybe he could find out what he needed to know.

Or better yet, find out that there was nothing to know.

This, unfortunately, seemed unlikely. It was just too big a coincidence for Yuki to show up at Laurel's school, especially when the woman who put her there belonged to an organization that hunted non-humans. Except for picking up Yuki after the troll attack, Klea had not shown her face since delivering the wild faerie to Laurel's doorstep. She *could* be off hunting, as she claimed, but both times sentries sent to follow her had come back empty-handed, having lost her trail within two or three miles of Laurel's house. Just like with the trolls—another "coincidence" that put Tamani's teeth on edge. What was their connection? Klea always wore sunglasses, as though she were sensitive to light, or hiding mismatched eyes, but otherwise she didn't look like a troll. Still, troll clans had been known to squabble over territory, which would explain her killing Barnes. But Tamani was at a loss to explain how Yuki ended up with a group of human troll hunters, never mind a clan of trolls posing as troll hunters. Laurel's suggestion that Yuki might not be the only wild faerie definitely had merit, but what could possibly motivate such creatures to ally with the likes of Klea or Barnes?

There were still too many questions, but whatever the answers, Tamani didn't see any way for Klea to be anything but a threat. She was hiding. Tamani didn't know if she was hiding from him or from Laurel, but she was definitely hiding.

*Animals hide when they are guilty—or afraid.* Klea didn't seem the type to cower in fear—so she was guilty. Tamani just needed to figure out what she was guilty *of*.

It wasn't that he didn't like Yuki—over the last few months, as he wormed in close, he'd found her company more than tolerable. She was smarter than she generally let on, and had a quiet confidence he admired. Which made his subterfuge all the more challenging. He was increasingly certain she actually liked him and it made him feel like a villain to be using that against her. If it did turn out that she knew nothing, he was never going to get over the guilt of this moment. But if she was a danger to Laurel in any way, it would be worth it.

"I thought maybe I could walk you to school this morning. Car's in the shop," he tacked on, scrambling for an excuse. In truth the car was parked at the head of the trail he and Shar had taken last night.

"I thought you 'knew a guy,'" Yuki said coyly.

Tamani grinned. "I do, that's why it will be done by this afternoon."

"Sounds good," Yuki said, snapping her lock shut and dropping the keys into her skirt pocket. "Oh," she said, stopping, then taking another step forward, then stopping again.

"What is it?" Tamani asked, bemused. She could be so awkward sometimes.

"It's stupid, I . . . I forgot my lunch," she admitted.

As a fellow faerie Tamani knew how important midday nourishment could be to making it through school hours. He nearly laughed thinking of the mental war she must have waged between not embarrassing herself and trying to make it through a whole day with no food.

"Go ahead," Tamani said brightly, gesturing toward the house. "I'll wait."

"You can come in for a sec," Yuki said, not meeting his eyes. "I'll just be a minute."

He hesitated. There was something about entering this unknown faerie's lair that felt like walking into a trap, but the tiny house was practically a training exercise in harmlessness. Not to mention the fact that they were surrounded by sentries. Still.

Yuki had swung the door wide open and the crisp autumn air wafted pleasantly through the front room. A small television set rested on a coffee table next to a pile of books, and a plush purple couch adorned one wall, but the rest of the room was wall-to-wall greenery. Potted plants lined the floors and windowsills. At least one variety of creeper had found purchase in the drywall and was crawling up around the window, framing it like curtains.

"Nice . . . plants," Tamani said lamely, every cell in his body springing to attention. With a good-sized mortar, it could be a Mixer's armory—or simply the natural inclination of a wild faerie who longed for a flowering homeland she'd never heard of, and seen only in her dreams.

"I use them for *ikebana*," she said, before disappearing into the back of the house.

She'd mentioned the Japanese art of flower arrangement to him before, though he couldn't remember the context. He had thought *ikebana* was more understated, however. This place was practically a jungle. He yanked his phone out of his pocket and hurried to snap a few pictures of the green-laden walls, hoping Laurel could tell him a bit more about the kinds of plants Yuki was growing here. He barely managed to get the phone back in his pocket when she emerged from her room, her backpack in place.

"Sorry; I'm ready now."

He smiled, forcing himself out of thinking mode and into friendly spy mode. "Great!"

But Yuki didn't turn to go. He watched her take a few nervous breaths before blurting out, "You're welcome here anytime."

"I'll keep that in mind," Tamani said, offering her a crooked grin.

Yuki looked like she might say something else, but lost her nerve and walked past him onto the porch, waiting for him to pass through the doorway before pulling it shut.

"I hope it's okay that I just stopped by," Tamani said as they set off at a leisurely pace toward school.

"I'm glad you did," Yuki said, lowering her eyes.

The silence was building uncomfortably and Tamani was scrambling for something not-too-stupid to say when Yuki's phone started ringing. She pulled it out of her pocket and rolled her eyes, pressing the button that would send the call to voice mail.

"Do you need to take that?" Tamani asked. "I don't mind."

"It's just Klea; no biggie."

"She doesn't care if you don't pick up?"

"I'll just say I was in the shower. Or riding my bike—it's actually tough to ride and talk at the same time. As long as I call her back pretty quickly, she doesn't care."

"And you really don't mind being alone so often?"

Yuki flipped a lock of hair over her shoulder. "Not at all." She smiled. "I'm not afraid of the dark." Tamani cringed inwardly at how obvious it was that she was trying to impress him.

"And your parents don't mind?"

He saw something cross her face. It was wary, then decisive. He leaned closer, trying to look interested instead of eager. "My parents aren't around anymore," she said in a rush. "It's just me and Klea. And mostly, just me. The whole 'foreign exchange' thing just . . . eases the transition." Her eyes kept darting to him, clearly nervous. "I'm sort of here for a fresh start."

"A fresh start is good. My . . . parents aren't around either. Sometimes I wish everyone didn't know. They look at you, all pitying, and it just—"

"I know what you're saying. Hey, listen," she said, touching his arm. "Don't tell anyone? Please?"

He didn't push for more. Not today—not on this subject. "Of course I won't," he said with a smile. Then he leaned over and laid his hand over hers. "You can trust me."

She beamed at him, but there was something wary around her eyes. "So, how was your suspension?"

*Eye of Hecate, now who's awkward?* Tamani shrugged, looking embarrassed. "It was stupid. I'm glad it's over."

"Everyone's still talking about your fight with David," Yuki said, her tight laugh completely unconvincing. She hesitated for a moment. "Jun said that he heard you guys were fighting over Laurel or something."

"Laurel?" Tamani said, hoping he sounded confused. "Laurel Sewell? Why would it be about her?"

"I heard she broke you guys up and said something about choosing."

"Oh, wow," he said, leaning forward conspiratorially. "That's crazy. Laurel is cool; she helps me out in Government. Because I'm totally clueless, right? I think she and David both got the wrong idea. If you know what I mean," he said in a callous, almost mocking tone.

"So, you're not into Laurel?"

"Not like that," he said, hating the words coming out of his mouth. It felt like blasphemy. "She's really nice. But, I don't know. Not my type. Too . . . blond."

"What *is* your type?" Yuki asked, her eyes shy now.

Tamani shrugged and smiled a little. "I'll know it when I see it," he said, holding her gaze until she looked away, embarrassed but pleased.

# TWENTY-NINE

"DAD'S HOUSE FOR THANKSGIVING THIS YEAR?"
Laurel asked David. They were sitting at a lunch table with
Chelsea; their usual spot was a mudhole, thanks to last night's
storm, and Chelsea complained that it was too cold. It was
almost too cold even for Laurel, so today they were braving
the noise and bustle of the cafeteria.

"I wish," David replied. "If that were the case we would
order a bunch of Chinese food and sit around and watch
football for three days. Or, more accurately, he would
watch football and I'd study for finals. No, my grandparents called a family reunion in Eureka. They're sure this
is the year they're going to die and they have to see everyone
before they go."

"Didn't they pull that one at Christmas last year?" Laurel
asked.

"And the year before. They're not even that old. They're,

like, five years older than your *parents*."

It was nice, talking to David again. Laurel tried to get both Tamani and David to tell her what happened during their suspension, but Tamani insisted it was guy stuff and wouldn't discuss it and David was very adept at changing the subject. They seemed to have come to an understanding, a truce, *something*—Laurel couldn't guess what—but they no longer glowered at each other in the hallway, and even exchanged friendly greetings on occasion. They'd also stopped pushing her to choose between them, but Laurel doubted that could last.

"Still, a break's a break, right?" Laurel said.

"Psh. A zillion relatives in one house? I won't get any studying done."

"I think you're missing the point of *having* a break," Laurel insisted.

"Are you kidding? I'm way behind."

"Oh, sure, Mr. Four-point-oh."

"Four-point-four," David and Chelsea corrected in unison before looking at each other and laughing. When Laurel raised an eyebrow at him, he said sheepishly, "Honors classes are worth five points, remember?"

Laurel rolled her eyes and shook her head. "You're such a perfectionist."

"Yeah, but you love me," David said. He had the decency to blush and look mortified at having slipped into their old banter.

But Laurel only smiled and reached up to squeeze his

shoulder. "Yeah," she said genially. "I do."

Everyone was silent for a few seconds before Chelsea snorted. "Awkward much?" she asked with a grin.

Luckily, Tamani chose that moment to plunk himself down across the table from Chelsea, eyeing Ryan, who was standing in line for tacos. "Hey," he said softly.

"Where's Yuki?" Laurel asked, looking around. "Didn't I see her this morning?"

"Yeah, she said Klea was picking her up early. Taking a few extra days off around the break."

"Still nothing at the cabin?" Laurel asked. David and Chelsea glanced around for eavesdroppers, then brought their heads in close so they could hear what Tamani had to say.

"Not a sound, not a movement, absolutely nothing. I'm starting to think those trolls just ran through the circle and past the cabin."

"Your guys haven't gone in yet?" Chelsea asked, disbelief shading her voice. "What are they waiting for?"

*Leave it to Chelsea to ask the obvious question,* thought Laurel with a smile.

"Shar thinks it's more important to figure out what they're doing. If we bust in, they'll fight to the death, and we won't know any more than we already do."

"They're inside a cabin," David said. "Shouldn't Laurel's sleeping potions work?"

"They *should*," Tamani agreed. "But that's part of the problem. Nothing we've thrown at these guys the last few

305

months has worked. Nothing. And that makes us more than a little nervous about storming the place. Who knows what else is lurking in there?"

"Hey, guys," Ryan greeted them, sitting down next to Chelsea with his lunch.

Chelsea gave him a perfunctory smile and patted his shoulder.

"So, you guys must have been talking about me, huh?" he said with a grin when everyone was silent.

"Actually, we were talking about faeries," Chelsea said with exaggerated excitement. When Tamani's eyes grew wide and he glanced over at Ryan, Chelsea smirked. "I was just asking Tam about them. Since he's from Ireland—"

"Scotland, actually—"

"—he probably knows a ton about faeries and magic and stuff. Way more than we do, anyway."

Tamani's expression was a war between shock and awe. Laurel put a hand to her mouth and did her best not to laugh Sprite right out her nose.

"You know, Chelsea, just because someone's from Scotland—" Ryan began.

"Oh, hush," chided Chelsea. "Tam was just going to tell us about how faerie enemies can suddenly become immune to magic that has worked on them for centuries."

"Er . . . ," Tamani said. "Actually, I have no idea."

"Good answer!" said Ryan, holding up one hand for a high five. When Tamani stared blankly, Ryan dropped his hand back to the table. "Seriously, if you let her suck you into her faerie world you'll never escape. I swear, sometimes it's like she thinks faeries are real. You should see her room."

That remark earned him an icy glare from Chelsea. "Guess who *won't* be seeing my room for a while?"

"So," Laurel cut in, eager to change the subject. "What are you guys doing for Thanksgiving?"

"Grandparents' house," said David.

"Grandma's house," said Chelsea, nodding. "At least she's local."

"Dad's family is coming up," said Ryan.

They all looked at Tamani, and Laurel realized she had put him on the spot.

*Whoops.*

"It's not really something we celebrate," Tamani said smoothly. "I'll probably just lie about."

"You want to come to Thanksgiving at my place?" Laurel asked, catching Tamani before he got out the front doors. He'd been avoiding her the last couple of days and she wasn't really sure why.

He stiffened. "Really?"

"Yeah, sure, why not?" Laurel said, trying to make the invitation sound decidedly casual. "We're not having anybody else over. Yuki's gone. You're going to be hanging around in my backyard anyway, I assume," she said, forcing a chuckle.

But Tamani still looked concerned. "I don't know. Your parents are going to be there, right?"

"Yeah, so? They know who you are." She leaned forward, raising her eyebrows now. "And they know all about the kitchen floor."

Tamani groaned. "Thanks for reminding me."

"No sweat," Laurel said with a smile.

He worried his bottom lip for a minute before saying, "It just feels weird. You know, your parents, these humans who raised you. It's just kind of awkward."

"Awkward because they're my parents, or because they're human?" Tamani didn't answer right away and Laurel reached over to poke his arm. "Come on," she said. "'Fess."

"Both. Okay, because they are your human parents. It's just, you shouldn't have human parents. You shouldn't have parents at all."

"Well, you better get used to it, because my parents aren't going anywhere."

"No, but . . . you are," Tamani said hesitantly. "I mean, eventually. Right?"

"I certainly don't intend to be one of those forty-year-olds who still live with Mom and Dad, no," Laurel said, avoiding Tamani's real question.

"Sure, but . . . you *are* coming back to Avalon, aren't you?"

It was a little harder to avoid when he asked her straight out. She looked down at her hands for a few seconds. "Why are you asking me this now?"

Tamani shrugged. "I've wanted to ask for a while. It just seems like all this human stuff is getting more and more important to you. I hope you aren't forgetting where you . . . belong."

"I don't know if that *is* where I belong," she said honestly.

"What do you mean, you don't know?"

"I don't know," Laurel said firmly. "I haven't decided."

"What else would you do?"

"I think maybe I want to go to college." It was strange to say it out loud. She had kind of expected that, without David pushing her to stay in the human world, she would gravitate toward Avalon. But breaking up with David hadn't made up her mind about college, which had forced her to reconsider the possibility that she might want to go, not just for David or her parents, but for herself.

"But why? They can't teach anything at college that would be useful to you."

"No," Laurel countered, "they can't teach me anything in college that you think would be useful to *you*. I'm not you, Tamani."

"But really? More school? That's what you *want* to do?"

"Maybe."

"Because I gotta tell you, sitting through all my classes is by far the worst part of my day. I don't know how you could want more of that. I hate it."

"That's basically what I do in Avalon, too. No matter where I go, there's school."

"But in Avalon you'd be learning stuff that's useful. Square root of a cosine? How is that ever going to be useful?"

Laurel laughed. "I'm sure it's useful for *someone*." She paused. "But I won't be majoring in math or anything. Besides, I think anything you learn can help you."

"Yeah, but . . ." He closed his mouth suddenly and Laurel

309

was glad he wasn't going to drag her back into that circular argument. "I just don't understand. This human obsession with schooling, it doesn't interest me. I mean, humans interest me. *You* interest me. Even your"—he hesitated—"*family* interests me. Strange though they are," he added with a smile.

"So," she said, "Thanksgiving? Will you come?"

He smiled. "Will you be there?"

"Of course."

"Then that's my answer too."

"Good," Laurel said, looking studiously away. "It'll give me a chance to show you what I've found out about the powder," she added in a whisper.

"You found something out?" Tamani replied, touching the back of her hand.

"Not a lot," Laurel said, trying not to feel the calm pressure of his fingertips. "But a few things. Hopefully I'll know more by Thursday. I work on it every night after homework."

"I never doubted you for a second," he said, smiling softly, giving her hand a gentle squeeze.

310

# THIRTY

THANKSGIVING HAD ALWAYS BEEN ONE OF LAUREL'S favorite holidays. She wasn't entirely sure why—she couldn't eat turkey, mashed potatoes, *or* pumpkin pie, at least not the traditional varieties. But there was something about the festivities and the gathering of family that she had always enjoyed. Even when "family" only included the three of them.

This year, her mom was making two Cornish game hens instead of a turkey. "I don't see why I should bother, considering only half of the people here will even be eating it," she'd joked. It seemed like a good idea to Laurel, though, and the rosemary rub was creating a mouthwatering smell in the kitchen. If you could get past the smell of cooking meat mingled in.

Laurel's mom was working on a big vegetable tray while Laurel put the final touches on her fruit tray. She looked over at her mom to ask if she should slice the strawberries, but her mom was staring out the back window. "Mom?" Laurel said, touching her arm.

Her mom startled and looked over at Laurel. "Should we invite them in?" she asked.

"Who?"

"The sentries."

Man, *that* was a disaster waiting to happen. "No. Seriously, Mom. They're fine. When we're done I'll take the fruit and veggie trays out and see if they want some, but I don't think they'll come in."

"You sure?" she asked, gazing out at the trees, maternal concern in her eyes.

"Totally." Laurel could see it now, a whole bunch of grave, green-clad men standing in their kitchen, alert for danger, jumping at every sound. Very festive.

The doorbell rang and Laurel hopped up from her stool. "I'll get it."

"I bet you will," she barely heard her mom say under her breath.

"Mother!" she scolded just before rounding the corner.

She opened the door to Tamani, standing with the sunlight at his back, giving him an ethereal glow. She felt her knees start to wobble and wondered briefly if inviting him had really been the best idea.

He smiled and brought his face close to hers; Laurel took a sharp breath, but he just whispered, "I really don't know what I'm doing. I hope I wasn't supposed to bring something special or anything."

"Oh, no," Laurel said, smiling; it was nice to know that, beneath his cool exterior, he did worry about things sometimes. "I just wanted you to bring yourself." *Stupid, stupid! Like he could leave himself home.* She hated that he still made her tongue-tied.

Her mom was bent over the oven, checking the hens, when Laurel led Tamani into the kitchen. Laurel suspected they didn't really need checking, but it was nice to walk in and not feel like her mom was waiting expectantly. It was a little odd how supportive her parents were where Tamani was involved—her mom in particular was really making an effort. Laurel couldn't help but wonder why.

"Hey, Mom," Laurel said, "Tamani's here."

Her mom looked up and smiled, closing the oven. She wiped her hands on her apron and extended one toward Tamani. "We're so glad you could join us."

"My pleasure completely," Tamani said, sounding like a perfect English gentleman. "And . . ." he added, hesitating, "I wanted to apologize for the last time we met. The circumstances were . . . less than ideal."

But her mom waved his words away. "Oh, please." She put an arm around Laurel and smiled down at her. "When you have a daughter who's a faerie, you learn to deal with these things."

Tamani visibly relaxed. "Can I help?" he asked.

"No, no. Thanksgiving is football day. You can go sit with Mark in the rec room," she said, pointing. "And dinner will

313

be ready in about fifteen minutes."

"If you're sure," Tamani said. "I'm a great fruit slicer."

Laurel's mom laughed. "I'm sure you are. No, we've got this covered. You go."

Laurel wanted to protest, but Tamani was already smiling and heading toward the rec room. She followed him and lingered in the doorway, peeking in at the two men. Not that there was much to see; they shook hands, muttered some greetings, and then Laurel's dad tried to explain football to Tamani. Still, Laurel's mom had to call twice before she pulled herself away to finish the fruit tray.

When the meal was ready, they gathered around the kitchen table. After everyone was served, Tamani looked up and complimented Laurel's mother on her preparation of the game hens. "It all looks fabulous, Mrs. Sewell. Meat obviously isn't my thing, but it smells fantastic. Rosemary, right?"

Laurel's mom beamed. "Thank you. I'm impressed you recognized the spice. And please, Sarah and Mark. None of this mister-and-missus nonsense." She reached over and squeezed her husband's hand. "Makes us feel old."

"You *are* old," Laurel said, snickering.

Her mom raised an eyebrow. "That's quite enough out of you, missy."

"So, Tamani, tell me about being a sentry."

"Well—"

"Oh, Mark, don't pester him about work on a holiday."

"I don't mind, really," Tamani said. "I love my job. And

it's basically my life at the moment, holiday or not."

Laurel's dad peppered Tamani with questions, mostly about Tamani's position as a sentry, then moving on to growing up in Avalon, what sorts of foods they ate, and several questions about faerie economics that Tamani couldn't answer. By the time her mom finally pulled out the pie, Laurel was feeling more than a little awkward and Tamani had only managed to clear about half his plate—which had not been dished high to begin with. Laurel longed for an opportunity to smuggle him away before her dad asked too many more weird questions about Avalon's gross domestic product or political hierarchy.

"Let the boy eat," Laurel's mom scolded, shutting her husband up with a huge piece of pumpkin pie, smothered in whipped cream. For Laurel and Tamani she had small sorbet dishes filled with a sweet frozen fruit concoction.

"We usually watch a movie after dessert," Laurel's dad said to Tamani. "Care to join us?"

"I'm actually going to take Tamani on a walk," Laurel said, snatching up her opportunity before Tamani could respond. "But we should be back in time to catch the end."

"Personally," her dad said, rubbing his belly, "I would have to go on a waddle."

Laurel rolled her eyes and groaned. *Parents.* She grabbed Tamani's arm and practically dragged him toward the front door, wanting to escape before anyone else said anything.

"Anxious to have me all to yourself?" Tamani murmured with a grin as the door closed.

"I may have underestimated how awkward that was going to be."

"Awkward?" Tamani said, looking sincere. "I didn't think it was awkward. Well, at first," he admitted. "But meeting new people is always like that. Personally, I found the whole thing to be much *less* awkward than I expected. They're nice."

They wandered aimlessly for a while before Laurel realized her feet were heading down the familiar route to school. Instead of turning a different way, Laurel headed for the football field and climbed the bleachers. When she reached the top, she faced away from the field and held on to the railing, letting the wind caress her face and tangle her hair. Tamani hesitated, then came to stand beside her.

"I'm sorry you have to go through all this," he said, not looking at her. "You know, when I started as a sentry, I had pretty mild expectations. Some sentries go their entire lives never seeing a troll. You were always supposed to live a pretty normal life out at the cabin, come back to Avalon once you'd inherited the land, and . . . after that, my job would be pretty easy."

"Jamison said the same thing," Laurel said, looking over her shoulder at Tamani. "About me just living a normal human life until it was time to come back to Avalon. I guess nothing's ever as easy as we hope." She wasn't just talking about the trolls, either. Had they really expected her to walk away from her human life without so much as a backward glance?

"No," Tamani agreed, "but I keep right on hoping." He shifted, snugging in close behind her. He placed his right hand on the railing beside her, and, after a moment's hesitation, placed his left hand over hers, his chest cradling her back.

She knew she should shrug his arms off, walk away, break contact, but she couldn't. She didn't want to. And for once, she didn't make herself. She stood, unmoving, feeling him so close, and just drank it in—his presence as invigorating as the breeze across her face.

It seemed so natural that she almost didn't notice his cheek press against her neck, his chin tilt until it was his lips meeting her skin. But she couldn't ignore the soft kisses that trailed up her neck and touched her ear; the fiery sensation that coursed through her, begging her to turn and face him, to give him the permission he was silently seeking. She could hardly breathe with the weight of the wanting. Then his hand was at her waist, turning her gently toward him. He kissed the very corner of her mouth and sighed before brushing his lips softly against hers.

Summoning every ounce of self-control she had, Laurel whispered, "I can't."

"Why?" Tamani asked, his forehead pressed to hers.

"I just can't," Laurel said, turning away.

But he took both of her hands and pulled her back, looking into her eyes. "Don't mistake me," he said, so gently, so softly. "I will do anything you ask. I simply want to know why. Why do you feel so bound?"

"I promised myself. I—I have to make a decision. And being with you, kissing you, it makes my thinking fuzzy. I need a clear head."

"I'm not asking you to make a decision," Tamani said. "I just want to kiss you." He slid his hand up her neck, cupping the side of her face. "Do you want to kiss me?"

She nodded, very slightly. "But—"

"Then you can," he said. "And tomorrow I won't expect you to have made your decision. Sometimes," he said, bringing a fingertip to her bottom lip, "a kiss is simply a kiss."

"I don't want to string you along," Laurel said, her voice weak.

"I know. And I'm glad. But right now I don't care if it means nothing. Even if you never kiss me again after today— let's have today." His mouth was back at her ear, his whisper breathy and warm.

"I don't want to hurt you," Laurel said.

"How could this possibly hurt?"

"You know how it is. You'll hate me tomorrow."

"I could never hate you."

"It doesn't mean forever."

"I'm not asking for forever," Tamani said. "Yet. I'm just asking for a moment."

She had no more arguments. Well, there were little ones. Ones that didn't matter, couldn't matter when Tamani's hands were tight against her back, caressing her shoulders, his lips a breath away from hers.

Laurel leaned forward and closed the gap.

# THIRTY-ONE

EVERYTHING SEEMED FUNNY ON THE TEN-MINUTE walk back to her house. Sadly, though, Laurel's good spirits were not helping her hair at all. "Why can't you be a regular guy who carries a comb in his pocket?" she asked, trying to finger-comb through the tangles.

"When have I ever given you even the slightest impression that I am a 'regular guy'?"

"Point," Laurel said, poking his stomach.

He grabbed her, pinning her arms to her sides, and spun her around as she shrieked. He was different. Relaxed and casual in a way she hadn't seen him for weeks. Really, since the afternoon at the cabin in Orick. It was easy to focus on herself and forget that everything was at least as stressful to Tamani as it was for her. But today, in that long hour of letting themselves just *be*, they had both found a kind of rest they desperately needed. Laurel kept expecting the usual

319

guilt to settle in, but it didn't.

"This is not helping my hair," she said, gasping for breath.

"I think your hair is a lost cause," Tamani said, letting her go.

"Sadly, I imagine you're right," Laurel replied. "Maybe my parents won't notice."

"Uh, yeah, maybe," Tamani said, smirking.

"Oh, crap."

"What?" Tamani said, instantly sober and alert, stepping in front of her.

"It's fine," Laurel said, pushing him aside and gesturing to the car parked in front of her house. "Chelsea's here."

"Is that a bad thing?" Tamani asked, confused. "I mean, I think she's awesome, don't you?"

"No, she is. But she notices everything and won't hesitate to *comment*," she said meaningfully.

"Come here," Tamani said, pulling her backward toward him. "I can fix this."

Laurel stood still as Tamani smoothed her hair—detangling some knots that she couldn't see—until it laid flat again.

"Wow," Laurel said, her hands running down her smooth tresses. "Where did you learn to do that?"

He shrugged. "It's just hair. Come on." They walked, no longer hand in hand, back to the house.

Chelsea was sitting at the bar with a plate of pumpkin pie in front of her, spooning the whipped cream off the top first.

"There you are!" she said, turning as Laurel came in. "I've

been waiting for you guys for half an hour. What on earth have you been doing?"

Laurel smiled awkwardly. "Hey, Chelsea," she said, studiously ignoring the question.

"Sorry I didn't call," Chelsea said, gawking rather openly at Tamani. "I just had to get away; my brothers are a nightmare. Is he staying?"

Laurel looked up at Tamani.

"I can go," Tamani said. "I don't want to interrupt."

"No, no, stay!" Chelsea said, clapping her hands together. "A chance to dig into you all by myself. I wouldn't miss this opportunity for anything!"

"Not sure I like the sound of that," Tamani said slowly. "And we're not exactly alone."

"Oh, Laurel hardly counts."

"Thanks," Laurel said wryly.

"Not like that. I mean without the looming bundles of testosterone. You understand."

Sadly, Laurel did. "You really can go if you want," she murmured to Tamani.

"I've got nowhere to be," Tamani said, grinning.

"Don't say I didn't warn you. Mom, we're going upstairs."

"Keep the door open," her mom called reflexively.

"Yeah, 'cause *that's* going to be a problem," Laurel muttered.

"Thanks for the vote of confidence, Mrs. S." Chelsea laughed, bounding up the stairs in front of Laurel.

As Chelsea peppered Tamani with questions about faerie

longevity, garden mythology, and folk stories from around the world, Laurel's mind wandered. Wandered down to the football fields at the high school, specifically. Why couldn't she resist? Why couldn't she just be by herself for a while? Was she in love? Sometimes she was sure the answer was yes, but almost as often, she was sure the answer was no. Not while she still felt the way she did about David. She was starting to really miss him, even though she saw him almost every day. But if it wasn't love with Tamani, what was it? Not for the first time, Laurel wondered if she could be in love with them both. And, if she could, whether it mattered; it wasn't as though either of them was willing to share. Not that that seemed like any kind of an answer, either.

Pushing her dreary thoughts away, Laurel watched as Chelsea continued to grill Tamani with many of the same questions her father had asked, shaking her head as Tamani scrambled for answers thorough enough to please Chelsea.

"I give up!" Tamani said with a laugh, after about half an hour. "Your curiosity is insatiable and I find myself not equal to the task. Besides, the sun is setting and I have a cabin to visit, and before I leave, Laurel has promised to tell me about her research," Tamani said, looking at Laurel, his eyes begging for a rescue.

"I do have things to show you," Laurel said, making her way to her desk. Hoping Tamani wouldn't comment on the beaker of phosphorescent that she hadn't had the heart to touch in weeks, Laurel turned on her desk lamp and pulled forward several sparkling pots that appeared to be made of cut glass—but were actually solid diamond.

"I separated it into five samples. Hopefully it's enough." She gestured at three of the dishes as Tamani and Chelsea peered over her shoulders. "You can see I've tried some different things with these. I mixed this one with purified water to make a paste that I've been touching and tasting—"

"Tasting? Are you sure that's a good idea?" Tamani asked. "It might be poisonous."

"I checked for that first. Nothing poisonous in it. *That*, I can detect. Generally." When she saw his look of alarm she rushed on. "Besides, I've been tasting it for three days and nothing has happened to me yet. I haven't even had a headache. Trust me—it's fine."

Tamani nodded, but he didn't look entirely convinced.

"This one I've mixed with a carrier oil—that's a neutral oil that doesn't actually affect the mixture," Laurel explained to Tamani and Chelsea's blank looks. "I used almond oil this time, to settle it into parts. I was able to discover two ingredients that way."

"I didn't know you could do that," Chelsea said, her breath close to Laurel's cheek.

"I am experimenting a bit," Laurel admitted. "Breaking down a mixture into its individual ingredients is difficult. It requires me to figure out the potential of each component, then match the effects with the list of plants I know. Some are easy," she said, feeling her confidence grow as she explained the processes she'd been going through. "Plants I work with regularly, for example, like fichus and stephanotis. But there are so many components in this stuff."

"What are you doing with that one?" Chelsea asked, pointing to a dish cloudy with scorch marks.

"This one doesn't have any additives in it. I'm simply heating it over a flame and letting it cool and observing the kinds of residue it leaves. Sadly, it destroys the powder's effectiveness. But this is how I discovered the blueberry."

"Blueberry?" Chelsea asked, then tilted her head to the side. "It *is* blue."

"It's a mask. It's not doing anything in the mix. In fact, if there were much more, it would wreck the warding."

"Then why put it in?" Tamani asked.

Laurel shrugged. "No idea. I've identified eleven components, and I know there are a couple more. But the main issue is that I still haven't identified the dominant ingredient. This powder is more than half some kind of flowering tree, and I can't figure out which one."

"Like an apple tree?" Chelsea asked, but Laurel shook her head.

"More like a catalpa tree," Laurel explained. "Flowers only—no fruit. But it's not quite that." She pointed at a large stack of books beside her bed. "I've been going through those page by page trying to figure out what it is. The most maddening part is that I know I've worked with it before. I just can't remember." She sighed and looked up at Tamani. "I'll keep trying," she offered.

"I know you will," Tamani said, laying one hand on her shoulder. "And you'll figure it out in the end."

"I hope so," Laurel said, turning away from him to look

out the window. She shouldn't feel so disappointed with herself. She couldn't be expected to do what the master students at the Academy could. She hadn't even caught up with the acolytes yet, but she still kind of felt like she should have. She was the scion! She should have skills.

*Guess I've been reading too much fantasy.*

"Do you want me to bring you some more of the powder?" Tamani asked.

"Oh, no," Laurel said quickly. "It's not worth the risk. Especially when I've got two samples I haven't even tried yet."

"Let me know if you need it," Tamani said softly. "I'll find a way."

Laurel nodded, wishing they were alone. Not necessarily so she could do anything with him, but maybe just hug him good night without getting probing questions from Chelsea. But then, that might just lead to places she didn't want to go—had already gone once today.

"Well," Tamani said, before the awkwardness could set in. "I'm off. Chelsea, lovely to see you today. Be safe."

Chelsea nodded.

"And Laurel, I will see you . . . eventually." He looked at her meaningfully for a long moment, then ducked out the bedroom door.

Chelsea waited only half a second before turning to Laurel with sparkling eyes. "That was so awesome!" she said, just shy of a squeal. "He's not David," she added, "but he definitely has his own charm."

★ ★ ★

Tamani swerved to the side of the road when he saw lights wink on at Yuki's house. He had caught her just as she was arriving home. With luck, Klea might still be with her. Tamani killed the engine and silenced his phone, moving noiselessly on foot—but not so sneakily that a neighbor seeing him might call the cops. As he approached, he could hear her through the open window—it sounded like she was on the phone.

"I'm trying," Yuki said, the frustration evident in her voice. Tamani sucked in a breath and stilled, straining his ears. "I've *been* trying. But she can tell; I had to stop for a while."

Tamani held his breath, trying to catch every word. She was obviously upset and probably talking much louder than she realized.

"I know the old man can do it. That's all I ever *hear* from you. But I can't, and he's not exactly here to teach me, is he?"

Tamani tensed. Who was "she"? Who was "the old man"?

There was a long silence and Yuki sighed. "I know. I know, I'm sorry," she said, her voice small again. She said "yeah" several times and Tamani could tell the conversation was winding down. He took a couple of heavy steps and knocked on the door before she could catch him eavesdropping.

Yuki paused, then said, "I gotta go; Tam's here."

Tamani craned his neck at the window. Had she seen him? But then, who else would be knocking on her door this evening? Still, it was more than a bit uncanny. By the time she answered the door, he had a friendly smile plastered on his face.

"Hey," Yuki said, smiling winsomely. "I didn't know you were coming, did I?" She reflexively looked at her phone for some sign of a voice mail.

"No, I was just out driving and saw lights. I didn't think you'd be back yet."

"Klea got called away on business. Again. She dropped me off early and I got mad and took a walk . . . anyway," she said, thoroughly flustered now. "You want to come in?" Yuki asked, holding the door open.

"Why don't we sit on the porch?" Tamani asked. "The weather's great." She was mad at something and already sloppy. Tamani had every intention of using that to his advantage. But there was something almost sultry in her eyes tonight and Tamani didn't want her using that to *her* advantage.

"If you want," Yuki said after a hesitation that confirmed Tamani's suspicions. They sat on the steps of her porch, facing out at the street.

"What did you do for Thanksgiving?" Yuki asked.

*Lie or truth?* "Nothing," Tamani said with a grin. "It's not exactly something we celebrate in Scotland."

"We have a sort of Thanksgiving in Japan," Yuki said. "But *kinro kansha no hi* isn't celebrated in quite the same way. The break from school is nice, though."

"You can say that again," Tamani said, grinning now;

glad they were on a subject he could be honest about. "Was that Klea on the phone when I walked up?"

"Yeah," Yuki said, the bitterness back in her voice. "I'd rather not talk about it, though."

"No worries," Tamani said soothingly. Was she getting suspicious of him? Or was she just genuinely upset at Klea?

"Tam?"

"Yeah?"

She took a deep breath, as if fortifying herself for something truly painful. "Am I your girlfriend?" she blurted in a rush.

Tamani had to grit his teeth hard to keep the smile on his face. He tilted his head back and forth, as though considering. "I don't know," he finally said. "I don't really like to put labels on things. I think they get complicated when you do that. I prefer to just see what happens."

Yuki nodded. "Okay," she said, clearly nervous. "I just, I wasn't sure and I thought . . . I needed to check."

"You're welcome to check," Tamani said, smiling broadly and leaning back, propping his arms up behind him, resting one on the cement step behind Yuki's back. He felt like he'd crossed an invisible line.

He steered the conversation toward neutral ground—easy enough, all he had to do was ask if she'd seen any good movies lately—and they chatted for about an hour. Tamani still marveled at how natural it was to be with Yuki most of the time. She was easygoing and even laughed at his dumb jokes. Under different circumstances they might have been friends, and it made him a little sad to know it was never to be—even if she was innocent, if she ever found out how much he'd lied and pretended, she would never speak to him again.

He tried a few times to nudge the conversation back toward Yuki and her life, but she avoided his questions and changed the subject entirely if he so much as mentioned Klea. It was frustrating, but Tamani finally decided that he would chalk up tonight to an evening of building trust. Hopefully that would pay off eventually.

"I better go," Tamani said, eyeing the moon as it peered out from behind the clouds. "My uncle doesn't know where I am."

"Okay," Yuki said, rising slowly to her feet.

Tamani stood beside her for a second, wondering if he was going to have to hug her.

She took a deep breath, then stepped toward him and he steeled himself to return an embrace. But she wasn't aiming for his chest. He forced himself not to flinch as she planted a kiss against his lips. It was a nervous kiss, quick and tentative and not at all intimate. He quelled the urge to swipe his arm across his mouth.

"Oops," Yuki said coyly. "It just . . . happened."

# THIRTY-TWO

"ARE YOU OKAY?" CHELSEA JOINED LAUREL ON the floor, where she was slumped with her back against her locker, wracking her brain for some way to use the final sample. She'd decided to suspend one of the samples in wax yesterday and turn it into a candle to see what happened when she burned it. She had only succeeded in filling her room with a foul-smelling smoke that lingered in her curtains and bedding even after she'd left the windows open all night.

Which had made for a frigid night. Winter was still technically a week away, but a wet chill had descended on Crescent City and Laurel hadn't managed to really warm up all day.

"I'm fine," Laurel said, looking over at her friend. "Just a little tired. And I have a headache." After several headache-free weeks, they had come back with a vengeance after

Thanksgiving break. She hadn't experienced stress headaches like this since last year, when things had gotten sticky with the trolls.

"Do you need to go outside for lunch?" Chelsea asked.

"It's raining pretty hard. I don't really feel like it." She shrugged. "I should probably just eat something." She always got a little run-down toward the end of the semester, but dealing with David, Tamani, and Yuki was twice as exhausting as fighting trolls, which—as it was practically a holiday tradition now—might have been preferable.

But Shar wasn't going to let that happen. No matter how many times she or Tamani suggested they just raid the cabin and be done with it, Shar refused. After three weeks it seemed like a lost cause to Laurel, but Shar insisted it was too dangerous to barge in without knowing more, and would destroy their chance to learn something new besides. So they continued to watch and wait and wind tighter with every passing day.

Laurel tried to shake her gloomy thoughts away and smiled at her friend. "I'll be fine. It's just the end of the semester."

"Yeah, finals. I totally get it." Chelsea sighed. "I should just give up. I mean, unless David crashes and burns this semester there's no way I can beat his GPA." She laughed. "Of course, if I do slack off, this will be the one semester he does crash and burn, and then I'll know that I could have beaten him, but I was lazy. So, it's studyville for me," she said, giving Laurel a sarcastic thumbs-up.

Laurel smiled and shook her head. She was proud of her

good grades, but David and Chelsea took it to a whole different level.

The hallways were emptying out. Laurel thought about heading for the cafeteria, but she didn't want to stand up. She wasn't normally one for naps, but now seemed like a great time to make an exception.

"Can I ask you a really weird question?"

Laurel stared at her. "You just did. At least for you."

Chelsea chuckled nervously. "I just . . . I just wondered. You've been broken up with David for a while now. Are you guys done for good?"

Laurel studied the floor. "I don't know."

"Still?"

Laurel shrugged.

"So, if—hypothetically—I were to ask him to the winter formal next week, would that be a problem?"

Laurel gaped at Chelsea as a strange feeling settled in her stomach. "Did you break up with Ryan?"

Chelsea rolled her eyes. "No, no. Thus the hypothetical part."

"That's a pretty extreme hypothetical," Laurel said. Her mind was racing. It wasn't that she actually expected Chelsea to ask David. But . . . what if she did?

Chelsea shrugged.

"I—I . . ." Laurel couldn't even think of anything to say. The idea that David would go to any kind of formal dance with anyone but her was beyond comprehension. Laurel and David hadn't missed a formal dance since sophomore year.

"Forget it," Chelsea said. "I can see it bothers you. I'm sorry I said anything. Please don't be mad."

"No," Laurel said, climbing to her feet and extending a hand to help Chelsea up. "It's okay. I'm glad you said something. Really. Are things that bad between you and Ryan? You haven't said anything about his scores in a while. I figured that got sorted out."

"More like swept under the rug," Chelsea said, shrugging. "Anyway, let's go get some food in you."

But suddenly food wasn't even on the list of things Laurel was thinking about. With the mystery of the trolls' cabin, the unsolved puzzle of the blue powder, and Yuki's constant presence, Laurel hadn't had the time—much less the energy—to think about something like the winter formal. But now that Chelsea had brought it up, it somehow took priority. Laurel wasn't sure exactly what she was going to do, but her mind was screaming at her to do *something*.

The noise of the cafeteria assaulted her ears as she studied the tops of the students' heads, looking for David. He was pretty easy to spot, sitting beside Ryan, the two of them head and shoulders above most of the other kids around them. Chelsea got in the hot lunch line while Laurel strode over and tapped David on the shoulder.

"Hey!" he said, turning to her with a grin. So *friendly*. David was a model of platonic affection—except for the longing in his eyes. She wasn't sure she wanted to lose that. Ever.

"Can I talk to you? Somewhere quieter?" she asked.

"Sure," he said, getting up a little too quickly.

They walked together until they found a somewhat secluded section of the hallway.

"Is everything all right?" David asked, touching her shoulder.

"I—" Now that she had him here she wasn't sure she'd be able to squeak out any words at all. "I was wondering . . ." She took a deep breath and blurted, "Have you asked anyone to the winter formal?" Only as the words tumbled out of her mouth did she realize she'd made up her mind.

Surprise was evident on his face. She wondered if it was mirrored on her own.

"I was just thinking . . . I was hoping maybe we could go. Sorry if it seems awkward, I just think we shouldn't let this . . . stuff . . . totally destroy our social life and I figured maybe—" She forced her mouth shut before she babbled any more.

"What exactly are you asking me, Laurel?" David asked, studying the tops of his shoes.

And with those few words, Laurel realized what she'd just done. She'd asked David on a date. What did that mean for them? What did it mean for Tamani? Her head spun and she was confused again. She looked down, avoiding his eyes. Not that it really mattered; he wasn't looking at her, either. "I just want to go to the dance with you, David. As . . . as friends," she tacked on, thinking of Tamani.

He hesitated and for a moment Laurel thought he might turn her down.

"Okay," he said at last, nodding. "That would be great." Then he was smiling and his eyes were shining with hope. Laurel wondered if she'd made a huge mistake.

But part of her was just glad he'd said yes.

"What day do you finish finals?" Tamani asked, flipping idly through Laurel's Government textbook while she rummaged through the fridge for something to eat.

"Friday," Laurel said, wondering if Tamani had ever done more than flip randomly through any of his schoolbooks. "Friday *morning*. After that I get the rest of the day off."

"Are you going to go to that dance on Saturday—the winter formal?"

Laurel looked up at him, butterflies fluttering in her stomach. "What exactly are you asking me?" She knew they couldn't go together—it was too dangerous—but she was suddenly feeling a painful sort of déjà vu.

"Well, Yuki sort of . . . expects that we're going together. I never asked her, but she's practically planned the whole thing already. She wanted me to ask if we could go as a group again. I guess she really enjoyed that, in spite of how it ended. I know you're not with David anymore, so it's okay if—"

"No, it's fine," Laurel said. She wondered how hard it had been for Tamani to even imply that she ought to pair up with David for something. "I actually already talked to David about it. We're going together. As friends," she added, before Tamani could read too much into this bit of news.

"So a group thing would be nice. But let's not invite the trolls this time."

"Don't worry," Tamani said. "I've got it all figured out. No more troll ambushes. No more last-minute rescues by persons of questionable integrity. We'll have two squads shadowing us all night, in addition to the ones behind your house, watching the cabin, making rounds through the city, watching traffic on the 101 and the 199, plus reserves standing by."

Laurel stared at him, mouth agape, eyes wide. "How many sentries are here now?"

"About two hundred."

*Two hundred!*

"I'm done playing games," Tamani said darkly. "We had two squads in Crescent City when Barnes tried to grab you and David last year. We had three behind your house when he lured them off and snatched Chelsea. There were almost a hundred sentries in place two months ago and we *still* had trolls ambush us within a mile of your house. Any troll that tries to crash *this* party will be dead before it lays eyes on you."

"Or Yuki," Laurel added.

"Or Yuki," Tamani agreed. "Or Chelsea, or anyone. It doesn't matter who they're after. The only thing I want trolls doing in Crescent City is dying."

"Does that mean Shar is going to raid the cabin?" Laurel didn't like talking so directly about killing—even trolls— but she had to admit she wasn't feeling very sympathetic lately. Absently, she picked up a petal—one of her own—from a decorative silver bowl on the counter. Her mother had preserved several with hairspray and left them out where the sun could hit them, lending a hint of their beautiful perfume to the kitchen air.

"He keeps saying we should wait. I hate waiting," Tamani said, "but I doubt he'll wait much longer. It's been almost a month and we haven't learned anything."

"Maybe we can start a club," Laurel said ruefully. "I haven't learned anything useful about the powder, either."

"What about the phosphorescent?"

"Honestly? I haven't tried anything new since I mixed it with your sap. I think individual faeries of the same season might differ as much as faeries of different seasons. I'd probably have to test half of Avalon before I could draw useful conclusions."

Realizing she was digging her fingernails into the petal, Laurel forced herself to relax. She'd left four little half-moon gouges in the otherwise unblemished field of blue. Dropping it back into the bowl, Laurel rubbed her fingers together, wiping away the tiny droplet of moisture that hadn't yet dried out of the preserved petal.

She paused for a second, and then rubbed her fingers again.

"No way," she whispered, almost to herself, half forgetting that Tamani was even in the room.

He started to talk, but she held up one finger and concentrated on the essence that lingered at the tips of her fingers. It had to be. She was amazed she hadn't figured it out before.

*Talk about the answer being right under your nose.*

Snatching the petal back out of the bowl, Laurel bounded out of the kitchen and took the stairs two at a time. She pulled her last dish of blue powder forward and forced herself to breathe evenly.

"Is everything all right?" Tamani asked, appearing in her doorway.

"I'm fine," she said, trying to stop her hands from shaking. She licked her finger and collected a few grains of the blue powder. She rubbed them against the fingers on her other hand. The sensation was almost identical.

"What—"

"The main ingredient of the powder. The one I've been looking for. The flowering tree. I can't *believe* I didn't think of it sooner. I even knew it was possible," she said. "I knew after you kissed me that day, that faeries could be used as ingredients, and I never even considered—"

"Laurel!" Tamani said, placing his hands on her shoulders. "What *is* it?"

Laurel held up the long, light-blue petal she'd taken from the bowl. "It's this," she said, hardly believing the words coming out of her own mouth. "It's faerie blossom."

"But . . . Yuki hasn't blossomed—at least, not since we started hanging out. If she had . . ." Tamani wiggled his fingers, where telltale pollen would have exposed Yuki's secret. "Unless she's a Spring or Summer, there's no way that blossom is hers."

"I don't know," Laurel interjected. "There's something

about this powder. I think—" Laurel forced herself to relax, trying to trust her intuition, no matter how it horrified her. "I think the petals have to be fresh. Not dried or wilted. . . . Tamani, somebody cut these petals off," she said, the macabre proclamation sending a shiver up her back. Cutting tiny pieces from her own blossom had stung; losing a fourth of it to a troll attack had hurt for days. She couldn't imagine how badly it would hurt to cut off the entire blossom—but a warding large enough to hide a cabin in the forest would need that many petals.

"Cutting off a blossom would still leave some kind of . . . texture. I felt Yuki's back very carefully when we were at the autumn dance and there was nothing but skin there. So even if she is the Fall faerie who made this, the blossom couldn't have come from her."

Was that hope in his voice? Laurel tried not to think too hard about that. Hadn't she, at one point, hoped for Yuki's innocence herself? "But that doesn't make any sense. Why would she make a hideout for trolls? I thought they were after her!"

Tamani was quiet for a moment. "What do we know about Klea? For sure, I mean."

"She likes guns," Laurel said. "And she's got those stupid sunglasses she never takes off."

"Why would anyone wear sunglasses all the time?" Tamani asked.

"To hide your eyes . . . ," Laurel said, realization dawning.

"And you said there would be no way to hide a blossom

under the fitted clothing she wears, but—"

"But if she *cut it off*, she would have nothing to hide." Klea. A faerie. Laurel's mind was racing now. Faerie poison had been used to make her dad sick. Faerie blood had been used to lure Laurel's sentries away last year. And now there were trolls showing up who were immune to faerie magic. There was evidence of faerie intervention thrust deeply into everything that had happened to her over the last two years. The thought made Laurel's stomach churn. Everything had been so much simpler when she could tell friend from foe just by looking at them. But when your enemy's face could practically be the one you looked at in the mirror every day . . . ?

"If she's working with the trolls, why did she kill Barnes?" Tamani asked, talking as much to himself as to her.

"Barnes said he made a deal with a devil," Laurel said, recalling the troll's strange words. "That's exactly how a troll would see working with a faerie. What if he tried to go back on his deal?"

Tamani nodded. "And if for some reason Klea wanted you alive—which she must, because she's had plenty of opportunity to kill you—"

"She'd have to protect me by finishing him off," Laurel said, half in shock. "And if she saved my life, maybe I would be more likely to . . . what? Help her with something? Barnes was trying to get to Avalon. What kind of faerie would want to get a bunch of trolls into Avalon?"

"The kind with a grudge," Tamani said darkly, pulling his iPhone out of his pocket. "I think we need to seriously

340

consider the possibility that Yuki is nothing but a distraction, that there are no troll hunters, and that the trolls have been working for Klea all along."

"But . . . a distraction from *what*? What is she after?"

"I don't know," said Tamani, putting his phone to his ear. "But I think it's long past time for us to find out what she's keeping in that cabin."

# THIRTY-THREE

LAUREL KNELT ON THE FLOOR, SCRUBBING OUT THE bottom of her locker with a wet paper towel—something every student had to do before leaving for winter break. Technically she was required to clean it with the can of heavy-duty cleaner, but that stuff wasn't exactly faerie-friendly. Besides, the teachers didn't watch very closely. If anything, they were more anxious for winter break than their students.

"Hey, slowpoke, let's go!" Chelsea said teasingly. "You have to come over and help me pick out a dress!"

Laurel smiled her apology. "I'm almost done," she said, gesturing at her locker.

"You want some help?" Chelsea asked, reaching for a roll of paper towels that had been left in the hall for them by the janitorial staff.

"Sure, you can clean my locker and I'll pick your dress;

how's that for a trade?"

"Hey, sounds fair to me," Chelsea said. "Are you going to wear that one dress?"

"I think so," Laurel said. Chelsea was referring to the dress Laurel had brought back from Avalon and worn to the Samhain festival. Ever since Laurel had told her about it, Chelsea had been pestering her to wear it to a dance. "I don't—"

Laurel just managed to bite off a scream as her head exploded with literally blinding pain. An eerie, whistling wind filled her head with sound and pressure and darkness.

And then it was gone.

"Laurel? Laurel, are you all right?"

Laurel opened her eyes to discover she had fallen backward and was now sprawled on the floor. Chelsea was kneeling next to her, concern written all over her face. Laurel sat up and glanced furtively around her, embarrassed. She hoped nobody else had seen her fall over like a moron.

Her eyes met Yuki's. She was in the middle of cleaning out her locker across the hallway, and looked away immediately, covering a smile with one delicate hand.

Momentarily, Laurel wondered if Yuki might be the *cause* of her headaches. She'd often been around when they struck . . . but then, she'd practically invaded every aspect of Laurel's life, so she was *always* around. Besides, "causing headaches" was not a faerie power, and even if it was, there were easier ways to distract Laurel from whatever it was Yuki was supposed to be distracting her from. Not that it mattered. If Yuki was doing something, it would all be over in a few days. Shar had arrived and was even now strategizing with Tamani.

"Let's get out of here," Laurel muttered, embarrassed.

Chelsea put a protective arm around her and they walked out toward Laurel's car.

They drove in silence, which at first Laurel thought was weird, but she quickly realized it was restful. All week she had been jumping at every sound, waiting for something to happen. For Yuki to realize they'd found out about Klea— for trolls to come barreling through the school wall—she didn't even know what. But something! The world had changed and no one else seemed to sense it. Yuki still clung to Tamani; Ryan still hung around cluelessly; Laurel and David and Chelsea tried to talk and laugh normally. Not to mention pass their final exams.

At Chelsea's house, Laurel did her best to put all of this aside. She had always liked Chelsea's house. No matter what happened in her own life, at Chelsea's house it was only her brothers who were the monsters, her room that was the mess, and the most difficult decision Laurel would be asked to make was the black dress or the red one.

"The red, I think," Laurel said, as Chelsea put it on for the third time.

"Why are we going to the dance with her, anyway?" Chelsea asked, examining herself in the full-length mirror that doubled as her closet door. "If we know Yuki's a distraction or whatever, then why does it matter if we keep her occupied? I so want to just ditch her. And what's she distracting us from, again?"

"The cabin," Laurel said, though she wondered what could be in the cabin that was worth keeping from them. "For all we know, Yuki doesn't even know the role she's playing. Klea is some kind of puppet-master, I'm telling you. But just in case, until they actually raid the cabin, we're supposed to act like nothing has changed."

"When are they going to raid?"

Laurel shrugged. Shar had been characteristically vague about that. The way he kept putting it off was driving Tamani crazy.

"Hmph. Well, Tamani's boss. Or is it Shar?" She looked at the mirror as Laurel shrugged again, twisting her curls up on top of her head. "You don't think it clashes with my hair?"

"Actually, I think it brings out the auburn," Laurel said, grateful to be done talking about Yuki. "I think you look gorgeous in it. Ryan is going to swoon," she said with a grin.

Chelsea's face fell.

"What?" Laurel said. "Is it the college thing? You won't even know for sure on that for a couple months yet."

Chelsea shook her head.

"Then what?" Laurel asked.

Chelsea turned and sat silently on the bed beside Laurel.

"Tell me," Laurel said, her voice soft.

Laurel saw tears gather at the corner of Chelsea's eyes.

"Chelsea, what?" she asked, a hand on her shoulder.

"I've been thinking for days how to tell you and make you understand. And not lose you in the process."

"Oh, Chelsea," Laurel said, her hand immediately on Chelsea's shoulder. "You could never lose me. You are my best friend in the whole world. There is nothing you could tell me that would change that."

"I'm breaking up with Ryan after the dance."

Laurel blanched. She wasn't sure what she had been expecting, but this wasn't it. "Why? Did something happen?"

Chelsea laughed. "Besides me constantly running off at inopportune times and keeping half my life a secret from him?"

But Laurel didn't laugh. "I mean, did he say something? Did *you* say something?"

Chelsea shook her head. "No, he's been fine. *We've* been fine. I mean, he didn't apply to Harvard, but so what? I might not even get in there. Just because he doesn't want to go to Harvard doesn't mean he doesn't care about me," she said, bitterness coloring her tone. "It just means he cares about staying in California more." She paused, taking a slow breath. "But really, I can't expect him to throw his dreams away for me. It's because of you, actually."

"Me?" Laurel asked, shocked. "What did I do?"

"You broke up with David," Chelsea said softly.

Laurel looked down in her lap. Now she knew what was coming.

"I thought I was over him. I really did. And I was happy

with Ryan. Very happy. But then you broke up with David and he got so sad and I realized that when the two of you first got together, I was okay letting him go because he was *happy*. Now that he's not, I—" She paused, taking a moment to compose herself. "If he's not happy, I can't make myself be happy."

Laurel was silent. She couldn't even muster up any jealousy. She just felt numb.

"I'm not going to chase him," Chelsea said, as if reading Laurel thoughts. "It's not fair, and it's disloyal, and I *won't* do that to you. But," she said, taking a deep breath, "if *he* decides to actually notice me after all these years and I miss it because I'm forcing myself to stay with Ryan, I . . ." She blinked back tears. "I would hate myself. So I'm just going to—to be there, if he needs me. And since you're my best friend, I thought it was only fair to tell you."

Laurel nodded, but couldn't meet Chelsea's eyes. She was right; it was only fair. In fact, it would be easier. If things worked out between David and Chelsea, then everyone would have someone.

So why did it make her weep inside?

They sat in silence for several seconds before Laurel threw her arms around Chelsea, hugging her tightly. "Wear the red dress," Laurel whispered in her ear. "You look best in that one."

# THIRTY-FOUR

LAUREL STOOD IN FRONT OF THE MIRROR, STUDYING her reflection. The irony of wearing the dress she'd worn to the Samhain festival with Tamani last year to a human dance with David this year was not lost on her. But it was her favorite dress, she hadn't had a chance to wear it since then, and she didn't really want to go out and buy something new. She'd pulled her hair up in a sparkling clip—also from Avalon—and then let it down again about six times. She didn't have much longer to make up her mind.

In ten, no, seven minutes, everyone would be downstairs, all dressed up and pretending to like one another before heading to the dance. In separate cars, this time. Tamani insisted. Just in case.

The cold, rainy fall had given way to a less rainy but even colder winter and Laurel hoped she wouldn't look too weird with just a light wrap. Without the sun to rejuvenate her, she couldn't handle wearing a jacket. It was too confining, too tiring.

She wondered what Tamani would wear. He'd never been to a human formal dance and she wondered if she should have stopped by his apartment to make sure he had something suitable. The black getup complete with cloak that he had worn when he escorted her to Avalon last year had been stunning, but not exactly appropriate for a high school dance.

Deciding that the sparkling clip would probably take at least some attention off her face—and therefore away from the concerned expression she couldn't seem to erase no matter how she tried to smooth it with a smile—Laurel stuck the clip back in her hair and forced herself away from the mirror and down the stairs.

"You look gorgeous!" her mom said from the kitchen.

"Thanks, Mom," Laurel said, smiling over her stress. She put her arms around her mom's neck. "I really needed to hear that right now."

"Is everything okay?" her mom asked, pulling back and looking at Laurel.

"The whole David and Tamani thing—remember he's Tam in front of Yuki—is just . . . stressful. On top of everything else, I mean." She had warned her parents that Klea was probably a faerie and not to be trusted, but there wasn't much they could do but play along like everyone else.

Turning Laurel gently around, her mom lightly rubbed her back, just the way Laurel liked it. "How's your head?"

she asked, kneading her neck now.

"Fine," Laurel said. "It got pretty bad yesterday, but with finals out of the way I'm hoping for a nice, relaxing break."

Her mom nodded. "I admit, I'm a little surprised it's David who's coming to pick you up tonight."

"Why is everyone surprised!" Laurel said in exasperation.

"Well, you did break up with him."

Laurel said nothing.

"After Thanksgiving, I thought for sure you were going to be with Tamani."

"He has to watch Yuki."

"And if he didn't?"

Laurel shrugged. "I don't know."

"Listen," her mom said, turning Laurel to face her now, "there's nothing wrong with taking time to just be yourself. I'm the last person to tell you that you need a guy to make you happy. But if you're not moving on because you're afraid you'll hurt David, maybe you need to remember that you're hurting Tamani by *not* moving on, and you might be hurting David by not letting *him* really move on. If—and I'm not saying you should choose him, but *if*—you really love Tamani, and you keep putting him off because of David, by the time you're finally ready to be with him, you may find that he's moved on. That's all I'm going to say," her mom finished, smiling now and turning back to the desserts, which she was piping out of a pastry bag into little edible works of art.

"No one's going to eat those, Mom."

Her mom looked down at the beautiful desserts with concern. "Why not?"

"They're too pretty."

"Just like you," she said, leaning in to kiss Laurel's forehead.

A knock sounded at the door and butterflies started up in Laurel's stomach again. She was chagrined to realize it didn't matter who was actually at the door. They all made her nervous.

She opened the door to find Tamani waiting on her porch. He was alone, wearing a black tux with full tails, a shimmering white vest and bow tie, and had topped it off with shiny black shoes and white dress gloves, as though headed to a white-tie affair. Despite being called a winter *formal*, Laurel knew that most of the guys in attendance would be, at most, wearing dress suits and ties. Tamani probably wouldn't be the only one in a tux—David seemed to enjoy wearing them—but he would still be the most formally dressed person at the dance. In wondering whether he'd wear the wrong clothes, Laurel had not considered that he might dress *too* well.

While taking in his appearance, Laurel realized that he looked almost as nervous as she felt—more than a little unusual, for Tamani. "Are you okay?"

Tamani leaned close. "Is anyone else here yet?"

Laurel shook her head.

"Good." Tamani ducked into the foyer and pushed the door shut. "Yuki asked me not to pick her up."

"Like, she canceled?" Laurel asked, her stomach clenching. Had she found something out?

"No, she said she was running behind and would meet me at the dance. But something isn't right."

"She knows I planned dessert. Maybe she doesn't want to draw attention to the way she eats. I mean, she has no idea we all know what she is. Well, except Ryan. Honestly, it sounds like something I would do," she added in a quiet voice.

"Maybe. But she sounded . . . weird. On the phone."

Laurel looked up as the doorbell rang. "You have sentries watching her house?"

Tamani nodded. "But her house is practically a fortress tonight—all curtains drawn, a sheet thrown over the front window. It just doesn't sit right."

"There's not much we can do until we find her at the dance," Laurel whispered. She paused, then added, in an even quieter whisper, "You look incredible."

Tamani looked startled for a second, then he smiled. "Thanks. You look amazing too. Just like you do every day."

The doorbell—practically next to her ear—startled her and Laurel shooed Tamani into the kitchen. Then she opened the door to David, Ryan, and Chelsea.

"Look at you!" Chelsea said, rushing forward to hug Laurel. She was wearing the red dress Laurel had recommended. It set off her complexion perfectly and brought out the gray in her eyes. "You look fabulous. Is this the . . . the dress you were telling me about?" she asked, her eyes flitting to Ryan for just an instant.

"Yeah," Laurel said, spreading the skirt a little. "I was really happy to find it." *Find it. Ha!* In Avalon you literally did just find clothes in the marketplace and then take them home.

"Well, the dance starts in, like, fifteen minutes and I was promised dessert," Chelsea said, smiling playfully. "Ryan wouldn't let me get dessert with my dinner, so there better be some here."

"Don't listen to her," Ryan said, pushing her gently toward the kitchen. "I told her she could have two desserts—she just didn't take me up on it."

Chelsea grinned at him and they both headed toward the kitchen. Laurel looked wistfully after them. It had been hard even looking at Ryan since talking with Chelsea, knowing what was coming. He still seemed completely head over heels for her. A niggling voice in the back of her head reminded her that he had lied to Chelsea about college applications, but did he deserve being totally blindsided by a breakup because of that?

Laurel turned to David, who had just stepped into the foyer. He was wearing a neatly cut tuxedo jacket over a black, mandarin-collared silk shirt with a shiny black button at the throat instead of a bow tie. He was different from the boy she'd met two years ago. Tonight, elegant and handsome in all black, he looked like he could take on anything.

"Hi," Laurel said, feeling strangely shy. He was looking at her dress and she could practically see him connecting the dots in his head. But when his eyes met hers, she couldn't tell what he was thinking.

"You look beautiful" was all he said.

Laurel was a nervous wreck as David pulled into the crowded high school parking lot. Despite her calm words to Tamani, it *was* weird for Yuki to be so late. Especially now that their only job was to keep her out of the way until they could figure out what to do about Klea. But there was nothing to do but take David's arm and try to appear calm as he escorted her to the front door.

Tamani brushed past Laurel, closing the distance between himself and the gym doors in a few loping strides. Yuki was there, waiting, in a silvery formal that must have been custom made. The dress folded around her, resembling a traditional kimono, complete with a V-neck that Laurel found shockingly low-cut. But instead of heavy brocade, Yuki's dress was a light satin with a chiffon overlay that blew around her ankles in the light evening breeze. Its top sat almost off her shoulders, with little cap sleeves that were lined with something sparkly, and a lace-covered obi wrapped around her waist and tied in an intricate knot that covered most of her back and came just high enough that her black hair, hanging in soft ringlets, brushed against it. Dramatic black lined her shining green eyes and her lips were painted a luscious red. She looked exquisite.

"Are you okay?" Tamani asked, one hand running down her shoulder in a way that made Laurel clutch David's arm a little tighter. There was obviously nothing wrong with her. *She probably just didn't want to admit it took her four hours to get into that thing*, Laurel thought, frustrated now that Yuki had made both her and Tamani worry so much when there was clearly no reason. She was radiant in the twilight, not to mention the glow of Tamani's attention. Her whole face lit up when he looked at her, talked to her, and it made Laurel want to slap that smile right off her face.

Laurel forced herself to turn away from Yuki and Tamani and focus on David. He *was* her date tonight, after all. She took a few calming breaths as she walked into the gym on his arm. The student council had definitely outdone themselves. The ceiling was draped with black tulle that melted into cushiony piles on the floor, with icicle lights hanging every few inches so the effect was a dark sky blazing with starlight. Instead of regular folding chairs, every chair had been covered in fabric, the way Laurel occasionally saw at weddings or really nice restaurants, and there was a huge display of petits fours at the refreshment table that looked lovely, although Laurel couldn't eat them. There were even two fans with curled ribbons tied to them to keep the air circulating as the gym filled up with people.

"Wow," David said, "this is way better than last year."

As a new song started up, David picked up Laurel's hand from his arm and pulled her out toward the floor. "Come dance with me," he said softly. He led her far onto the floor, to where the entrance was out of sight—something Laurel was quite sure was not an accident. Then his arms tightened around her and they began to sway in time with the music.

"You really look incredible tonight," he whispered, close to her ear.

Laurel lowered her eyelids and smiled. "Thank you. You too. Black looks good on you."

"If I admit my mom helped me pick it out, will you laugh?"

Laurel grinned. "No. Your mom has always had excellent taste. But *you* are the one who wears it. You get all the credit for that."

"Hey, I'm just glad you noticed."

# THIRTY-FIVE

TAMANI HAD TO ADMIT, FOR AN INDOOR PARTY THAT lacked any Summer illusions, the humans had done a good job. He couldn't help but smile at Yuki's seedling-like enthusiasm as she gasped and smiled at the splendor. It was easier to be around her now, knowing she wasn't the danger—she was just the distraction, and she might not even be aware of that. "This is amazing," she said, her eyes twinkling with the reflected sparkle of a hundred strings of lights.

Without saying a word, Tamani walked Yuki onto the dance floor, just at the edge, where the crowd was thinner. "You're lovely tonight," he said.

Yuki looked immediately shy. "Thank you," she said softly. "I—I hoped you would like it."

"Very much," Tamani replied. That, at least, wasn't a lie. Her dress was stunning. A different style than he'd ever seen before, but all the more beautiful for that. He forced himself not to think about what Laurel would look like in it. He shook his head a little, a physical reminder that he had other things to concentrate on. "I was sorry to not be able to pick you up," Tamani said, his voice low enough that Yuki had to lean forward a little to hear him. He laid one hand low on her waist and ran his other all the way down her arm, then folded her hand into his and pulled her close—a traditional dance pose, rather than the strange, leaning bear-hug the humans seemed to prefer—and stepped softly to the music.

"I'm sorry too," Yuki said. "It . . . it couldn't be helped." She glanced down, and Tamani thought she looked embarrassed. Then, very quietly, she added, "I was packing."

Tamani felt his whole body tense. "Packing?" *Of course she wouldn't stay here alone during the winter break*, Tamani chided himself. *Calm down.* Hopefully she had interpreted the tight squeeze of her hand as a sign of affection. He led Yuki into a spin under his arm, and then back close where she stepped evenly, expertly, matching him with a delicate grace that marked her as unmistakably fae.

"Klea is coming for me tomorrow," she said evenly, her voice strained, but controlled.

"When will you be back?" Tamani asked, his voice calm. It wasn't that unusual.

"I . . . I—" she said, but looked down, avoiding his eyes.

She was supposed to lie, he could tell. But he wanted the truth. In another few hours it might not matter, but for once, he wanted the truth. He tilted his face close to hers and let his cheek touch her face, his lips just brushing her ear. "Tell me," he whispered.

"I'm not supposed to come back at all," she said, her voice catching.

He pulled back, not having to fake the horror written across his face. "Never?"

She shook her head, her eyes darting around the room as if afraid someone would catch her dropping her secret. "I don't want to leave. Klea—she wasn't happy that I came tonight at all, but I was *not* going to miss this."

This was an act of rebellion then—and one of which Yuki was clearly proud.

He was silent for a moment and Yuki looked up at him, waiting for him to say something, do something. He gave himself another moment to think by pulling her close and listening to her shallow breathing as he again brushed her earlobe with his lips. "Can't you stay?" he asked, digging now. "Won't she listen to you?"

"Klea doesn't listen to *anyone*," Yuki grumbled.

He stopped now, stopped dancing entirely, letting the other couples swaying around him make room for them. He reached out a gloved hand and ran his fingers down the side of her face, her heavy lashes fluttering closed at his touch. "How far will you go?"

"I don't know."

"Back to Japan?"

"No, no, not that far. I'm pretty sure we're staying in California."

He looked over his shoulder when someone bumped him;

instead of pulling Yuki in close, he led her into a graceful stretch, then held out his hand, inviting her to come near this time. She jumped at the chance, pulling herself against his chest, lifting her face up close to his as they resumed swaying. "She won't take your cell phone, will she?" Tamani asked, his mouth only a breath away from her lips.

"I . . . I don't think so."

"Then I can call you, right? And I have a car. I could come and see you."

"Would you?"

Tamani leaned just a little closer, his forehead brushing hers. "Oh, absolutely."

"Then I'll figure out a way," Yuki promised.

"Why now?" Tamani asked, leading Yuki backward in a slow, waltz-like circle around the human dancers. Even as he pushed her for secrets and signs, she followed him easily, and he found that he enjoyed dancing with her. "Can't you stay till Christmas? It's only a few more days."

Yuki shook her head. "I can't. It's . . . not a good idea."

"Why?" Tamani asked, injecting a hint of longing into his voice, hoping he wasn't prodding too hard.

"I—" Her gaze faltered and she looked down again. "Klea says it's too dangerous."

The music changed and Tamani led her a little faster now, into a series of more complicated steps. *Take her mind off her mouth*, Tamani thought to himself. "I don't want you to go," he whispered.

Yuki's face lifted, her eyes soft. "Really?"

Tamani forced himself not to grit his teeth. "There's something different about you."

Her expression was momentarily guarded, but she smiled his words away. "I'm not different. I'm just a regular person."

She was pretty good. But Tamani had been lying since before her sprout opened its petals. "No," he said sweetly, pulling her tight against his body, feeling her erratic breathing as he did. "You're special. I can tell. There's something amazing about you." He laid his cheek right on hers now, and felt her hand tremble in his. "And I can't wait to find out more."

Yuki smiled and opened her mouth to say something, but Tamani felt his phone buzzing in his pocket.

"Just a sec," Tamani muttered, pulling his phone out just enough that he could see the display. Sure enough, Aaron's number was lit up on the screen. Tamani looked up at Yuki and apologized with his eyes. "It's my uncle. I'll be right back." He squeezed her hand. "Why don't you go get something to drink?" He smiled at her for another second before walking quickly from the dance floor.

"I'm really glad I came with you," Laurel said, looking up at David.

"Really?"

"Yeah. It was good to clear the air. I—" She paused. "You have to know that I hadn't planned to break up with you. It just happened."

"I do know that. But I was so riled up. You were justified."

"I kinda was, wasn't I?"

David rolled his eyes. "I'll do better," he said. "If you'll just give me a chance."

"David—"

"I'm going to keep hoping," David said, raising her hand up to his lips and kissing her knuckles.

Laurel couldn't help but smile. Over David's shoulder, she noticed Tamani striding out of the gym, his phone held to his ear, his face unreadable. "Something's happening," Laurel said. "I'll be right back."

Trying not to draw too much attention to herself, Laurel followed Tamani out into the lobby.

"You raided without me?" Tamani whispered, his eyes darting left and right as he backed into a dark corner, locking eyes with Laurel for a brief instant as she approached. "Well, I'm glad you're still alive. Goddess only knows what could have happened. What was in there?"

"We raided because I knew you wouldn't be able to join us." Shar's voice sounded in Tamani's ear. Through *Aaron's* phone. Apparently Shar had "forgotten" his iPhone back in the forest. His *human trinket.* "I told you—you've been spreading yourself too thin."

"You had no right—"

"I had every right. I am in command here, though you seem happy to forget that when it's convenient to you."

Tamani clenched his teeth; when it came to matters concerning Laurel, chain of command was not the only

362

consideration, and Shar knew it. "What did you find?" he asked emotionlessly.

"It was empty, Tamani."

David walked up and stood beside Laurel.

"Empty?" Tamani asked in disbelief. "What do you mean, *empty?*"

"Well, not *completely* empty. The trolls we chased down are still here."

"A month later?"

"I didn't say they were alive."

"Dead?"

"One looks like it starved to death. But not before eating part of the other one. The stench was . . . well, let's just say I'm not going to be able to smell properly for a long time."

"Why didn't they just leave?"

"They must have seen us, known they were surrounded. It was death if they left and I was more patient than they were." He coughed. "Earth and sky, but they reek."

Tamani sighed. He had several choice words for Shar, but now was not the time. "Well, thanks for letting me know, I suppose. If you'll excuse me, I have a job to get back to." Without saying good-bye he pulled the phone away from his ear and jabbed at the END CALL button on his screen, once, twice. *Blighted glove!* Suppressing a growl, he bit down on the middle finger of his glove and yanked it off, poking hard at the phone to hang it up. He looked up at Laurel and David.

"Why did you follow me out here? I'm making some headway with Yuki and you two hanging around could ruin everything. Go! Dance!" he said, gesturing toward the door.

"Tam," Laurel said, her eyes wide. "Your hand. *Look at your hand!*"

Tamani looked down at his hand.

It was covered with sparkling powder.

*Not powder. Pollen.*

David raised an eyebrow. "Happy thoughts?"

Tamani could see Laurel's chest heave as she sucked in a nervous breath. "I'm not in bloom," she hissed.

"No," Tamani said, terror growing in his chest. "No, no, no! It's not possible!" Tamani exclaimed.

"Tamani," Laurel said, her voice eerily calm, "it's the first day of winter."

"No!" Tamani felt like about twenty gears had clicked into place in his mind. He shoved his glove back onto his hand, concealing the damning evidence. He reached out to grab Laurel's arm, not too tight, but tight enough for her to recognize how serious he was. "If Yuki is a Winter faerie, then we are all in very serious danger. She doesn't just know you're a faerie. She knows *I'm* a faerie. There's no way she couldn't. Every word out of her mouth since she arrived has been a lie. Every word." He swallowed. "And she knows how much I've been lying to her, too."

He placed his phone in Laurel's hand, curling her fingers around it. "Call Shar. He's on Aaron's phone. Tell him everything. I'll keep Yuki at the dance as long as I can. Then I'll find a way to bring her back to my apartment. You and Shar have to think of something by then."

"Can't we wait till tomorrow?" Laurel asked, panic creeping into her voice. "I don't think we should rush—"

"There's no time," Tamani interrupted. "Klea is coming to pick Yuki up and she's not coming back. Whatever she was sent here to do—it's done. It has to be tonight." He hesitated, wanting to stay in the lobby with Laurel. But he gritted his teeth and stood tall. "I've spent too much time out here already—she's going to be suspicious. You guys need to go."

Laurel nodded and turned to David. "I'll call Shar from the bathroom—I'll be right back."

Tamani watched her walk off. Then he grabbed David's shoulder, looking him hard in the eye. "Keep her safe, David."

"I will," he replied soberly.

It wasn't good enough. But then, where Laurel was concerned, nothing ever was. It was as good as it was going to get. The human boy hadn't failed her yet. Tamani could only hope his luck would hold.

He took a moment to try to calm himself as he headed back into the gym. Yuki was standing by the punch bowl and hadn't noticed him yet. He watched her with new eyes—seeing her as the dangerous creature he now knew she was. She looked so innocent in her sparkling dress. Only now did he fully understand. The large bow in back was just perfect for hiding a blossom.

It took everything he had to smile seductively as he approached her. She had to know his words were a lie. But there was one thing—even from the beginning—that she had always believed. He pulled her back in his arms possessively and his cheek went to hers, his lips pressing softly up her neck and to her ear. "Come home with me tonight?" he whispered.

She pulled back a little, looking at him with wide eyes.

"It's our last night," he said.

A long moment passed and Tamani could feel a single bead of condensation building up at the back of his neck as she continued to say nothing—to look into his eyes, searching for truth. "Okay," she whispered.

# THIRTY-SIX

TAMANI SLID HIS KEY INTO THE LOCK AND STARTED to turn the handle when Yuki placed her hand over his.

"Tam, wait," Yuki said softly.

Tamani felt his gloved hands start to shake and he tried not to imagine all the damage a Winter faerie—especially one not bound by the laws and traditions of Avalon—could inflict upon him. The kind of damage that would make death a reward by comparison. He turned to her and touched her arm as tenderly as he could manage. "You okay?"

She nodded shakily. "Yeah, absolutely, I just . . ." She hesitated. "I need to tell you something."

Was she trying to come clean? How much was she going to confess? She knew he was a faerie. She must; a Winter faerie could sense plant life at a distance, as well as control it. Did she know he was a sentry too? That he was Laurel's guide, warden, and protector? How much did she suspect he knew about her?

Tamani smiled casually and ran a hand down her cheek. It was too late for confessions. "Come inside first—you've got to be freezing."

He could almost see her reach out and cling to the excuse to wait just a few more minutes before unveiling her secret. Tamani turned the knob and pushed it open, wondering what Shar had waiting for them inside. Would Yuki be dead before she drew her next breath? To kill a Winter, even a wild one, struck Tamani as a kind of sacrilege. He trusted Shar—trusted him with his life—but this was bigger than anything they had ever encountered and Tamani wasn't ashamed to admit there was an icy pit of fear in his stomach.

He reached for the light switch and flipped it up.

Nothing happened.

"That's weird," Tamani said quietly, but loud enough for both Yuki and anyone who might be lurking in the dark room to hear. "Come on in," Tamani said. "I'll go grab the light in the kitchen, see if that one works." He felt rather than saw Yuki pause, before crossing the threshold. As if she sensed the danger that was lurking.

Tamani felt his way to the kitchen, running his hand along the wall and reaching for the kitchen light switch. A warm hand—a human hand—covered the switch. He felt someone grab his shoulder and a hand cup around his ear. "Tell her to come over to you," David whispered, as he carefully repositioned him a few steps to the right. "Tell her the

368

electricity must be out."

"Come this way," Tamani said. "The electricity must be out." She was still standing in the doorway, silhouetted by a dim streetlight that scarcely touched the murky blackness.

"I can't see." Her voice sounded strange, like a little girl's. There was something inside her, telling her this was wrong.

"I'll catch you if you fall," Tamani said, making his voice purr.

Hesitantly, she took a few steps toward him.

"I'm right here," Tamani said, as David nudged him just a little more to the right.

He heard a clang and Yuki let out a frightened yowl. There was a flurry of motion and David was gone from his side. He heard a couple of dull thuds, two sets of staccato clicks, then more shrieks from Yuki.

The light overhead burst to life, making Tamani cringe and screw his eyes shut against the onslaught. He blinked and surveyed the scene, his eyes searching for Shar.

But Shar wasn't there.

It was David, pulling off a pair of night-vision goggles. Chelsea, too, standing at his side, a length of rope in her hands. Some kind of backup plan. It was strange to see them standing in their finery with tools of capture in their hands.

Yuki was gasping as she struggled to escape from a metal chair someone had bolted to the floor, her hands cuffed securely behind her, one set for each wrist, with the other end locked around the back of the chair. Enough slack to throw herself against them pretty hard, but not enough to lean forward more than about a foot.

Tamani's jaw dropped. "What have you done? She's going to kill us!" Tamani hissed. But David wasn't talking. His face had gone white and he was staring at Yuki in horror. Tamani suspected he'd never tied someone up before.

But now was not the time for speculation. He threw himself in front of the humans, bracing himself for whatever was about to come.

Yuki stopped struggling for a moment to glare at him. Her eyes narrowed dangerously, then her head snapped back and she howled, not in anger this time, but pain. And then she was gaping at the floor around her.

It was the first time Tamani had noticed the circle of white powder that surrounded her chair. He took two steps forward and bent to examine it.

"Don't touch that." Shar's breathless voice came floating in through the doorway.

"What is it?" he gasped, drawing his hand back.

Shar stood with his chest heaving—Tamani wondered where he had run from—and Tamani could see him hesitate for a second; something that frightened him even more than the trapped Winter faerie not inches from him. "It's exactly what you think it is," Shar finally whispered.

Tamani looked back to the circle, now recognizing the granular crystals as salt. "It's too simple," he said, his voice soft.

"It's hardly foolproof, and difficult to invoke. A Winter faerie must walk into the circle willingly, or it won't work.

370

If you couldn't get her to walk in on her own, I guess we'd all be dead."

"Let me go!" Yuki screamed, her face tight, the sharp angle of her cheekbones standing out.

"I wouldn't make so much noise if I were you," Shar said, his voice deadly calm. "I have a roll of duct tape and I'm not afraid to use it. But I promise you, it hurts coming off. A lot."

"That won't matter when the cops come," Yuki said, and she drew in a breath to scream.

"Oh, please," Shar said, chuckling. The humor in his voice startled her enough to stop her scream before it began. "You mighty Benders always underestimate the power of Enticement. The cops wouldn't get past the front door even if you were screaming your head off ten feet away. My request for you not to scream is to keep me from wasting memory elixirs on the entire population of this apartment complex, not out of any kind of fear of retribution."

Yuki growled and glared at Shar, then her head snapped back again and she screamed through clenched teeth. Then she slumped forward and her body shook with sobs.

"Why is it hurting her, Shar?" Tamani said, feeling strangely desperate to stop her pain. "Make it stop!" Tamani was no stranger to pain; in fact, he'd spent a lot of his life learning how to inflict it—but never on another faerie, let alone a female faerie, and so young. He was shocked that he had to suppress an urge to run to her, to comfort her, even though he knew she could kill him with a glance.

"Any magic used within the circle rebounds. As soon as she stops attacking *us*," Shar said, raising his voice a little, "the circle will stop attacking *her*."

Yuki shot a dirty look at Shar, but she must have gotten the idea, because she didn't scream again. Tamani was glad. He turned to Shar and pushed him back toward the wall. "This is black magic, Shar. It must be forbidden."

"Beyond forbidden," Shar said, his eyes darting to the side. "It's Forgotten."

Forgotten. Magic from before memory, too dangerous to be passed down.

"You learned this from your mother, didn't you?" Tamani didn't try to hide the accusation in his voice.

"The Unseelie have always remembered things best forgotten."

"She told you this the day Laurel and I went to Avalon."

"I thought she was taunting me. I told her about Yuki, and she started babbling on about killing all the Winter fae. I thought she was telling me to assassinate Marion," Shar said, his voice still deadly calm. "Maybe my mother loves me after all."

"Shar, you can't do this. I won't let you turn Unseelie."

Shar laughed, a quick bark of disdain. "Please, Tam, you know where my loyalty lies, and it is not with the Seelie or the Unseelie. It is with Avalon. I will do whatever it takes to keep her safe."

Tamani knew Shar wasn't referring to Laurel, but his companion, Ariana, and their seedling.

"I will protect them by any means necessary. Think about it, Tamani. The only thing standing between her and Avalon is the fact that the gate is hidden. The moment she knows where it is, there is *nothing* we can do to keep her out."

*What have I gotten myself into?* He felt like someone was strangling him. But what choice did they have? "For Avalon," he said softly. Then he glanced around. "Where's Laurel?"

"Home," Shar said, his attention fixed on Yuki again. "If this didn't work, I wanted her as far away as possible. The sentries were told to do whatever it takes to not let her leave." He hesitated. "She put up a bit of a fight."

Tamani swallowed, trying not to think about that. "Where were *you*?" Tamani asked.

"You know as well as I—better, I suspect, considering your friendship with Jamison—that a Winter faerie would sense if another faerie was in your apartment. I was waiting less than a kilometer away, just close enough to see the light turn on." He shook his head. "This was a job for human hands, and I have to admit, they performed admirably."

But both of the humans seemed deaf to Shar's praise. David was still pale, and Chelsea looked scared, though not quite so horrified.

"All right," Shar said, pulling a knife from his pocket. "It's time to find out once and for all."

Yuki's eyes widened and she opened her mouth to scream again, but Shar handed the knife to David. "Go cut open her dress. I need to see her blossom for myself."

"Let me," Tamani said, stretching out his hand. But Shar's wrist closed around his.

"You can't," Shar said simply. "If you enter that circle, you will be under her power. No plants enter that circle, or we all die."

Tamani reluctantly withdrew his hand.

David stared at the knife in his hand, then pursed his lips and shook his head. "No. It's too much. Cuff her to the chair. That's all you asked me to do. Cutting clothes off a defenseless girl? Do you have any idea what that sounds like? I won't do it." He started to make his way toward the still open door. "Y-you're insane. She hasn't done anything. And this circle?" He glared at Shar. "You didn't tell m-me it would hurt her. Protecting Laurel is one thing, but I—I can't be a part of this." David turned and stormed out the door.

Tamani took a step to follow him—to bring him back—but Shar put a hand on his chest. "Let him go. He's had a rough night." Then he turned to Chelsea and—after a moment of hesitation—offered her the knife. "Would you . . . ?"

"Men," Chelsea muttered derisively, ignoring the knife. Carefully, and with remarkably little trepidation, Chelsea stepped over the white line. As soon as she entered the circle, Yuki started to thrash again, but Chelsea stood behind her, hands on hips, and said, "Yuki, hold still."

To Tamani's surprise, she did. Maybe it was finding herself so helpless before a human, but something in her broke, and she sat quietly as Chelsea carefully untied the silver obi and lowered the zipper of her dress several inches. Then she folded down a wide ACE bandage that Yuki had wrapped around her torso.

Everyone gasped as Chelsea pulled the bandage away from four broad, white petals. It resembled—and was not much bigger than—an ordinary poinsettia.

Tamani had seen the pollen on his palms, but to see that classic white Winter blossom spread out in front of him filled him with a terror that nearly brought him to his knees.

Shar's whispered oath was Tamani's fervent prayer.

"Goddess help us all."

# ACKNOWLEDGMENTS

KUDOS ALWAYS GO OUT FIRST TO MY BRILLIANT editors, Tara Weikum and Erica Sussman, who make me look good, and to Jodi Reamer, my awesome agent, who, well, also makes me look good! Thank you for being constants in my career. There are so many people at Harper whose names I don't even know who work tirelessly on this book—thanks to every single one of you! And my foreign-rights team, Maja, Cecilia, Chelsey, the degree to which you rock cannot be described! Alec Shane, trusty agent assistant, your handwriting on my mail always means something good.

Sarah, Sarah, Sarah, Carrie, Saundra (now aka Sarah)—I would go crazy without you guys. Thank you for everything! Especially the ninjas. I mean . . . what ninjas?

To my aunt Klea, credit and an apology. Somehow you didn't make it into the acknowledgments of *Spells*! (I blame my faulty memory.) Thanks for letting me blatantly steal your name. And don't worry, the name is where the likeness both begins and ends! Other names I stole: Mr. Robison, my high school counselor who managed to get me a diploma despite . . . issues . . . with my transcripts, thank you! Mrs. Cain—you taught me to love literature of all kinds. The use of your name in this book is a tribute; my time in your class is so appreciated, even now. Aaron Melton, Realtor extraordinaire, who lent his name and likeness to Tamani's second-in-command. I told you I'd do it and you didn't believe me! Ha! And to Elizabeth/LemonLight, the very first person to recognize me in a bookstore—just because I know she'll notice.

Kenny—words cannot describe. You are my rock. Audrey, Brennan, Gideon, Gwendolyn, you are my greatest achievements. My family and family-in-law: I could not ask for better cheerleaders.

Thank you!